The Wicked Widow

ALSO BY BEATRIZ WILLIAMS

The Wicked Widow

A Wicked City Novel

BEATRIZ WILLIAMS

wm

WILLIAM MORROW
An Imprint of HarperCollins*Publishers*

THE WICKED WIDOW. Copyright © 2021 by Beatriz Williams. All rights reserved. Printed in the United States of America. No part of this book may be used or reproduced in any manner whatsoever without written permission except in the case of brief quotations embodied in critical articles and reviews. For information, address Harper-Collins Publishers, 195 Broadway, New York, NY 10007.

HarperCollins books may be purchased for educational, business, or sales promotional use. For information, please email the Special Markets Department at SPsales@ harpercollins.com.

FIRST EDITION

Designed by Diahann Sturge

Library of Congress Cataloging-in-Publication Data has been applied for.

ISBN 978-0-06-314244-2 (paperback)
ISBN 978-0-06-314473-6 (library edition)

21 22 23 24 25 LSC 10 9 8 7 6 5 4 3 2 1

To the real Aunt Julie,

who had nothing to do with bootleggers

(so far as we know)

The Wicked Widow

ELLA

Ella KNEW that watching the *Today* show during prenatal yoga tended to defeat the purpose of yoga. But even while pregnant, she was a morning person—the kind of person who judged her day by how much she'd accomplished by lunchtime. Anyway, she mostly tuned it out. Just a pleasant background noise as she moved diligently from pose to pose and told herself to meditate, dammit. She only really listened when something caught her attention.

Like now.

We turn live to Faneuil Hall in Boston, Massachusetts, where Senator Franklin Hardcastle is expected to announce his candidacy for his party's nomination for president of the United States. Reporter Mary Jane O'Sullivan from our local affiliate WGBX is on the scene—

Ella's cell phone rang.

"Are you watching this?" said Ella's mother.

"Mumma, I'm trying to do my yoga. Can you call back later?"

"You know he used to be married to your aunt Tiny."

"For God's sake, that was the Dark Ages. Before I was even born. You all need to get over this."

"I *am* over it. I just think it's *interesting,* that's all." Short pause—probably for coffee, because Mumma mostly gave up cigarettes when

Ella was ten, and she hardly ever drank liquor before noon. "And the 1960s were *not* the Dark Ages, Ella. Honestly."

"Whatever."

"Don't *whatever* me. You'll see how fast the time goes once that baby's born."

"Look, can I get back to my yoga and we can discuss this later?"

"You can't tell me you're not interested. He was almost your *uncle*."

"I'm happy with Uncle Caspian, thanks. And I'm pretty sure Aunt Tiny feels the same way."

"Why? What do you know about it?"

"About what?"

Mumma's voice went all husky and secretive. "About the divorce."

"I don't know. Nothing, I guess. Aunt Tiny never talks about it."

"And you never *asked*?"

Across the room, the door opened. Ella heard the unmistakable nail-scrabbling noise of a brown-and-white King Charles spaniel bounding across a wooden floor. She had just enough time to brace herself before Nellie skidded to a halt at the yoga mat—Ella lay on her back—and coated her face in dog saliva.

"Nellie! Bad girl! What did I just tell you?" Hector's arms appeared out of nowhere to scoop the dog from Ella's face. "I said Ella's doing her yoga, leave her alone, and what did you do, Nellie? *What did you do?*"

From the telephone: "Ella? Ella?"

"Yes, Mumma! Everything's fine!"

"Is that Hunky Hector I hear? Back from fetching your milk and newspaper?"

"Mumma, please! Don't call him that, it's so weird."

"Call me what?" Hector bent to drop a kiss on Ella's lips.

"Nothing! Hold on, Mumma. It's the other line."

"Ella! Don't you *dare* put me on—"

"Hello?"

A voice cackled down the line, like a cross between an elderly Katharine Hepburn and a seagull. "Ella! I hope you're watching this."

"Aunt Julie, for the love of God—"

"The *nerve* of that family! I won't stand for it!"

"Aunt Julie, can I get back to you? I'm on the line with Mumma."

"I *know* you are! I'm right across the *room* from her! Now listen. I need you to come out here *pronto*—"

"Pronto? Like *today*?" Ella sat up and stared at the handsome, all-American face on the television screen. Senator Frank Hardcastle, charismatic yet reliable, intelligent yet likeable, dignified yet every-man, the conscience of the Senate, worked across the aisle yet argued his principles passionately and eloquently. What better man for the highest office in the land? "I'm kind of busy, Aunt Julie. Can't it wait until the weekend or something? You have Mumma and Aunt Viv looking after your every whim—"

"This has nothing to do with them. I need *your* help. That *man*—that *family*—"

"Really, Aunt Julie? You have some vendetta against Frank *Hard-castle*?"

"It's not a *vendetta*, darling. We're not the damn mafia." Then muffled, as through a palm covering the receiver: "Vivian! Where's my Bloody Mary?"

"Aunt Julie, I have to go. Really. Mumma's on the other line."

"No, she's not. She's hung up. I can see her from here."

A strange noise came from the kitchen. Ella turned from the television. Hector was putting away the groceries—milk and oranges, bananas and a bunch of spinach and what looked like some kind of fancy granola. A blush seemed to be creeping up his cheeks.

"Aunt Julie, look. Much as I'd love to just drop everything I'm doing and rush out to East Hampton and gossip about Senator freaking *Hardcastle*—"

"Drop everything, *indeed*. What exactly have you got to do around there, except jump in the sack with Horny Hector—"

"Ack, *gross*. What is *wrong* with you guys? All this Horny Hector and—oh, screw it. Never mind. Bye. See you this weekend. Or not."

Ella threw the cell phone into the sofa and lay back down on the yoga mat. "Don't say a word," she called to Hector.

"I feel so objectified."

"It's just them. They can't get past your good looks."

Hector's feet padded toward her. "So I'm just your sex toy? Is that it?"

"I mean, that's a big part of it. Yes."

"Orange juice, banana, prenatal vitamin." He laid each one on the coffee table and picked up the remote. "How many times have I told you, Ella? You need to turn everything else off. Focus your mind. Yoga's sacred to peace and quiet."

Ella held up her arms. "It was just this once."

"Liar. We need to talk about your workaholic issues." Hector dropped onto his hands and knees and kissed her again, more thoroughly. "How are you feeling?"

"Still good. The worst is definitely over."

He took her hands and pulled her up. "Then eat your breakfast, okay? We need some meat on those bones."

"The doctor said everything was fine, remember?"

"Can you just indulge me? I spent the past six weeks holding your hair back over the toilet. Like having a permanent dorm party in the apartment but without all the fun and games."

"You weren't worried. Were you?"

Hector handed her the orange juice and the vitamin. "Not *worried*? Are you kidding me? Like someone punching me in the gut all day."

Ella swallowed back the vitamin with the juice. "I am fine. *We* are fine. Thanks to you."

Hector nodded to the television screen, now dark. "So what was this about Frank Hardcastle?"

"He's running for president, apparently."

"Yeah, I heard. No big surprise, right? So what's it to your crazy aunts?"

"Kind of a weird family connection, actually. You know my aunt Tiny? The one who lives in San Diego with all the kids? Mumma and Viv's sister."

"Dying to meet her. She sounds like the only sane one."

"Well, before she married my uncle Caspian, she was married to *that* guy." Ella stuck her thumb in the direction of the television screen.

"Senator Hardcastle? She was married to Franklin *Hardcastle*? You're kidding."

"No, it's true. They divorced right after he was elected to the House, back in 1966 or something."

"My mind is seriously blown."

"I never mentioned it? Sorry. It's ancient family lore. I forget what a random connection it is."

"So what happened? Was he sleeping around?"

"Probably. Don't they all?"

"Well, you don't see a lot of divorced senators out there. Kind of supposed to stand by your man, right? So it must have been some pretty big shenanigans."

"I honestly don't know. It's one of those topics everyone in the family understands we don't discuss. Also, I think Aunt Tiny's the only one who knows what really happened? And she's *definitely* not telling." Ella set down the empty glass and reached for the banana. Hector sat next to her on the floor, knees up, hands linked between them. His head tilted a bit to one side as he watched her.

"But you have a theory," he said.

"What makes you say that?"

"Because I *know* you, Dommerich."

"Aren't you smart."

Hector opened his legs and held out his arms. Ella turned around and scooted back against his chest. He leaned with her against the sofa. He wore a soft, worn blue T-shirt and soft, worn chinos, and his heart thudded comfortably against her spine. He folded his arms across her chest and stomach and rested his chin lightly on her shoulder.

"Okay, here's my theory," Ella said.

"Tell me your theory."

"I think *she* was the one who had the affair. I think she fell in love with Uncle Caspian and that was that. She wanted to be with him in San Diego and raise a bunch of kids, instead of being some East Coast politician's wife."

"Hmm. I think I like this theory. What's he like?"

"Uncle Caspian? He's the *best*. He fought in Vietnam and lost a leg. From the knee down, the left leg. Won the Medal of Honor and everything. He's a photographer now. And they're so in love with each other it's almost gross."

Hector kissed her neck. "*That* I understand."

"So Aunt Tiny's happy, and obviously Hardcastle didn't have much trouble finding a replacement, so everyone came out a winner, I guess. But Mumma and Aunt Viv and Aunt Julie are in a tizzy for some reason."

"They like the drama, maybe?"

"Oh, they *love* the drama. *I* couldn't care less. Never met the guy. He seems to be a great senator and all, and I wish him well, but I don't feel any kind of . . . kind of . . ."

"Any kind of what?"

Ella stared at the television screen. *Franklin Hardcastle*, she thought. FH. Cambridge, Massachusetts.

"Nothing." She reached out to drop the banana peel on the coffee table, turned around to face Hector, and looped her arms around his neck. "Lost my train of thought, that's all."

"Not *again.*"

"The doctor said a return of sexual desire is perfectly normal during the second trimester."

"I don't think you've explained the full extent of the problem."

Ella traced his bottom lip with her thumb. "I don't remember you calling it a *problem* last night. *Is that enough or can I get you another?* Those were your words."

"It's a tough job," Hector said, "but someone's got to do it."

AS FAR AS ELLA was concerned, there were few upsides to unemployment. No paycheck, no routine, no sense of purpose. No latte on the way to work, no dinners on the expense account. No fiendish puzzle of income statements and balance sheets and cash flow burning on a screen before her, which she searched for some anomaly, some malfeasance, some crime against shareholders and the public at large.

Still, there were compensations. For example, she could spend all Tuesday morning in bed with her—well, what *was* he, anyway? There were no words for Hector. *Boyfriend?* Too casual. *Lover?* Too sexy—not that Hector wasn't sexy, but he'd spent much of their relationship holding back her hair as she vomited her way from the second through the fourth month of pregnancy, which was loving by any measure but hardly loverlike. *Partner?* Too businesslike. *Fiancé?* Well. They had scrupulously avoided any reference to marriage, for the simple reason that Ella was still technically married to another man—the father of this baby.

Well, whatever Hector was, now that the worst of the morning sickness was finally over, Ella seemed to be in the grip of another sickness altogether—a fever, let's call it. (The obstetrician had some clinical explanation about hormone balance that Ella forgot.) So being home all day *did* have its compensations. She could relish this freedom to pull off Hector's clothes after breakfast and kiss his skin by the light of the warm June sun pouring through the windows and the skylight, when—before her life imploded—she would ordinarily be sitting before her laptop in a fluorescent-lit office cubicle. The freedom to take all this *time* with each other—oodles of luxurious time, ticking away lazily around them—nowhere to be, nothing pressing to do, every worry forgotten, while Nellie sat on the rug nearby with her head on her paws, looking anxious.

"Ella's all right, girl," Hector said. "Never mind the banshee wailing."

"I was not *wailing.*"

"Don't be embarrassed. A man likes his work to be appreciated."

Ella grabbed a throw pillow and hit him on the shoulder. He laughed and sat up, pulling her with him. Parted her tousled hair away from her face.

"It's good to have you back, dream girl," he said. "Playing the piano with me again. Singing. Cracking jokes. Tearing my clothes off and having your wicked way with me."

"No more midnight bourbon, though."

"I can live without the bourbon. Can't live without my girl." Hector gave her a kiss and squinted at the clock. "Didn't you say you had an interview at eleven?"

"What time is it now?"

"Ten fifteen."

"*What?* How is that even *possible?*"

Hector called after her as she bolted for the bathroom. "Look, this is a full-service restaurant, all right? Not a drive-through!"

HECTOR WAS THE ONE who'd urged Ella to head back into the working world. Well, maybe *urged* wasn't the word. Ella had stoically endured about a month of the *hyperemesis gravidarum*—that was the technical term for unstoppable morning, noon, and night morning sickness—when she melted down completely after yet another three A.M. barfing session and sobbed in Hector's arms about how her life was over, she would never be herself again, she was going to be a slave to this *creature* inside her womb for the rest of her days.

Hector had wisely kept his mouth shut while she ranted. Cuddled her close and handed her the electrolyte water to sip from time to time. When she ran out of breath, he said look, they were in this together. Whatever she wanted to do, he would support her. She could go back to work if she wanted, if she *needed* work to be herself. He'd stay at home with the baby. Why, he was great with kids! When his sister had hers, they went right to sleep in his arms, like they were drugged. Martha said it would've made her sick if she wasn't so grateful.

So they decided that when she was feeling better—fingers

crossed—she would brush up her résumé and give it a try. They would find a way to make it work. Totally modern couple.

What could possibly go wrong?

LUCKY FOR ELLA, THE interview was downtown, nestled inside the warren of streets around Bowling Green, at a small accounting firm that specialized in midsize investment banks. She caught the 9 train just in the nick of time and emerged into the smoggy heat of lower Broadway—summer had arrived early this year—with five minutes to spare.

Ella wasn't quite showing yet, at least not unless you were actively *looking* for a bump and happened to know it wasn't just gas or too much cheese. She considered this a blessing. She could button up her navy suit jacket and walk into a job interview and nobody could tell she was now weeks into her second trimester. Still, she couldn't quite shake the awkwardness of her too-snug waistband, the pumps with the three-inch heels she hadn't worn since April, the pantyhose clinging to her skin in the June heat. She'd suited up twice already—the first interview last Friday, the second yesterday—and she'd hoped the uniform would seem more natural this time, that she would feel like herself again instead of someone putting on a Career Woman costume for Halloween or school spirit day.

But no. The first interview had gone really well, a pair of senior project managers, great rapport, they'd promised to get back to her—though she hadn't heard from either of them yet. The second had been canceled at the last minute, they'd follow up soon with a new date—again no word. So Ella, pushing her way through the revolving door on her too-high heels, belly straining against the superfine navy wool that had once been her workwear mainstay, felt out of rhythm. Rusty. Not *herself.*

She crossed the lobby and checked in with reception. Twenty-second floor, they told her. Elevators to the left.

At eleven o'clock in the morning, Ella had the elevator to herself. The building was an older one, and the cab moved laboriously past the floors, one by one. A smell of sweat hung in the air, like someone had gone up in gym clothes. She looked at her reflection in the polished metal door. Lipstick, hair. You've got this, Ella. You're a professional. Done this a billion times before. Look at you, shiny and confident!

The doors opened. Ella stepped through. *Strut,* she told herself. Strut to reception. She strutted to reception and gave her name. The receptionist had straight black hair parted down the middle and gathered in a plain ponytail. Her skin was the same color as Hector's skin, an enviable golden olive. Her eyebrows knit together as she looked down the list of names on her clipboard. She glanced back at Ella.

"I'm sorry, who did you say you had an appointment with?"

"Diana Church," Ella said. "Eleven o'clock."

"Hold on just a moment, please."

The receptionist picked up the telephone and punched a couple of numbers on the keypad. Ella shifted her weight. Her shoes were just a little too tight, probably the heat. And the skirt! Definitely tighter than Friday. Maybe she was popping out already. Damn. She wasn't ready to shop for maternity clothes, she wasn't *ready* to look pregnant. She needed a job first. She needed some normal back. She needed—

"Mrs. Gilbert?" said the receptionist.

Ella tried not to wince at her married name—Patrick's name. Hector called her by her maiden name, but she hadn't changed it officially, yet. Still, it didn't feel like hers anymore. *Gilbert* sounded contaminated. Unclean. Alien.

"Is something the matter?" Ella said.

"I'm sorry, there seems to have been a mix-up? Her assistant tried to reach you on your cell phone?"

Ella patted her laptop bag, checked a pocket or two, found the cell phone buried under a mini umbrella. "What kind of mix-up? I'm afraid I didn't catch the call."

The receptionist tried to disguise her pity with sympathy. "Ms. Church had a last-minute conflict and unfortunately can't do the interview after all. She said she'll be in touch later this week to reschedule."

ELLA WAITED UNTIL SHE was outside the building before she checked her voice mail. She had her dignity, after all. She found the message from Diana Church's assistant but didn't bother listening. What was the use? *They would be in touch later that week to reschedule*, which was the polite, businesslike way of saying *buzz off*.

She also found two messages from Patrick. Ella was supposed to meet her husband tomorrow morning in a last-ditch effort to hash out the big issues before the lawyers got involved, and Ella was looking forward to it about as much as a colonoscopy. In the first voice mail, Patrick made some rambling, repetitive sentences about his expectations and lines in the sand, how there was no way in hell he was going to settle for daytime visitation for six whole months, for God's sake, she could just pump some milk if she was so worried about goddamn formula during the night. The second came an hour later—he apologized if he sounded frustrated earlier, it was just that he wanted this baby *so much*, Ella, he was *heartsick* that it had come to this, he wished they could go back to where they were so he could show her what a *changed man* he was, could she meet him for lunch instead of coffee, Le Bernardin at noon, his treat, see you then.

Ella counted to ten before she called back. He answered on the first ring. "Ella. Love hearing that sweet voice of yours. Are we all set for lunch?"

"No, we're not. I've already got plans for lunch. You should have asked first. Ten o'clock at the Starbucks on Madison and East Forty-Third Street, like we agreed."

"Ella—"

"Sorry, Patrick. You're breaking up. What's that? Sorry, I can't hear you. Tomorrow at ten, okay? See you then!"

Ella shut her phone and stared at the round metal shell, half expecting him to call right back. But the phone remained silent. The sun burned the side of her face. Not even noon yet, and the hot, thick, lifeless air stank of a thousand rancid metropolitan odors. It was going to be one of those summers, apparently. Mumma and Aunt Viv had already moved out to The Dunes—the ancestral Schuyler summer house in East Hampton—where Aunt Julie visited regularly from Maidstone Meadows, the assisted living facility in which she'd set herself up for the golden years. Their glamorous heads would be stuck together in the final throes of wedding planning right now. This time the bride was Lizzie, Aunt Viv's youngest, who was supposed to get married over July Fourth weekend, just over three weeks away. The whole clan would be there, and Ella would stroll around sipping ginger ale, looking thick-waisted but not quite pregnant—wouldn't that be marvelous. At least Hector was going, too. Ella had already negotiated that with Aunt Viv. Absolutely no *way* she was sitting at the singles' table at a Schuyler family wedding at nearly six months preggo, only her brother, Charlie, to dance with.

Ella checked her watch and slipped her cell phone back into her tote bag. Turned down Broadway toward the subway stop at South Ferry and felt the vibration of the phone next to her ribs.

Dammit, Patrick.

But when she lifted the cell phone back out of the bag, it wasn't Patrick's number, after all. It was a number she didn't recognize, a Manhattan cell phone. She stared at the LED screen and debated whether to pick up. Probably just a wrong number.

She answered it anyway. "This is Ella," she said.

"Hello, Mrs. Gilbert? I don't know if you remember me. This is Rainbow Stevens? Travis Kemp's assistant at Parkinson Peters?"

"Rainbow! Of course. How's everything? Can I help you with something?"

On the other end, Rainbow made a brief, nervous chuckle. Something about the sound made Ella's skin prickle. She'd always liked Rainbow. She was competent, she was discreet, she never made you feel like you were burdening her with some stupid, tedious chore, even when you were. Also, when Ella marched out of Kemp's office, having delivered what might be called a preemptive resignation with the kind of panache usually seen only in movie scripts, she was pretty sure Rainbow had sent her a look of approval. Of solidarity, you might say.

Still. That nervous chuckle. Something was up.

In the background, Ella heard street noises. Rainbow wasn't in the office; she was probably on her lunch break already, making this call where no one could overhear her. Was she switching jobs? Needed a reference for a headhunter?

"Actually, is there somewhere we could meet in person?" Rainbow said. "It's something I've been wanting to tell you for a while, something I need to get off my chest, and I think—I'd rather not do it over the phone, if you know what I mean?"

"Um, sure. Do you mean now?"

"Sooner the better. Are you downtown or midtown?"

"Downtown. But I can hop on the express—"

"No! I'll meet you there. There's a Starbucks in South Street Seaport. Half an hour?"

"Well, yes, but—"

"Thanks. Great. And Mrs. Gilbert?"

"Yes, Rainbow?"

"Just—you know. Don't tell anyone about this, okay? It's about what happened to you in March."

ELLA HADN'T BEEN TO South Street Seaport in ages, not since she was working on a project at the bottom of Wall Street and used to go there on lunch breaks. She liked the fresh salty air off New York Harbor, she liked the crowds of tourists—normal people from the rest of America, black-clad Eurotrash types dragging cheap, giant suitcases full of clothes from Century 21. She liked the old ships and the gritty buildings across the East River. Plus, there was shopping and a food court. It was like a mall, which was somehow comforting, like a piece of suburban New Jersey had dropped onto Manhattan. It was a place where New Yorkers wouldn't go if you paid them, which was probably why Rainbow had suggested it.

Ella arrived first and ordered a decaf iced mocha. Even if she weren't pregnant, she didn't need the caffeine—her nerves jangled, her pulse thudded in her throat. She felt the same rush of adrenaline she'd felt on that Friday evening back in March, when she'd sat in the Sterling Bates conference room, puzzling over some anomaly in the accounts about a firm called FH Holdings, and Travis Kemp had called her cell phone out of the blue. Had shouted and sworn at her for failing to disclose that her husband worked at Sterling Bates, told her to wipe her laptop and leave all the project documents behind in the conference room.

Back then, her adrenaline was the juice of outrage. Because she *had* already disclosed that Patrick was a managing director in the investment banking department of Sterling Bates, dammit! And corporate investment banking stood behind a Chinese wall from the municipal bond department where *she* was working!

All of which insulted her sense of honor, but even worse was that Ella had been *on* to something! She'd found something shady, like she was supposed to do—this was her *job*—and now that shady thing was going to get buried forever, and as Ella marched home that Friday in March, she was so outraged—so offended—she'd resolved to fight back.

But by Sunday morning, she'd found out that Patrick had bestowed a parting gift on her, and right after *that* she was deluged with nonstop morning sickness. No more adrenaline, no more outrage. Not even curiosity. She didn't want to *think* about what had happened at work. She didn't have the time or the energy for the nefarious shenanigans of investment banks. What was the point? Like Patrick, they would just find some other way to screw around. She wanted to close the door on the past. She wanted to focus on the future, on Hector and the baby and some shining new career.

Until now.

It's about what happened to you in March.

Ella's fingers buzzed. Her mouth was dry. She sipped her mocha and checked her phone. No messages.

Rainbow hurried into view about ten minutes later, flushed pink and out of breath. She wore a navy suit nearly identical to the one Ella was wearing, her light brown hair in a ponytail. Ella asked what

Rainbow would like to drink and Rainbow looked flummoxed, like she hadn't given this any thought—didn't know what to order for coffee in the middle of the day. At last she said she'd have what Ella was having, so Ella ordered another iced mocha, except with regular coffee instead of decaf.

"So how are things at PP these days?" Ella asked, when they were seated with their drinks.

"The usual. Really busy. Still a lot of fallout from the Asian thing last fall, I guess." Rainbow cast a quick, furtive glance around them, like a secret agent might. "We really miss you around the office."

"Really?" Ella was genuinely surprised.

Rainbow nodded her head vigorously. "You were the *decent* one. Treated the staff like actual human beings instead of peons. You know I have a degree in art history? So this was not supposed to be my forever job, and—well, anyway. Not to tell you my life story. I wouldn't have called you if you were like the others, right? But this has been, like, weighing on my heart."

"Weighing on your *heart*?"

"I mean, I've seen a lot of crap going on, you know? Like my illusions were already shattered. But you were one of the good guys. You didn't deserve it. And I just figured if I didn't say something, I was no better than the rest of them, right?" Rainbow fingered her green plastic straw. "So a couple of days before you left I was in Kemp's office going over his travel schedule with him. And somebody called him on his direct line. I could tell it was somebody important, right? Because of the way he talked. And he had this expression on his face, like he'd been called into the principal's office at school. It was very *Yes, sir. No, sir. I understand, sir.*"

"And he let you sit there and listen?"

"Ella, I'm barely even human to him. He probably thinks I don't understand any of the shit that crosses his desk. Anyway, the conversation seemed super weird—I mean, Kemp doesn't scare easily, he's the one who likes to call up *other* people and make them cry—so I leaned over the desk to take back the travel schedule, like I was going to mark it up or something, and I memorized the number on the telephone screen."

"Wow. You're good."

"You have to be, working in a snake pit like that. Meanwhile I'm listening to Kemp's side of the conversation. I remember he said something like, *I don't know if we can do that, she's one of our rising stars,* and then, *All right, I'll find something.*"

Ella slammed down her drink. Rattle of ice against the blond wood. "Are you *kidding* me?"

"Then he picked up his pen to write something down. He literally wrote it on the fucking schedule I'd just handed back to him, because he's a tool whose wife probably puts his toothpaste on his toothbrush in the morning. And he's like, *Okay, I'll make sure it's all deleted over the weekend,* or something like that. And *then*—" Rainbow sucked down her drink, rattled the ice around, sucked some more. Glanced at a nearby table, where a man in a gray suit was busy with his laptop. She leaned toward Ella and said, in a low voice, "*Then* he said—I remember this so clearly, because I almost wet myself—*Who the hell are you protecting, anyway? I could go to jail for this.*"

"Holy shit."

"Right? And I was sitting *right there*! But the guy on the other end wouldn't tell him. So he hangs up the phone and kind of sits there, staring down at the travel schedule. He's forgotten all about me. You know, stunned. Then he looks up and tells me to have your HR file pulled and on his desk in ten minutes."

Rainbow sat back and stared left, where the East River glittered and rippled under the June sun. She finished the mocha and set the plastic cup on the table. The remaining ice settled and drooped. Ella and Rainbow sat on the covered terrace overlooking the water, and the heat smothered them, even in the shade.

"Sometimes I hate this city," Rainbow said. "I was hoping to get a job at Sotheby's or Christie's or something, or one of the museums. Just took this job to pay the rent until something panned out. That was four years ago. Now I feel like I'm one of them, you know? Like the dirt is on me and won't wash off. I've been dating this guy at Goldman. Hot nerd type. He's a good guy, but he's not that into art, you know? Just as an investment. Everything's about money. How nice an apartment can you afford. What fancy restaurants do you eat at. Where do you go on vacation. He loves that I studied art at college, but honestly? I think it's because he figures I'll supply the good taste in the relationship, you know? Decorate the house. Make him look classy."

"I know," Ella said. "I was married to one of those."

"So it's true? You divorced that prick?"

"Divorc*ing*. Best decision I ever made."

Rainbow turned back to her and frowned—not displeasure, just concentration. "Anyway, I gave Kemp your HR file, like he asked. Then I tracked down that phone number—it was a D.C. area code—and found out the call came from the SEC. That's all. I wish I had more for you there, but you know how it is. I didn't want anyone to get suspicious. But I do have this."

Rainbow reached into her tote bag and rummaged around in the interior pockets. Drew out a clean, unmarked CD in a paper sleeve, which she laid on the table between them.

"What's this?"

"Kemp's really bad with computers, so I take care of his files for him. Before I wiped all the Sterling Bates spreadsheets you emailed him in the last client update, I burned a copy on a CD-ROM."

HECTOR'S APARTMENT—*THEIR* APARTMENT, he reminded her daily, so Ella almost felt like this was true—covered the entire fifth floor of the building at 11 Christopher Street, a typical nineteenth-century Greenwich Village town house converted into apartments. Only not so typical, once you got to know the place. For one thing, you had the peculiar jazz orchestra that struck up around nine or ten in the evening. Best jazz you ever heard, seeping through the walls and the floorboards from no earthly jazz orchestra you could discover, no matter how long or hard you searched for it.

For another thing, the residents were related to each other. All descendants of a legendary bass player named Bruno, who used to live there between the two world wars, according to family lore. Hector's grandfather, he said. Ella was the first inhabitant from outside the family. And now look—they'd practically made her family, too. Jen in 3C said hello from her doorway, from which she was about to take down the trash. Asked how Ella was feeling, and Ella said much better, thanks. She turned down the landing and up the next flight to the fourth floor, where the door to her old apartment—the studio into which she'd moved after discovering her husband having sex with a prostitute back in February—stood open.

Ella stopped and poked her head in. "Hello?"

Hector's face appeared around the corner of the kitchenette. "Hey! There you are. Everything okay?"

"Interview got canceled. What's up in here?"

Ella stepped into the apartment and found Hector in his T-shirt and chinos next to a tall, spindly man holding a clipboard and a metal measuring tape.

"This is Mike, the staircase guy. Doing some measurements for the renovation. Mike, this is Ella."

Mike held out a calloused palm. "Ella, pleasure. Hear you two are expecting a baby in November. Congratulations."

"Um, thanks."

"I've got three, myself. Out in Flushing. Just enjoy every minute, they go by fast."

Hector said quickly, "Mike's promised to get started ASAP so the paint's dry and the dust is clear by the time we get back from the hospital. Right, Mike?"

"Aye aye, sir. You have my word."

Hector squinted at Ella. "Listen, Mike. You all set in here? Need anything else from me?"

"I'm good. Just take down a few more numbers and I'll be out of your way."

"Thanks, man." Hector made the phone sign next to his ear. "Give me a call with the estimate and everything."

"End of the day." Mike stuck out his hand and Hector shook it. "Ella? Nice to meet you. Good luck with everything. I'll lock up behind me."

They stepped into the hall. Hector took Ella's bag. "So what's the deal?"

"Well, like I said, the interview was canceled."

"What, seriously?"

"They left a message on my cell phone."

"That's weird, right? Two in a row."

"You know what? It *is* kind of weird. But not as weird as what happened after."

"*What* happened after?"

"Rainbow," Ella said. "Rainbow is what happened."

"You mean like leprechauns? Pot of gold?"

"I don't know about leprechauns, but I'm pretty sure there's a pot of gold in it somewhere."

They reached the top of the stairs. Hector opened the door and stepped back to let her in. "Okay, be mysterious. You okay, by the way? You look kind of pale."

"I'm fine. It's just hot out."

"Sit down. I'll get you some water."

Ella slung her tote on the kitchen counter and kicked off her heels. Settled on one of the counter stools. Nellie came up and licked her foot through the pantyhose. Hector filled a glass with water and ice and added a lemon slice from the bowl in the fridge. He sat on the stool next to her and handed her the glass. Ella had learned how to drink all over again the past couple of months. Teeny, tiny sips. Hector's face was drawn with familiar worry. She forced a smile.

"Don't look like that. I'm fine, okay? Just dehydrated."

"I didn't overstep down there, did I? Telling Mike about the baby?"

"Of course not. It's not a secret or anything. I mean, we *are* having a baby."

"I left out the complicated part. Even though it made me look like a schmuck who isn't doing the right thing by you. You should have seen the look he gave me."

"Little does he know. So how did things go?"

"Good, good. He said he can put the staircase in, no problem.

We'll keep the bathroom where it is and wall in a nursery. Then the kitchenette becomes a little sitting room. I mean, obviously the baby sleeps with us at first—does that sound okay?"

"It sounds a little freaky, actually."

He laughed. "If you keep yourself busy, you don't freak out so much. I can do most of the work myself if you give me a hand with the drywall, but a staircase is a little out of my league. Anyway, that's my update. So what's all this about rainbows and pots of gold?"

"Not *a* rainbow. Rainbow Stevens. She's one of the assistants at Parkinson Peters? Called me up out of thin air, wanted to meet for coffee. Turns out I was right. There *was* something fishy going on." Ella reached inside her tote bag and pulled out the CD-ROM. "She gave me this. All the spreadsheets I was working on when they booted me off the Sterling Bates audit. And I'll bet you anything it's why these other firms keep canceling interviews on me. Apparently I'm kryptonite or something."

Hector whistled and plucked the CD from her hand. "Have you taken a look?"

"Not yet. I have to dig up my notes first. Also, I had to relinquish my company laptop, so I'm currently computerless."

"Use mine."

"Hector, your computer belongs in a museum. It can't even *run* Excel."

"You say that like it's a bad thing." He set down the CD. "So what happens if you find out something big?"

"I really don't know. Depends on what it is. Right now the question is whether I'll ever be able to find a job again." Ella put her head in her palm. "Which plays right into Patrick's hands with custody and everything."

"Whatever happens, we'll find a way, all right? We've got a roof over our heads. You've got the best lawyer around, thanks to your mom." He drew her hands into his. "Everything will work out, okay? Just stick to your guns. And remember I'm right here in your corner if you need me."

"What, so you can go at each other like a pair of silverbacks, like the last time?"

"Hey, I was just trying to make nice. He was the one swinging from the vines. Not that I could blame him. Must be downright emasculating, watching another man go home with your wife."

Ella leaned forward and laughed into Hector's T-shirt.

"So another thing," Hector said. "Not the best timing, maybe, but here goes."

"Uh-oh."

"No, it's good. It's about the movie."

Ella lifted her head. "Oh gosh, the movie! What's going on? You haven't said a word—I didn't want to *ask*—"

"No, no. Everything's great. In fact, while you were out, it so happens I got a call from the director. They're pretty eager to get me in the studio and record that score."

"How eager?"

"As soon as possible. They've delayed things as much as they can, worked around me, but now it's crunch time. Final edit's ready. They need the music in."

Ella spoke slowly. "Are you telling me that you put *all this* on hold for me? Recording the movie score? For the past two *months*? And they *let* you?"

"What was I supposed to do? Take off for three weeks of rehearsals and studio time in L.A. while you were barfing your brains out?"

"*Yes!* I could have stayed with Mumma or Aunt Viv! Hector, this is your *dream*!"

"*You're* my dream, dream girl." Hector grinned. "But yes, okay. The movie's still kind of a close second, if you put a gun to my head."

"How soon do they need you?"

"They wanted me to fly out tonight, but I said no way, tomorrow at the earliest."

"So you're leaving tomorrow?"

"Ella, I'm not going to book a flight to California for three weeks without talking to you first. You tell me. Is tomorrow okay? You're feeling well enough?"

"I'm feeling *fine,* Hector. It's a pregnancy, not a fatal disease. Go out to L.A., for God's sake. Record your music. I can't believe everyone's been waiting for me all this time while I've been a selfish jerk—"

"Don't say that."

"—obsessed with my own idiotic hormones. *Go.* I mean, not that I *want* you to go. But I have Nellie for company. And I'll call you every day to make sure you're not having a steamy affair with some gorgeous not-pregnant actress."

He leaned forward and kissed her mouth. "You're the best, you know that?"

HECTOR WANTED TO TAKE her out to dinner, but Ella said no, she wanted to make dinner there in the apartment, just the two of them. So they made dinner together and washed up. Took Nellie for a short walk in the balmy June twilight. Sat down together on the piano bench with a bottle of Martinelli's and a couple of old-fashioned champagne coupes and messed around, playing and singing and laughing. Ella asked about the movie. Hector said how nice of you to finally ask, it's a historical thing, Poland just before Hitler invades.

This Polish air force pilot falls in love with a Jewish girl, kind of a Romeo and Juliet vibe except instead of killing Mercutio he flees to join the RAF and asks his family to protect this girl from the Nazis. Then she starts working for the Jewish resistance in the Warsaw ghetto.

"So what happens? Do they survive?"

"Ah, you'll have to watch it and find out," he said, running a few scales.

"So play me some of the music."

"Already have. You just didn't notice. Like this. Played it about a hundred times while you were right there groaning on the sofa." Hector strummed a few bars. "This is when he meets her for the first time in Warsaw. She's just started at the university, meets him at a party. Love at first sight. Crowded room so they can't really talk. So the music has to say it, right?"

Ella closed her eyes and listened. "It's kind of jarring, isn't it? Sweet but jarring."

"Well, that's what it's like. Your whole life changes in a second. Like an earthquake, you can't do anything about it, it's just fate—scared and excited." The music shifted. "This bit is when the Nazi planes come in. She's sheltering in the basement, knowing he's up there in the air dogfighting these guys."

"God, I can't even imagine. If that were *you*? I'd be in pieces."

"Well, it's war, right? You do what you have to do. Sorry, the piano doesn't really give you the full effect. It'll sound a lot better coming from a symphony."

"You hire a whole symphony to record the score?"

"Yep. The Los Angeles Philharmonic."

"Seriously? The L.A. *Philharmonic*?"

"I know, right? Director pulled some strings. They've started rehearsing in sections already. We're scheduled for our first combined run-through the day after tomorrow."

"Wait a second. Does that mean you're *conducting* them? The L.A. Philharmonic?"

"That's kind of how it works with new music. The composer stands on the podium."

"I think I just came."

"Don't get too excited. Haven't done much conducting since conservatory. Could be a bloodbath." He shifted into something else, more lyrical. "Now this was the hardest theme. They just got married, city's in ruins around them, he's leading the remains of his squadron out of Poland to London later that night."

"Wait, I know this. I *love* this bit. I didn't realize—this is *yours*? For the movie?"

"They're young, right? Never felt this way before. They're shy and eager and desperate, but there's this edge of grief. They might never see each other again."

"It's like a waterfall, almost. A series of little waterfalls—then more and more—scales on scales—"

"Last thing I wrote. Kept putting it off. Tried out this and that and nothing seemed to work. It just wasn't authentic, like I was faking it somehow. This was the end of February, beginning of March. Then this woman turned up in my laundry room one morning."

"Oh, stop."

"Sweaty and messy and flustered and perfect. And my heart might have stopped beating for a minute or two. And when it started again— well, I had these notes in my head. This idea. This sound. The whole piece started coming together. I would get snatches, phrases in the middle of the night. Finally wrote it all down the night that . . ."

"The night that what?"

The music fell from its peak—ebbed to a trickle. "The night before I broke up with Claire, actually. Finished this part at four in the morning and crashed. When I woke up I knew I couldn't be with anyone else but you." He stopped playing and cocked his head. "Listen."

Through the floors and walls came the sound of a trumpet, lonesome and longing. A clarinet appeared, playing chase, in and out. Then a double bass. When all the instruments joined together, the music shifted seamlessly into a waltz.

"Hey, that's not jazz," Ella said.

"They're playing for *us,* that's why." Hector stood up and held out his hand. "May I have the honor, Miss Dommerich?"

USUALLY ELLA WAS THE first to drift off to sleep after sex, but this time she lay awake next to Hector, sprawled on his stomach, out cold—or maybe *awake* wasn't the word for it, but she wasn't asleep, either. She watched the movement of his back as he breathed, the occasional tiny flicker of an eyelid. His lips were parted. His warm breath touched her forehead. In the distance, the jazz orchestra still played, but so faint it was almost gone. The music always faded away like that. At three o'clock the last strain vanished. Like closing time or something. Ella yawned and shut her eyes. Music washed over her ears.

Then something else. Another noise, a human noise. Someone crying. A woman.

Ella opened her eyes.

Was it real? The sound was louder now, but not *loud*. The way you cry when you can't help crying because your heart is broken, but you don't want anybody to overhear your anguish.

Ella whispered Hector's name, but he didn't stir. She snuggled a little closer and shut her eyes. Tangled her fingers with Hector's fingers and tried to block this noise, but it was no use. The weeping ebbed and flowed. Hector's eyes cracked open. "What's the matter?" he mumbled, half-asleep.

"Do you hear that?"

"Hear what?"

The sobs weren't loud, but they were clear—so clear and real it was like the woman sat on the bed with them. "Nothing," Ella whispered. "Go back to sleep."

Hector closed his eyes and Ella stared at his shadowy face until she was sure he was out. Then she lifted the covers and slipped out of bed.

HECTOR HAD MOVED ELLA'S things upstairs two months ago, after that first wave of hyperemesis gravidarum had flattened her on a train platform in East Hampton. She'd left all the furniture behind when she left her marriage—hadn't wanted so much as a stick she and Patrick had bought together—and her new futon, chest of drawers, table, and chairs were all cheap and junky, made of flimsy particleboard covered in fake veneer. Hector took most of it to the thrift store. (*I hate to kick you when you're down, Dommerich,* he'd said, shaking his sad head, *but this is the crappiest furniture I've ever seen.*) Besides, his own apartment was already fully furnished with bed and table and sofa and chairs, all of which he'd made himself.

Still, Ella *did* need somewhere to put her clothes, so he'd built her a dresser to match his—four large, deep drawers, cast iron hardware, simple lines. He found original chestnut boards from this dealer in Connecticut who took apart old, falling-down barns; Hector sawed and planed and fit it all together without a single nail, just seamlessly notched together. He polished and finished until the wood was the color of maple syrup. Took him hours and hours. His gift to her, he said, because while he couldn't afford to shower her with jewelry or fancy vacations, at least he knew his way around a miter clamp.

He wouldn't let her see it until he'd finished. Carried it upstairs to their bedroom and told her to open her eyes. Ella had stared speechless at this handmade chest of drawers. Not just because it was so beautiful and marvelous, not just because it matched his chest of drawers exactly—a perfect pair—but because she was so humbled that somebody would devote so much time and skill and care just to please her. Nobody had ever done anything like that for Ella. She didn't know how to thank him, how even to express how much she loved it, how much she loved him for creating it for her. She was sick and utterly drained from the constant nausea, despite the pills they'd given her and the electrolyte water. She couldn't remember the last time she and Hector had made love; she couldn't summon the energy or the will for sex, for any of the ways you would usually show your lover how much you appreciated him.

So you like it? he'd asked. *Yes, I love it,* she'd replied—desperate to say more, to kiss him or throw her arms around him or anything, paralyzed by love and gratitude. *Good, because I gave it my awl,* he said solemnly, hands on hips, and after a second or two she had burst into laughter so hysterical that Hector had swooped her out of the room and onto the sofa, where he blew raspberries into her still-flat tummy until she cried uncle.

The next day, during one of her better spells, she'd folded her clothes carefully into the drawers, which opened and closed weightlessly on their runners, and from then on, every time she got dressed, she remembered how Hector had lovingly constructed this beautiful, useful object in her old apartment while she was upstairs vomiting in his toilet or lying gray-faced on his sofa. Sometimes she would just run her hand along the delicate pattern of the wood, would stare at this simple chest of drawers like it was a work of art, which it was, and she felt so much love for Hector she couldn't breathe, almost.

And because she loved her chest so much, she kept her treasures there, too—an enamel box filled with peculiar old-fashioned buttons she'd found under a loose floorboard in her apartment downstairs, and a larger cardboard box her aunt Julie had given her that same day she'd wound up in the hospital. The box contained a cache of rare antique photographic plates depicting a flame-haired woman in novelty poses—*Redhead Bites the Bullet*, *Home Run for Redhead*—that displayed her stupendous knockers to nakedly creative effect. To her obsessed collectors, she was simply known as the Redhead, and an original Redhead photograph card might be worth tens of thousands of dollars, depending on its scarcity.

But Ella knew better. Ella knew that the Redhead's real name was Geneva Kelly, and she had once lived in this very building at 11 Christopher Street, in the studio apartment where Ella had taken shelter four months ago when she left her husband.

IN THE DARK BEDROOM, the quiet sobs seemed to be coming from everywhere, from the air itself. Ella put her hand on the smooth, slender bedpost to steady herself. She closed her eyes. Nearby, Hector's sleeping body was like an anchor that tethered her to safety. She felt his weight, his comforting gravity. If she concentrated, she could detect a faint direction to the weeping, a thickening of sound in one corner of the room. She released the bedpost and stepped toward it, eyes still closed, hand outstretched, because when she opened her eyes, she lost that tug of direction. That instinct guiding her footsteps.

She wasn't afraid. She was used to the building by now—the benevolent music that played for her when the sun went down, comforted her even. In the early days, before she'd started spending her evenings with Hector, she'd heard a terrifying screaming, a gunshot, when she was down in the laundry room one night. But that happened only once. Just slipped out. Everyone had a dark side, an uneasy history, even this building. It would never, ever hurt her. Hadn't it given her Hector? So she wasn't afraid.

Another step. One more.

Her hand met the perfect edge of the chest of drawers. As she knelt before it, she slid her fingers down the silky wood, the ridges of the drawers, until she came to the bottom drawer and found the round cast iron knob on one side, found the other, eased the drawer open. Here it was, the sobbing. It came from *here*. She burrowed under the sweaters, neatly folded, until her fingertips met the cardboard sides of the box containing the photographic plates.

A voice spoke in her head, a female voice, clear and pleading.

Don't go.

HECTOR LEFT AT DAWN the next morning. As soon as the door closed behind him, Ella got out of bed. No way she was going to mope around for three weeks! She took a shower and ate some dry toast and took Nellie around the block. Just as she came back through the door, the phone rang from East Hampton.

"Out of bed already, are you? How's Horny Hector?"

"Good morning, Aunt Julie. Hector's headed out to L.A. right now, as a matter of fact."

"Los *Angeles*? Why would anybody go *there*?"

"He's working on a movie, remember? He told you about it when we came out to visit you last month. He's written the score for a movie? And now he's going out there to record the music with the Los Angeles *Philharmonic*. It's a pretty big deal."

"Philhar*mon*ic, huh. You're not worried he's got a woman out there?"

"Honestly, the thought never occurred to me."

"Really? After what happened with Peter?"

"Patrick. And Hector's different. He's *loyal*."

"Honey, men are loyal the way dogs are loyal. Someone else feeds him, he'll go right home with her."

Ella looked down at Nellie, who was waiting patiently by her food bowl—head cocked to one side, eyes soulful. Ella opened the drawer filled with Science Diet and dug the scoop deep.

"I'm sure you had a reason for calling, Aunt Julie? Other than spreading your usual pixie dust?"

"Don't sass. As a matter of fact, I did. Are you all done with your yoyo?"

"Yoga."

"Whatever. This is important, Ella. I need you to come out to The Dunes right now and help me."

"But I'm coming this weekend. Can't it wait?"

There was a note on the counter, next to the metal canisters of flour and sugar. Ella picked it up. *Don't forget your OJ and vitamin!!! H*

"Honey, I'm ninety-six years old. You wait for the weekend, you might miss me. And if I go to my grave while *that man* gets off scot-free—"

"Hold on. Are you back on this Frank Hardcastle business?"

"Who else?" There was a pause, as of a Bloody Mary being sipped.

Ella trudged to the fridge and took out the orange juice. "Are you serious? You actually think you have dirt on Frank Hardcastle?

Senator Frank Hardcastle? Something nobody else in the world—journalists, *opposing party,* for example—has ever figured out?"

"That's right. You think your generation invented scandal? You don't know the meaning of the word. This is big, I tell you. Goes way back." Aunt Julie cackled into the telephone. "Oh, there's going to be dead bodies all over Washington by the time I'm done."

Ella swallowed back the vitamin pill with a swig of orange juice and glanced across the room at the CD-ROM lying on the rolltop desk, waiting for a new computer. "Okay. Let's assume you're not completely nuts. You have about a hundred other great-nieces and nephews with plenty of time on their hands. Why me?"

"Because *she* chose you."

"*Who* chose me?"

"Her. Gin. The Redhead. *You* were the one she picked. God knows why."

Ella set down the empty orange juice glass. The nerves buzzed at the tips of her fingers. In her head, the sobs echoed back from the night before. The brokenhearted voice.

Don't go.

"I'm sorry, you lost me. What does the Redhead have to do with this Hardcastle business?"

"Darling," Aunt Julie said in the way you explained dental hygiene to a kindergartner. "*Everything.*"

ACT I

There's No Place Like Home

(and thank the good Lord for that)

LONG ISLAND, NEW YORK

June 1924

1

THIS WOMAN leans against one of the pillars in the lobby of the St. George Hotel in downtown Brooklyn, wearing a suit of lean brown tweed and a tiny cloche hat of ivory felt. Beautiful she be. Face sculpted in marble. Eyes the color of glacier ice. Tall and slender as one of them mannequins you see in the picture windows at Lord & Taylor. She stares toward the revolving door and smokes a cigarette in sharp, nervy jerks of her arm. So marvelous diligent she studies on the morning trickle of humanity through that door, she don't see me coming until I tap her bony shoulder and scare the living daylights out of her.

"Why, hello, Luella," I say. "If you're waiting for Anson, I'm afraid he's already left."

2

WE STEAMED into New York Harbor last night, Anson and me, aboard the *L'Oiseau* out of Nova Scotia. Ship arrived late, due to some furious weather off Long Island, and yours truly emerged from her stateroom somewhat to the left of bilious, much to my companion's dismay. Be only recent recovered from losing about half my store of blood, you see, and Anson is what you might call the nervous type where my health is concerned. Still, I was not so bilious

I didn't notice Anson sign us into the guest register as *Mr. and Mrs. Oliver Marshall*—just the same as he signed us into the steamship the day before—which is a downright lie, possibly the only lie Anson has ever told.

The two of us be no more married than a pair of swans, for all we've mated for life.

But what choice did we have? After what happened in Canada, neither me nor Anson can stand to spend the black hours of night without the other. He don't sleep much anymore. Only thing to knock him out reliable is me, offering up my flesh as a sanctuary, a vessel of blessed relief, and even then I might deliver him but a few hours of precious oblivion before he wakes again for good. Sometimes I stir and sense his watchfulness, the soft burr of his anguish spinning in the dark, and I reach my hand to touch him on the arm or leg or stomach so that I might possibly tap off some of that sorrow into myself. I think it helps. He will entangle himself back around me, lay his hot skin to melt against mine, so that we seem to leach into each other, almost to share the same bones.

Last night I don't believe he slept at all, curled safe though we were in the shelter of that warm hotel bed. Who could blame him, when such a terrible ordeal lies before us today? All the night I felt him at my back, holding me snug the way you might clutch some treasure for solace, and though he wanted me desperate hard, he never would take me, howsoever I made him to understand I was willing. I woke just as the gray dawn slid between the curtains. Opened my eyes to see a crack of light, a hint of steam from behind the door of that exemplary white hotel bathroom. Anson had already risen, already bathed.

I reached for my wristwatch on the table beside the bed and saw the hour was but half past five o'clock. Stole naked across the carpet to the bathroom. Inside, Anson stood before the mirror, white towel wrapped around his middle, shaving his cheeks and jaw in long, contemplative strokes of the stainless steel safety razor he bought in Halifax to replace the one he'd lost at sea to a gang of liquor pirates. We stared at each other in the patch of clear glass he had smudged away from the fog. How pale-skinned I looked, how frail next to him. Shoulders like a bull, wide grim sunburned face. I took the razor from his hand. Without complaint he let me have it. I made him to sit on the stool, where I straddled his lap stark naked and shaved him tender. Wiped away each speck of soap with a square of washcloth. Kissed the sweet, damp, sleek skin of his face until he couldn't stand it longer, poor man, and carried me back to bed.

Lord Almighty, how I do but live to feed the carnal fury of my beloved! To bury my hands deep in his hair when at last he arches his back and comes off in terrible shudders. Expression of tortured rapture murders me every time. Be all or nothing with that man. Once he gave up his virtue to me, why, he could no more restrain himself than suffer his heart to quit beating, nor could I suffer him to try. There will be hell to pay for this, mark my words. Hell to pay. And worth every nickel, too, just to clasp his dead slack weight against me, while my own nerves dazzled like stars. I would have stretched that moment of tranquil conjoinment into eternity, if I could.

But there be no such thing as eternity here on earth. Eventual he came to. Raised his head and asked me anxious if I was all right, was my arm all right. I said I was just fine, I was better than fine, don't worry so much. He said he couldn't help but worry. Face all hung with remorse. Dropped his head back down next to mine and said to me soft, so his words brushed my cheek—*I can't stop myself. I try, but I can't. Can't survive anymore without this.*

"My goodness," I told him, "then it's lucky you don't ever need to. Now lie here comfortable and bide awhile. You need to rest."

He shook his head and rolled away. Had to go into Manhattan and retrieve his car, he said, so we could drive out to the other end of Long Island in time for the funeral.

Well. I watched him rise and dress, and I thought about the slip of paper in my pocketbook, stashed there hurriedly as we disembarked the ship last night, and I told him he had better get a move on, then. Can't be late to your own father's funeral.

Which is how I came to encounter Luella Kingston in the lobby of the St. George Hotel at seven in the morning, because I'd happened to read this radio telegram that was meant for Mr. Oliver Marshall, Stateroom 22, and was instead delivered into the hands of the so-called Mrs. Marshall, because her so-called husband was out taking a walk on the rain-dashed deck when he ought to have been safe in bed. And if you tell me what a wicked, unscrupulous creature I am, practicing such deception on this fellow I profess to love as I love to breathe, why, I will tell you I never pretended otherwise.

Before Almighty God, I would trade my last scruple, barter my last scrap of immortal soul, for to give Oliver Anson Marshall but a single hour of tranquility.

3

THIS WOMAN, on the other hand. Seems to me Luella Kingston lives to give Anson nothing but trouble, though she loves him near as fierce as I do. How she hates the sight of me. She didn't save his life out there on the North Atlantic for *my* sake, that's certain. At most, she saved him for himself. More likely, for her own use.

Still, save him she did. I owe her for that, at least.

She recovers her composure right quick. "So much for private telegrams, I guess."

"No secrets between husband and wife, after all."

"He hasn't *married* you, has he? The idiot."

"Well, not quite. Sort of a temporary measure, you might say, to observe the niceties. Anyway, I'm not the marrying kind."

Luella wiggles the cigarette and regards me, ice cold. "Still, you're the *jealous* kind, aren't you? Did you even bother to tell him I needed to see him?"

I nod to the cigarette. "I don't suppose you've got a spare?"

Baleful she glares at me, but she takes a handsome gold cigarette case from her pocketbook and holds it out. I light myself with the matchbook in my pocket and suggest we make ourselves comfortable. Anson won't be back anytime soon.

We settle ourselves on a pair of plush chintz armchairs, the kind you find in hotel lobbies and nowhere else. I start the conversation friendly. "I want to thank you for what you did, out there. You saved his life, and I won't forget that."

"Don't thank me for yourself," she says. "I did it for him."

"That's what I figured. All the same, he's alive. If you need a favor, it's yours."

Luella sits back in her chair and crosses one antelope leg over the other. "I don't need any favors from you, Ginger Kelly. But I appreciate the thought."

"Do you really? Because it seems to me you're in an awful fix, just now. Does your lover know you betrayed him for the sake of his mortal enemy?"

"*Does* he. As a matter of fact, I hear he wants me dead. Offered a flattering price for someone to do the dirty work, too, so if you're in need of a little dough to start your nest egg—well, be my guest." She opens her arms wide and smiles at me with her crimson lips, the only single color on that exquisite face of hers.

"Is that why you're here? To ask for Anson's help?"

"Certainly not. I don't ask favors from other women's lovers, sweetheart. I only meant to give him this." Luella reaches into her jacket pocket and produces an envelope. "If you really mean that nonsense about paying me back, you can play postman for me."

I reach between the armchairs and pluck the letter from her long fingers. "Can I ask what's inside?"

Luella makes this brittle laugh. "It's not a declaration of love, if that's what you're worried about. It's just that I'm off to strike that monster first, before he can strike me, and I thought someone should know about it in case things don't work out as planned."

"You mean to murder him? Your bread and butter? Head of the whole damn northeastern racket?"

"What have I got to lose? He knows what I've done. Anyway, I'll find someone else, never fear. Why, I might even turn straight. I guess even those skinflints at the Bureau'd pay a pretty penny for all the information I've got up here." She taps her temple and sucks pleasantly on the cigarette.

"You think so? I figure the Prohibition bureau might not be so quick to trust you again, since it turns out you was nothing more than a rat in agent's clothing. Carrying every crumb of information back to your lover. Protecting his business and all."

"Of course they'll trust me. What more proof do they need? My God, I'm going to hand them their prize head on a platter." She stubs out the smoke in a bronze ashtray and stands. "Well, I must say, I've enjoyed our little chat more than I should. I trust you'll pass that letter along to Marshall? Some juicy gossip inside, which I'm sure he'll be glad to know. Particularly in the event of my death."

"I'll give it to him, never fear. I want that murderous bastard dead as much as you do, believe me."

"Well, then." She holds out her hand and bares her teeth. "I'd say *until we meet again*, except I really hope we don't."

I shake her hand. Hard, bony fingers. Remarkable cool. "No hard feelings, though?"

"Oh, I've got plenty of hard feelings, believe me. But you won him fair and square. If he's happy with you, why, good luck to him. Anyway, I've got my own fish to fry."

"I wish you luck."

"Sure you do. I'm off, then. Long drive ahead."

She's about to depart and turns back. For an instant, her face softens. The hat cradles her head. The chandelier light touches the side of her cheek, so she seems almost human.

"Take care of him for me, will you?"

4

LORD ALMIGHTY, how I do dread a funeral. The last time I endured the requiem for some poor soul, called premature to the house of our Father, I came only to bear witness they buried my mother so deep in the consecrated dirt of River Junction, Maryland, my step-daddy could never see nor hurt her again.

To look upon the face of my beloved, you might not plumb the depth of his sorrow on the occasion of his father's burial. His expression is so hard as the side of a cliff, and his eyes are the same cold navy as the most pacific ocean. He quivers not, neither does he sigh. Still, I guess the grief beneath Anson's skin runs deep enough to have no end.

He drives conscientious, both hands gripping the wheel, speed never once exceeding the legal limit. All around us, the first new sunshine of June sheds its warmth upon the meadows and the orchards of Long Island. The sky is a giant, clear blue, as yet uncorrupted by the sultriness of midsummer, and so placid I can scarce recall the heaving seas of yesterday. We don't speak much, but then we have hardly spoken at all these past weeks. Too much to be said to say even a word, sometimes. We are as a pair of soldiers in the late Great War, fixing our bayonets to go over the top at dawn. On the battleground before us stands this funeral, for one thing, which we must somehow survive before the sun arcs its way to the opposite horizon. The agony of Mrs. Marshall will strike us deep.

And then what?

When this sun rises again, where will we be? What will we do?

Under fraud of making myself more comfortable, I glance over my shoulder at the road behind us. The gray, sunbaked strip of asphalt lies empty behind us. The hour's early, after all, and most folks are heading into the city, not out of it. One of them rushes past right now. The sunlight flashes on the windows, then he's gone. Funeral starts at eleven sharp, down the other end of Long Island, yet Anson—as I've already said—does not ever push his fine automobile beyond the speed ordained by the county commissioners. Oh, my beloved shoots straight as an arrow, all right, whereas I be so crooked as the little notches at the end, holding that arrow to its course, so you see we make a perfect combination.

Needless to say, his mama don't agree. His mama sits this moment in her fine house by the ocean, checking the clock, dressed in some fashionable black frock, wondering where she went wrong. Mrs. Marshall will shortly bury a husband, killed by those same high-seas pirates who abolished Anson's razor and tried also to murder me. Last

I heard, her other remaining son was not long for this world, either—consumed by fever from a wound he acquired in my defense. For all these calamities, she will hold me to account.

I'll be straight with you, I don't look forward to staring at *her* face-to-face.

Her hard eyes will remind me that her family affairs were all in perfect order before a bastard child named Geneva Kelly rode down from her mountain holler into New York City and commenced to seduce Mrs. Marshall's two sons, one after the other. She will not admit mitigating evidence. She has condemned me, I know it, and in the rumbling peace of the black automobile's passing, I contemplate Anson's thick fingers around the steering wheel and wonder if she's right. Whether I ought to open the door of this Packard and roll honorably out of Anson's life, out of his mother's way, out of New York City altogether.

Then I remember I've left something of my own behind at the Marshall lair. Kind of a thing you can't leave behind, ever again.

I uncurl my fingers from the door handle. Anson stares at the road before him. By the set of his brows, I can tell he's rassling with some monster inside that brain of his. Grief, maybe? Guilt? What will he say to his brokenhearted mama?

Inside the pocket of my jacket, Luella Kingston's letter lies flat and hot against my blouse. I figure I'll give it to him after the funeral. One damn thing at a time, that's all a man can swallow.

5

HIS NAME is Grendel. That's all I know about the man who was Luella Kingston's lover, who runs the vast bootleg racket that once included my stepfather. The name was slipped to me accidental by one of his associates—a banker named Benjamin Stone, whose job it is to distribute lettuce to the hungry rabbits of certain local municipalities, in order to ensure the smooth flow of booze up and down the Atlantic Seaboard. At the time, me and Benjamin worked for the same particular bank—me in the typing pool, him heading up the municipal bond department—an august institution named Sterling Bates & Co., headquartered in one of them handsome neoclassic towers that line the downward slope of Wall Street, neatly cornering the New York Stock Exchange, and I leave it to you to determine which of us does the least credit to the American system of capital finance.

Funny name, Grendel. You might remember it—as I do—from some literature class in college. Terrible monster, that Grendel. Required so great a hero as Beowulf to put him to his bloody end. As I understand it, the sobriquet was fixed on our modern beast by his schoolfriends, which is why I introduce the subject now, as we motor toward this church full of blue-blooded mourners.

You see, Grendel's one of them.

That's right, you heard me. Anson's mortal enemy acquired his fearsome nickname at one of them legendary American boarding academies, where the great and good drop off boys like Benjamin Stone not just to fashion them into honorable manhood, but to encourage those lifelong friendships without which no man ever achieves the pinnacle of anything, from presidencies to investment banks to bootleg rackets. Hardly needs saying this tribe is a tiny, exclusive one—otherwise, what's the point of belonging? So it stands to reason we shall find any number of them gathered in this church today to grieve their fallen brother.

Why, Grendel himself might even now be arranging his necktie and a sober, mournful expression, preparing to take his seat on one of the pews, and I wouldn't know him from Adam. Who among us can tell a man from a monster, at first glance?

6

WE ARRIVE at the church at five minutes to eleven. Already the music swells from the organ. Cars parked for miles around. Anson wedges us into some impossible slice of grass and leaps out to open the door for me before I can so much as straighten my hat. Hands me out on his firm, dry palm and keeps hold of my fingers so we face the music as one. "Nearer, My God, to Thee," like they played on the deck of the poor old *Titanic*.

At the foot of the steps Anson pauses to stare at the humble wooden face of the church, pure white lines clean against the blue sky. His hand grips my fingers so snug, I can't find the nerves at the tips. I ask him what's the matter. He turns his earnest face to me. Snatch of breeze ruffles the hair that hangs above his forehead.

"We should get married," he says.

"What, *now?*"

"As soon as we can." He recollects himself and covers our knit hands with a broad palm. "If you'll have me, that is."

"Lord Almighty, Anson. You pick a strange moment for a marriage proposal."

"Can't go in there without it."

Music swirls around us. How pious they sing—*Darkness be over me, my rest a stone*. My whole field of sight contains nothing but Anson's grim face. The sun and sky have washed the color of his eyes, somehow, to a clear true blue that implores me so desperate keen, the scruples scatter right from my brain. From inside the church, some

childish soprano pipes out of tune above the other voices—*Nearer,
my God, to Thee, nearer to Thee.*

"Well, then," I whisper, "since it means so much, I guess I'd best
make an honest man of you."

The gust of his relief washes over us both like salvation itself. For
an instant, he shuts his eyes above our clasped hands. Then he turns
and mounts the steps so fast, it requires me to scramble like hell just
to keep up. At the door stands an usher, shooting fire from his eyes.
Still, the fellow opens up the Lord's house for us. He was bred up
proper and all.

Likewise, the congregation of admirable rich folk minds its man-
ners and turns not to witness the humiliation of the latecomers. All
the way up, souls sing lustily toward the altar, except in the very first
pew, where a small blond head breaks off at *Angels to beckon me* and
shrieks out *GIIIIIIIINNYYYY!* at the top of her wee lungs. The dark-
veiled woman beside her grabs an instant too late. Off the bench my
kid sister, Patsy, leaps—down the aisle she hurtles her darling self—
until she reaches my arms and throws herself trustful upon me. A few
singers soldier on—*Nearer, my God, to Thee, / Nearer, my God, to
Thee, / Nearer to Thee!*—but the rest just hang there in almighty hor-
ror and some amusement, while the organ plows through to the end.

7

MERCY UPON us, what a scene. Patsy having drug us to the
front pew, we make to sit with all eyes upon us. The minis-
ter delivers some thunderous lecture about divine retribution raining
down upon the heads of the wicked—he looks hard at my red hair as
he says this—after which I simply stop listening for reasons of health.

I feel the words strike blows upon Anson's skin, however. Patsy sits wedged between us, one of our hands in each of hers, so we connect through her like an electrical current. *We are engaged*, I think. Another of them light-headed waves crashes over me, and I realize I have forgot to breathe.

One after another, men stand to eulogize the departed. Sylvo Marshall was an important fellow, you understand, a leader of New York society. To begin with, I don't pay much attention. One eulogy is like another, anyhow. Then I focus my attention on the man who stands before us, speaking with some emotion of the fine qualities of the departed, and I realize I know this face particular well. Belongs to a fellow named Charles Schuyler, who happened to accompany us on our adventures two weeks ago, along with his sister Julie, and was lucky to escape with his life. Upon Schuyler's yacht we sailed north-northeast to Nova Scotia, and upon Schuyler's motor tender we met the pirates who had murdered Sylvo Marshall, who plied those fateful waters only to save his son.

Now Schuyler speaks movingly of his friend and neighbor—how bravely he fought to rescue Oliver Marshall from a dirty ambush, how willingly he gave his life so that his beloved son might live. As he says this, he gazes down at me and Anson in our front pew, so warm and sad your heart might break. Then he lifts his head and says that Sylvo Marshall's sacrifice must not be in vain. We must all recall what killed him—the ring of bootleggers Agent Marshall was on the high seas trying to break—and *no decent person* should rest until the man who gave that order to ambush Oliver Marshall and kill him dead was dead himself.

The words *no decent person* he says with particular emphasis, and it seems to me he searches through the congregation and rests his gaze upon somebody in it, just as he utters the words *was dead himself*, and the recollection comes to me sudden—I was dreadful injured, don't forget, and certain details fell from my attention—that I *do* know another man who went to boarding school with this unknown, anonymous monster named Grendel.

Charles Schuyler.

8

NOW MY ears commence to buzz, so I don't hear the rest of Schuyler's speech, just the dread silence that meets the end of it. Schuyler steps away from the pulpit and returns to his pew, where his wife and his young son doubtless wait for him, and a man rises from the other side of Mrs. Marshall—a man I didn't notice before, on account of my own shock and misery.

A man I recognize well, though not as he now appears.

He stands and shambles to the pulpit, a shrunken, pale fellow, scarred and disfigured, jaw all hollowed out on one side. At one time, not long ago, I was in the bad habit of joining this young man upon a sinful bed, which I now regret more fierce than any bad habit I've ever picked up. Not because he wasn't a sweet, good boy, a fine lover who adored me much beyond my deserts, but because his name is Billy Marshall, Mrs. Marshall's other son, younger brother to my beloved.

The thing is, though, he ain't supposed to be alive at all. I left him two weeks ago on his deathbed, burnt to a crisp with fever on account of certain wounds to his face, as I told you, which he received at the vengeful hand of my stepfather, Duke Kelly. You've heard of Duke, maybe? It was all over the papers some months ago. Duke Kelly, the notorious Appalachia bootlegger, caught at last by that intrepid agent of the United States Bureau of Prohibition, Oliver Anson Marshall.

And now Billy stands alive. What miracle is this?

So shocked as I am, I croak out *Billy!* without a thought in the world. Next to me, Anson jerks to life. Takes my elbow with his hand, the better to hold me back from making a fool of myself. I guess I might cry with relief. Poor Billy looks my direction and swiftly away. A ruined face like that, you can't tell what it's thinking, no more than you can divine the thoughts of a carnival mask.

But I expect the price of his life is steep, and this is how I pay it.

Patsy tugs my other hand and casts me back to present. I know by the grip of Anson's fist that he's as shocked as I am. That his mama, in her brief, curt telegrams, never told him this—your kid brother, Billy, has risen from the dead, maybe at the exact moment Sylvo Marshall was felled. A life for a life. Dear old Sylvo, darling father of my beloved, who made himself a sacrifice to rescue Anson from death.

How would it feel, I wonder, to possess a father who loved you so much as that?

Billy saws his throat and starts to speak. His words aren't so clear, but they arise straight from his heart. I don't listen to what he says, however. My mind's too a-jumble with all these ideas, these shocks struck one after another—all different yet related—Luella in the lobby of the St. George Hotel, Schuyler's vow of justice and Billy still alive, me engaged to marry Oliver Anson Marshall for so long as we both shall live. I cling to Patsy's wee hand. On the other side of her, Anson sits straight and shares his brother's sorrow. Somewhere behind us, that monster lurks. Right here nerveless at the very funeral service of the man he caused to be murdered! Charles Schuyler knows

who he be. Benjamin Stone knows who he be. Luella Kingston—
well, she knows better than anybody.

And I swan before this sacred altar I shall murder him myself, the
instant his face is known to *me*.

9

WHEN THE service ends, we file out of the family pew. I become aware of the stony stares of the rest of the congregation, for am I not but a cuckoo in this nest? A red-haired Appalachia
hillbilly possessed of no morals whatsoever, burrowed among these
august Marshalls?

Anson gathers Patsy's wee hand in his paw and gives me his arm
to hold as we walk past those hostile stares of his friends and neighbors. All the way down that aisle we follow the elegant black figure
of Mrs. Marshall, leaning on the arm of her son Billy, holding the
hand of her small daughter, Marie, while the organ plays some familiar hymn I can't quite place. Through the door and down the steps.
When we reach the bottom, away from the eyes of the congregation,
Mrs. Marshall stops at last and turns to face us through her black
veil. The veil is nice enough. Sheer black netting edged with lace
knit by a hundred diligent novices at some convent atop an Italian
mountain, the kind of veil that costs a lot of kale. Shows a proper
respect for the deceased. You can just see Mrs. Marshall's handsome
face behind it, her cherry-red lipstick, though you can't see her expression. Puts you at a disadvantage, and don't imagine for a second
she doesn't know this. She waits rigid for Anson to address her.

Anson leans forward to embrace her. "Mother, I—"

But she steps away. "We'll speak later," she tells him, and she turns with Billy and tiny Marie and proceeds to her stately black car, where the chauffeur waits respectful next to the open door.

For an instant, Anson stands absolutely still, watching her go. My own face is numb with shock. Because one thing I know about Mrs. Marshall—know *for certain*, or thought I knew—is she loves her children with a fierce, uncompromising love. She will forgive them anything.

Anything, it seems, except this.

Or maybe Anson *himself* is the exception? I do recall a time, not long ago, when Mrs. Marshall commanded me to do a despicable thing for the sake of Billy Marshall—to marry Billy instead of Anson, to give Billy a reason to live after his terrible injuries. At the time, I figured she just knew Billy was the weaker one, the one who needed our help, and maybe she was right about that. But now I wonder if maybe Anson is simply the least of her fierce loves, for some reason I cannot fathom. Some reason that hides deep inside the pages of her history.

Just as I open my mouth to say something, Anson starts himself into action—takes back my arm and Patsy's hand and leads us to his car. Opens the door for me and Patsy to climb in for the drive to Windermere, the fine house by the ocean where Marshalls have summered for decades now, and where all these mourners will proceed for a short, tasteful reception to remember Sylvester Marshall, before the internment tomorrow in the family plot at Calvary Cemetery in Queens.

10

LUCKY FOR us both, Patsy's happy to fill the dreadful silence with chatter. Rattles off a whole list of tactless questions for

Anson, like where has he been all this time and did he know poor Mr.
Marshall got killed by a gang of wicked pirates, which he answers
with his usual solemn patience. Then Patsy goes on to tell him how
she's learned to swim and to ride Mrs. Marshall's pony, about the shell
collection she's amassed in her weeks by the sea, and then out of the
blue, just as we're turning down the drive to Windermere, she asks if
him and Ginny got married while we were away.

"My goodness, why would you think such a thing?" I ask her.

"Because you *looked* like you was married. Holding his arm and
everything."

"Well, we're not."

"Why not?"

"Because we didn't have time," Anson says. "But Ginny's promised to marry me just as soon as all this is over."

Patsy squeals loud and jumps up on the seat. Anson and I both
reach out to steady her. "Really, Ginny? You really *is* going to marry
Anson?"

"I really am."

"Praise the Lord, I was that afeared you was going to marry Billy
instead!"

"I was never going to marry Billy, you know that. Just being kind
because he was so sick and all. Now sit back down before you fly right
out of the car."

"Can I be bridesmaid?"

"Can't think of anyone else to do the job."

"And you'll take me to live with you? Like a real family?"

"Why, of course we will, my wee round sweet apple. We're a family deal, I said to Anson. Isn't that right, darling?"

Now, as you know perfectly well, I said no such thing, there on
those church steps before the funeral service. In my shock, I didn't

think to mention Patsy, who has no one left but me in the whole wide world to raise her, now that our mama and her daddy rest deep together in the earth of River Junction. But Anson shows no surprise at all, either to his newfound responsibility for raising my kid sister or to that unaccustomed *darling* that popped from my lips. Just pulls Patsy down from her precarious perch on the cloth seat to a comfortable position against his side, while he pilots us down the gravel lane with his competent left hand. Leans down to kiss her gold hair.

"Why, that's why I asked Ginny to marry me in the first place," he says.

We reach the house, where Mrs. Marshall's giant black automobile sits right before the entrance. Anson rolls to a stop and sets the brake. We sit silent for a moment. Patsy still cuddles into Anson's middle, so delirious with joy she can't yet speak.

"Billy will be just fine," I say softly.

"Still, I've betrayed him."

"You didn't do any betraying. That was your mother. She knew which brother I loved. And me, *I* let him think I was still his, on account of he was so sick. None of this is your doing. You've got the only true heart among us."

Anson turns his head to look at me. Eyes dark with anguish.

I reach across Patsy to lay my hand on his knee. "You know what? Let's just go. Turn around and head back to the city. We'll get hitched, go off somewhere, come back again when it's all blown over and Billy's happy married to somebody else—"

"No. I won't run away. I'll face them, all right. Tell them straight."

"Then I'll go with you."

Anson takes Patsy by the shoulders and sits her back up. "No need for that. Just take care of our girl while I'm in the lion's den."

"Lioness, you mean. Don't let her maul you to pieces, now. Stick to your guns. Me and Patsy need something left of you when she's done."

A car pulls up behind ours, and another one right behind. Anson leans over Patsy to kiss me on the lips. "I'll survive. I've faced her before."

"Be careful anyway," I tell him. "I hear they're specially dangerous when wounded."

11

TRUE TO Anson's command, I lead Patsy away from the house and down the lawn to the ocean. I have no desire to mingle among a shocked New York high society. Not the slightest inclination to take Patsy anywhere that monster Grendel might be lurking, all unknown to us. Instead we take off our shoes and wander in our stockings along the sand, examining shells and whatnot. Off the coast, you can just make out the hazy shapes of the liquor ships, anchored outside United States territorial waters where the daring motorboats can reach them by night. But I don't care about that now. Don't care in the slightest about this illicit trade in booze for a thirsty nation. Let them drink, I say. Patsy and Anson, that's all I care about, and how soon we can depart this place and find some peaceful corner to live together.

The hot sun strikes my shoulders and the back of my neck. Patsy says she's thirsty, can we get a drink. I stare unwilling at the great house, where there be food and drink aplenty, and consider whether the price is too high. Then my eye falls upon another building, next to the glimmering swimming pool at the bottom of the lawn. A summer house, small and perfect, which I know offers shade and shelter and running water and a little kitchen, where you can fill yourself a glass of water. Also a couch that sometimes serves as a bed, where me and Anson first lay together, during a cold March night that seems to belong to another lifetime.

I take Patsy's hand. "Come along. I've got just the place for us."

12

WE DRINK some water, cool and fresh. Then Patsy says she needs to wee. I show her the tiny bathroom and wander around while she does her business. Room shows no sign of that midnight hour when I stole Anson's virtue from him. Poor fellow had just been stitched up from a gunshot wound and prescribed whiskey for his pain, so I had him at my mercy at last, and didn't I take advantage of *that*. Still he was altogether willing. You might say that whiskey did no more than melt away his scruples, so nothing remained but what he wanted more than anything in the world, which was me.

All these thoughts float in my head—the precious remembrance of that night, the sorrow for what followed, the anxiety for Anson, who even now settles our future in the lion's den across the lawn—when a noise reaches my ears, the noise of a door hinge squeaking open.

Quick as a cat, I fly across the room and join Patsy inside the bathroom.

She turns from the sink, where she be washing her wee hands like I taught her. "Ginny, what—"

"Shh!" I lay my finger over my lips. She claps her damp palm over her mouth and nods, like we have played this game before.

I reach for the switch on the wall and turn off the electric light above the mirror. Peek through the crack of the door, which I have left ajar for this purpose. Above all things I hate to be surprised. The door opens at such an angle to afford me a view of exactly half of the room—the half that contains the wide couch and the windows overlooking the hot blue ocean, but not the door from the terrace surrounding the pool. Patiently I wait. A man comes into view, smoking a cigar. A fine-looking man, though unfamiliar to me. Maybe forty or forty-five years old. Trim, tall figure. Dark, expensive suit. Fair hair, curling a bit in the humid summer air. Skin tanned a fine leathery gold, the kind of man who spends his time outdoors for recreation, tennis or golf or sailing or what have you. Can't see but the side of his face, but you have to admire the shape of his long, triangular nose and trustworthy jaw. One hand smokes the cigar, other hand curls to a fist in the pocket of his trousers. Seems to frown as he stares through the windows to the ocean and the ships dreaming on the horizon. I have the notion he's waiting for somebody.

A minute passes, maybe two. He wanders a bit, kind of paces across the room and back. Still can't get a good look at his face. At one point he passes perilously close to the bathroom door, so I draw away from the inch of space between door and doorframe and try not to breathe. Seems I can feel his gaze searching through the dark air, the way an animal senses the presence of another. But the footsteps continue back across the room, and an instant later I hear a man's voice call a single word, too muffled for me to hear it.

"It's me," says the man in the room.

Patsy leans forward like to whisper something in my ear. I shake my head and put my finger again to my lips. She frowns. Won't be silent much longer, I guess. Only so many minutes a wee round sweet apple can keep from expressing herself, howsoever great the danger.

When I turn back to the crack in the door, another man steps into my line of sight. I swallow back a gasp. Long, pale, skinny stick insect of a man.

Benjamin Stone.

They commence to talking in hushed voices. Can't pick out more than a word or two. I close my eyes so I can better hear them. Settle my ear as close to the door's edge as possible. Stone speaks in a high, agitated voice; the other man a calm bass. Shallow and scarce lies my breath in my lungs. Wild thoughts race around and around in my head.

. . . *live with myself,* says Stone, almost sobbing. *He was my friend.*

The other man replies in cold composure, too low to understand.

. . . *doesn't matter. He's dead,* Stone says.

The other man asks a question.

Stone sobs back, *But I can't do this any longer, I just can't. I'm out, do you hear me?*

I'm afraid that's not possible, says the other man, firm enough that the words reach me whole.

Patsy tugs on my sleeve. I hold up my hand and shake my head.

But Ginny, she whispers. I place my hand on her arm to hold her still.

Stone turns away and says something toward the opposite wall.

You've profited handsomely, Stone. Surely you understand this comes with a price.

Now I owe Benjamin Stone exactly nothing, and if he feels remorse for his involvement—however incidental—in the death of poor Sylvo Marshall, why, it's no more than he deserves. Still, I feel this peculiar urge to shout some warning—*My God, don't turn your back on this man! For God's sake, turn around!*

Stone tilts his head upward. *No more. I can't. That's it*—unintelligible—*I just can't do it any longer.*

The other man—Grendel, let's call him—stands quite still, staring at the back of Stone's pepper-and-salt head. The sunlight drifts through the window, bathing him in this unearthly glow like an angel.

Without a sound, he steps in the direction of Stone's pale, tender neck.

Patsy throws off my hand. Both men whirl toward the bathroom door.

"Who's there?" shouts Stone.

I gather my breath, take Patsy's hand in mine, and burst cheerfully from the bathroom.

"Why, hello there! My goodness, I didn't hear you come in. I was just helping my little Patsy here in the bathroom. Tinkle, tinkle, little star."

Stone and Grendel stare in shock. I put my hand to my mouth.

"Oh dear! Did we interrupt? Can't apologize enough. We'll just scamper right out of your—"

"Miss Kelly!" gasps Stone.

"*Kelly?*" says a startled Grendel.

I drag Patsy across the room. "Ta-ta, gentlemen! Just pretend you never—"

A hand grips my arm and spins me around. Face-to-face we stand, me and Grendel. My every nerve thrums with the electric desire to kill this man, to close my hands around his throat. Only Patsy's small fingers stop me. How striking he looks, how *good*. A fine honorable specimen of American manhood. Wife and kids at home, so I understand, and I bet they adore him. A miniscule muscle twitches beneath his right eye. His blue eyes stare me down.

"Miss Kelly," he says softly.

Patsy tugs my hand. "Ginny, come *on*! I has to change my drawers!"

"Change your *drawers*?"

"What I was trying to *tell* you! There wasn't any *paper*!" Then she tugs me down to whisper loud in my ear: *Diarrhea!*

Grendel barks with laughter. "Go on, Miss Kelly. Never fear, I'll be sure to find you once you've tended to this emergency."

13

WHEN I have tended to Patsy, I race through the house in search of Anson. Rooms full of festive mourners I find, but no bull-shouldered beloved. At last I come to the sunroom, which is peculiar empty—maybe because the French doors trap the heat like it's noon on the equatorial line. Just one man in a chair, staring through the glass. I pull up short.

"Billy?" I whisper.

He turns and looks at me. Can't tell what he's thinking, his face so mauled as it is.

"I'm glad you're up and about," I tell him. "I was afraid for the worst."

"I'll live."

"Does it hurt bad?"

"Better than it was."

"I-I'm awful sorry. About all this. I've always cared for you so much, Billy, always will—"

He turns away. "'Sall right. Guess I knew all along, deep down."

I might go up to him, I guess. Might could touch his shoulder or kiss his hair, some kind of good-bye or commiseration, at least. But I don't. Heart still pounds with fear. Head still whirls. Anyway, what good would it do? He's got his pride, after all. I open my mouth to ask him has he seen his brother, Ollie, anywhere, but I snap it shut just in time.

"All right," I say instead. "See you around, I guess."

I slip out of the room and into the way of Mrs. Marshall. She's discarded both hat and veil, and her face looks about ten years older than I saw it last, just two weeks ago. Pale and gaunt, swipe of crimson lipstick. Right behind her, Anson about staggers against her back when she stops short before me.

"Is it true?" she demands.

I guess I don't need to ask *what*. "You can't say I didn't warn you."

"What did you say to Billy?"

"Just good-bye."

Anson steps around his mother and snatches my hand. "We were just leaving," he tells her.

"I think that's best," she replies, cold as ice.

He leans forward and kisses her cheek. "Good-bye, Mother," he says soft.

Her eyelids flutter, so brief as a heartbeat. Then she draws away and says good-bye. Walks straight past us into the sunroom. Anson slumps against the wall and closes his eyes.

"Where's Patsy?" he asks.

"Upstairs."

"We should leave. Your trunks are already in the car. Mother had them packed."

"Well, don't start the engine just yet."

He opens his eyes and straightens from the wall. "What's the matter?"

"He's here," I whisper. "Grendel."

"*Here?*"

"He was with Benjamin Stone in the summer house a moment ago. I took Patsy inside for a drink of water and—"

Anson grips my arms. "You saw him? You spoke to him?"

"I couldn't help it. We hid in the bathroom, and then Patsy made a noise. He knew who I was, Anson. He means to find me. You, too, probably. God only knows what—"

"But *who?* Who is he?"

"I don't know! Never seen him before. About your height but slender. Dark blond hair, blue eyes, deep voice—"

"That might be half the men here."

"Maybe forty, forty-five. He was smoking a cigar."

Anson paces down the hall and stops. Squints through the window at the lawn. "Is he still there, do you think?"

"I doubt it. Half an hour ago now, at least. He said he was going to find me."

Anson swears and turns to face me. "Go back up to Patsy, right now. Wait for me there."

"Oh no you don't!"

"Just once, Gin. Just for *once* can you do as I ask? Stay put when I tell you to?"

"If I'd stayed put—"

I catch myself. Because if I'd stayed put right here at Windermere, instead of tearing off to rescue Anson—as I thought—Sylvester Marshall would still be alive. And so would Anson, because Luella Kingston had already gone to warn him about Grendel's trap.

Luella saved him, not me.

All I brought was tragedy.

The realization jolts me silent. I stand there and stare at him hopeless.

"Gin. Gin, I'm sorry. That's not what I meant—"

I turn for the stairs, for Patsy's bedroom, but he catches me and pulls me close. Arms fold snug around me. "Listen. Let's just leave. It doesn't matter anymore. I've quit the Bureau. It's not my lookout, is it?"

"Quit the *Bureau?* When did you quit the Bureau?"

"Back in Halifax, before we left. Sent my resignation to Washington by telegram. For good, this time."

"You never said."

"I'm saying it now. Nothing's going to bring Dad back. Nothing I do for the Bureau is ever going to make a bit of difference. You were right, all along. No such thing as justice in this game. Someone else'll just take Grendel's place, take over his racket. I don't care. Come along." He steps back and takes my hand. "Let's get Patsy and get out of here."

"You don't really mean that."

"I have never meant anything more."

He says it so fierce, his eyes so keen, I can't help but to believe him. His face and his hair have this wild look to them, like of a prisoner attempting an escape, and I myself be his fresh air, his freedom, his whole new life beyond bars. Me and Patsy. He pulls me toward the stairs. Got no choice but to follow him.

14

So IT comes to pass that we're flying out the front door, Patsy skipping joyously between us, when the ambulance tears down the drive in a spray of Mrs. Marshall's carefully tended gravel.

Anson skids to a stop. The ambulance men jump out of the ambulance, a Model T truck painted white with a red cross on each side, like in the war.

"What's the matter? Can I help you?"

"Got a call there's a man in the stables, been stabbed or something? You know where that is?"

"Follow me," says Anson. He takes off at a run, followed by the ambulance men, followed by me and Patsy. Well, we can't just stand here by ourselves in the driveway! Anson and the ambulance men outpace us fast. As we turn the corner of the house, the stables come into view. Crowd gathered around. Anson pushes his way through, the ambulance men right behind with their black leather bags, their spotless white uniforms. Mouth so dry I gasp for air. Come to a stop with Patsy at the edge of the crowd.

"What is it?" I ask a blonde in a navy-blue dress.

She turns her head. I realize in shock that it's Julie Schuyler, Charles Schuyler's kid sister, my old nemesis and sometime ally.

"As if you didn't know," she says.

"Tell me anyway."

Julie measures me up and down. I start to turn away, find somebody else to tell me what the hell's going on, but she reaches out and snags my arm.

"It's Louis Hardcastle, you bumpkin," she says. "Somebody stabbed him to death."

ELLA

East Hampton, New York, 1998

IF YOU asked Ella, she would say she wasn't a Hamptons person, not at all. She hated the scene, top to bottom—the relentless traffic, the competitive socializing, the conversations studded with oblique status markers, the passive aggression, the aggressive aggression, the clothes and cars and shopping and house renovations—in short, the people who drove out from Manhattan every summer weekend and ruined a perfectly lovely beach town because they couldn't sit still and just enjoy what Nature had provided, free of charge.

But The Dunes was another story. Built more than a century ago by Mumma's great-grandfather, the house occupied two dozen prime beachfront acres and hadn't been renovated since Mumma's mother had made her husband wire it for electricity as a wedding present. That was in 1938. Needless to say, there was no air conditioning at The Dunes—why waste power when you had a perfectly good ocean in your backyard, as Ella had heard over and over when she was a kid—and the Hotpoint range had to be lighted with a match on the rare occasions when somebody could be bothered to cook.

Ella and Hector had driven out two weekends ago to help Mumma and Aunt Viv open up the place for the summer, and Hector—who went a little reluctantly, not being a Hamptons person himself—had fallen in love at first sight. Had repaired the loose paneling in the dining room and tightened the leaky ancient bath fixtures and opened all the windows at night so the ocean breeze washed over them. When he laid eyes on the 1911 concert Steinway gathering dust in the sitting room, he nearly passed out. Spent the afternoon painstakingly tuning it and put out a tip jar. He took requests all evening and made ninety-three cents. "For God's sake, Ella," Mumma said afterward, "why couldn't you have met this one first and saved us the trouble?"

All this and more occupied Ella's mind as she drove down the gravel drive in the secondhand Audi she and Hector had bought from a friend of his who'd gone to Vienna for a year to study piano. The sky was hot blue and hazy, the grassy dunes rolled in a daze to the sea. Out popped the house—gray-shingled, rambling in every direction, turrets and gables poking up all over the place. Nellie stuck her head out the window and yelped joyously at the familiar scent of the nearby beach, to say nothing of Aunt Viv's two Labradors, who'd welcomed her into the Schuyler pack after a rigorous initial inspection.

Ella reached over and stroked her ears. "I know what you mean, doll," she said.

"BUT WHY LOS ANGELES?" Mumma wanted to know. "Couldn't he have recorded his music here in New York?"

"I don't know. The director hired the symphony, probably."

"I was hoping he could do something about the banister on the front stairs," said Aunt Viv. "And that wobbly chair in the dining room."

"For God's sake, he's not a *handyman*. Not *your* handyman, anyway."

"Darling, he *enjoys* it. Why not give him something to do?"

They sat on the terrace with drinks and a cheese log from the supermarket. Aunt Viv was layering orange-pink cheddar spread on a Ritz cracker with an ivory-handled silver knife that had probably arrived in the kitchen drawer eighty years ago as a wedding gift from one of the Roosevelts, and really you could not express the entire Schuyler ethos better than that. Mumma and Aunt Viv drank identical vodka tonics, Ella drank seltzer with lime. Lizzie had taken Aunt Julie to a doctor's appointment in Southampton. The exhausted dogs lay in a pile on the nearby grass, drenched in afternoon sun, by all appearances dead.

"Vivian," said Mumma, "you're an awful snob, you know."

"Pot, kettle."

Ella studied the bubbles rising inside her seltzer. She had the feeling Mumma was staring at her again, and she didn't know where else to look. To stare back at Mumma was to acknowledge that things had changed between them, that a new current had disturbed the equilibrium of their relationship, and then Mumma—being Mumma— would demand to know what it was.

And just how was Ella going to respond to that?

Well, Mumma. It's just that I learned a few months ago that Daddy's not my actual biological father, and I'm having a hard time with that, I really am. I have questions. What's the story? Why didn't you tell me?

Who the hell is my father, anyway?

Daddy had confessed that he *wasn't* present at Ella's conception, but he hadn't said who *was*. They hadn't really talked about it since— morning sickness had the single virtue of giving Ella a pass on difficult, soul-baring conversations. Besides, before she could talk to Daddy, she had to talk to Mumma, daughter to mother. She had to know the truth. She had to know everything.

But how did you even *start* that conversation with your mother?

Especially Mumma—vibrant, beautiful, mettlesome Mumma, whose love was electric and all-encompassing but hardly comforting.

"Ella?"

"Yes, Mumma?"

"Look at me, darling. Is something wrong?"

Ella looked up. "Wrong? You mean other than being pregnant with one man's baby while you're in love with someone else?"

Mumma took in a neat little gasp of air, like a hiss. Then her face relaxed. She took a sip of vodka and said, "Yes, I mean other than that. You've been so *distracted* lately."

As if on cue, Ella's cell phone rang. Mumma gave her a dirty look.

"It's Hector," Ella said, by way of apology, and opened the phone.

"There you are. Out and about?"

"*Actually*, I'm in East Hampton, surprise! Came out early instead of waiting for the weekend. The city's just too hot and Nellie needed a vacation."

"Genius. How are you feeling?"

Ella rose from her chair and walked to the edge of the terrace. "Hundred percent fine. Even the drive was okay. How was your flight?"

"Flight was late, but I'm all set now. You should see this hotel. Right on the beach. They scored me this crazy suite with a baby grand in the sitting room. Everyone's coming over this evening for a nightcap to hear some of my stuff."

"Who's everyone?"

"Director, producers, couple of the actors. Dog and pony show, basically. God, I miss you."

"I miss you, too."

"Listen, I have to go. Hop in the shower and head down the freeway to squeeze in some rehearsal time before dinner. Just wanted to check in and tell you how much I adore you."

Aunt Viv called across the terrace: "Tell him he'd damn well better be back for the wedding!"

"Aunt Viv says you'd better not miss the wedding."

"What, miss the entire Schuyler clan gathered together for the party of the century? Not for a million bucks," Hector said.

"SO WHAT'S THIS DOCTOR appointment?" Ella asked, when she was back in her chair at the teak garden table.

Aunt Viv rose to refill her vodka tonic. "Oh, Julie hasn't been taking all her meds, apparently. That's the trouble with having her stay here over the summer, she goes right off her schedule without an aide to keep her straight. We have to call over to Maidstone Meadows and get her nurse on the line."

"But she's okay, isn't she?"

"Oh, she'll outlive us all, I'm sure." Mumma cocked her head. "I think that's the car now, isn't it?"

"Now, listen, Ella," said Aunt Viv. "Lizzie wants to talk to you about something, and I hope you'll hear her out. Personally, I think it's a terrible idea, but it's her wedding."

"What idea?"

"Oh, I'll let her tell you. Don't want to spoil the surprise."

Ella looked at Mumma, but Mumma just shrugged. Their charged exchange a moment ago seemed to have been forgotten, thank God. Lizzie was a sweet kid, only twenty-six and divinely pretty, youngest of the four Salisbury siblings. She was getting married to an old colleague of Patrick's—in fact, Lizzie and Owen had first met at Ella and Patrick's wedding, four years ago. He was a nice guy, for a banker. A perfect match for sweet-natured Lizzie. Sometimes Ella had trouble remembering what he looked like. He was attractive in an utterly unremarkable way, and Ella struggled to hold conversations with him because he just didn't seem to be interested in much besides finance and sports. But he made Lizzie happy, and he was apparently going along meekly with all the wedding planning, so what more could you want?

Lizzie came bounding up to the terrace from around the side of the house, makeup-free and glowing.

"Ella! Omigosh! I'm so excited you came early! Omigosh, look at you! You're so *pregnant*!"

"Please. This? Too much cheese log, that's all. Hector keeps complaining that the bump is too small. I think he wants me waddling around like a fertility goddess."

"Forget him, you look amazing. *Glowing*." Lizzie glanced to Aunt Viv, who shrugged her elegant shoulders and jiggled her ice. "Mom? How long before dinner?"

"Dinner's at the club at seven, darling. As always."

Lizzie took Ella's hands. "Can we talk for a minute?"

THEY WALKED DOWN TO the beach, where all Serious Talks were held at The Dunes, by tradition. It was June and the sun was still high, shedding hazy gold heat over the sand. Lizzie sat on the bleached log that had drifted up after a storm last winter and patted the space next to her. Twisted her diamond engagement ring, which was four or five carats and reminded Ella of a Chiclet.

"So I *know* this is a super big ask," said Lizzie.

"Lizzie, it's your wedding. You can ask what you want. The one time in your life. As long as it's not murder or something."

Lizzie giggled. "It's not. But you'll want to murder me for asking. Okay. Here goes. You ready?" Deep breath, then *Owenreallywants-Patricktobeoneofhisgroomsmen.*

Ella squinted. "*What* did you say?"

"Owen and Patrick. We wouldn't even be together without him. He was the one who put us at the same table at your wedding—"

"That was me, actually."

"Was it? Patrick said—well, whatever. It's been breaking Owen's *heart*. He asked Patrick to be his groomsman, and then you two broke up, and we just *assumed*—you know—and then Patrick called him up last month to ask about what he's supposed to *wear* and everything, and Owen didn't have the *heart* to say he was out of the wedding—"

"Are you saying"—Ella was almost laughing, it was so absurd— "are you saying Patrick actually *invited himself* into the wedding?"

"No! It wasn't like that! He just thought—you know, because he and Owen are such good friends and everything—it just never *occurred* to him that he wouldn't still be groomsman."

"Lizzie, honey. You're such a sweetheart. I hate to tell you this, but Patrick always knows *exactly* what he's doing. He waited until the last minute to call Owen, because he knew Owen couldn't say no to him. I can just about tell you what that conversation sounded like. Played Owen like a violin."

"Oh, Ella, *no*! I know you're not *thinking straight* right now, because of the baby and everything, and I know you're, like, not in the *mood* to cut Patrick any slack, which is *fine*, I get it—"

"Any *slack*? Lizzie, you *do* know the story, right? I mean, nothing's secret in this family. You know I caught him fucking a prostitute in the stairwell of our apartment building? And it wasn't the first time he'd done it, either. He'd been cheating on me from the beginning, before we even got married."

Lizzie sprang from the log, twisting her ring frantically on her finger. "I'm sure there was some—look, they're *best friends*, the two of them—"

"No, they're not. I can name ten of Patrick's friends he's closer to than Owen."

Lizzie turned. Her face was like the face of some actress on a poster for a disaster movie. "Ella, this is, like, the hardest thing I've ever had to do. I just want everyone to be happy, okay? He came to see us. He was in *tears*, Ella! Won't you please give us your blessing? I swear to God, I'll seat you on opposite sides of the tent! And you'll have Hector with you!"

"Trust me, that won't make it any less awkward."

"Ella, please! He'll be so *hurt* if we exclude him!"

Lizzie's blue eyes welled with tears. The breeze riffled her red-blond waves, the color of cinnamon toast. Aunt Viv's husband was a renowned and extremely attractive pediatric surgeon, and the genes were strong in this one. Ella sighed and rose from the log. Held out her arms and pulled Lizzie close.

"Liz, it's your day. If you and Owen really want Patrick to be part of your wedding, I can suck it up for a few hours out of my life."

"Omigosh! *Ella!* Really? You mean it?"

"My God, weddings are hard enough without guests bringing in their hang-ups. Just have the best day of your life and don't worry about me, okay?"

"You're *amazing*. Seriously, you *are*. Thank you, like, a *billion*. I can't tell you how much this means to both of us. Omigosh, I've been dreading this so much and you just—you just—"

"It's okay, all right? No big deal."

"I owe you forever. Seriously."

"Tragically, I won't be able to drink down a bottle of champagne to wash away the woe, but I'm a big girl. I'll find a way to deal. Just please don't seat us at the same table, all right? Bloodshed would be so unseemly."

Lizzie hiccupped. "I promise. I promise! Okay. Whew. All right, I'm going to run and tell Mom. Thank you again, Ella. *So, so* much."

Lizzie kissed Ella on both cheeks and snatched up her sandals. Ran up the beach and onto the lawn. Ella stood watching her. She stuck her hands in her pockets and curled her toes into the warm sand.

"Shit," she said.

ELLA FOUND AUNT JULIE in the library, on a stepladder next to a wall of jam-packed bookshelves. She slid a book from between its neighbors, leafed through it, and dropped it on the growing pile on the floor. Ella dashed over.

"You get down from there *right now*!" she exclaimed. "You'll break your bones!"

Aunt Julie handed her a book. "Here. See if you can find something."

"Not until you get off that ladder!"

"Good luck," said Mumma, coming in behind her. "She's been at it all day. Won't say what she's looking for."

Aunt Viv crossed her arms. "Lizzie had to *drag* her to that appointment."

"Never you mind what I'm looking for. This is none of your business, you two. Not *yet*, anyway. *You*, however"—Aunt Julie gestured to Ella with a book and stepped down nimbly from the ladder—"you do the upper shelves, if you care so much about my bones."

"Ella can't go up there, she's got a bun in the oven," said Mumma.

"Good grief, Mumma. It's only a stepladder."

"And it's *only* my grandchild. I'll do it."

"You!" Aunt Julie pointed the book at Mumma, then at Aunt Viv. "You! Out! This is between me and Ella."

Mumma was affronted. "Well, I don't see *why*."

"That's right," said Aunt Viv. "Pepper and I know all there *is* to know about the Horrid Hardcastles. Why bring poor Ella into all that?"

"Because," said Aunt Julie, "this has *nothing to do* with where Frank Hardcastle was sticking his pecker back in 1966, all right? So I'll thank the two of you to mind your own beeswax."

"*Well,*" said Aunt Viv.

Mumma wasn't giving up. "Family business *is* our business. And don't forget I spent that whole summer with Tiny at the Hardcastle place on the Cape. I've seen it all."

"Trust me," said Aunt Julie. "You don't have the least idea. Now get the hell out of here and close the door behind you."

"But it's *my house!*" wailed Aunt Viv.

"Vivian Schuyler Salisbury, I lost my virginity right over there on that window seat back in 1919, when your father was still pelting guests with his slingshot. If anyone's got a right to privacy around here, it's me."

"SO WHAT EXACTLY AM I looking for?" asked Ella, as she thumbed her way through a leather-bound set of Trollope. The

Schuyler library was a bewildering archive of popular novels and earnest treatises and dirty periodicals, enlarged thoughtlessly each year by family and guests and then forgotten.

"A key," said Aunt Julie.

"A key? To what?"

"To that." Aunt Julie nodded toward the enormous Victorian desk at the southern end of the room, overlooking the ocean. "Your great-grandfather died suddenly, you know, and nobody could ever find the key to his desk. It's been locked up ever since."

"Couldn't they have forced the lock or something?"

"His wife wouldn't hear of it. Oh, she gave us some drivel about its remaining sacred to her husband's memory and so on, and the desk being too valuable, but I expect she just didn't want certain things to come to light."

"Certain things?"

"He kept his personal affairs here, you see? The family business stayed in the city. The Dunes was where he came to escape all that."

"This was your brother, right? Charles Schuyler?"

"Yes," she said sharply.

Ella finished the Trollope and started on a bound collection of *The Federalist Papers*. "What was he like?"

"Hmph," said Aunt Julie.

"What's that supposed to mean?"

"It means I don't want to talk about it, what do you think?"

"Why not? Since we're trying to raid his desk and everything."

"Because he was my favorite person in the entire *world*, that's why. The only one in this damned family who understood me. And that's all I'm going to say."

"But what does he have to do with Frank Hardcastle?"

Aunt Julie sat back on her heels and reached for the tall glass of vodka tonic on the lamp table. "Ella, for God's sake. Just help me find the damned key."

Ella slid *The Federalist Papers* back in its place. Her fingertips prickled, her head whirled with some idea, some emotion that had been gathering since yesterday, since the *Today* show, since Frank Hardcastle's all-American face beamed down earnestly as she did her yoga and a tiny electric charge connected two separate wires in her brain.

"But you *said* it has to do with the Redhead, right?" she said.

Aunt Julie set down the glass. "Ella. Is there something you want to tell me?"

"I don't know if it's important or anything. Might just be a coincidence."

"There's no such thing as coincidence, darling. Everything's fate. Well, except when it isn't. But that's not interesting."

Ella turned to look at Aunt Julie. What a relic she was, what a living monument. Had she really lost her virginity on the library window seat eighty years ago? When the First World War had only just ended, and women couldn't yet vote for the laws that bound them, and speakeasies hadn't been thought of. Now here she sat on a worn tapestry footstool she'd probably sat on as a child, when the tapestry was fresh and the colors bright. The whole twentieth century contained inside her head. Depression and war and baby boom and civil rights. The things she knew. A whole lifetime of secrets. People who had lived and loved and schemed and died. All lurking there behind that powdery forehead.

Ella climbed down from the stepladder and sat on the bottom step, face-to-face with Aunt Julie. "This is going to sound a little weird," she said.

"Please. I lived through poodle skirts."

"So about a week or two after I moved into the new apartment—the one you say the Redhead used to live in—I was pulled into this new assignment at work. Big, high-profile deal. Do you know anything about Wall Street?"

"A little," Aunt Julie said.

"Have you heard of an investment bank called Sterling Bates?"

Aunt Julie's blue eyes narrowed. "Go on."

"Well, there was this big scandal in their municipal bond department a while back. Turns out the bankers were giving kickbacks to local officials to get their business—you know, underwriting municipal bonds. So my firm was called in to audit the accounts. Figure out just how big the problem was, how many bankers and municipalities were involved. And while I was doing that, I came across some transactions that struck me as—I don't know, *off* somehow. Nothing to do with the scandal we were investigating. At least, I didn't think so. Because the payments were going the other way. *This* firm was paying Sterling Bates."

"Paying the bank? How?"

"Well, it was classified as commission revenue. But commissions should vary from transaction to transaction, depending on the value of the trade, right? And it's episodic. Sometimes a firm will trade ten times in a week, then once the next week. But this payment occurred on the *same day* every month, the *same amount every time*."

Aunt Julie lifted the pencil lines that had once been eyebrows. "This is what you do for a *living*, Ella?"

"Pretty much. Cool, huh? Like solving a murder mystery."

"I'd rather stab out my eyeballs with a chopstick."

"All right. Fine. But listen to this. As soon as I flagged this transaction to my boss, told him I thought this needed more investigation, guess what? He fired me. For that made-up excuse I told you about, because Patrick worked for another division in the bank, which was supposedly a conflict of interest."

"Fascinating," Aunt Julie said. "Is this a long story? Because I could use another drink."

"I can cut it short."

"Please."

"Well, as you know, I've been putting my résumé out there, trying to find a new job. And I've had no traction at all. Two interviews canceled. Another went really well, but they never called back. And yesterday, out of the blue, I get a call from this assistant back at Parkinson Peters, where I used to work—"

Aunt Julie stifled a yawn.

"—and she said—are you ready for this?"

"Tenterhooks."

"My boss took a call from the SEC before I was fired." Ella leaned forward. "Somebody *ordered him to fire me.*"

"Darling," Aunt Julie said, "I don't mean to imply you're naïve or anything, although you are, but these things happen all the time. Somebody's misbehaving, he gets found out, he calls up old Scooter he used to go to Princeton with, who works at the SEC now—"

"Would you listen to me a second?"

"I've been listening to you for half an hour, and I still haven't found your point."

"This firm that's paying Sterling Bates is based just outside of Boston. And I went inside the file Rainbow gave me—"

"Rainbow? You got a file from a *rainbow?*"

"No, that's her name. My boss's assistant. So I bought myself a new laptop and opened up the file to refresh my memory. I remembered the name wrong, I thought it was FH Holdings, but it's actually called FH *Trust*—"

"FH?" Aunt Julie said. "Like the initials?"

"I mean, I know it's probably nothing, it just seemed like a funny coincidence that—"

"My dear," said Aunt Julie, "you *do* know that Gin Kelly used to work for Sterling Bates? In the typing pool, back in the old days?"

"*What?*"

"Well, she couldn't just make a living from those photograph cards, after all. She did have *some* sense of decency, however faint."

"You're kidding. *Seriously?* Why didn't you *tell* me?"

"Because it made no difference until now."

"So why *now?*"

Aunt Julie braced herself on the corner of the lamp table and hoisted her frail body to its feet. Walked back to the bookshelf and pulled out a volume at random. "As I understand it, she wasn't some ordinary typist. When Ginger worked at this bank of yours, she kept busy supplying money from a certain bootlegging racket to a fellow in the municipal bond department, whose job it was to deliver bribes to various local officials—"

"Oh my God! To keep them quiet! So they looked the other way instead of arresting the bootleggers!"

"That's how she explained it to me, anyway. I might have the details wrong. It's been a year or two, after all. What I know for sure is the head of the racket—biggest bootlegging racket on the East Coast, for a time—was a man named Louis Hardcastle."

"*Hardcastle?* You mean—"

Aunt Julie nodded. "Grandfather of a certain candidate for nomination to the presidency of the United States. Also happened to be a friend of my brother's. And I'll never forget the day he was murdered, right in the middle of old Sylvo Marshall's funeral reception."

OVER A CENTURY AGO, Aunt Julie's father had founded the local club—there were other clubs, of course, but this was the one that mattered—with several dozen of his closest friends, and Schuylers had dined there most summer evenings ever since. At five minutes to seven, Ella and Mumma and Lizzie crawled from the back of Aunt Viv's car, a ten-year-old Mercedes station wagon that stank of wet Labrador, wearing colorful shift dresses and Jack Rogers sandals. Aunt Julie had sat up front with Aunt Viv, giving her advice about driving until Aunt Viv told her to shut up already.

"I *won't* shut up when somebody's trying to *kill* me." Aunt Julie took Vivian's arm to heave herself out of the car.

"For God's sake, nobody's trying to kill you," said Aunt Viv.

"Yet," said Mumma.

Aunt Viv tossed the keys to the valet. "Ella, honey, you'll drive us back, won't you? So tedious having to count one's martinis when the men are away."

"All this modern drivel about drinking and driving," said Aunt Julie. "In *my* day we could hold our liquor."

"Here we go," said Mumma.

"Why, one Midsummer Ball I drank two bottles of champagne, danced all night, jumped straight in my little Nash roadster—oh, she was a swell car, that Nash Six, cherry red—and drove all the way home from here to Manhattan just so I could sleep with Jack Bouvier without my husband finding out. Though he did, after all. Peter always could tell when I was up to no good. Still, it was worth it. That man could outlast a Wagner opera. Peter, I mean. Jack was done in six minutes flat. No, the thing about Peter, you had to get him good and jealous first, but once he located the caveman within, so to speak—hell's bells, is that your *husband*, Ella?"

Ella's mind snapped back to the present. "Patrick? Where?"

"Oh Christ," Mumma muttered. "He's at the bar, with the Hendersons. That Mamie."

Aunt Viv was aggrieved. "It's a *Wednesday*, for God's sake. He should be at work."

"He quit, remember? He's starting a new business."

"A new *business*? Doing *what*?"

"I *told* you, Aunt Viv," said Ella. "This whole World Wide Web thing."

"Ha! I told you he was a spider," said Aunt Julie.

"A snake, you said."

"The snake's in his *pants*, Vivian."

All the while they'd been following the maitre d' across the dining room to the usual table, overlooking the ninth hole. Ella offered up a hopeless prayer that Aunt Julie's voice hadn't carried over the hum of noise to where Patrick Gilbert stood at the bar with Mamie and Joe Henderson in his tan chinos and navy blazer and tasseled loafers, his tie with the Harvard crests in a repeating pattern, his neat, short carpet of dark hair. But of course it had. And even if it hadn't, Patrick knew perfectly well that the Schuylers dined at the club most nights at seven sharp, seven thirty on weekends.

Ella's head still churned with everything she'd learned from Aunt Julie. Things nobody else knew, Aunt Julie said, because the Hardcastles had kept it all out of the papers. But who murdered Louis Hardcastle? Ella had asked, and Aunt Julie shrugged and said nobody was ever charged with the crime.

But that's terrible! Ella said, and Aunt Julie cackled. Not as terrible as the whole world knowing what old Hardcastle was up to. Anyway, she would've taken care of justice herself.

Who? Ella said.

His *widow*, of course, said Aunt Julie. Old Granny Hardcastle.

Ella had clapped her hand over her mouth. You mean *Rose Hardcastle*? The *matriarch*?

But there was no time to elaborate. Aunt Viv came bustling into the library to hurry them to dinner—Aunt Viv was one of those people who hated to miss any fun—so Ella didn't get to hear this juicy snippet of gossip about Rose Hardcastle, "America's Matriarch," as *Metropolitan* magazine dubbed her, in a lavish spread about the family a few months ago. Nowhere in that hagiography had the writer mentioned any rumors about bootlegging money, but of course Ella had heard the whispers. Everyone had. How the family had lost all their money in the 1907 panic and built a brand-new fortune during Prohibition. Plenty of whispers about Frank Hardcastle's father, sure, which had supposedly tanked his own political career—but *Rose*? Mother of eight, held the family together after the premature death of her husband, instilled in her children and grandchildren that Puritan ethic of great achievement and public service? Floating like spun sugar above all those rumors of ill-gotten gains?

But surely she *must* have known where the money came from.

If Aunt Julie was right. If the Hardcastles really *were* bootleggers.

Well, that was the great thing about America, right? You could reinvent yourself with every generation. Whitewash your sins with public virtues. New money aged into old money in a couple of decades. Who really cared where the money came from, all those years ago? Wasn't Frank Hardcastle's fault. That was all in the past.

Unless it *wasn't* in the past. Unless those payments from FH Trust to Sterling Bates weren't just commission revenue. Unless some SEC official wasn't just motivated by public spiritedness when he demanded some midlevel accountant be fired for no good reason.

Ella stood up from the chair in which she had just sat down.

"Go ahead and order for me," she said. "I'm just going to go have a word with Patrick."

THE LAST TIME ELLA had seen Patrick, he had stormed out of the restaurant where he was supposed to be forming an amicable relationship with Hector. That was two weeks ago.

Ella had spent most of the past four months doing her best to avoid her husband. When she left him, she left without a word—in shock, to be fair, since she'd just witnessed him having sex with a prostitute in the stairwell of their apartment building when he was supposed to be picking up the pizza order from the lobby. They'd done most of their divorce negotiations over the phone, partly because Ella was so sick and partly because she just didn't want to face him in her exhausted, frayed state—didn't want to face the fact that this baby would tie them together forever, when all she wanted was to cut him out of her life with a pair of gigantic divorce scissors.

But then she was feeling better, and she couldn't avoid this first careful introduction of the baby's two fathers to each other. Patrick had been—well, *hectoring* her about it for a while. Who *was* this guy she was *shacking up* with? How *dare* she impose this *total stranger* on their *child*? What if he was a *psycho abuser*? A *con* man? So Ella asked Hector if he'd mind having coffee or lunch or dinner with Patrick and prove he wasn't a psycho con man abuser. (Hector: *How do you know I'm not?* Ella: *Because you run out to buy me ginger ale at three in the morning.* Hector: *Could be part of my con.*) After some back-and-forth, they'd all agreed to meet at the Village Atelier on Hudson Street, a French bistro type place a few blocks away from Hector and Ella's apartment.

Sometimes Ella thought it might have gone better if the two men hadn't been too polite to order themselves drinks in front of her. On the other hand, things might have turned violent if alcohol had been involved. Of course, the fault was mostly Patrick's. Patrick at his worst, bragging and posturing and practically flexing his gym-honed muscles. In the beginning, Hector had gone for conciliation. By the time the waiter came with the roast chicken and duck confit and seared salmon, though, he couldn't resist a nudge or two, the kind of remark that might have sounded like a compliment but was really an insult, like *So did you always want to be an investment banker? Since you were a little kid?* Eventually Patrick caught on and started asking Hector about his Birkenstock collection and how many of his musician friends had died of AIDS, and Hector said quite a lot, actually, he was pretty sick of going to the funerals of better men than himself, and it all went downhill from there.

Finally Ella stood up and said she was leaving, they could duke it out just fine without her there, and Hector apologized and said he didn't mean to be such a jerk, awkward situation and all, let's just start over for Ella's sake. Patrick said no, he was *out*, wasn't about to apologize to the jackass faggot musician who was screwing his wife—the whole restaurant fell silent—and off he stormed into the May twilight, leaving Ella and Hector to face alone all those sympathetic gazes, plus the bill.

The next day Patrick sent Ella flowers and a note of apology, both of which Ella was about to throw in the trash until Hector pointed out that it wasn't the *flowers'* fault and put them in a vase with water. Hector said this was a metaphor for their relationship—Ella and Patrick and Hector—and they should try again, they were all going to be parents together and they had to make this work. He was truly sorry for being a dick, swore he wouldn't let Patrick get under his skin next time—it was that stupid AIDS crack that did it, even though he knew it was just Patrick's way of dealing with the insult Hector had inflicted on his masculinity, sleeping with his wife and all.

But Ella didn't want to see Patrick again. She'd been relieved to call him up this morning to reschedule their meeting. She hated conflict. She hated these exhausting competitions into which these encounters had degenerated. They'd loved each other once! Couldn't Patrick just let her be *happy*, for God's sake?

BY THE TIME ELLA rose and turned toward the bar, Patrick was already on his way to their table, drink in hand, smiling his emollient social smile. Right from the start of their relationship, Patrick had loved that Ella came from an old New York family. He'd made the absolute most of her connection to the club and its members, schmoozing and boozing their summer weekends at The Dunes for all he was worth. Hence his friendship with the Hendersons, for example. His smile grew wide and genuine when he saw Ella turn and walk in his direction. He reached her in a couple of strides and leaned forward to kiss her cheek, the way you did with close friends.

"Ella! Thought I saw you walking in. You look beautiful. Blooming. Come early for the weekend?"

"Yes. I actually have a question for you, if you don't mind. Can we sit for a second?"

"Sure! Of course! Always have time for you, babe. Out on the terrace, maybe?"

Ella would rather *not* go on the terrace with Patrick, actually, but she didn't want to waste time dickering over alternatives. So she said sure, and Patrick offered to order her a drink, and she realized she was thirsty and said a club soda with lime would be great. Patrick bounded off to get the club soda and Ella walked out on the terrace to breathe the good salt air coming off the beach to settle her nerves. A peculiar anxious feeling had come over her, like she was somehow cheating on Hector, speaking to Patrick alone like this.

Well, she'd call Hector right after dinner. Once they were out of the clubhouse, where cell phones were strictly forbidden.

The club soda appeared before her. "Here you go, babe," said Patrick. In the other hand he held his own drink, half-finished, an old-fashioned by the look of it. His usual. He always specified some expensive brand of whiskey; Ella couldn't remember the name.

"It's *Ella*, actually," she said.

"Oops! Sorry. Force of habit. So what's up? Where's Hector-boy?"

"He flew out to L.A. this morning. They're recording his *movie* score? He has to conduct and everything. The *Philharmonic*."

"Nice. Love California. Lucky him. Poor you, getting stuck behind. How long is he away?"

"Three weeks, he said."

Patrick whistled. "Three *weeks*, huh? Long time to go without. You didn't want to chaperone?"

Ella couldn't exactly say that Hector hadn't exactly asked. "Not really. He'll be too busy. I'd just be sitting around in the hotel room by myself, what's the point?"

"You could see that aunt of yours, right? The one in San Diego, used to be married to Frank Hardcastle?"

Ella sputtered her club soda. "How'd you know that?"

"Steel trap." Patrick tapped his forehead. "Pretty cool, though. If he ends up being elected and all."

"I've never even *met* him, Patrick."

"Ella, seriously. What did I always tell you? You have to work these connections. She's kept quiet all these years, right? So he *owes* her. And by the transitive property, he owes *you*."

"Actually," Ella said, "that's really what I wanted to talk to you about. All those little connections dangling around inside that steel trap of yours."

"Aha. What's the matter, need to pick the lock or something? Gonna cost you."

"Haven't I already paid enough?"

He tilted the glass to her. "Touché. I was just kidding, though. In all seriousness. You need a favor, you got it. I mean that."

Ella leaned her elbow on the railing and sucked on her straw. "It's about this investment firm I came across, when I was doing the Sterling Bates audit."

"Ah, the fishy muni books. What's the deal?"

"Firm called FH Trust, based in Cambridge."

Patrick frowned and leaned his elbow not far from hers. "FH, huh? I see what you're getting at."

"Well? Have you heard of them?"

"Nope. Never."

"You're sure?"

"Doesn't ring a bell. Although that tells you something right there."

"How so?"

"Because I'm pretty sure I've met just about every shop out there running more than twenty million, say. One deal or another. You're sure that was the name? Not a front for something else?"

"I guess it could have been. But it was the transaction itself that looked off to me. The bank put it down to commission revenue, but it came in the same day every month, exact same amount, as far back as the accounts went. Like a retainer."

"Whoa. That *is* weird. How much?"

"Seventy-five a month, I think? And as soon as I flagged it to Kemp, that was when they took me off the account. Apparently some SEC guy called him up and gave him orders."

Patrick finished off his drink and set it on the railing next to his elbow. "Tell you what, Ella. You must have dug up some serious shit. FH Trust, right? Cambridge, Mass.?"

"That's it."

"I'll ask around and see what I can find."

"But quietly, right?"

"Of course. Don't want to get my own ass in trouble, do I?"

Patrick flashed her a smile, the old smile, and for an instant Ella felt the old connection. The answering warmth in her middle. And relief, too. He'd help. He was on her side.

"Thanks," she said.

"Anytime. So how are you doing? Still feeling okay?"

"Much better."

"You're kind of showing a little, I think. Just a—you know." He made a motion with his hand.

"You got the ultrasound picture I sent, right?"

"I did. Hanging up on my office wall. Thanks for that. I—well, I know I should've said thanks before. I mean, I *did* say thanks, but not very well. I really, *really* appreciate it."

"Look, Patrick," Ella said. "Whatever's going on between us, it's still your baby, right? I wouldn't ever just cut you out."

Patrick blinked and looked away, toward the ocean. The sun was falling somewhere behind him, to the west, and the gold light touched his hair. "I have been a total dick," he said. "I know that. Believe me, I know what I did and how wrong it was. You have literally every right in the world to cut me off."

"Not really. I gave up that right when I decided to have this baby.

Who has a right to know its dad. So I'm stuck with you. That's just the deal."

Patrick parted his lips like he was going to say something. Caught his breath on whatever it was and pressed them together again.

Ella went on. "You know, if you want to come to the next ultrasound, you can. It's pretty cool. You hear the heartbeat and everything. I literally shook, it was so surreal. Hector had to . . ." She trailed off.

"It's okay. You can say his name."

Ella looked down at her bare fingers. "Had to hold my hand because I was shaking so hard."

The words hung there. The breeze came in quietly. From the dining room came the clink of glasses and the hum of voices. Down the terrace, a pair of couples were laughing over some joke. They were all drinking martinis or something. Ella remembered going out with other couples, that wonderful secure feeling of a double date, going home with your husband afterward, everything so simple, the relationships drawn in neat lines.

"That was decent of him, I guess," said Patrick.

"He's a decent person. I wish you'd just give him a chance."

"Look, I'm sorry about that shit I said. I really am. You know that. I was just acting like a jackass because I was so mad, seeing you with him."

"It's early days, I guess. We'll get used to it."

"I don't want to get used to it. I'm not going to lie. I hate seeing you with another guy. And just like *that*, right? Like you didn't even need to get over me first. Seeing you and him together, happy as shit, it's like—I don't know, like drinking acid or something. I lie awake at night and just wish to God we were back to where we were."

"I'll bet you do."

"I don't mean *that*. I mean someone knocking me over the head and telling me to grow up and treat you like you deserve. But that horse is out of the barn. I know that. So I apologize in advance for any future asshole behavior. It's not you, it's me."

"I'll try to keep that in mind."

"And I will definitely see what I can find out about this FH Trust deal, okay?"

Ella sucked down the last of her club soda. "I appreciate it. And I appreciate your acting like a human being, finally."

"I swear I'll try to do better, in the future. Get my inner caveman under control."

Patrick grinned at her. She found herself grinning back.

"Anyway, I'd better get back inside."

"Yep. Right. Definitely. Can't keep the aunts waiting."

Ella turned to leave.

"No, wait!"

She turned back.

Patrick hesitated. "No, shoot, never mind."

"What is it?"

He made a sheepish smile and gestured his palm toward her. "Do you mind if I, like, you know. Just for a second."

"Oh! Yeah, sure. If you want. I mean, I haven't felt it moving or anything yet. Hector—Hector's always got his hand on it, trying to feel something."

Patrick took a step toward her and laid his palm lightly against the pastel monkeys covering her midriff. "Wow," he said.

"See? Nothing moving around yet."

"But there's definitely a bump there. There's definitely, like, an actual baby on the other side. Our actual baby."

"Oh, believe me, there is," Ella said darkly.

They both laughed. Patrick rattled the ice cubes in his glass. "Very cool," he said, drawing his hand back.

"Ella?"

They snapped in unison to the open French doors, where Lizzie stood, staring at Ella's nose. Deep pink cheeks. Trembling lower lip.

"I'm, like, so sorry to interrupt?" she said. "Mom sent me to find you? Appetizers are here."

DINNER TOOK FOREVER, BECAUSE dinners at the club always took forever, especially at the beginning of summer—old friends coming up, lives brought up to date, food eaten, drinks drunk. Ella drove everyone home. Aunt Viv and Mumma traded dirty stories about their old days in Manhattan, before they got married, while Lizzie stared out the window in embarrassment. By the time Ella reached the peace and quiet of her room, it was past ten o'clock. She took her phone out of her pocketbook and turned it on. There were three voice mails from Hector. She listened to the last one, which had come in at half past nine, when she was just sliding behind the wheel of Aunt Viv's Mercedes.

Me again. So I guess you're probably at the club having dinner with the girls. No worries. Just give me a buzz when you're back safe. Missing you like nuts right now. Gang's coming over in a few minutes so I might not hear the phone ring. Just leave me a message so I hear your voice at least. Love you. Bye.

Ella called back but the phone rang and rang and went to voice mail. She left a long, complicated message about The Dunes and Aunt Julie and dinner at the club. *Oh, and you'll never guess who we saw with the Hendersons. Patrick, right? Enjoying his time off from banking,*

I guess. He was actually pretty nice, though. Apologized for everything. Sorry, I'm rambling. Enjoy your party. I miss you so much. Love you. Bye.

She closed the phone and set it down on her nightstand. Put her hand on her belly where Patrick had put his hand, for a second or two. Small, firm mound the size of her palm.

The phone rang, making her jump. She snatched it off the nightstand. "Hector?"

"Sorry to disappoint. Just me."

"Aunt Julie? You're, like, ten feet away from me."

"No, I'm not. I'm downstairs in the library. And I need you to join me, pronto."

ACT II

Joined Together in
the Eyes of the Lord

(shall no man put asunder)

UPSTATE NEW YORK

June 1924

1

TWO DAYS after his father's funeral, me and Anson are married at City Hall by the actual mayor of New York City, no fooling. Seems he owes my beloved a favor or two—God knows what—which Anson has never collected until now. Patsy is my bridesmaid, inasmuch as you can call a girl a bridesmaid when she's just standing next to you in the mayor's office while you repeat some promises that tend to get broken by most husbands and wives, somewhere along the line. Still, I mean what I say, I really do. Forsaking all others and worshipping him with my body and that kind of thing, and I can see he means it right back.

My, he cleaned up well for the occasion, all sleek-shaven and sweet-smelling and bull-shouldered and earnest. He wears a plain gray suit of lightweight wool and a pale pink rose in his lapel. I wear a green silk dress that comes all the way down to my ankles—the best I could find on short notice—and a wee cream-colored hat festooned with pale pink silk roses to disguise the overbright color of my hair. In my hand I carry a half dozen pale pink roses tied together with a green satin ribbon, and Patsy carries the same. When Anson seals the deal with a kiss, she loses her head a bit, squeals, and tosses her bouquet. A quick-witted clerk in a brown suit catches it. He hands the flowers back with an air of bamboozlement.

Outside, the noon air has grown sultry. Anson hands us both into the spruce-green Packard and starts the engine. I ask him where we're headed.

"Don't ask so many questions, Mrs. Marshall," he says, and it takes a moment for me to realize that his mother's name is now my own.

2

WE HEAD north out of Manhattan to follow the wide Hudson River. I fall asleep around Poughkeepsie, curled up on the seat with Patsy tucked in my arms and Anson's jacket draped over our frail wedding day frocks—me and her not being the kind of females who own such a thing as a going-away dress.

When I wake, the first thing I notice is the smell of pine mixed in with automobile exhaust, and next I notice the luminous twilight sky like the color of Anson's eyes. I sit up. Patsy's still asleep, so exhausted by excitement she might be dead.

"Are those mountains?" I whisper.

"Adirondacks. Thought you'd like to go somewhere that looked a little like home."

He says it modestly, like a thing any man might think of. I lay my head back down on the seat, up against his thigh. He curls his warm right hand around my shoulder. Patsy sighs into my chest. I ask him how much longer.

About an hour, he tells me. Maybe less.

"What did they say in Washington yesterday?" I ask him. "Do they know who did it?"

"No. Still investigating."

"But who do you think?"

"Could be anybody, I guess. Stone. Schuyler, maybe. Someone

we don't even know about, an inside job. Doesn't matter. He's dead, that's all. Someone did us the favor. He's dead, and we're free." His hand squeezes my shoulder. I reach up and lay my own hand over his, the left hand that now bears my gold wedding ring. I think about the letter tucked inside my pocketbook, which I haven't yet shown to Anson.

"Free as birds," I murmur. "Flying north for the summer."

The mountain wind slides familiar along my cheek. If my geography serves, the Adirondack Mountains rise up from the earth of New York state, hundreds of miles from River Junction, but I feel that warm stir in my stomach that says I'm somewhere I belong. Steep winding roads and chill wet breezes—how well I know them. Scent of pine and fresh water. Lord have mercy, we might could stay forever, and nobody would ever know what become of us.

3

COMES THE moon, hung above the eastern hills, three-quarters full. The car makes a last turn and rolls to the gentlest stop. I do my best to sit up without disturbing Patsy. The headlights illuminate a dark, giant building made of logs, porched on all sides. I ask where we are.

Anson switches off the engine and sits for a moment, hands on the wheel, staring through the windshield glass. "Friend's cabin. Friend of my father's, actually. Said we could stay as long we liked."

"Nice of him."

"Wait here a moment." Anson gets out of the car and walks up the steps to the porch. His legs ripple across the headlight beams. Seems to be searching around for something, I can't see what. At last he finds it—the key. He unlocks the front door and swings it wide. Comes back down the steps and opens the passenger door. Leans in and takes the slumbering Patsy in his arms, lifts her like she's made of air. Offers his hand to me. I take it gratefully, for the long journey has stiffened my limbs considerable. Once I'm on my feet, he keeps hold of my fingers and leads me up the rough steps to the porch and through the door to some wide, moonlit room that smells of wood. I guess there's no electricity, because he asks me for a match. I rummage in my pocket until my fingers find the edge of the matchbook. Meanwhile he's settling Patsy on some lump of a sofa. She wakes and says his name, asks where we are. I perch beside her and say we're in the north country, pumpkin. Together we watch Anson light the kerosene lamp and replace the glass chimney. The room takes on a warm, gold glow. *What* a room. The entire downstairs might be one giant log box, except for a pair of doors on either side of the opposite wall. Table and chairs, sofa and armchairs—all of them rest on patches of worn, comfortable rug.

"What do you think?" Anson asks me. His face is worried, like he's afraid I might not appreciate the rustic qualities of this honeymoon lodge he's discovered for us.

Honeymoon, I think. There's a funny word. Who would imagine Ginger Kelly on a honeymoon? Least of all me.

I untangle Patsy from my side and circle my arms around the waist of my beloved. Tell him I reckon it's just about perfect.

4

C OMES THE sun, streaking white through the crack in the blue calico curtains. I lift my head to a most extraordinary sight—

Anson deep asleep. So deep, in fact, I stare for some time at the muscles of his back, just to be sure he's breathing.

Now, I don't mean to shock you, but it happens I had nothing to do with his current state of exhaustion. That was Patsy. Having napped all the way up the Hudson River and into the mountains, she commenced her waking hours with a vengeance. Patiently Anson trailed behind her to visit every nook and cranny, dash hither and thither in a state of febrile excitement, while I aired the beds and put away our clothes and filled the washbasins from the hand pump in the kitchen. On the kitchen table sat a big basket full of food—fruit and bread and cheese and nuts and a ball of salt butter, along with a note from some caretaker who lives in town when the owner ain't around, offering instruction on such matters as the operation of the stove and the care of chickens. I rustled up plates and so on and called on them to eat a bite of supper, just like my mama might have done. Cold fresh water pumped straight up from the mountain earth. Then we washed the dishes—Anson at the sink, sleeves rolled up his massive forearms, Patsy at the dish towel, me at the cupboard. You would think Patsy might now yawn and declare herself ready for some shut-eye, but no. I figure it might have been three o'clock before she settled at last on the trundle bed in the big bedroom—this after rising eight or nine times like a jack-in-the-box from the child's bed down the hall. Anson got up the last time and carried her back with him. "Can she sleep in the trundle, do you think?" he asked me sheepish, and I said I didn't give a damn if she slept hung from the ceiling, so long as she slept. Wouldn't you know it, the little fury was out cold the instant he kissed her good night. Then Anson collapsed next to me, on top of the quilt. This was our wedding night, chaste as the moon. They say it's bad luck, but surely we've used up our allotted quantity of misfortune by now?

Anyhow, I allow myself a minute or two to admire this rare view of Anson's sleeping face. His unshaven jaw, a fleck of sleep crust tucked within the inside corner of his dear eye. He wears no shirt, just a pair of white linen drawers, because he sleeps ferocious hot. I lean over to kiss the soft skin between his shoulder blades and rise to check on Patsy, who is yet more unconscious than her brother-in-law, if such a thing be possible. Then I steal downstairs to the kitchen and out the back door.

Lord Almighty.

Though my mother told me I was born in New York City, and I have no reason to disbelieve her, the landscape of my earliest memory is a mountain valley, tucked between peaks, thick fertile green in summer and frozen gray in winter. I hardly knew what a horizon was until I left for convent school, age eight. But I left all that behind when I ran from home, and save for two brief, agonizing visits—my mother's funeral and the final reckoning with my bootlegging stepdaddy—I became a metropolitan girl, the skyscrapers my mountain peaks, the streets my straight, narrow valleys. I never thought to love a mountain again.

So why does the breath stick in my lungs at these long, deep slopes tumbling from an ultramarine sky to a lake of glass? Why does the sight of a few scraps of mist clinging to a ridge make my heart climb through my ribs? We are alone. Not a soul inhabits this place but us. The lawn before me spreads to the lake, and a boathouse of worn gray clapboard, and a short, low dock. By the shore stands a pavilion made of logs, maybe fifteen feet square, where you might enjoy a picnic sheltered from the squalls. The air is mountain chill and tangy. Bits of grass cling to my bare feet as I walk through the dew to the lake. I shed my nightgown the way a lizard sheds an old skin and dive from the end of the dock into the cold water that washes me clean.

5

I GUESS I can swim, all right. When a girl's bred up alongside four hulking brothers, she best know how to swim, and fast. I stroke about a hundred yards out and pause to tread water, turning in a slow circle to take in the thick forested slopes. This lake is marvelous deep. Currents of primeval water come up icy from the bottom of it to numb my legs. I half expect some ancient monster to take hold of me and drag me under, but then Mama always said my imagination was too strange for this world. A pair of common deer sip from the opposite shore. One of them lifts her head and stares curious across the water, as if she senses some unusual fish breaking the surface.

When I spin back, I'm surprised by the size of the house. *Camps,* they call them, these mountain retreats for rich folk—and with a straight face, too. I recollect escaping that weather-beaten clapboard shack we called a house with my brother Johnnie from time to time, couple of days out in the wild with a canvas tent and an iron skillet and a sack of cornmeal, and believe me, *that* was camping. Whatever soothes your soul, I guess, and mine does grow and grow out here in the middle of this Paleolithic lake, until it might could touch the sides of the valley, because I am here alone with my true married beloved and my baby sister, safe and sound at last, nobody to hurt us.

6

J UST AS I commence to stroke back the way I came, I catch sight of some movement on the lawn. Big strong fellow walking toward the dock, wearing not a stitch but his white drawers. I bend my body to its task. After a minute or so, I hear a splash, whistle-clean. I wait until he reaches me to pull up, smiling.

"You're shivering," he says.

"So're you."

"I brought down some towels."

"Regular Boy Scout, aren't you?"

Beneath the water, I kick furious to stay afloat. Above, I loop my arms around his neck and kiss him. The heat of his mouth warms me, the slick of his pale skin against mine. He hasn't yet shaved. The bristles rasp my chin. I break away and stare at him. Can't hardly speak for gasping.

"Why, it's true. It's really true."

"What's true?"

"You and me. Bound together. Husband and wife."

Husky he says, "Let's swim back to shore."

Side by side we stroke to the dock. He wraps his big hands around my waist to hoist me up, which is not strictly necessary, or maybe it is. We kept separate rooms at the hotel, you see, in the days before the wedding—me with Patsy, Anson by himself like a monk—and we are mortal starved of each other. He climbs up behind me and gathers me against him so hard and fast, the two of us nearly stagger down together to the wooden boards. The cold water might have shriveled his parts, I guess, but not his ardor. We kiss like lunatics. I mumble something about the towels. He says goddamn the towels and swings me up to carry me to the pavilion. We kiss all the way there. The kindling beneath my skin burns away the lake water. Coal hot I be. Anson's parts unshrivel hasty. Under the roof of that pavilion, on some convenient bench, we scramble to consummate this holy union of ours in the manner ordained by God as a remedy against sin and for the procreation of children.

7

Once WE are collapsed one against the other, panting hard, I gasp—*Patsy?*

Asleep, he gasps back.

Takes some time to come back to yourself after a thing like that. Somewhere in the middle of the business, we contrived to tumble off the bench to the wooden floor, and I imagine Anson might have cracked a vertebra or two, though he don't complain. The chill breeze is a blessed relief. At last Anson peels himself away and props up against the wall, grinning like a little boy for maybe the first time since I met him. I climb on his lap and tell him I have a question for him. He closes a pair of contented eyes and says anything, Gin. Anything you want.

"What do you think about a little playmate for Patsy?"

Eyes flash open. "*Gin!* Are you saying—"

"No! Jehosaphat. Not that I know of, anyway. I'm only saying we've done exactly nothing to halt the course of Nature, so to speak. So I want to make dead sure you know what you're doing. The birds and the bees."

"What do you take me for? Of course I know."

"Well, then?"

He runs a sheepish hand through his wet hair, and for a moment I don't know whether to shake him or marry him all over again. "I guess I figured—if you *didn't* want one—you would say something. Wouldn't you?"

I take a little time to answer him. Discover some speck along the line of his jaw. When I choose the words, I choose them careful. "What I figure is you're a family man, through and through, for all you seemed bent for a while on getting yourself killed, one way or another. I figure the good Lord created Oliver Marshall to sire a whole litter of young and raise them responsible. And you have drained the cup of sorrow dry, your poor loyal heart is about bruised to death, and what you want from the bottom of your soul is to make some new life to fill the terrible hole inside you. That's what I think, anyway."

"You figured all that out on your own?"

"I did."

"All right, then. Maybe I wouldn't mind a kid or two, if God allows. Now we're good and married. What about you?"

"Me?" I hear myself laugh, the way a sick woman laughs. "Anson, haven't you figured it out yet, with that trick brain of yours? I am dead frightened of babies. My mama died of it. I always swore I would never."

Now he sits up and takes hold of my shoulders. "Gin, for God's sake, why didn't you say something? You know I'd never—I would've—"

"I know all that. I also swore I'd never hitch myself to any fellow, ever, no matter how sinful handsome, and now look where I be. Your lawful wedded wife, for better or worse. So I been lately thinking the Almighty maybe sent you to me that I might learn to forsake all my old sworn promises for new ones. Might stop feeling so paralytic fearful for myself and start fearing for someone else."

He looks so lost when I say this. Like I punched him in the gut or something, instead of confessing some raw secret from deep inside the solar plexus. When he can't take it anymore, he leans back against the wooden wall and makes me to lie against his chest. We remain there silent and sacred until Patsy cries our names out the back door and says she needs to wee real bad.

Anson bangs the back of his head against the wall and swears. I ask what for.

"Towels are at the end of the dock," he says.

8

AS CHANCE would have it, two days later I am able to inform Anson that he is not about to become anybody's daddy, at least not until next month. From the look of him, I can't tell whether he's relieved or disappointed. Nor me neither, to say the truth.

9

COMES JULY, before we know it. So blessed content we abide in these mountains, all by ourselves, we scarce count the hours at all except to note their passing. Since the third night, Patsy sleeps happily in her own room. She discovered the chicken coop and loves to run outside first thing to see how many eggs were laid. Makes a basket of her nightgown and bears them careful inside, legs all wet and grassy from the dew. On Tuesdays Anson drives the Packard into town, ten miles away, and returns with fruit and vegetables and meat. The milkman leaves four glass pints on the front porch at dawn, without our even asking, and takes away the empties. Plenty of tea and coffee and flour and cornmeal and spices in the pantry. We want for nothing. Some days we paddle out the canoe, or swim, or lie sprawled in the grass reading some book from the shelves in the library, or maybe play some cards or mah-jongg. They keep a nice mah-jongg set in this house, real ivory and bamboo. Anson's a terrible cheat. It's because he looks so square and innocent, he can get away with murder. Don't worry, I make him pay for it later. Always make them pay. You can't let a man get away with cheating, ever, on account of it's bad for morale. Also Anson is of a musical bent. In the evenings he might pluck out some song from the spinet, or else me and Patsy rummage through the records and play a ragtime tune or a polka or some such on the old Victrola, the kind with the windup box, and how can you help but to get up and dance to something like that? Anson taught Patsy how to waltz. You should see them together, it's the sweetest thing. He bows gravely and asks if she will allow him the honor, et cetera, and you never met such a blushing little coquette as my sister, Patsy, accepting his kind offer. Every so often he discovers some old cornball love song in there and pulls me in close, cheek to cheek, while Patsy drinks her milk and works a jigsaw. That's our evenings. Some might call it dull, I guess, but we like the peace and quiet pretty well. We like to fall to bed in the blessed night, starshine spangling the sky outside, good mountain breeze tumbling through the window, nothing to see nor hear nor touch nor love but each other. Sailors who have ridden out some hurricane to arrive safe in port at last. In my whole life I have never known a quiet so deep as this, so deep as the inside of my own bones, and I expect I never shall again.

10

NOW TODAY happens to be the last day of eternal July, and to celebrate me and Patsy take to paddling the canoe while Anson sits fishing for our dinner at the end of the dock. We can hear him whistling all the way across the cove. Patsy rattles on about something, I don't remember what, you know how she gets to chatter sometimes. I'm afraid I'm paying more attention to the particular note of Anson's whistle, which always makes me to smile till my stomach gets warm. As I lift my paddle from the water to stroke again, I discover that feeling you get when somebody is watching you.

You might say I have an instinct for these things. Well, we all do. Nature endows us human animals with senses we don't even know, which is puny enough protection against the types of predators you run across in the valleys and alleys and low-down joints of lower Manhattan, if you ask me, to say nothing of the four clapboard walls of your step-daddy's house in Allegany County, Maryland. Well I know the sensation of some hidden person laying his greedy eyes upon your skin. The electricity runs down the stalk of each hair upon your hide until it finds your blood, whereupon your heart pumps it *swish swish* into the waiting muscles of arm and leg, so you can fly or fight or die trying.

Yet I keep on paddling that damn canoe, though my hair stands on end. Though my skin ripples and my heart pounds and my muscles keen. I turn my head casual to sweep the shore. Nothing but thick green brush and proud trees. Patsy looks back at me and asks what's wrong.

"Just thinking I might coulda left that lamp burning in the kitchen," I tell her. "I guess we best head back to shore and make sure."

"All right," she says, no argument, because Patsy has her own set of instincts, believe me, for all she be innocent as a wee round sweet apple.

We commence to turn the canoe and paddle back to the dock, and all the while my pelt just prickles and stings, my pulse liketa burst from my throat.

Then Patsy says, *Where's Anson gone?*

I realize sudden the whistling has ceased, and sure enough An-son sits no longer at the end of the dock with his fishing rod and his bucket.

I keep my voice steady, I don't know how. "I guess he had to visit Mrs. Murphy or something," I say, and hope it's true. Paddle to a steady rhythm, so fast as I can without making to *look* as if I be pad-dling fast. Patsy keeps up valiant. On and on we stroke, till the empty dock looms. The hair on my neck no longer stands on end, but my heart and lungs pump so hard as ever they had, maybe because of the exercise but also this alarm—Anson gone at the exact moment the premonition of danger settled on my nerves.

I throw the rope around the bollard at the end of the dock and hand Patsy to shore. She holds the canoe while I step on solid boards. Re-markable levelheaded is our Patsy, when calm is called for. Anson's bucket and rod stand where he left them. A couple of trout twitch bewildered in the bucket. The line still dangles in the water, and from the tugging I guess it's found a bite. I tell Patsy to wait in the boat-house and not make a peep while I run to find Anson, nor come out until we tell her to. She nods her sweet head like she understands me. I take a knife from the cupboard and hurry out along the western shore. I can't say why I pick west over east, it just comes natural. I wear but my plain old black bathing suit and straw hat to protect my redhead's complexion. The knife I grip in my hand. As blades go it's hardly fearsome, made for cutting rope and cleaning fish, dust of rust near the handle, hasn't been sharpened in years, I bet. Still it's some-thing to hold in my hand, and I know how to use it, all right. I reach the ground where the meadow runs into the trees and call out Anson's name. No answer. Bare feet sink into the damp leaves. I tighten my grip on the knife and walk in among the saplings.

Anson! I call out again.

Again the woods send nothing back. I take a few more steps where the trees grow in thick, maple and oak and birch, making a canopy of luscious green above my head. A brief shower did pass through our valley an hour or two ago, and the leaves still drip rain here and there. The birds yammer. To my right, the sunshine flashes on the lake. I venture on. My bare feet make no sound on the leaves, I am like a wild Indian how I walk through a forest. The straw hat hides the unnatural brilliance of my hair. Nothing I can do about my milky limbs, so pale as to glow luminescent in that shade, except for the unfortunate freckle or two.

Then I hear the crack of a firing gun, and my caution flies. I scream out *Anson!* and commence to run in the direction of that terrible, familiar sound. Tear my feet up good on a branch or two. Grip my knife for dear life. When all of a sudden a man appears through the trees, loping toward me. Big, thick male in a white shirt, just like Anson. It *is* Anson. I drop the knife and hurtle into his arms. Demand to know why the devil he must scare a girl so. He says he just went for a walk, that's all. I figure he smells a lot like sweat for a fellow who's just walked through the woods.

I slide back down to the ground. "What about that gunshot?"

He shrugs and says he guesses it was a hunter or something.

I tell him I'm not some city-bred dimwit who don't know when is hunting season. He looks down stony at me and I forgive him, just because he's alive and all. He retrieves the knife, takes my hand, and leads me back through the wood, till he happens to look down at my torn feet and swears mightily. Up I swing into the cradle of his arms. He bears me silent back to the house and sets me on the back porch steps. Says don't move, he'll be right back. I cup my hands around my mouth and call to Patsy in the boathouse. A moment later she comes out running.

"Ginny, is you hurt? Is you hurt?" she cries.

I open my arms and haul her into my lap. "Not a bit, my pumpkin."

"I heard a gun!"

"So did I. Must have been some men out hunting, I guess. Poaching off season or something, the dirty scoundrels."

"Oooh, Ginny! What happened to your feet?"

"Just a scratch or two. They're all right." I bury my face in her sweet-smelling hair and stretch out my legs to the cool sunshine. Anson comes back out of the house with a bowl of soapy water, a roll of white gauze, and a bottle of Old Grand-Dad. Medicinal purposes, he says. Perfectly legal. Commences to wash my feet himself, tender as can be, then rinses them off with a generous splash of whiskey. You might could hear me yowling all the way over at your place, only you imagine it's the neighbor's cat. Anyhow Patsy wants to know what for Anson put the whiskey on my foot instead of in a glass for drinking.

"Because Anson don't believe God gave us whiskey for to ease our sorrows, my wee round sweet apple. He thinks he might better torture his wife with it."

Anson unrolls a length of gauze and winds it gentle around my foot. "Don't listen to your sister, Patsy. Alcohol kills the germs, you see, so those cuts don't get infected. Wouldn't want Ginny to get blood poison, would we?"

"No, Anson."

"Now, if Ginny's very, very good and doesn't complain, I might pour her a glass to drink when I'm done. For the pain, you understand."

"Going to need more than just a glass," I tell him. "Maybe the whole bottle."

With her solemn blue eyes Patsy looks at Anson and then the bottle. "Don't worry, Ginny. If you run out, there's lots more in the boathouse."

Anson stops rolling gauze. The two of us look at Patsy's guileless face. Her grassy bare feet swing careless from my lap.

"*What* did you say?" Anson asks, quiet-like.

11

THERE BE about twelve or fifteen crates altogether, stacked underneath a couple of horse blankets at the back, except Patsy took off the horse blankets while she was waiting for me to retrieve her and opened up one of the crates with the claw end of a hammer to see what was there. My Patsy knows her way around a toolshed, all right. Now she runs right up to this open crate like she owns it and pulls out a dark bottle. "See?" she says, triumphant.

I take the bottle from her hand and examine the label. "I'll be damned. Canadian rye whiskey, distilled legal and everything. Did you notice anything here before?"

"No, but I can't say I was looking." Anson rolls another bottle in his hands and frowns at it. He looks again at the pile of crates in the back corner and fingers the edge of the horse blanket. "I could kick myself. Probably they've been landing cargo here for years. Sheltered cove like this, right on the edge of Lake Champlain. Nobody for miles around."

"You don't mean to say they've been carrying on right under our noses!"

"Probably. At night, dark of moon. When we're all sound asleep."

I lift my head and meet his gaze, because the pair of us don't necessarily just sleep under the dark of moon, being rightfully married as we are.

"So what do we do about it?"

He takes the bottle from my hands and puts it back in the crate, together with his own. "Nothing. We seal it back up and cover it with the blanket and forget we saw a thing."

I snake my hand inside the crate. "Now hold on just a minute."

"*Gin*. Put that back."

"But it's good whiskey. They left it here, didn't they? Finders keepers."

"Put it *back,* I said."

He speaks sharp. Reluctant I lay the bottle back in its crate and watch him set the lid on top. Lift the hammer and pound the nails back in.

"They can count," he says, "and you don't want them to come up short, believe me. Not by a single bottle."

"Now that's not neighborly."

"These men don't come around to beg for a cup of sugar, Gin. You know that as well as I do." He pounds the last nail and sets the hammer back on the shelf. Sets his hands on his hips and stares down at Patsy, who watches the whole business wide eyed. "As for *you,* curious cat. I don't want you playing in here by yourself, do you understand? And if you find something funny in here, or see something funny out on the lake, come find me or Ginny, right away."

"Yes, sir."

"All right, then." He bends down and swings me back into his arms. "Now let's get your sister inside to put her feet up."

"They Lord, it's nothing but a scratch or two! I can walk myself."

My beloved makes no reply but to carry me out of that boathouse and up the lawn to the giant log house. Patsy tags at his heels and fires him a fusillade of questions, which he answers patient and truthful, while I lean back against his rumbling chest and figure walking is overrated, anyhow.

12

ANSON AND Patsy fix up supper together in the kitchen, while I recline magisterial on the sofa in the company of a dirty novel purloined from one of the bookshelves, like the invalid I am. Anson's remarkable handy in the kitchen, owing to his years as a bachelor in a cheap studio apartment on East Thirty-Third Street, and I overhear him instructing Patsy on the proper way to clean a fish for frying. After supper he sits down at the spinet, stretches his fingers, and plays a couple of rollicking polkas, followed by that Beethoven sonata, the terrible sad one, followed by "Maple Leaf Rag" in honor of our friends up north over the lake water—all of which he taps out from memory, being a natural-born musician and all. Patsy cuts the rug up good. She does adore to dance, my baby sister. When Anson's plumb out of tunes he hoists her on his shoulders and bears her upstairs for bed, belting some aria in his honey baritone while my heart fixes to burst from its cage. Then it's my turn.

"You know, my feet be just fine for walking," I murmur in his ear as he carries me along the gallery hall to the bedroom.

But Anson shakes his head grave and tells me he's just not prepared to take that kind of chance with a brand-new bride.

13

THE NEXT afternoon is warm and unsettled, clouds thick overhead. Storm weather, Anson says. He suggests we take out the rifles from the gun cabinet and shoot some targets ahead of the tempest. I ask what gun cabinet, he says the one in the library. Well, blow me down. We each select a fine handcrafted Winchester Model 1892 and tramp out through the still, greasy air to the woods. Patsy tags along important with the bag of cartridges. Turns out my wee round sweet apple does know a thing or two about loading guns. Anyhow we spend a pleasant hour picking targets. I'm afraid Anson's no match for a hardscrabble mountain wildcat when it comes to blasting off the acorn from an oak tree a hundred yards distant, but then few men are. Still he comports himself credible. Patsy squeals delighted whenever he hits his target, for he is her almighty god by now, you understand, can do no evil.

On the way back to the house a strange cold puff of wind riles our clothes. Anson squints up at the jostling clouds and says there's a storm brewing, all right. We hurry our way indoors, where Anson cleans and oils the guns himself and puts them back in the cabinet and locks it tight. Snatches me around the waist and kisses my neck and warns me he will put Patsy to bed early tonight. I ask to what do I owe this warm behavior, sir, and he nibbles the other side of my neck and tells me it must be something to do with the way I blasted that acorn to kingdom come, figures a man would do wise to keep such a woman blissful content.

After supper Anson plays backgammon with Patsy while I lounge on the sofa with my dirty novel and a glass of fresh creamy milk and listen to the rising gale. Then the first wave of rain hits the windows like a handful of dashed pebbles. Patsy runs to look. Reports back there be a real big storm outside, *awful* big, just as a flash of lightning turns the air white. Crack of thunder follows directly.

Anson jumps up and swings her in his arms before she can scream. "I think it's about bedtime, don't you?"

"I won't sleep a wink," she promises.

"That so? Well, I guess we might as well start polishing the silver, then. Or waxing the floors? What do you think, Gin?"

"Wash and iron the linens. That needs doing."

So Patsy drags herself up the stairs, followed by Anson with the two giant cauldrons of water heating themselves up on the stove this past hour. I wander around the big room and the kitchen, put out the lamps, bank the fire in the giant coal stove. Upstairs Anson's honey baritone serenades Patsy in the bathroom. Sound of splashing and Patsy's bell laugh. I open the door a crack to find a flotilla of rubber duckies and a great many soap bubbles. "Don't be too long, now, children," I tell them, and Anson looks up, sleeves rolled to his elbows, expression so marvelous droll as to strike me down dead from joy.

"Can't you see we're busy here?" he says to me, this fearsome former special agent of the Prohibition enforcement bureau, this man sleepless with sorrow but eight weeks before, and I instruct him to make sure he don't track any water on my nice clean floor and close the door.

By the time he climbs into bed and gathers me up lascivious in his arms, the hurricane beats furious on the window glass, and I swan it's invaded his spirits as well. Arrives between the sheets in full rut, so doped up with libido I don't scarce know how to keep pace. Toward the end I find myself pinned for dear life to a bedpost and bite my own fist to keep from hollering the good news to the whole neighborhood, such as it is, while Anson labors vigorous behind me. We expire at exactly the same instant and crash bang to the mattress, panting and perspiring like a pair of racehorses that just won the Derby in a dead heat.

When I have air to breathe again, I demand to know what's got into him.

Nothing, he says, can't a man enjoy a honeymoon around here?

Still we remain joined together. Lie on our sides, hearts galloping. I reach up to finger his soft hair. Flash of lightning sends an instant jagged light across the room, log walls and chintz armchair, empty stone hearth. Anson's thick arm wrapped snug across my belly.

"Some honeymoon," I say. "Here you be stranded smack in the middle of nowhere, not a room service waiter in the whole county. Washing your own dishes. Minding your wife's kid sister. Playing the piano and backgammon and rubber duckies."

"Sounds like heaven to me."

"Honest? You don't mind?"

"Me? I was born for this. It's you I worry about, Ginger Kelly. Not too bored up here in the woods, are you? Nobody to amuse you but your sober old husband?"

Before I can answer him, a brilliant flash of lightning illuminates the whole room like noon, making me to jump straight up. Rain pours against the window. Anson reaches down for the quilt and sheets, all bunched up at the foot of the bed. Draws them over the both of us and tethers me back safe against him. *Bored?* My God, I'm so happy I could die. So grateful to fall asleep with this man's skin laid against mine, to know we shall wake together in seven or eight hours' time, sound rested, scarce an inch of empty space betwixt us. Not another human being for miles around to disturb our sacred peace. Me and Patsy tucked safe inside his steadfast heart.

"I guess you keep me amused, all right," I tell him.

Then I lay my hand over his hand where it rests flat against my belly and hold him there snug, so he knows how pure this joy runs inside me.

I am just drifting to sleep when Anson speaks up. "I've been meaning to ask you something."

"Hmm?"

Wind rattles the window glass. Anson strokes his thumb along my rib, paying special attention to the ridge where it meets my bosom, for he does worship that bosom regular, as a pilgrim before a shrine.

"What do you think if I adopted Patsy?"

My eyelids flash back open. "*What* did you say?"

"She's an orphan, after all. If she were legally my daughter, her position would be more secure. And then—well, if we *should* have any additions to the family, she'd be no different than them."

We lie there listening to the mad symphony of the storm outside, wind and rain and bang of almighty thunder. The air smells damp and uneasy, yet Anson's thick arm holds me still against his chest. Tear rolls from my chin to his fingertips.

After a while, he ventures, "What do you think?"

I wait some more till I can answer him back in a steady voice.

"Not up to me, Anson. You best ask her yourself, in the morning, and see what she says."

14

SOMETIME IN the night, I wake to the noise of a thunderclap. Or maybe it's the absence of Anson in my bed, which I feel like the absence of a limb or something. I sit straight up and call his name soft, so I don't wake Patsy down the hall, though on second thought she couldn't possibly hear that one word over the noise of the storm. Could she?

No answer, but I didn't expect one. If he was still in the room with me, I would know it. I throw off the covers and feel around the armchair nearby for my dressing gown. Slip my arms through the armholes and belt it up good. Toe my slippers onto my bandaged feet and steal out the bedroom and down the stairs. No sign of him in the big room, nor the kitchen. I take a battery flashlight from the shelf, raincoat from the hook. Change my slippers for the rubber boots next to the back door. Head out into the storm, heart pounding for two.

Outdoors is pitch black and wild, riven by sheets of invisible rain. I do love a good hurricane so much as the next floozy, but this is something else. When I yell out Anson's name, I scarce hear my own voice. Still I sense him out there. Sense some terrific struggle taking place in the wilderness. Down the lawn to the boathouse I chase the glittering beam of my flashlight. Call his name frantic. Already I be soaked through and frozen cold. Rain thunders against the boathouse roof, but no shadow lurks inside, no human being shelters here. Horse blankets still cover those crates of contraband. Out I fly, down the slippery dock. Like a lighthouse I throw out the beam of my lamp, but there's nothing to see, no object close enough on that roiling, spitting lake to illuminate. On my knees I fall and pray to Almighty God, though I well understand He has but scant reason to hear the prayers of a wicked floozy like myself in the middle of all that magnificent tempest He has kicked up. Still He must surely desire to cast His loving shelter over His servant Anson? Anson, who strives always to do what is good though it kills him.

Even as the unaccustomed words pass my lips, a shudder of lightning turns the night to stark day, and I see some flash of something in the distance, on the eastern shore of the cove. I jump to my feet.

The world goes black again. Still I strain toward that thing I saw, whatever it was, and it seems to me a light flashes there, a pinprick in the middle of the night.

In the next instant, I run heedless along the rim of the shore. Trip over some object and land hard on the grass. Bounce straight up and go on running, flashlight bobbing just ahead of me, trees now closing in. Whole world wet and howling around me. Branches slice my cheeks. Throat all hoarse from shouting Anson's name when at last I hear some answering shout. Between the trees ahead, some flashes of light. I run bang into a tree trunk and stagger dizzy to the side. Pair of hands takes me by the shoulders. "Gin! What the hell are you doing here?"

I drum my fists against his chest. "*Me?* I went after *you*, you dumb lug!"

He swears mighty and makes me to sit. Sticks something under my nose and tells me I'm bleeding. I push his hand aside and ask what's going on.

Shipwreck, he says.

15

SEEMS THE ship's a total loss, but the sailors are just banged up and incipient hypothermic. *Sailors.* Bootleggers, *that* I see plain, as they drip rainwater all over my nice clean kitchen floor. There be three of them, haggard and pale. Anson gets blankets while I build up the fire in the stove and boil a kettle of water for coffee. My nose has stopped bleeding, but it don't look so good. Still, the men are grateful, at least. The captain is a man called Standish. Won't tell me his first name, and I suspect the Standish ain't real, either. Well, we are all desperate wicked and inclined to evil as the sparks fly upward, as the Good Book says.

When they have drunk their coffee and eaten down the remains of the apple pie Anson and Patsy made for dessert, they bed down on the floor of the great room, wrapped in wool blankets, and commence to snoring. Anson hustles me upstairs and clucks like a mother hen over my nose. I tell him that should learn him for the last final time, running away like that into the woods without saying why.

You don't have to follow me, he says stern. I can take care of myself, believe it or not.

Then I must take his face in my hands and look him straight in the eye, so he don't mistake my words for jest.

I will *always* follow you, Oliver Anson Marshall. I will follow you to the ends of the earth, *always*. So you better make sure you know what you're doing before you leave.

16

WHEN ME and Patsy troop downstairs to hunt the eggs for breakfast, the bootleggers are still passed out cold before the giant empty fireplace. Patsy stops dead.

"We had some unexpected visitors last night," I tell her. "Come in for shelter in the storm."

She nods understanding and expresses a hope that the hens weren't too frighted by the storm to lay their full measure of eggs.

Say what you will about the character and habits of scoundrelly bootleggers, they are right grateful for the eggs and toast and bacon and coffee we lay before them, and mighty sheepish to have imposed on our hospitality. Standish makes apology for my nose and hopes it ain't broken. I am happy to inform him it's only bruised, not broken—according to Anson, anyhow, who has played enough football to become expert on all matters olfactory—and should recover its straight lines nicely in a week or two.

When the last of the drizzle clears, Anson takes out the canoe and helps them haul what they can from the wreck to the boathouse. Standish assures us someone will be along later to pick up the cargo, not to worry, and they do certainly appreciate our kind understanding of business matters. Anson offers to drive them into town so they can telephone the news to their friends. Off they go down the muddy road, jolting through the potholes, Anson and a pack of affable bootleggers. When he returns a couple of hours later, I ask what on earth *that* was all about. Don't tell me he's thinking of entering a whole new line of work or something. Changing sides altogether.

"No," he says, "but it never hurts to do some fellows a favor or two, now that it's not against professional ethics."

Sure enough, the next morning the entire stock of crates under the horse blankets is clean gone, except for a single case of the finest fifteen-year-old single malt Canadian Club, together with a note that says simply *Help yourself.*

17

SECOND WEEK of August. I wake at dawn to the kissing of some tender lips down the knobs of my spine, one by one. Crack my lids. Sleepy gray light between the curtains. Though I make some half-hearted effort to turn on my back and conduct this interview face-to-face, Anson holds me still till he done what he came for, which is to render me howling into the pillow while he attends to my nethers like the most conscientious cat. Then he plants his palms on either side of my shoulders and by mighty strokes he delivers us both our heart's desire till I cry for mercy. In the dizzy silence afterward, you can hear every creak of that giant log house, every twitter outside it, which is how I come to startle upward, launching my tranquilized beloved clear across the bed.

He asks why, respectful as hell.

"Car in the driveway!" I hiss.

What I love about Anson, he don't tell me I'm a hysterical female and go back to sleep, for God's sake. Not this fellow. Next instant, he's on his feet, hand laid against the bedroom door, listening fierce. I throw on my nightgown and toss him his trousers from the back of the chair. He tugs on one leg and the other, listening all the while. Soundless he turns the knob. Opens the door an inch. Holds up his hand to signal me to stay where I am, bless him, when he knows full well I don't mean to obey.

Now I don't believe I've yet described this lodge in proper detail. Pay attention. That giant room I spoke of, the one into which you enter from the front door, reaches two stories high, and a gallery runs all around that second story, overlooking the giant room and its contents. The bedrooms all open up to this gallery. So when Anson steps out of our bedroom, he puts his hands on the rail and looks down upon the neat arrangement of heavy dining table and chairs in one corner and sofa and armchairs in another, and doors and shelves and tables and cabinets and what have you. He turns his head and signals me to go to Patsy, just as if he was expecting me to be standing there outside the bedroom like he told me not to.

This time I do like he says. I fly to Patsy's room and peek inside, where my sweet baby sister be spread akimbo in her bed like a starfish, pink-flushed and innocent. I lock the door and slip the key into

the pocket of my dressing gown and fly down the stairs to find Anson, emerging from the library with a pistol and a grim expression.
He don't so much as glance at me. Just strides to the front window
and lifts the curtain a bare half inch with his left pinky finger. What
he spies, I can't say for certain. What I heard before, I couldn't tell if
it was a big car or a small car, one car or a half dozen. I don't even
remember did I hear it, exactly, or just pick up the vibration through
earth and stone and wood.

He stares through that crack for a moment or two. I figure I might
as well back him up. I steal into the library and open up the gun cabinet. My fingers are dead steady. My nerves are ice cold. I discover a
pistol, old but useful, unloaded. The boxes of cartridges are labeled
careful, I'll give them that. I load the gun in a matter of seconds and
hurry back into the main room, where Anson—to my surprise—has
his hand on the knob of the front door, ready to open it. I want to
ask him whether he might better go around back in an ambush, but I
guess he knows more about this kind of business than I do, for all I'm
a better shot. The muscles of his back flex magnificent. He opens the
door and steps to the porch. I hear his voice, asking a question. I
think I might hang back and defend the staircase, on account of Patsy.
Then I think to hell with that. Quick as a whisper, I whisk across the
room to the front window and peer out as Anson did, through the
crack in the red-checked curtain. The sun hasn't yet risen above
the neighboring mountains. The headlights cut through the gray air.

He stands on the porch, my beloved, covered by nothing but the
trousers he wore yesterday. I never thought to see such a sight, Oliver Anson Marshall greeting some guest—invited or otherwise—
half-naked. It's a bruising sight. His rope muscles coil in all the right
places. The pistol sits comfortably in his palm. I don't doubt it's
loaded.

In the driveway before him sits a large black car. A man climbs slow and cautious out of the driver seat. Holds up his hands. Shouts something to Anson. Anson shouts back. Incredulous, sounds to me. Like he don't quite believe what the man says.

The rear door cracks open on the left side. A woman's shoe pokes from beneath the frame. I drop the curtain and run to the door and come up behind Anson in my plaid dressing gown. Morning air be frightful cool. The woman now slides out from behind the door. She's not what I thought. Maybe forty years old, rectangular jacket buttoned over prim white blouse, plain skirt hemmed somewhere near the middle of her calf. Not so much as a smear of lipstick. That stern face—I know it. I'm sure of it. I seen her before, all right, but not face-to-face. On the page of a newspaper—a number of newspapers, to say nothing of the weekly magazines.

I think I might be sick.

At the same instant I realize who she is, Anson lowers his gun, steps forward into the headlights, and makes respectful apology for his state of undress. Explains he had no warning she was coming to call at such an ungodly hour. (He doesn't actually say *ungodly*, but you can see he means it.)

"I'm sorry to arrive unannounced, Mr. Marshall," says Mabel Walker Willebrandt, "but as you haven't done me the courtesy of replying to my telegrams, I was forced to invite myself."

18

NOW, IN case you've had your head in a basket for the past five years, Mrs. Willebrandt is the assistant attorney general of the United States, in charge of prosecuting violations of the Volstead Act.

I guess she might be the most celebrated woman in America, after Mary Pickford. Well might Anson offer her a sheepish expression, though his dignity remains intact.

I consider that sheepish expression and think—*Telegrams?*

What telegrams?

"Mrs. Willebrandt. You'll excuse me a moment to dress." He turns to find me standing there, shocked stiff. He clears his throat and adds, "My wife will show you inside."

He disappears so instant as a haint, and me and Mrs. Willebrandt are left to regard each other wary. You can see the word *floozy* in her head, though she don't say it aloud. I imagine the state of my hair and skin and suppose I do look like a woman who's just been tumbled good, but isn't that Anson's fault so much as mine? Still, nobody judges a woman so harsh as another woman.

"Won't you come in, Mrs. Willebrandt," say I, in my best convent-educated voice, tinted with just a shade of Bryn Mawr. (I only spent a year among the fine females in that institution, you see, before they kicked me out on account of I busted up somebody's tip-turned nose for her.)

Once I usher Mrs. Willebrandt to a seat on the sofa, crumbs brushed specially, I repair to the kitchen to brew up some coffee and gather my composure. Strictly speaking, this is the boss. Anson's boss, though the Prohibition bureau is technically a unit of the Treasury Department. Why, don't they fondly call Prohibition agents Mabelmen? He's as much hers as mine.

Was, I remind myself. He quit, remember?

I bang the sugar bowl and the creamer on the tray. Pour the coffee beans into the mill and turn the handle vigorous.

Well. What if she refused to accept his resignation? What if Prohibition enforcement is the kind of work you can't just leave if you want to? Maybe she's here to drag him back to Washington for some kind of dressing-down. Maybe they need him to find the fellow who killed Louis Hardcastle, after all. Maybe she's here to arrest him for dereliction of duty. Absconding with a red-haired mountain floozy.

Maybe I should just head out there and ask her outright.

The water in the kettle starts to boil. I pour in the ground coffee and stir it up a bit, like my step-daddy learned me to do. Today's Wednesday, so Anson brought home fresh beans just yesterday, which I roasted up slow and careful in the big iron skillet. Makes a difference, how you roast them. I pour the coffee through a strainer into the coffeepot and carry the tray into the big room, where Mrs. Willebrandt sits ladylike on the sofa where I left her, stifling a yawn.

I lay the tray on the table. "Drive all night, did you?" I ask, air of sympathy.

"Yes."

I pour coffee into her cup and ask does she take cream or sugar. She takes both. Hand her the cup, pinky all crooked like I was born to it, for I have no intention of allowing this Willebrandt woman the satisfaction of pitying her former agent because he did marry beneath him.

"Thank you, Mrs. Marshall," she says.

Again, I experience the shock of my new name. Mrs. Oliver Marshall, that's me. Funny how a woman's name gets swallowed up altogether when she marries. Nothing but a single lonely *s*, curved like a snake, to signify her individual existence. I pour myself a cup of coffee, add sugar, drink. Burns my tongue. I set down cup and saucer in my flannel lap.

"Must be important, then, to drive all the way out here, straight through the night."

"Yes, it is. This is a fine lodge, isn't it? I expect you're on your honeymoon?"

"I expect we are."

"I apologize for intruding."

"We'll get over it." I lift my coffee back to my mouth and sip more cautious this time. Pretend I don't notice the sharp stare of Mrs. Willebrandt from the neighboring sofa. Then some devil makes me add—and you must admit I've been very, very good until now— "Thank the Lord Almighty you didn't arrive ten minutes before."

She chokes on her coffee. I offer her a napkin. Enter Anson down the stairs, all pink and shaved, wearing the dark suit he last wore at his father's funeral, two days before we were married. He pulls up short to witness his assistant attorney general in the middle of a coughing fit, me patting her solicitous on the back. Shoots me a look of accusation. I shrug back my shoulders at him, innocent as a lamb.

While the two of them confer—and Mrs. Willebrandt made it plain that the discretion of wives is not to be trusted in these secret matters—I climb upstairs to attend to Patsy, who's been locked in her room all this time. She sits reading a book on her pink rag rug and looks up ingenuous when I open the door.

"Is that a friend come visiting?" she asks.

"No, my wee round sweet apple. Just business. Anson's business. Come along with me and we'll fetch those eggs together."

I hold out my hand. She hauls herself up. Together we clamber down the back stairs and through the kitchen and pantry to the sparkling outdoors. The wet grass chills my feet. Patsy sticks on her garden clogs to enter the coop while I stand outside, not wishing to dirty my peachy toes with chickenshit. The gray dawn has lit to pure silver. The sky be shredded with luminescent cloud. In a moment that

August sun will crest the eastern peaks to warm the earth. I close the lids of my eyes and return to the instant of waking, the sweet damp kisses along my spine and my nether parts before this Willebrandt arrived, the earth-bending shudder of my beloved at the height of our wedded bliss. Had better not be the last time, is all.

But then, you hardly ever know when is the last time for anything. Nobody ever warns you such a thing. It just ends.

19

THIS MORNING the hens are pleased to bestow eleven plump eggs upon us, just one short of an even dozen. That fool sister of mine is so delighted by this prodigious haul, she must gallop straight into the big room before I can stop her and tell Anson the astonishing news.

"*Eleven eggs!*" he exclaims, like we have won first prize in the county raffle.

"Me and Ginny is going to make a custard. Ain't we, Ginny?"

"*Aren't* we. I guess we might, if I can find some vanilla beans. Mrs. Willebrandt? Would a fresh poached egg suit you for breakfast?"

The assistant attorney general of the United States looks from Patsy to Anson to me, and you can see what she's thinking, all right, that her incorruptible agent must have sired this secret love child with his floozy, and the best that can be said is he's done the right thing at last and made an honest pair of us both, though she don't much care for his taste in floozies, nor hold out hope for his future happiness.

"Thank you, no," she says.

"No, I insist," Anson tells her. "You must eat. It's ninety miles back to Albany."

Mrs. Willebrandt rises to her feet and gathers her pocketbook. "Then the earlier I set out, the better. Thank you for your time, Mr. Marshall. Mrs. Marshall? May I have a word?"

We are both startled, Anson and me. I look to my beloved and lift my eyebrows. He frowns and makes a slight nod.

"I don't see why not," I tell her.

Patsy tugs Anson's hand. "Come on, Anson. You can pick out your egg."

I take the lead and escort Mrs. Willebrandt onto the front porch. The driver climbs out of the car and stands by the door, watching us hawklike from beneath the peak of his cap. Now the sun drenches the valley in melted gold, enough to break your heart. Mrs. Willebrandt turns to me and makes a seam of her mouth. I just wait till she picks the words she wants. No point rushing a lawyer, she'll harangue you eventual.

"Congratulations," she says at last.

"Why, thank you."

"No, I'm perfectly serious. He's the finest agent in the Bureau, one of the finest men I know. I hope you don't ruin him."

"Likewise."

She sighs. "Of course, I'm pleased to see him happy in his choice of wife. But I do need him urgently. His country needs him."

"His country didn't seem to appreciate him when it had him. Whereas I do."

Mrs. Willebrandt glances at the wedge of sky that meets the porch roof and back at me. "In a country of eighty million men, I can't seem to find a single one who isn't above taking the pay of the other side. Except your husband, who seems to believe he's under the obligation of a promise to you, which lies somehow higher in his account than his duty to his country."

"You wouldn't want him any other way. A man who honors his wife is the exact same man who won't take a dime from a bootlegger to look the other way when a truckful of Wild Turkey comes down the Jersey turnpike at two in the morning without a certificate."

"I suppose that's true. Which means *you* hold all the cards, Mrs. Marshall. I am reduced to appealing to *your* sense of duty to your country. If you have any."

"As to that, I can't see what my country's done for me lately, other than attempt to shame and murder the fellow I love."

"That was an unfortunate misdirection."

"*Unfortunate?* Damn near killed us both. His own father died for it. No, Mrs. Willebrandt. You had your chance and you squandered him. Go find yourself some other sucker. He's mine. And I do swan I'll take better care of him than you ever did."

Prideful as I am, I reckon I've struck the final blow in this duel. I don't consider I'm squabbling with a lawyer. No garden variety lawyer, either. She has argued her case before the Supreme Court of the United States and won it, too, whereas I'm but a poor mountain-bred bastard with nothing but animal cunning to guide me.

She fixes her clever eyes upon mine. "Have you considered, Mrs. Marshall, that all honeymoons must end sometime? Eventually your husband must decide what he's to do with his life. This is all very *pleasant,* naturally"—she gestures to the house, the valley, Anson himself—"and I even admit I envy you for it. I wouldn't mind a little peace and quiet myself. But we must all come down from the mountain. And you can hold a man like that with a promise, but you can't make him happy in his work." She holds out her gloved hand. "Good-bye, Mrs. Marshall. I believe you know where to find me."

I take her hand and shake it, because my mama brung me up to act polite with strangers. But no power on earth will drag a *Good-bye* out of me for this woman. We are mortal enemies, me and her, and I don't wish her well.

20

A PALL DRAPES over the rest of the day. We don't so much as mention the phantasmagoric arrival and departure of the most powerful woman in America, but her apparition kind of hangs there in the air, wherever we turn. In the afternoon another colossal thunderstorm rolls through the valley. Claps of thunder like the splitting of boulders. Explosions of rapid light one after another. Down pours the rain. For a moment or two you might think the end of the world comes nigh upon us sinners. Patsy's scared stiff, though she don't say a word—just burrows into Anson's ribs so her small white face near enough disappears in his shirt. Then it's over, so sudden as it begun. The sun comes out, gold and watery. The clouds boil past to expose an innocent blue sky. We squish down the lawn in our bare feet and watch the distant flashes on the other side of the hilltop until they're gone.

After dinner and custard for dessert, I play a polka on the phonograph and send Anson and Patsy whirling around the room until they collapse laughing. Patsy changes into her clean white nightgown and brushes her teeth. She makes Anson read her three stories before she will suffer the darkness. We take turns kissing her good night, tucking her quilt more snug around her shoulders. In our own room, my ardor takes Anson by surprise, though he don't complain. Nor does he ask me what for, when we collapse back some time afterward, damp and exhausted. Maybe he guesses I want to hold him close, after the day's frights, and that's true. But I think also of my premonition outside the chicken coop. I mean to prove it false beyond redemption, to incinerate doubt in giant bolts of carnal electricity—to borrow a metaphor from our recent weather. From the face of my beloved on the pillow, I'd say I done what I came for. I tell him he has the look of a contented man.

"I wouldn't say contented," he replies.

"What would you say?"

"I don't think there's a word for what it's like to be married to you. I just know that contented ain't it."

I poke him in the ribs. "You said *ain't*."

He just grunts and pulls me close, like he means now to catch a wink of well-earned sleep after all that, and no more talking. But I'm not through. I have a question for him, right this second when he can't tell a lie, not that he ever would.

"How did she know where to find us?"

He hesitates only a fraction. "Because I told her where we'd be."

"This wasn't about that booze in the boathouse, was it?"

"Of course not. What do you take me for?"

"Then what?"

"It doesn't matter, Gin. It's none of our business."

I squirm right out of his arms to sit up. "Now, hold on a second! What do you mean, none of our business? What happened?"

"Nothing more than you'd expect. The old racket's running again, under a new head. It's what I said would happen, that getting rid of Hardcastle wouldn't make any difference."

We speak low, because of Patsy, but I can't keep the ferocity out of my voice. "And Mrs. Willebrandt came all the way up here to beg you to help her take the racket apart. Is that right?"

He says not a word, which tells me all I need to know. I fold my arms until he sits up and drags my hands into his.

"Gin, I said no, remember? I told her I quit and I don't mean to come back. It's none of my business, not anymore. The only business I have left is keeping you safe from harm."

"Oh? And just what happened to all your fine ideals about upholding the law of the land? All that nonsense you used to tell me about our duty to respect the will of the majority, and how the wicked bootleggers undermine the sanctity of the Constitution?"

"I was a pompous idiot. You were right about everything, Gin. All the time you were right, and what happened out there—to Dad, to you—that was my fault, his blood's on my hands, because I didn't listen to you. Well, I don't give a damn about the Constitution anymore. I'm *your* man, Gin. *Yours,* I swear to God. That's all I am."

Well, I can't say much to that, can I? Can't tell him he takes too much on himself, can't explain that Mr. Marshall's death does not belong to Anson's own soul but to the bastard who did the deed. There is no burden left lying aground, howsoever impossible heavy, that Anson will not undertake to heave upon his own great shoulders, even though it break him. All I can do is help him to bear it. Hang my arms around his neck and lend him the use of me.

21

I DON'T RIGHTLY know what wakes me, whether it be the actual smell of smoke or the female instinct that something's amiss in her home. I sit bolt upright out of a dream and stare at the black night. A queer glow seems to creep around the edge of my vision.

Fire! I whisper.

And then—*FIRE!* I shout.

Anson bolts straight out of bed. "Where?"

"I don't know!"

Already he's tugged on his trousers and shirt. He shouts at me to cover my mouth and get Patsy while he runs downstairs, where the smoke already billows from some unknown blaze. Talk about dreams. I race down the gallery to Patsy's room like I'm inside the worst kind of nightmare, the kind that won't let you wake. Impossible, impossible. Every night we put out the kerosene lamps, one by one! The pile of wood inside the great stone fireplace has sat unlit since we arrived! The coal fire in the cookstove was banked careful by Anson himself, lids and damper shut tight! No electricity for miles, no gas, not a blessed thing that could spark a flame. Yet here I stand, throwing open the door to Patsy's room and gathering up my baby sister in a quilt. Cover her sweet astonished face with a patchwork corner. Reek of black smoke falling on everything. I figure I should grab a few things so she don't lose all she has, but a quick glance cast around the room reminds me she has not got much— some clothes and hair ribbons, the beaten-up stuffed lamb already clutched to her ribs, the watchful devoted love of me and Anson to protect her. And the greatest of these is love.

I hoist my Patsy into my arms with the strength God gives mamas to save their young. Together we thunder down the gallery to the back stairs. But the smoke is worse here, so thick you can't see the bottom. I turn back and head for the front stairs instead. Heart like a dynamo. Smoke not so terrible here—fire must be in the kitchen— now I hear it roar beast-like and ravenous. Lick of flame finds a rug and sweeps across. Hideous rancid reek of burnt wool. We reach the bottom of the stairs—wide wood floor to cross—flames erupting in the giant cauldron of oxygen that is this enormous double-height room. We can't go back. I shield Patsy as best I can and lower my head and dash for the door, scalded by heat and spark and smoke—*don't touch that metal doorknob*—brace my shoulder and knock that door down straight into Anson's waiting arms.

He snatches Patsy from me and says to run down to the lake, fire pump by the boathouse, hurry, he's right behind me. I leap from the front porch and circle around the burning tinder, dark lake flickers orange from the flames that shoot into the night. Fire pump waits outside the boathouse where Anson left it. Saw how fast the house burned and ran back in to fetch us himself. Together we roll out the hose and sink one end in the lake—Anson carries the other end so close as he can—I commence to pump with all my might, pump and pump, the might to pump just flooding my muscles natural. Patsy waits by the lake shore in her quilt, wide eyed, beaten-up stuffed lamb clutched to her chest.

22

BY DAWN it's all over. Nothing remains of our beautiful honeymoon lodge but a pile of wet charred timber and ash. The fire brigade showed up maybe half an hour after we started pumping, me and Anson taking turns with pump and hose, though the weight of that fire hose liketa killed me. Seems the smoke showed up real good in the moonlight and they spotted it from the fire tower next peak over. Too late to save the building but at least they kept it from spreading elsewhere. Now me and Patsy huddle in the pavilion as a shower drizzles down upon the steaming wreckage. Patsy has fallen asleep in my lap. I stare awestruck at the building that no longer exists, and at Anson, who confers earnest with the firemen. They point fingers hither and thither while the rain sparkles in the air and on their hair and clothes, and the smoke drifts aimless around them. The chickens run amok, having been set free by some humane soul.

After a while, when the shower lifts and the sun pokes over the ridge to shed a buttery glow over the ruins, Anson joins us where we sit on the floor. He crouches down and touches Patsy's sleeping cheek, then my own face, stunned and listless.

"Seems to have started in the kitchen," he says, "though not in the cookstove. They can't say how. No lamp or anything."

"We put the lamps out anyway."

"You must be exhausted. The way you kept on pumping."

I shrug. "I did what I could, that's all."

He looks at me, sober and warm. "Come with me. Garage wasn't touched. We'll take the car and drive into town and get something to eat. Find somewhere to stay."

"So how did it start? If it wasn't us?"

"What do you mean?"

"I mean who else knows we're here? Those bootleggers, for one. Your Mrs. Willebrandt."

Anson squints back toward the smoldering pile. "I don't think Mrs. Willebrandt told anyone."

"But what if the bootleggers saw her come to visit? Thought you had asked her to come on purpose, so you could rat on them?"

"It's possible, I guess."

"And what about the fellow who owns the place?"

"You can put that out of your head, Gin. Trust me."

We stare at each other.

"Look, I know what you're thinking," Anson says, "but I'd trust this man with my life. *Your* life. He's a friend."

"You're sure about that?"

"Dead sure."

"Anson, somebody started that fire, and it wasn't us. You know it and I know it."

"I know," he says, quiet and tired.

He holds out his arms for Patsy. She wakes up a little as I pass her over, but falls back asleep against that thick, smoke-scented shoulder. Wouldn't you? Together we make our way to the carriage house, which no longer holds carriages but rather Anson's spruce-green Packard roadster. I haven't been inside that car since we drove up to this mountain holler some six weeks ago. I scarce even remember that new-mint bride, skittish as a yearling Thoroughbred at her new way of life, wondering would she make her beloved miserable or happy.

Well. I have made him happy, I guess. But now *this*. Honeymoon finished in a blaze that stinks to high heaven.

Still dreaming, I wait for Anson to settle Patsy on the seat betwixt us. Then I slide in and set my bare feet on the floorboards, where they discover something lumpy. I reach down. My pocketbook. For the Lord's own sake, how have I not missed my own pocketbook in six weeks? No lipstick nor compact, no greenbacks nor subway nickels have I required in all that time. Not Luella Kingston's letter, tucked in its crisp envelope. I rummage around to count the money, which is likely all we can call our own until we locate a bank with corresponding privileges to my own, or Anson's.

My fingers bump against something cool and hard, half-smooth and half-ridged. I lift it out.

A key.

Uncomprehending I stare at it, until my memory clicks and a door cracks open in my head. A possible light inside, who knows. I slide the key back inside the pocketbook and fasten it shut. Patsy mutters and falls in my lap, clutching her lamb. Anson starts the engine and looks at me.

"All set?"

"What's his name?"

"Whose name?"

"Whose? The man whose house just burned down, that's who. This man you'd trust with our lives."

"Oh. Well, I guess he wouldn't mind my telling you."

Anson puts the car into reverse and backs it slow and careful out of the garage. When we reach the gravel drive, he casts one last look at the smoky ruins of the main house, the firemen still crawling over it, and heaves an old sigh.

"Charles Schuyler," he says.

ELLA

East Hampton, New York, 1998

ELLA WOKE up to the Nokia music of her ringing cell phone. Sunshine burst around the edges of the window shades. She flung her arm to the nightstand and knocked the phone across the floor.

Dammit, she groaned.

She lay on her stomach, in her nightshirt. Head still groggy. When had she gone to bed? Four in the morning or something. She tried to sit up and felt a wave of nausea, the old vertigo feeling, like she was hung over. *Dammit,* she said again. Staggered to her feet and swayed out the door and down the hall to the ancient bathroom, where she heaved bile into the toilet and cried. *You probably won't get over it entirely,* the doctor had said, trying to sound sympathetic. *You'll likely have bouts throughout the pregnancy.*

Bouts. Terrific word. Like a boxer or something.

When her stomach was done, Ella climbed to her feet and snagged a washcloth from the stack. Ran it under some warm water and held the wet cloth against her face. Stared at her wan face, her puffy eyes, her matted hair, all frizzed from the humid beach air, the absence of air conditioning. Thank God Hector couldn't see her like this.

Only he *had,* hadn't he? Seen her at her worst and still loved her. Hector.

She put down the washcloth and ran back to her room and the cell phone on the floor. It had fallen on the rug, thank God, so it was still intact. She picked it up. Hector had called twice around midnight, while Ella was downstairs in the library with Aunt Julie, and once this morning, four minutes ago.

UNTIL A WEEK AGO, Ella had known next to nothing about her great-grandfather. Now she was adrift in the detritus of his life— newspaper clippings, social invitations, club newsletters, personal letters—and she felt a little queasy about it all, to be honest, as if she were eavesdropping on a conversation not meant for her ears.

Aunt Julie had no such scruples. Of course, he *was* her own brother. She'd remembered about the desk key during the drive home from dinner at the club, that first evening. How he used to drop it into the recess of a peculiar lamp on the side table, shaped like a red English postbox, and sure enough that key was right there where he'd dropped it for the last time, decades ago, never knowing it was the last time. Aunt Julie said never mind feeling guilty—if Charles hadn't wanted his sister to know what was inside the desk, he would've made damn sure she didn't know where he kept the key. Anyway, he was dead, wasn't he? Dead for ages.

Worse, Ella didn't even know what she was looking for. The desk drawers were a mess, everything jumbled together. She spent the first three days just sorting everything into piles. Now she was organizing the newspaper clippings, mostly because they weren't personal, while Aunt Julie rummaged through the letters. She'd arranged them in chronological order. The earliest was dated May 1922 and had to do with an art exhibition just opened at some small gallery in Greenwich Village, featuring works by a painter known only as Anatole.

Another had to do with a series of police raids on speakeasies all over Manhattan: "Local Bureau Chief Confident Liquor Trade Will Be Shut Down 'Once and for All.'" (Ella snorted.) A few articles had to do with the apparently sensational murder of Louis Hardcastle at the Marshall residence in Southampton, two from the *New York Times* and one from the local rag, the last one dated two weeks after the event—"Still No Suspect in Hardcastle Slaying," it read. Then several articles from the summer of 1925, about the upcoming trial—the Trial of the Century, one of the papers called it—of some bootlegger named Bronstein, who ran a liquor smuggling operation that seemed to cover the entire northeastern United States. Ella skimmed a few of the columns, but she saw no mention of anyone named Hardcastle.

One name caught her eye, though.

"Look at this," she said to Aunt Julie. "Blah blah, here it is— *according to evidence obtained by Special Agent Oliver Marshall, operating under disguise for the Prohibition enforcement bureau at enormous personal peril.* You see that? *Marshall.* You don't think that's the same family that owned that place in Southampton where Louis Hardcastle was murdered, do you? I mean, I know it's a common name and all, but—"

"Let me see that." Aunt Julie snatched the clipping and squinted at it. Fumbled for the readers perched on top of her head. Her mouth moved as she scanned the page, exposing the line between faded magenta lipstick and the wet skin of her inner lip. As always, she was dressed impeccably in a pink sweater of summer-weight cashmere and cropped white pants. On her feet she wore tan Tod's; she said it was immodest to wear sandals indoors, although Mumma said the truth was she didn't want anyone to see her bunions. Her gold bouffant fluffed around her head, suggesting far more hair than actually existed—she'd had the hairdresser over to touch her up yesterday—

and her legs were long and skinny as a pair of chopsticks. Aunt Julie belonged to the tribe of women who would rather shrivel into nothing than weigh a pound more than she had at twenty-two. When she finished reading the article, she looked over the rim of her glasses at Ella. "No," she said. "It's not a coincidence."

"Wait, seriously?"

Aunt Julie handed back the article and removed the glasses from the bridge of her nose. "Oliver Marshall was Sylvo Marshall's son. He was there when Hardcastle was murdered. I remember it clearly, because she was there, too."

"Who? The Redhead?"

"Yes. He was the love of her life, you know. The only man she ever loved. Ollie Marshall. Now there was a *man*, all right. Positively *dripped* with sex appeal. If you liked them dark and silent, anyway."

"*What?* Why didn't you tell me any of this before?"

"You never asked."

"You're saying her lover was a *Prohibition* agent?"

"Her husband, actually. Yes, he was."

"So what happened?"

Aunt Julie put her glasses back on top of her head and reached for the pile of newspaper clippings. "He betrayed her, that's what. Are you done sorting these?"

"Hold on! *Betrayed* her?"

"Men always let you down in the end, darling, no matter what kind of promises they make in the beginning. Now, how are you coming along with your sheet spreads?"

"My what?"

Aunt Julie made a movement with her fingers. "On your computer."

"Oh. *Spreadsheets*, Aunt Julie. Not so much since you put me to work organizing all this paperwork."

"Well. Why don't you get to work on that?"

"Because I want to know more! *You* were the one who said she *chose* me, right? Ergo, she wants me to find out about all this."

"Not *that*, believe me. She would never in a million years want some stranger poking into her private life. What she *wants* is the justice she never got. The justice nobody dared to get back then, because you would've ended up dead like the rest of them. So you just let *me* take the walk down memory lane while *you* work on the bedsheets."

"Spreadsheets."

"Whatever."

"But what happened to her? What happened to Oliver Marshall?"

Aunt Julie stared down at the clippings in her lap. "They're gone, darling. That's all you need to know."

THAT WAS THREE DAYS ago, and Aunt Julie hadn't let her peek at the clippings—or the letters, or the invitations or receipts or any of the rest of it—since. During the day, Ella sat with her laptop under the terrace awning, drinking glass after glass of seltzer and lime as she drilled through the spreadsheets she'd put together four months ago, with the help of the yellow legal pad she'd smuggled out that last day in the office. In the evening, after they returned from dinner at the club, she moved her work indoors. She hated how rusty she'd become in the past four months, how squeaky the hinges of her brain. She kept having to look up formulas and go back and check her mistakes, refresh her memory, retrace the lines of logic again and again. Last night she'd fallen asleep in the armchair while Aunt Julie frowned and hummed over the letters written in her brother's scrawling handwriting, making illegible little notes on lined index cards as she went.

Meanwhile, Hector had called. Twice. And she'd missed him both times, and again this morning. He hadn't left any voice mails. Just checking in, then. Usually he called in the morning and the evening—his days were hectic, naturally, and Ella didn't want to interrupt him in the middle of a rehearsal or something. This was his dream, his calling! She was happy to be nudged into ten or fifteen minutes' conversation at the beginning and the end of his day, so that he could pursue that dream without distraction by the quotidian details of his pregnant girlfriend's Hamptons summer.

Or so she told herself, anyway. On the other hand, she couldn't quite ignore a low, subcutaneous unease whenever she hung up the phone. Oh, he *said* all the right things. Loved her, missed waking up with her this morning, missed the smell of her skin and hair, the sound of her vomiting over his toilet. Missed playing the piano with her at night. Missed Nellie! Was desperate to see how their bump was growing. That kind of thing. And he said it all the right way, too! He didn't sound rushed—at least, not often—or impatient or uninterested in what she was doing while he was Mr. Big Shot out in Los Angeles. He asked her about the club, about the crazy aunts, how the wedding plans were shaping up. Laughed and said he wished he was lying on the beach with her right now.

She couldn't put her finger on it, exactly. Just that he didn't seem to share that many details about *himself.* She would ask him about his day, what was it like, where did they go for dinner or drinks—he seemed to take most meals with what he called *the team*—did he have any fun insider gossip for her to chew on. And he would answer—

well, not evasively. Just not expansively. They ate at Spago. He had the sea bass. Gossip? He laughed his warm, dark laugh that made her think of coffee, for some reason. He wouldn't know, he said. All went over his head.

So Hector had been in L.A. for a week now, and she still didn't have a clear idea who his friends were and what they did and how, exactly, you recorded a score for a movie and edited that sound into the movie. Maybe she should have asked better questions? But she had the feeling it wouldn't have made any difference.

And it was a strange feeling, because she and Hector shared everything. Food, air, music, stupid jokes, small random thoughts, silences that said more than words. It just unsettled her, that he existed right now in a world he didn't seem to want her to know much about.

HE ANSWERED THE PHONE on the first ring. "*There* you are, sleeping beauty."

"I'm so sorry. Aunt Julie kept me up until four with this—this *project* of hers."

"Four in the morning? Are you insane? How are you feeling?"

"Not so great." Ella wandered to the bookshelf and found the box of saltines she'd left there two weeks ago, for just such an emergency. "I'll be all right, though. How's everything?"

"Fantastic. Wrapped up rehearsals yesterday, now we're headed out the door to the studio to record. Hold on a second."

Ella unwrapped the stack of crackers and pried one loose while Hector traded words with somebody. She glanced at the clock—five minutes to ten—and subtracted three hours for Pacific time. "Wow. You're off early."

"Sorry, what's that?"

"I said you're an early bird," she said, nibbling the cracker. "Was that room service?"

It seemed to Ella that there was the slightest pause.

"What? Oh. No, it's just Lulu. She's giving me a ride over to the studio. Grabbing some breakfast before we start."

"Wait, who's Lulu? Did I miss something?"

In the background, somebody laughed. A woman. She said something to Hector. Ella put down the cracker sleeve.

"You know, my director," said Hector. "The film director."

"Oh. Oh, of course. Sorry, I never caught the name."

"Really? I'm sure I mentioned it. So what are you up to today? More of the same?"

"Just hanging out on the beach with a laptop. Exciting times. Probably head over to the club at some point so Mumma and Aunt Viv can kill each other over tennis."

Somewhere in the background of Hector's hotel room, the woman said something.

"Yeah, yeah, I know." Hector lowered his voice. "Look, kind of a tight schedule this morning. I'm sorry. Have to get moving."

"Of course. Get going. Don't keep the musicians waiting, they'll eat all the doughnuts."

Hector laughed. "It's L.A., nobody eats doughnuts."

"Another reason I could never live in L.A."

"Damn, I miss you."

"Miss you, too."

"I'll call you as soon as we have a break, okay? You're doing good? Feeling all right? You know how much I worry about you."

"Fine. So—I'm sorry, what's her last name? The director? Would I have heard of her?"

"Oh—yeah. I don't know, maybe? You've probably heard of her dad. Goring? Carroll Goring?"

"Wait, Carroll *Goring*? She's his *daughter*?"

"Yeah. Louisiana Goring? It's her first solo feature. You'd like her, she's cool." Again, the vibration of background laughter, some throaty female voice. Hector made an exasperated noise. "All right, all right. Gotta hop. Love you. Love you like crazy. Call you soon, okay?"

"Okay. Love you."

But he'd already hung up by the time the words came out. Ella shut the phone and stared at the cracker sleeve. Swallowed back some dry, masticated cracker. From the corner of her eye, she caught her reflection in the mirror—her frizzed hair curling around her face in an erratic light brown cloud—her pale, splotchy face—her puffy, reddened eyes—her limp jersey nightshirt clinging to her swollen breasts, her thickened waist. She thought of Hector, fit and fresh in his spacious Santa Monica hotel suite overlooking the Pacific Ocean. Headed off into the sunrise with Louisiana Goring. Daughter of Carroll Goring. *The* Carroll Goring, Oscar-winning film director, owned a vineyard or something. Or was it a baseball team? The Angels? He'd directed that epic Vietnam film, the one that won some record number of awards a few years back. The old Ella would've remembered the name of that movie. The new Ella, the pregnant Ella with the rusty, squeaking brain, could hardly remember her own name anymore.

Louisiana Goring, on the other hand. Was a film director herself now! Wasn't that wonderful, a great victory for women in Hollywood and everything. She appeared regularly on Page Six, though Ella couldn't remember much about her, other than that she was glamorous and beautiful—of course—and had dated Brad Pitt at some point. Of course, *of course*.

Her stomach swam. From nowhere came the echo of Aunt Julie's wobbling, raspy, cocksure voice—*Men always let you down in the end, darling.*

But not Hector, Ella told herself firmly. Hector was different.

What had he called this woman? *Lulu.* My director.

Ella picked up the half-finished sleeve of crackers and hurled it against the mirror.

LAPTOPS WERE FROWNED UPON at the club, almost as much as cell phones, so Ella brought her yellow legal pad and calculator and pen and found herself a lounge chair near the pool, under a blue-and-white striped umbrella, thinking about Hardcastles and Oliver Marshall the hunky Prohibition agent, who had married and then betrayed the Redhead, and the article about the Bronstein trial that Charles Schuyler had carefully clipped from the newspaper for some reason. Something bothered her about that, some connection between them she couldn't put her finger on. Hadn't Aunt Julie said that the Hardcastles ran the main bootlegging gang in the northeast? So why was this Bronstein on trial as the kingpin, only a year after Louis Hardcastle was murdered? It didn't add up.

Next to her, outside the circle of shade, Lizzie lay on her stomach in a white bikini. She was working on her tan for the wedding, which was now only two short weeks away. On the lounge chair, next to her head, sat an upside-down copy of *A Widow for One Year*, pages splayed. She'd been reading it since Ella arrived a week ago and didn't seem to be making much progress.

"Ella, question," she murmured, eyes closed. "Did you and Patrick take dance lessons before the wedding?"

"Dance lessons? Why?"

"Um, so you don't look like a doofus when you're doing your first dance together? Everyone takes lessons now. But it's probably too late, right?"

"Just have your mom show you. She knows all that stuff. Your mom and my mom. Or Aunt Julie. Or your dad, even. He's coming out this weekend, right?"

"Yeah." Lizzie propped herself up on her elbows. "But Owen's got to work all weekend. You know, wrapping stuff up before the honeymoon and everything. He's only coming out, like, two days before."

"You'll be all right, don't worry. Nobody cares by then. Everyone's all drunk and happy."

"But the video. The video lives *forever*."

"Video? You're having a *video* done?"

Lizzie picked at her cuticles. "I know it's kind of cheesy, but there's this really great videographer—totally classy, like, really artsy angles and editing and stuff—everyone's using her."

"And your mom *agreed* to this?"

"She's not thrilled, I have to say. Wedding videos are definitely not, like, the Schuyler Way. But she was, like, whatever, it's your day."

"It's good to be the youngest, I guess."

Lizzie rolled on her side to face Ella. "*You* don't approve."

Ella looked at Lizzie's lithe young golden limbs, splayed with unconscious grace down the length of the lounge chair. Her sun-streaked hair, held back by a yellow silk headband. Her long neck, her blue Schuyler eyes, tip-tilted at the corners. The enormous Chiclet glittering on her finger. The pristine swimming pool behind her. She looked like a Slim Aarons photograph come to life. Ella turned back to the yellow legal pad propped against her raised knees. The bottom edge rested against the gentle swell of her belly, covered by a pink crepe beach tunic.

"Honestly, your mom's right," she said. "Whatever makes you happy. And if it's a thing now, it's a thing, right? Even *this* family has to keep up with the times. I just . . ."

"Yeah?"

"Just remember it's about you and Owen, right? All this other stuff, the dresses and party and cake and videographer, you won't remember any of that. It's all over in a few hours, anyway. But the rest of your life is the rest of your life."

Lizzie caught her breath, like she meant to snap something back. She bit her lip and made an exasperated noise and plopped back on her stomach. Just as she closed her eyelids, a shadow fell over her. The eyes flew open again.

"*Pat*rick! Omi*god*! You're blocking my *sun*!"

She didn't seem mad, though. Her face turned pink beneath the tan.

Patrick laughed and moved around to the other side of the umbrella, next to Ella. "Sorry, babe. What was I thinking?"

"You're forgiven if you can convince Owen to come out here and take a couple of dance lessons with me."

"What for? My man can dance."

"Like *real* dancing, okay? Foxtrots and stuff?"

"Jesus, you're not doing foxtrots at the *wedding*?"

"Ugh! Nobody under*stands*!"

Patrick made a helpless gesture and looked at Ella. His smile took over his face. "Hey there, mama. You're looking especially blooming today."

"Liar. I was up until four in the morning. I still feel like hell. What's up?"

His eyes shifted to Lizzie and back. "Can I talk to you for a minute?"

IF THE FOUR YEARS of their marriage had been close and loving—or so Ella thought at the time, anyway—and the past four months had been separate and loathing, Ella didn't know what to think of the relationship that existed between her and Patrick right now. It wasn't like friendship, and certainly not like romance. What could you call it, really?

She'd seen him almost daily since that evening at the club a week ago. It turned out Patrick was staying all summer with the Hendersons—in their guest cottage, God only knew how he'd worked that one out—who had also proposed him for the club, which gave him an excuse to eat and drink there every day. He said he was working on his World Wide Web thing with a friend who'd taken a summer house share in Sag Harbor, but he didn't seem to spend much time on it. He seemed to be on vacation. He was relaxed and carefree, all the old resentments and aggressions wiped nearly clean from the slate of his personality. His hair was ruffled and growing a bit long, his skin had tanned, his tennis game was sharp. His chinos were laundered and pressed to a knife-edge crease by the Hendersons' housekeeper. He treated Ella with the affectionate ease of a cousin, almost.

That was it. Cousins. It was like they had leapfrogged past acrimony to an ideal state of ex-hood in which they were still family but without the sex or the cohabitation, committed to parenting their child in perfect cooperation. Patrick had agreed to an even more generous child support payment than Ella's lawyer had proposed and backed off his conditions about overnight visitation in the early months. He would ask friendly questions about Hector and how the movie was coming along, like he bore no jealousy at all. It was all a little bewildering, like he'd had some born-again secular conversion.

54

Beatriz Williams

Now he sat down with Ella on a pair of pool chairs near the snack bar and asked if she was comfortable, did she want anything to eat or drink. Ella said no thanks. Patrick leaned forward and linked his hands between his knees.

"So. This investment firm of yours. I did some asking around, like you said."

"And?"

Patrick cast a quick glance around them and spoke in a hushed voice. "I'm going to be honest. I think you should back off."

"Back off? Why?"

"Because there is some weird shit going on here, and I don't want you involved, okay?" He held up his hand. "Not because I don't think you can handle it, all right? Because I don't want you getting hurt."

"Oh come on. Like *physically* hurt?"

"Yes. Physically hurt. Listen up." He leaned forward. "I called up a couple of guys I know in the muni department. We were in the same analyst class, right? So we stayed in touch. Found out which trader was handling the FH Trust account."

"And did you get hold of him?"

"Nope. No can do, Ells. He's dead."

"*What?*"

"Fell out of his apartment window last April. Eighteen stories, tore right through the bodega awning down below. Story was that he was drunk. Two in the morning kind of thing. Case closed."

The day was hot and sultry, the usual kind of late June weather. Only the riffs of onshore breeze from the nearby ocean kept you from melting out of your own skin. Still Ella felt a chill creep over her, freezing the fine hairs on her arms. She stared into Patrick's sincere blue eyes and didn't say a word.

"Look," he said, "I realize I'm the world's worst asshole, okay?

Mea culpa. Mea maxima culpa. But I still believe in doing business the right way. You can make your pile without cutting off any toes. And whatever's going on with these guys, they have no problem cutting off toes. Fingers, heads, whatever. I can smell it, Ells. You need to back off."

"How can I back off? If it's even worse than I thought?"

"Because I care about you, okay? I fucking *love* you, Ella. If something happened to you, I'd—I don't know." He looked away. "Just let it go. It's not your problem. No skin off your nose if some family makes its dough off the books."

"Patrick, somebody *died* for this. Don't you *care*?"

"Of course I care! But I care about *you* more. That's just a fact. I'm sorry, I know you don't want to hear it, but it's true. Plus, you know, the baby."

For some reason, Ella had brought along the yellow legal pad and her Cross pen, the one Daddy had given her when she started her first job at Parkinson Peters. First and last. She looked down at her hands and saw she was throttling both objects, notepad and pen, and that her knuckles were white and the hairs on her forearms stood on end from each tiny goose bump. "Aunt Julie says—"

"Fuck Aunt Julie. Sorry. I didn't mean it like that. But she's what, a hundred years old? You have your *life* ahead of you, Ella. She shouldn't be dragging you into a pile of steaming shit that has nothing to do with you."

Ella thought about the Redhead photographs in her drawer. Her box of antique buttons. The jazz that played from the walls of the apartment building on Christopher Street, so ghostly and beautiful that her bones ached with longing *right now* to go back and listen to it.

None of this she'd told to Patrick. Not his kind of thing.

But how could she otherwise explain that this *did* have something to do with her? Had everything to do with her. She wasn't sure what, but it was there. In her bones, like the longing to return to the apartment building. Like the way she felt about Hector.

At her silence, Patrick made a rueful laugh. "Yeah, I guess I can't have it both ways, can I?"

Ella looked up. "Have what both ways?"

"You being you. Wanting to see it through. But if you *weren't* you, I wouldn't be so shit-scared of something happening to you. So, yeah. There you go."

Patrick's brow was creased, his eyebrows almost touching. He looked not at Ella but at the snack bar, where a group of young boys jostled each other while they waited for their ice cream. He looked like he was in pain, like he'd hit his funny bone and was trying to muscle through the agony without saying ouch.

"I don't understand," Ella said. "If you cared so much, how could you do it?"

"Do what? Cheat on you? Oh, Ella. *Babe.* Don't you think I've been spending the past four months trying to figure that out? Why I fucked us up?"

"Well?"

Patrick fiddled his fingers. "I wasn't trying to hurt *you*, believe me. I was trying to hurt *me*. Like, I knew you were too good for me. You're too good for anybody, Ells, but especially me. I didn't deserve you and I knew it, right? So I guess what I was trying to do was—I don't know, punish myself for not deserving you? Make it worse. Prove over and over what a jerk I was. I know that doesn't make sense. Like those penitents back in the Middle Ages? Flagellating themselves? I would check out some random attractive woman and think these horny male thoughts and feel so guilty about it I would just go off and"—he made another self-deprecating laugh—"commit adultery. Like, *revel* in how bad I was. Relish my own self-hatred. Because I am an ass-hole, Ells. Don't even think of getting back together with me."

"I'm not."

"That being said, I would trade my soul to get back with you for even one single night. Just making that clear."

"Not gonna happen."

"I know. Anyway. I know you've probably been driving yourself crazy wondering why. That's the best I can give you. I wish I had more. Seems like there should be more, right? But that's all. It wasn't you, it was me."

"No, I guess it makes sense. As much as anything makes sense. Except I'm not too good for anybody. I'm just Ella. I'm just a nice girl who tries hard and screws up and—you know. Like everybody."

"Not like everybody, believe me." He looked back at her at last and smiled. "So if that Hector guy screws up with *you*, I will person-ally shoot him in the balls, right? And in the meantime, could you just please *not* go after the entire fucking Hardcastle racket all by your-self? Okay? Just for me?"

Ella folded her arms over her knees and leaned toward him. "Can you just please try to understand why I can't promise that?"

"*Shit*, Ella."

"Please? I have to see this through. I can't explain why, I just do."

Patrick sat back and threw up his hands. "So what am I supposed to do, huh? Just watch you throw yourself in front of the bus?"

"No." She laid her hand on his forearm. "You're going to help me."

AUNT JULIE WAS NOT surprised at the news. "They'll stop at nothing, that family," she said. "Why, they tried to have poor Tiny committed to a loony bin. We're lucky she made it out alive."

"A *loony bin*? You mean, like, a *psychiatric* hospital?"

"Whatever you call them these days. Of course, by the time they had her committed, she just about belonged there." Aunt Julie shook her head. "Threw her to the wolves with that marriage. I told your grandmother. I said, Vivian, that poor lamb will be eaten alive once she figures out how her father-in-law does business."

It was cocktail hour—an hour that stretched into two or three at The Dunes, where the summer heat tended to warp the space-time continuum. The dogs had collapsed on the grass, the humans had collapsed in chairs with tall glasses of vodka tonic, except Aunt Julie, who stuck to gin, and Ella, who stuck to soft drinks. In the distance, the horizon boiled with possible thunderstorms, but for the moment the air was tranquil and sea-scented, and Ella's laptop burned the tops of her legs. On the table next to her, a glass of lemonade sweated into the teak while she absorbed this information about Aunt Tiny.

"But I had no idea," she said. "Why didn't I know about this?"

"Oh, I expect your mumma likes to keep it secret or something. I don't know the particulars myself, but I imagine Tiny stumbled on the dreadful truth or something and couldn't stand it. Sweet thing, Tiny." Aunt Julie said this like it was a shame.

Ella worried her lip with the end of her pen and thought about this Sterling Bates muni trader, and how it might have felt to plunge eighteen stories from your apartment window. Especially if he hadn't wanted to do it. Did you black out? Or did time slow down? Ella had fallen off a horse once and it seemed like forever before she hit the ground. A terrifying forever she didn't want to live again.

"So how *did* Aunt Tiny make it out alive?"

Aunt Julie didn't have much left in the way of eyebrows, other than a pair of thin lines she penciled in carefully each morning. They came together now, into a point right above her nose. "Well, I don't exactly know," she said. "I guess she made them an offer they couldn't refuse."

Ella looked down the terrace at her mother, who was locked in intimate conversation with Aunt Viv on a pair of lounge chairs, long bare legs spilling everywhere. "That was the summer Mumma spent with Aunt Tiny, wasn't it? The summer before I was born. When she was pregnant with me."

Aunt Julie frowned at the horizon. "Why, yes. I guess it must have been."

At that instant, Ella's cell phone vibrated in her pocket. She drew it out and looked at the screen.

"Excuse me," she said.

Aunt Julie made an offended noise and reached for her drink.

"Hello there," Ella said. "You're checking in early."

"Hey, sweetheart. Where are you? Can you talk?"

"On the terrace. What's up?"

"I'm standing here on my balcony staring at the Pacific Ocean, wishing you were standing here next to me, and it just occurred to me. Why not?"

"Why not what?"

"Why not have you standing here next to me?"

Ella's heart smacked into her ribs. "You mean there? In California?"

"Here in California. Under the sunshine. Big luxurious hotel suite right on the beach. King-size bed with all the trimmings. Room service ginger ale in a bucket of ice. Devoted manservant waiting on you hand and foot. What do you say?"

Ella looked at the green lawn at the edge of the terrace, where Nellie lay on her side surrounded by Labradors. "What about your work? Won't I be in the way?"

"Tomorrow's Sunday. Day off from the studio. And come Monday I promise I'll do my best not to let myself get distracted on company time. Besides, everyone wants to meet this girl I've been raving about all week."

"Everyone who?"

"The team."

"Oh, the *team*."

"Come on. Just for a few days. You need a vacation."

A faint laugh sounded in the background.

"Is someone there with you?"

"Just a couple of folks from sound production. Director."

"You mean Lulu?"

"Yep. Hanging out and drinking up my minibar."

"Hold on a second. Aunt Julie's waving at me like I'm landing on her aircraft carrier." Ella put the phone on her shoulder. "Whaaaat?"

Aunt Julie spoke in slow, loud words, the way you'd talk over copper cables to a friend in Hong Kong. "How far away is San Diego from Humphrey's hotel?"

Ella stared at Aunt Julie's glittering eyes. Her penciled eyebrows, now raised all the way up to her hairline. Ella put the phone back to her ear.

"Humphrey, darling?"

"Yes, my treasure?"

"I'll see if I can get a flight out first thing tomorrow morning."

ACT III

For Better or Worse

(and worse and worse)

GREENWICH VILLAGE, NEW YORK

October 1924

N OW I know what you're thinking. An immoral low-down gin joint is no place for a six-year-old girl, especially one so impressionable as my sweet Patsy, but this particular dive is owned by a friend of mine, the kind of fellow who looks out for a girl, and anyway Anson plays in the orchestra so trust me, nobody would dare.

The name of the gin joint is Christopher's, and it happens to thrive right next door to us, which is another reason to treat the premises like our own front parlor. Certainly Patsy regards these tables and chairs and sleek mahogany bar as her very own, and Christopher himself she has wrapped diligent around her little finger so many times, he might shoot halfway across Manhattan if she let go. I never seen the like of it. Christopher is one hard-bitten fellow, you understand, not much given to living under the thumb of a wee round sweet apple—or should I say the *stem*?—but he seems to like the view all right. Pours her a tall glass of milk when she swings onto the barstool at eight P.M. and asks for a nightcap. Sticks one of them candied cherries on top. Never seen the like of it.

Of course, at eight P.M. Christopher's is not even properly open, not even to regulars, and Patsy's back in her own bedroom by nine, listening to Anson run up and down scales on his clarinet through the common wall between our two buildings while she drifts off to sleep. Me and Patsy and Anson have taken up residence in the same exact house where I used to pay rent for a postage-stamp room on the fourth floor, back when it was a boardinghouse, except now I own the whole building, it seems.

Strange to climb up and down the stairs and poke into the closets and cupboards, the kitchen and parlor and dining room and six spare bedrooms, and all of it belongs to me. In the fuss over Anson's perilous mission to Nova Scotia, I clean forgot—or maybe I never quite believed it was true to begin with. A gentleman bought it for me back last spring, lock, stock, and barrel, and turned over the key to Christopher and said to keep it for me. A gentleman! What gentleman, you say?

Here's the funny part. I don't *know* who he is. Honest to God. Christopher won't say. Just shrugged his shoulders and said I had an admirer, apparently, of the kind who prefers to remain anonymous. Why, this benefactor even fixed it up nice for me, as I discovered eight weeks ago when I unlocked the door with that key I'd tossed in my pocketbook and forgot about. Everything new-painted and clean, furniture polished, leaky bathrooms replaced with fine new plumbing and porcelain. Fine new electric coffee percolator in the kitchen, too. Anson and me and Patsy, we blundered inside and wandered about the rooms in a daze, until we got to the top and looked out over Christopher Street peaceful beneath us, and Anson growled (kind of suspicious) who was this fellow again, and why might he have had the generous impulse to leave me an entire house of my own, just so happens to be next door to a low-down joint like Christopher's?

I said I didn't know for certain, which was true. Then I added— because I feel I cannot lie to my beloved, not anymore—that I thought it was maybe my father.

2

NOW, I be a bastard child, as I've reminded you a dozen times before. I guess in my secret heart, I take a kind of pride in it. Nobody gave me a hand up, not so much as a fingernail. Right here in the bowels of the wicked city was I conceived some quarter century ago, during a sordid love affair between a chorus girl and a rich admirer, and I *relish* my hatred for this fellow who abandoned us both to our fate—our fate being Duke Kelly and a soggy mountain holler back in Allegany County, Maryland, where my mama was bred up.

On the other hand. From the raw age of eight, I was sent off to a convent for my education, and just as I prepared to complete my education and return to my step-daddy's house for good, the mother superior called me into her formidable office and delivered the improbable news that I was to continue my education in the fall at a place called Bryn Mawr College in Pennsylvania, where so many of the finest families sent their finest female offspring, and I ask you: How the devil did a lazy, no-account wastrel like Duke Kelly afford a thing like that? At least before the Twenty-First Amendment offered him the right opportunities for a man of his particular gifts. The mother superior told me the trustees had awarded me some kind of scholarship, but I didn't believe that for a second, my record of discipline being what it was and all.

Naturally I locked these doubts deep inside my heart, because—as I said—I relished my hatred too much to give it up. But when Christopher handed me the key to the next-door house last May, a funny flutter came to life in my stomach, and when I came at last to take stock of these rooms with Anson and Patsy, that flutter returned and blossomed. Oh, I pressed it down, all right. Stuck my boot right in the middle of that fluttering butterfly and said *Stop it, Gin*. You despise and abhor this man. He abandoned you and Mama, and Mama died because of that, and you are a damn fool to imagine for *one second* that your life has turned into some kind of fairy tale, and you this man's little princess.

But the butterfly squeaked back, *Who else, then?*

Who else had a reason to give me this house? Who else possibly stood so deep in my debt as that? Who else has means and opportunity and most especially motive?

My father, that's all. He knows what he done. Whoever and wherever he be.

3

THIS IS not Anson's first stint in the orchestra at Christopher's. But last winter he tootled his instrument undercover, for purposes of surveillance, so maybe it don't count. These days he plays for real money, wearing his own regular hair and face and clothes, and I'll be damned if he hasn't took to it natural. Why, he has laid his scruples so far aside, he'll even order us each a whiskey and soda and park himself on a barstool by my side, where we sip our drinks slow and enjoyable and listen to Christopher shoot the breeze with Patsy at the end of the bar. (Nobody knows the boss's real name, you see, so his patrons just took to calling the joint after the street outside, and the owner after the joint.) In another half hour the other musicians will start to filter in, and Anson will take his clarinet out of the case and start to warm up, and that's our cue for me and Patsy to slip off our stools and kiss him good night and steal through the door in the back larder that connects our two buildings—more on that later—so that Patsy can have her bath and repair to bed at a godly hour. Some nights Anson don't follow us home until two in the morning, maybe three, but in that case he might return with a hundred dollars in tips, so I forgive him extravagant.

Even now, sipping his whiskey and soda, he looks so heated and handsome, I can't help but adore him even more. I imagine for a second I could get used to this way of life. Anson kisses the top of my carroty hair and signals to Christopher for seconds. Christopher ambles over and the two of them get to talking while Christopher delivers another Scotch and soda. Anson bends his head to mine and asks what I think.

"Think about what?" I say, because I wasn't paying much attention to the conversation, to tell the truth. Anson has a way of idling your fingers that makes you think of taking him to bed.

"This fellow Remus, out in Cincinnati."

"I don't know anybody from Cincinnati," I tell him.

"You haven't listened to a word I've said, have you?"

"Because I'm enjoying the sound of your voice, that's all."

Christopher makes a noise like he might be sick. "Don't you have time to read the newspapers these days? George Remus used to run the biggest distillery racket in the country."

I snap my fingers. "Oh, *him*. The King of Bootleggers, that's what they call him. Kind of a grand title, if you ask me, for somebody who makes his dough outside the law."

"Now he's king of a cell in the Atlanta Federal Penitentiary," says Christopher, "though from what I hear, he don't do too bad for himself. Bribes the warden for filet steak and what they call conjugal visits from his lady wife."

"Must have cleared a lot of lettuce, then."

"He did, all right," says Anson. "Bought up dozens of distilleries so he could get his hands on their bonded inventory. Then he bribed federal officials for withdrawal certificates so he could sell his stock to drugstores. Plenty of men running that racket, of course, but Remus did it better and bigger than the others. A genuine businessman."

"How big?"

Christopher shrugs. "Maybe a third of the liquor in this country, for a while. What he did right is he sold the good stuff. You could trust a shipment of Jack Daniels from Remus. It was the real deal, not watered down or adulterated or labeled one thing when it was maybe something else, like with the other gangs. He was on the level, that Remus."

"What a shame. I guess our Mabel decided she needed a prize scalp." I examine the bottom of my whiskey glass. "So what do you do for supply now?"

"Oh, I got my sources."

I laugh. "None of my business?"

"I just hate to put the pair of you in an awkward position, see. Nice square married pair like you." Christopher jabs a thumb at Anson's chest.

"A lot less square than he used to be. Look how I've corrupted him."

Christopher glances down at the Scotch and soda at Anson's elbow, nearly empty. Anson lifts the glass and drinks it off. Sets the glass on the counter and winks mischievous. He never takes more than two, but they do loosen him up some. Fingers depart my hand and wander to my leg, under the overhang of the bar, where they walk on down to my knee and back up again.

Christopher leans forward. A short, muscular fellow, our

Christopher—could be any age from thirty to fifty, wears a black wool vest buttoned over a crisp white shirt rolled to the elbows, your average New York City bartender except he's anything but. He owns the forearms of a Navy boilerman. I don't know, maybe he *was* a Navy boilerman. His pleasant brown eyes fix on mine. "See you keep him busy, that's all. This husband of yours blows the best stick of licorice in the Village. Can't afford to lose him to some piece of human garbage like in the northeastern racket."

"The northeastern racket?"

He squints at the gleaming oil-slick mahogany bar and wipes away a speck of condensation from my Scotch and soda. "You want another or do I close out your tab?"

"I don't have a tab."

"Pretend you do for once."

"Close it out, then."

"Fine choice. I'll just leave you two stinking lovebirds to your goddamn billing and cooing and talk to my best girl over there."

Christopher slides down the bar to where Patsy perches on her stool with her glass of milk and her deck of cards that Christopher gave her. That wicked man has took to learning my baby sister to play poker. Seems she has a knack for it, sorry to say. Just look how she shuffles that deck with her nimble wee fingers.

Anson drags me onto his lap. Breath hints of whiskey, which is a thing I can't seem to get used to, coming from Anson. Smells pleasant, don't mistake me. But I don't ever feel that it properly belongs to him. "What are you thinking about, Mrs. Marshall?" he asks me.

"Nothing. You."

"What about me?"

"How much you've changed since the day I stood against this very bar counter and met you. Whether it's my fault and all."

He shrugs. "And here I figured you'd prefer a man more relaxed in his habits than I was then."

"Not a question of do I prefer you one way or another. I'm bound to love you, whatever you are. What I can't figure is whether this is the real Anson, all freed from scruples and what have you, or some kind of act. Some kind of penance, maybe."

"Penance for what?"

"For what happened upstate."

We speak softly, on account of me sitting right there on his lap, mouths nearby each other. How I love that wide warm slab of chest I lean against. Seems nothing can hurt a person who relies upon a chest like that. His thick left arm holds me gentle. His right hand plays with the ring on my finger. "What makes you say that?" he asks me.

"Because right after that's when you took to the sauce. And— well, other things. Playing your clarinet for money in a joint like this. I can't help feeling you've got things in your head you don't care to share with your lawful wedded wife."

"I share everything with you."

Now I turn to straddle this idiot of mine while he sits on the stool and leans back against the edge of the bar. Traps me from sliding off again by means of a pair of broad paws attached to my hips. "Somebody fixed to burn us to a crisp out there, and you're saying you don't think upon it at all? Don't wonder who did it?"

"Sure I wonder."

"Well, who? That bootlegger Standish? Schuyler?"

"Not Schuyler, believe me."

"Why not? He's the only one who knew we were there, outside of Mabel Willebrandt. *And* Standish and his men."

"It's just not. Why would he burn down his own house? Anyway, if I thought there was even a chance Schuyler tried to kill you and Patsy, do you think he'd be walking carefree around New York City right now?"

"Well, somebody did it, and you and me ain't exactly hid away since. *You* of all people, playing clarinet inside the one place in town every low-down seedy bootlegger is going to hear about you."

"Sweetheart, nobody's going to set fire to Christopher's joint. He's got friends inside of friends."

"I don't mean setting fire. I mean maybe you have some trick up your sleeve, with your clarinet and your Scotch and soda, just like you've joined the club."

"Why, is that why you think I took this gig?"

"I don't know. Why *did* you take this gig?"

"Because it's right next door. Because this way I can blow my horn for a few hours and then come straight home to bed with my lawfully wedded wife, right there on the other side of this wall, with a hundred dollar bills for the cookie jar."

"And that's all?"

"That's all. Easiest job I ever took."

"What about the future?"

"What about it?"

"You're made for big things, Oliver Marshall. Not clarinets and cookie jars."

"What have I told you? I'm made for you, Gin. That's all I'm made for."

I ought to kiss him for that, but I don't. Instead I look sober into his eyes and inhale the whiskey trace of his breath. Take his face betwixt my palms and run my thumbs along the ridges of noble cheekbone. Whisper sadly, "What have I done to you, Lucifer? You have fallen from the firmament for me."

Anson pulls my hands down and folds me against his chest. "You've got it backward," he tells me. "You're my salvation."

4

BY HALF past ten Patsy lies fast asleep in her little bedroom and I curl myself up in bed with a mug of cocoa and another dirty novel, waiting for to be drowsy enough to turn out the light and sleep. Listen to the jazz orchestra dance through the walls. I can pick out the notes of Anson's clarinet like it was the voice of my own infant calling to me. Sometimes I hear the raucous joy of the sinful, too, breaking the law with conscious abandon, and it seems to me incredible that I was once among them, and Anson now keeps them company. You know that feeling you got, when you first saw some clown sitting on top of a flagpole for no reason? Like the universe around you has taken on some crazy meaning you don't understand.

Anyhow, I don't recollect falling asleep, but I stir as I always do when Anson climbs into bed, clarinet tucked in its case for the night. Without hardly knowing myself, I turn and reach for him. He likes to scrub down each night after work. Render from his skin and his hair the smell of cigarettes and sweat inside a ritual bathtub of strong soap. How I love the pure smell of him at night. I love that he cleans himself for my sake. I lay my palms on his shoulders, my lips on his.

Seems he feels the same itch, for he gathers me right up and rolls to his back, so I ride his hips, nightgown rucked up around my waist, breathing the particular fumes of bourbon whiskey—an awful lot of fumes, now that I notice, and Anson himself more than a little reckless. Grips me hard. Tears the nightgown up over my head and onto the floor. Then we roll again and he acts on me ferocious, like some demon snaps at his heels. Well, sometimes it's like that with Anson. Lucky for him he has married a wicked mountain wildcat like me, who knows how it is with demons. I give his trouble straight back to him, ride him so ferocious as he rides me, so that together we be more beast than human. How he *yowls* at the end. Wake the dead, I swan. Collapses upon me like the end of the world. Mutters some incoherent bourbon-scented apology. I lie on my stomach and savor his hot damp satisfactory weight, don't move a muscle for to keep him safe inside me. As for me, I have long since achieved my bliss in the onslaught of his vigor. So much bliss it hurts my heart.

5

IN THE morning he pays for it. Sits at the kitchen table with a cup of coffee and bends an excruciating smile at Patsy, who jabbers on regardless. I bustle about making eggs. Anson once suggested we hire some girl to help, but I said no, why spend the dough, the three of us hardly make enough trouble to keep me busy. Anyway, Anson's been taking care of himself long enough, he does the dishes and picks up his socks. Doesn't yet occur to him that he might ask a wife to iron his shirts for him. Hasn't yet occurred to me that I should.

Patsy is presently in the middle of some disquisition about a horse. Anson listens attentive, or looks as if he's trying to. Coffee seems to pour back some life into him, though seems to me there's not enough coffee in the world to restore it all. Upstairs, the telephone jangles. He winces just a fraction. I wipe my hands on a dishcloth and hurry up the back steps to the little room behind the parlor we call the study, because it has a desk and chair and telephone. Lift the receiver and say *Marshall residence.*

"Gin, darling? That you?"

I plop down hard on the chair. "Julie Schuyler. What on earth?"

"Why, good morning to you, too. You're not busy or anything, are you?"

"Awful busy. Fixing up breakfast for my husband. Eggs'll burn any second."

"How charmingly domestic. I'll be quick. As you know, I don't like to pry in the affairs of others—"

"Well, that's rich."

"—but I have a special affection for you, Gin, after all we've been through together."

I snap my fingers. "Say. How'd you know where to find me?"

"I asked around. Now listen. I just so happened to stop by Christopher's last night for a naughty little nightcap, and you'll never *guess* who was holding up the bar."

"My husband?"

"Well, yes. But he had a friend with him. An *old* friend. Awfully *chummy,* the pair of them, if you know what I mean. Heads bent together."

"There's no law against friends."

"Of course not. And I'm not a *snitch* or anything, I mean heaven *knows* I've shared enough drinks with enough husbands—"

"Say, have you got a point, Julie? Or are you just enjoying yourself?"

"I'm enjoying myself immensely, darling. But not nearly so much as Luella Kingston last night, sucking down champagne cocktails in the company of her old partner Oliver Marshall."

6

SMELL OF burning eggs finds me as I reach the bottom of the stairs. Through the door of the kitchen I spy Anson at the sink, cloud of smoke, Patsy laughing her head off. The table's covered with a cheery red-checked cloth, bowl of zinnias in the middle. You never saw such domestication.

I step through the doorway. "Patsy, honey. Now you're finished eating, why don't you go upstairs and read your new book?"

Patsy stares up puzzled in the middle of a giggle. She must read something in my face, because she says a nice meek sober *I guess* and drags Muriel (that's her battered stuffed lamb) from the table. For a minute I listen to the soft thump of her footsteps on the stairs. As I am opening my mouth to say something—I don't even know what— Anson turns around from the sink.

"Sorry about the eggs. Patsy was rattling on about something and I didn't—" He catches the look on my face and stops. "Something wrong? Who was that on the telephone?"

"Julie Schuyler."

"Julie? What did she—" Again he stops. A gentle flush climbs up his neck and invades the pasty skin of his face.

Funny, I could *swear* the room moves around me. I mean I am downright *light-headed.* Anson stares at me, dish towel hanging from his big hand. White shirtsleeves rolled up to his elbows.

He takes a mighty breath. "Gin, there's something I need to tell you."

"Let me guess."

"Last night . . ." He looks down at the dishcloth, bunches it between his hands, shakes it out, and folds it over the side of the sink.

"What about last night, Anson?"

He looks back up and says defiant, "Luella turned up."

When I don't speak—well, I *can't* speak, can I?—Anson elaborates.

"We talked, that's all. Between sets. She wanted to talk."

The room stops whirling at last. "Did she buy the drinks, or did you?"

"Gin."

My fist comes down on the kitchen table. "Why didn't you tell me before?"

"Me? You're asking *me*? *You* saw her in New York, she said. At the hotel in Brooklyn. She gave you a letter for me, which I never saw. All those weeks, you never told me. Do you know what a heel I felt like? After what she did for us?"

"For *you*, you mean."

"I had to apologize. Tried to explain."

"You want the letter? I'll give you the letter."

"I don't need to see it. She told me what was inside. She killed Hardcastle, Gin. *She* was the one who lured him into that stable and killed him, so he couldn't hurt us again. She's been on the run ever since, one step ahead of this lieutenant of his, the one who's taken over the racket, and *all this time*—"

"Dammit, Anson. When will you learn your lesson with her? The woman was stringing you all along. All along Hardcastle was running her. You was nothing but her patsy until she decided she had the most insatiable crush on you—"

"That's *enough*, Gin."

"It's the plain truth, and you know it! She only turned on him because she decided she wanted you more. And I don't know what kind of game she's playing now, what she wants from you, but trust me, she wants *something*. She's got her own fish to fry. She'll use you like she used you before."

"She wasn't using me. She was doing her best in an impossible situation."

"My God, is *that* what she said to you? An *impossible situation*? She was sleeping with him for money and for luxury, you idiot—for *power*—she was his creature, she's got nothing but cunning in that ice heart of hers. She knew exactly what she was doing then, and she knows exactly what she's doing now. I don't know how you can *think* of trusting her again."

"I'm not saying I trust her entirely. But she's changed, she's redeemed herself."

"Baloney. Bird like that don't change her feathers on a dime."

"You don't *know* what kind of woman she is."

"I know her enough. Not so well as you do, that's obvious."

"Yes, because she was my partner for two years."

"And all that time she was sleeping with Hardcastle! She was his mistress! Betrayed your every move to him!"

"But she left him. She felt sick about what she was doing, and she ended it. She killed him herself, with her own hands."

I throw up my hands. "Well, I guess that goes to show a nice sensible fellow will forgive a woman just about anything. Specially when she about blinds him with sex appeal."

"*Sex* appeal—"

"You don't think I've noticed?"

"I never *once*—"

"I don't blame you for it. It's a natural urge for a red-blooded man like you—"

"—never *touched* her—"

"Of course you wouldn't touch her. Doesn't mean you don't think about it, sometimes. Can't control our carnal thoughts, can we? A man comes home so wound up with lust as you was last night. About split me in two—"

"Now hold on. You gave back just as good as you got—"

"Because I didn't realize it was *Luella* stoked your fire—"

"Luella had nothing to do with it."

"Oh, just a funny coincidence, then? You mounting me like a prize bull one particular night for no reason?"

"No *reason*? I'm crazy about you, isn't that reason enough? It's not *one night*, it's *every* night, we do it *every night*, I can't keep my hands from you, you've turned me into this—this—"

"What? *What* have I turned you into?"

Anson makes a terrible sound and spins to look out the kitchen window at the bare, paved courtyard. "Nothing," he says.

"I don't ask you for any of it. Don't put any drinks in your hand. Don't make you work for Christopher nor pummel me in bed when you're done. I don't know what's chasing you, Anson, but I wish to God you'd tell me."

"You don't have the slightest idea how—how desperate—I'm out of my mind . . ."

"With *what*?"

He stands there with his hands stuck in his hair, his face tilted up to the stairs that climb to the black iron gate and the sidewalk just above us. Nice quiet street, our street. Not too much foot traffic, except at night. His white shirt stands out bold against the charcoal vest. His broad, muscular back. I want to touch him, but I don't dare to do it.

"Forgive me," he says, quiet voice. "I didn't realize. It won't happen again."

"What won't happen again? Sharing drinks with your old pal Luella?"

"I mean in bed. The way I behaved."

"The way you *behaved*? Anson, if I wasn't enjoying myself I'd say so, believe me. It's *her*. Don't you see what she does to you?"

"*Does* to me? She doesn't do a *thing* to me—"

I throw up my hands and turn to march out of the kitchen. From behind, he snatches my hand.

"Don't go."

"I'm not going anywhere. I need to think, that's all. My husband crawls home last night from an evening out canoodling with that she-devil—"

"I was *not*—"

"And you had the *nerve* to climb into bed with me afterward and—"

He crushes me right up against his chest. "Stop it, Gin. Don't break my heart. Don't break the one thing I can't live without."

I want to ask him what, but my mouth is full of shirt. I sob instead. I don't know why. I never do cry, as a rule. Still the tears heave out of me for no good reason. Somewhere outside my body, a hard-hearted Gin Kelly fixes to take me by the shoulders and shake me, tell me what an unfathomable fool I be, allowing so much as a tint of suspicion to color my heart, when nobody else in the world understands so well the matter of the man I married. Still my brain seems taken over this morning by somebody else. Some mealy woman who sobs at the littlest thing.

7

NOW I don't know for certain what particular whim brung Lu-ella Kingston to Christopher's bar that night, but I'm beginning to believe that woman has kidnapped my husband and replaced him with some grim imposter. So taciturn is this stranger in my house, I might consider taking a rock for a lover, just for the conversation.

When he crawls into bed at half past three in the morning, he don't so much as touch me anymore. Lies there on his back like a corpse, and I can't say whether he sleeps or no. At half past six he rises and descends the stairs to start the coffee. I gather up Patsy from her bower so cheerfully as I can. Wash and dress. I find it helps to start her singing something, the sillier the better.

When we arrive in the kitchen that smells of good coffee and oatmeal and buttered toast, sometimes bacon or pancakes, Anson will hardly meet my eye. He makes an effort for Patsy, I'll give him that. She climbs on his lap and lays her little palm on his cheek and delivers him some verdict on the quality of his shaving this morning. He does smile at that—he's not made of granite all the way through. I figure some nice fresh air is what he needs, so I tell him to take Patsy for a walk to buy a newspaper or some oranges or something, and I guess that might be the best part of his day. He returns to our nest nearly happy. Then comes the gloom again. Spends his hours in the study reading, or practicing some new tune on his clarinet, some new trick of improvisation, or else he takes long, laborious walks by himself. Before he leaves, he reminds me to bolt the door behind him.

Now I know what you're thinking. *Just ask him what's wrong, for God's sake!* Husband and wife should *talk* to each other, *share* their burdens, that's the vital beating heart of any marriage. *Well.* I say *you* try getting Oliver Marshall to explain to you what's the matter, if you think it's so easy! Because I have chiseled and pried and begged every which way, cajoled and harangued and seduced and what have you, and all I achieve for my trouble is the same tired refrain—*It's nothing. Don't worry about it. You're imagining things. Of course I'm glad we got married. I thought I was showing you.*

After dinner, as usual, we troop next door to chew the fat with Christopher. Me and Patsy, anyway. Anson has taken to staying behind until the last minute, nine o'clock or so, when I shepherd Patsy back home for bath time. He gives us each a kiss and opens his clarinet case. All through the night I hear him playing and playing for those merry lawbreakers next door, each man Jack and doll Jill having the time of their lives, while I curl in bed like an infant with my cocoa and my dirty novel. When at last Anson staggers home, I sniff the air careful, just like any old dry matron who never touched a drop of the demon liquor except to pour it down a drain somewhere. Not a hint of a sinful fume, however, not bourbon or rye or plain Scotch whiskey. Seems he has quit the Wild Turkey cold turkey.

Been like this a week now, ever since that damned dame cast her spell over my beloved, and I'm at my wit's end. The worry is making me sick, to say the truth. I can't eat but a bite, it just boils there in my stomach like I have taken seasick or something. Last night I scarce slept a wink. I heard the noise downstairs when Anson quit for the night and came through the passage from Christopher's joint, and I lay there waiting for him to climb the stairs and wash and change for bed, to lie down next to me, even if he wouldn't touch me. Even the heat of him, that's all I asked. I think a tear of frustration actually came out the corner of my eye. Waited and waited. At last I got to worrying and slipped out of bed, tiptoed down the stairs. Heard his voice speaking low from the study. On the telephone to somebody. I couldn't hear the words, but it seemed to me his voice was tender— all the loving eloquence he hasn't spoke to me in seven long days. I felt a little sick. Climbed back upstairs and slipped back between the sheets, shivering a little, dizzy. Half an hour later Anson joined me.

Didn't kiss me or nothing. I lay silent and stiff while he settled himself
with excruciating care. This time some remnant of bourbon whiskey
did waft the skin of my face, like the memory of my childhood.

8

I N THE morning I feel sicker than ever, though I don't like to say a
word about it. Instead I ask Anson to play with Patsy while I head
out for meat and groceries. He looks up from the newspaper and asks
why can't I order the butcher and grocer to deliver something, kind of
sharp, and I say I crave a little fresh air, it's been raining the past two
days, been cooped up like a hen. He frowns at me for a second or two,
kind of pale, and says not to stay out long. He's nursing some sickness
himself, I think, on account of that bourbon whiskey the night before.

Off I go into the brisk new-washed October sunshine, that rare
moment when Manhattan don't stink to high heaven like a refuse
heap laid over with automobile exhaust and animal excrescence and
human vomit, but I don't lay my tracks for the butcher and the green-
grocer. Instead I walk to the doctor I used to visit when I lived here
before, nice woman doctor who understands a woman's needs, and
after a short examination and a few direct questions I am given to understand what I already know: me and Anson are going to be parents
together, come May.

9

A S YOU might guess, I have no opportunity nor nerve to deliver this news to the man responsible. When I arrive home, he

presents to me the same gruff face as usual, and my resolve dissolves away. I lay the brown-wrapped beef rump and the net of vegetables on the kitchen table and commence to make a fine slow pot roast, like my mama learned me to do, on those precious rare occasions when we had an actual rump of beef to roast. The doctor said I was to eat a lot of good meat, because the vitamins are good for the baby. Even Anson's moved to eke out a word or two on the subject of that pot roast, being so tender and rich as it is. My mouth opens to blurt out the reason for this treat, but his grim expression stops me. How do you blurt out a piece of news like that? Specially when your every instinct tells you he will not be best pleased by the turn of events. Not these days.

10

COMES THE night. Patsy be tucked safe asleep, and I look out the window at the moon and figure I can't survive another minute of this. Can't just lie back and wait for the storm to pass, not when some diligent seed of Anson's sprouts to grow up big inside me and require its real father, not this granite imposter.

I throw open the door of the wardrobe and yank out my one evening dress and squeeze myself inside. Seems I have layered on some additional bosom since September, and my bosom did not require enhancement, believe me, being so unfashionable lush already as to excite more than just comment. Well, it can't be helped. Brush out my too-long hair and arrange it in carroty curls around my face, contained by a glittery bandeau like I used to wear, back in my salad days. Swipe of lipstick the color of blood. One last peep around the edge of her bedroom door at my wee round sweet apple, perfectly content.

I blow a kiss into the air and hurry down the stairs.

On the other side of the basement opposite the kitchen is a store-
room with a door, and through that door is the vestibule that connects our two buildings, mine and Christopher's. I believe I have
mentioned this curiosity before. On Christopher's side, the vestibule
opens into a wall of shelves in the larder, so you wouldn't even know
it was there. Anson did all the work himself soon after we arrived,
on account of he didn't necessarily want to show his face to the world
every time he came and went from his place of employment. Also,
should the premises experience some unannounced raid by certain
agents of the Prohibition enforcement bureau—as occurs regular, just
to keep up the appearance of virtue—Anson can beat a hasty retreat.

By now it's nearly midnight, and the joint's starting to cook.
Through the wall comes the sound of the jazz orchestra. The nimble syncopation of Anson's clarinet weaves in and out, playing some
game of chase first with the trumpet and then the saxophone and then
the sonorous double bass. A low roar of voices complements the per-
cussion. I happen to know that bull fiddle player pretty well. Fellow
named Bruno. He used to look out for me in the days before I took
up with Anson. Once we slept together, some sultry drunken August night, an experience I now recall as through a pleasant haze. He
catches sight of me now as I emerge all sparkly black and crimson
from the back room, brushing a speck of dust from my dress. His
eyebrows lift high and he pokes an elbow into the rib cage of my husband, who sits beside him. Anson follows Bruno's nod and finds me.
Nearly drops his clarinet.

From long habit I take the measure of the population as I saun-
ter and jostle my way across the room. The usual Thursday crowd,
jaded Manhattanites and a wide-eyed tourist or two, tipped the hotel
concierge large to discover the password. The college kids turn up

weekends, predictable as the equinoctical storm. My experienced eye picks out the gentlemen in the expensive suits at the tiny round corner table, pretending not to be taking in every detail of me. Not on account of the globes up front, either. At least, not exclusive. I pounce on an empty stool and signal Christopher at the other end.

"What in hell are you doing here?" he asks.

"Club soda, squeeze of lime. I want to ask you about Miss Kingston."

"Blond knockout, legs to China?"

"That's the one."

Christopher grunts and walks away. When he returns with the club soda he says, "She came here to see Marshall about a week ago. Stayed an hour and left. End of story."

"Do you happen to know what they talked about?"

"What am I, a rat?"

"So far as I know, my dear, you got no principles to speak of."

He spreads out his hands. "I'm a busy man. I don't have time to listen to the private conversations of my customers."

"Oh? That's not what I recollect."

"Depends on the conversation, then."

"Look, all I want to know is, is she on the level. Does she work for herself these days or for someone else."

Christopher stares at me sullen. He's got what you call a poker face, because of his line of business and because he was born that way, I think. God only knows what kind of mother he was bred from. But he likes me. In the main, Christopher looks out only for Christopher, but still he likes me, and if it's no skin off that thick, woolly backside of his, he don't mind helping me out from time to time. I get the feeling he's reading some words written upon my eyeballs. When he's done, he tilts forward an inch or two, confidential.

"What I hear is she used to be in bed with the northeastern racket, that's all. *In bed,* you understand me?"

"Tell me something I don't know already."

"I hear she was the one that offed the boss, last summer on Long Island. And I hear she's got a bull's-eye bang in the middle of her forehead, on account of it."

"From who?"

"From the fellow that took over the racket, who else?"

"What's his name?"

He shrugs. "Some say it's the boss's son."

"His *son?* Why, he can't be but a baby, surely!"

"That's what I heard. Don't matter to me. I look out for myself. Without that racket running smooth, I got a supply problem, see? Remus is finished. Where else am I going to find half-decent liquor for all these thirsty people to drink? Reliable, I mean. Don't care if the new boss is his son or his pet schnauzer, so long as my product gets delivered on time."

"But I guess it matters to Anson, don't it? I guess my husband cares like hell whether she lives or dies for killing that snake."

Christopher shifts his glance over my shoulder. All of a sudden I feel the white hot glare of my bridegroom's eyes scorch the back of my neck, and it feels pretty good, to say the truth. Better than what I haven't been feeling lately.

"Anything the matter, brother?" Christopher asks. "That was an awful short set."

Anson leans heavy on the bar counter next to me, and I'll be damned if he doesn't carry the smell of liquor about him already. Lord Almighty, what the devil am I going to do? I feel a pain in my heart like it's stopped beating altogether. The black sight of his tuxedo sleeve right next to my bare arm is the last possible straw.

Full ignorant of my desperate state—Lord have mercy, they are obtuse, these husbands—he says to Christopher, "Make it two." To his credit, the words don't slur a note.

With dreadful effort I rise from my stool. Hold up my near-empty glass and rattle the ice. "Don't mean to disappoint you, but club soda is all. And I was just leaving."

I lay a kiss on Anson's cheek and brush right past him for the back of the room. I don't stop to turn and see what my better half is up to. Fellow named Orpheus did that once, remember, and you know what happened to *him*.

11

I HAVEN'T BEEN gone but half an hour altogether. Energy still kicks down my veins. I bound up the stairs to make sure Patsy's still snug—of course she is—and lay myself down flat in the dark on my marital bed to calm my nerves. I figure there's no chance in the world I'm going to sleep before dawn, the way my heart thuds frantic in its cage, but next thing I hear some banging, which at first seems like part of my present dream, in which I knit some giant stocking becomes a crepe myrtle becomes a whole woods in which some unseen hunter fires his gun after me, and I run and I run and still the gun goes *bang bang* after me until my lungs fix to explode right out my chest when—

I sit up. For a second I think it's gunfire, somebody firing a gun— *Where's Patsy*—but it turns out it's just banging like you bang on a wall or a door. Beyond that, some shouting and whistling, like Christopher has a fight on his hands. Happens more than you think.

I swing out of bed, put on my dressing gown, and run down the stairs to the door in the basement that connects to Christopher's. I guess Anson forgot his key or something. I unlock the door and swing it open, saying, "What the sam hill is going—"

A woman stumbles through the doorway, brings a whole commotion of chaotic noise along with her. She slams the door *bang* and slumps against it, face pressed hard upon the thick wood. I jump back scalded. Some tall blonde in a sequined black dress, ostrich feather stuck in a sequined band around her forehead, the works. Wheezes like she just run the Derby. I make to grab her arm.

"See here, you better go straight back where you came from, or I'll—"

She straightens and turns and opens her tip-tilted blue eyes at me. "Fraid I can't do that, darling," says Julie Schuyler. "It's a raid."

12

I GUESS I shouldn't be amazed that Julie Schuyler still stops by Christopher's regular for a drink or four. Back when I was a permanent resident, so was she, so we got to know each other well enough. For a bird who belongs to one of New York's oldest and finest families, Julie makes more than her share of trouble—and I say that as a compliment, having a nose for no good myself. Still, it hardly seems fair that *I* should be tucked up in bed with a mug of cocoa while *she* gets her kicks next door with my husband—

Christ. *Anson.*

I reach for the doorknob. Julie grabs my wrist.

"Don't you dare! He'll kill me!"

"Who'll kill me?"

"Ollie'll kill me!"

"Then why didn't he follow you to do the job right?"

"Because he was too busy helping Christopher shut the place down!"

I shake off her hand and lunge again, and the damn girl slides betwixt me and the door like she hides some terrible sin behind it.

"I swear to God, Gin! His exact words! *Julie Schuyler, I will kill you if she gets through*."

"*Me?*"

"You."

"He *said* that?"

"He *meant* it!" She shudders a little. "You know how he *looks* when he's dead serious!"

From the other side of the wall comes a familiar symphony of thumps and shouts and whistles, all muffled by brick and wood. Before, I thought it was your average Thursday night brawl at Christopher's—some drunk tries to cut in on another drunk's doll, that kind of thing—but now I hear the difference. It's those whistles, the whistles the police use—shrill like they mean business.

Anson's right. Too late for me to do a thing, except to get myself arrested, and who will take care of Patsy?

I'll be damned if Julie Schuyler hasn't already took her compact out of her dangly glittery evening bag to check the ravage to her face. Maybe she feels my disapproval on her skin. Returns my sideways glance with one of her own. "You don't have a bottle of something stashed away around here, do you?" she asks me.

"Happens I don't."

"You're kidding."

"No need, is there? All the booze you can drink right next door."

"You know, it's funny the way that husband of yours likes to toss back a couple these days, in between sets. I never thought I'd see the woman who could turn Ollie Marshall into a drunk. I see I've under-estimated you, although I guess if *anyone* could . . . Say, are you all right? You don't look so well to me."

"I'm fine."

She snaps the compact shut and tucks it away in her purse. She's got that lean, sharp, fair, Thoroughbred beauty and wears it well, down to the expression of calculated boredom that most certain hides all kinds of startling thoughts, except she'll never tell you what they are until she's too old to care.

"Do you like children?" I ask her.

"About as much as I like a root canal. Why?"

13

IT SO happens I know just the precinct house they'll be booking in Christopher's guests for the night. In a funny coincidence, it's how I met Anson to begin with. That was back when he needed somebody to help him take down my step-daddy, Duke, so he arranged a raid and also arranged to sneak one Ginger Kelly out of jail to make a deal. That's a long story. Still, I can't help but discover a kernel of hu-mor in all this, black though it is. Now *I'm* the one who heads square and virtuous to the clink in order to spring Anson out of it, assuming he's sober enough to say his own name.

Mind you, it's dollars to doughnuts they'll let him out the back door anyway, directly they realize he's an old pal. You know how it works with these fellows. I don't doubt Christopher's fixing to toast health with the warden himself, any minute. The fix is in, is what I'm saying, and Anson don't need his ball and chain to come drag-ging in at some inopportune moment. Which is the same exact reason

I hurry my way down the wet streets to the Sixth Precinct station house, where the paddy wagon ought to be rolling up to the loading dock right about now. The drizzle glitters inside the yellow pools of light from the streetlamps. My small felt hat wilts around my face. I might could murder him, I really might.

Nobody recognizes me. Before I left, I tore off my dressing gown and put on a regular dress of navy-blue gabardine, black stockings, black shoes, black hat. Drab as can be, except for the hair, and whatever remains of my lipstick. The receptionist bestows this pitying look and says I'll have to wait until they book him. I ask to see a sergeant, maybe one of the Bureau agents. I hint at powerful connections. The receptionist turns sour and tells me to take a seat. I give her a look that says there will be hell to pay. Settle myself on a wooden chair and observe the burr of activity in and out of doors. The tobacco color of the walls, which might once have been pristine white. The clickety-clack of unseen typewriters, a sound I remember well from my days in the typing pool at Sterling Bates. How my fingers twitch at the recollection. I lace them tight at the knuckles and close my eyes to imagine some future, months hence, when me and Anson will have moved out of the city altogether and set up housekeeping in some pretty cottage in the mountains somewhere, where the sun always shines and the creek runs full, and Anson ranges about outdoors, learning Patsy to catch fish, while I rock the baby in some handmade wooden cradle—wee sweet round-cheeked cherub who gave me no trouble as he slid into this world—

"Mrs. Marshall?"

I startle straight to my feet, nearly upsetting the short jowly fellow who stands before me in a blue policeman's uniform. Feel like I ought to recognize him somehow.

"Can I help you?" I ask stupidly.

"Follow me, please."

He turns and stumps out of the reception area. I scramble to follow him, past the reception desk and the secretarial desks, *clickety-clack*, through a couple of doors and down a cold passageway, until we reach a door that bears the number 3. For no good reason that detail sticks on me, the number 3. Anyhow, the policeman opens the door and steps back for me to enter. Instead of following, he closes the door behind me, leaving me inside the windowless room, staring at my husband, who stands with his hands clasped and his back turned, as if he cannot bear to look upon me.

"Anson?" I squeak.

He turns reluctant. His face looks sore, his eye socket bruised and swollen. All is forgiven and forgotten, that very instant. I dash up and put my hands to his cheeks.

"What have they done to you?" I whisper.

Anson takes my hands gentle by the wrists and lowers them back down. "I'm all right, Gin. It's all right. No harm done."

"No *harm*—"

"I need you to sit down a moment."

When I don't obey, he draws a chair from the table in the middle of the room and guides me into it. Draws out another chair and sits so he faces me, knees about touching. He takes my hands by the fingertips. By now I shiver in spasms like some leaf in a gale. Ends of my nerves buzz. Some dread thing comes my way, I know it. I stare speechless at Anson's lips, waiting for the calamity to drop.

"I need to go away for a little while," he says.

"How long?"

"I don't know, exactly."

"Where?"

"I can't say."

Fear rises in my throat. I try to swallow it back, but it won't go back where it came from. Bright and hard like a ball. Chokes me. I rip away my hands and stand up.

"Can't say? Your own wife?"

He stands, too, and looks sorrowful at me. "I'm sorry, Gin. It's for your own safety, and Patsy's."

My fists commence to beat against his ribs. He catches them and holds me firm, a foot or two away. I yell at him incoherent, how I knew it all along, I knew he'd go back, I knew it was all a lie, I just *knew* that cursed bitch Luella would—

Luella, he repeats, stone cold. *Luella's dead.*

14

H E EXPLAINS everything in the same stone-cold voice. By now I sit stunned in my chair again. He tells me how Luella came to warn him about the man in charge of the northeastern racket, Hardcastle's old racket. He's Hardcastle's son, all right, and he wishes with the fiercest possible determination to murder Anson and scatter his bones for the vultures. Because why? Because he thinks Anson's to blame for the death of his father.

Why on earth? I ask, though I believe I can guess the answer.

Because of Luella. Because Luella was Hardcastle's lover, and Hardcastle's son imagines Luella betrayed his father in carnal intercourse with Anson, and that's how his father came to be killed. Luella warned Anson of the ambush off Nova Scotia, and Hardcastle discovered her treachery, and Luella murdered him to save her skin and reunite with her beloved.

Did she really do it, though? I ask. *Did she actually kill him?*

Anson hesitates. *She did.*

I don't ask him what exactly passed between him and Luella a week ago. I don't want to know all the things she said to him, how *desperate* she must have been, ruthless avenging prince on her heels. Probably she begged him to run off with her, to protect her—appealed to him with all her wiles and her beauty, appealed to his sense of obligation because she betrayed her lover in order to save him, and Anson would have told her no on account of being a married man, his loyalty already pledged to another, but it broke his heart to refuse her because she done this thing for him, killed a man for his sake. Oh, I can see it. He watches her go and slings back some bourbon whiskey to numb the anguish, then stumbles upstairs to lose his mind in my bed. The next day he receives the terrible news. The wicked prince has tracked down Luella and murdered her, all because Anson forswore her. Anson wracked by guilt. Plots some desperate revenge.

We stare at each other, me and Anson. This scene passes between us, my imagination and his memory. How far they run alike, I never will know. That tormented face about destroys me. On account of *his* torment, of course, which strikes grievous upon my bones. But also mine. A new and mortal understanding that sucks the life from my chest.

So it was all delusion, after all. He never did belong to me alone. No man ever does. He belongs to the wide world first of all, and what's left over must be divided up among those with some claim upon him. Maybe I got the largest share. But at some point, a piece of that mighty heart was chipped off into Luella's palm, even if he never knew the loss until last week.

And what defense have I got? The woman has laid me bare. She sacrificed her life for him! How can I hate her for that? She saved my beloved, and I swan she did it for spite. Now he can't ever forget her nor renounce her. She has bought him with her own soul, the cunning bitch.

I wonder how they killed her. Gunshot? Knife? Automobile? Would've been something messy, that's just the way the rackets do these things. Something that sends a particular message. Something that spilt her youthful blood all crimson from that alabaster skin and pale hair. Think of the sensation, once the papers get wind of this! The dreadful photographs of the crime scene! Keep them going until Christmas at least.

"So I guess you're going out after them? Break your sworn promise to me and Patsy?"

Nods his head. Lord Almighty, he does not even see fit to remonstrate.

"And you've cooked up a plan? Kept yourself busy this past week, while I worried myself sick over you? This whole raid and all? Cooked it up with Christopher, I'll bet, and your Bureau friends. Mabel's in on it, I make no doubt. Everybody but me."

"I know it was wrong. I've been selfish all along, I know it."

"You never said a thing to me. All last week, grieving for her, plotting to avenge her, and you never said a thing."

"Because I know how you feel about her."

"You don't think I love you enough to understand? Why, you never once reproached me because I had lovers before you, your own *brother* even, yet you can't imagine I might give you leave to have cared for *her*? Maybe I never did like that Luella, Anson, but I swear I'd have took all your grief and your guilt into my own bones if you'd let me. If you'd *trusted* me."

"I do trust you."

"Not to love all of you, the dark parts the same as the light."

He turns away to face the blank tobacco-colored wall. "So far as you know, Gin, I was killed in this precinct house tonight. Witnesses will testify to seeing me drunk and resisting arrest. Beaten up by the police. Carried inside. The Bureau will handle all the arrangements; all you'll have to do is turn up at the funeral in a black dress—"

Now the rage overboils inside me.

"The *funeral*? Be you *tetched*, Oliver Marshall? Knocked in the *head*? You actually think to make them believe you're *dead*?"

"Better than sit around and wait for them to strike first. As long as I'm around, the two of you—I can't stand to think of it, Gin—what they'd do to you because of me . . ."

"Baloney. If you really only wanted to protect us, you'd pack us up and move us all to Mexico or Argentina or someplace."

He spins to face me. "Run away, you mean? I can't do that, Gin. You know I can't. No, I'm going back in. I'm going to take the whole racket down, once and for all. I've got no choice."

"It's the stupidest thing I ever heard. You're a dead man, do you know that?"

"Well, that's the idea."

"Oh, you're making jokes now, is that it? This is a fit subject for humor? You *swore* to me, Anson. You said you belonged to me and nobody else. I *trusted* you. Me and Patsy."

"I don't ask you to forgive me. I know what I've done."

I think I might could drown in the ocean of his grief. The ocean of mine. Blocks of stone bound to my limbs so I cannot even flail against this force that drags me under. I never dreamt a body could feel this helpless. Room stinks of stale cigarettes and fear. I don't blame it. I wouldn't mind a cigarette for my fears. I wouldn't mind a drink. I wouldn't mind to wake up and discover I was but dreaming all this time.

I whisper, "What's the matter with you, Anson? What terrible thing has worked upon you that you don't believe you deserve a lick of mercy?"

He stares silent at me. Skin mottled and swollen. Broad shoulders slumped. Dark ocean eyes of quiet despair. Both of us drowning, neither of us possessed of the mortal strength to save the other.

"Go, if you want, then," I tell him. "But don't you ever dare come back to me."

15

WHEN I stagger out of that precinct house, I am amazed to see the gray smudge of dawn behind the black rooftops. A man rises from the bench on the sidewalk and says my name. Takes a moment of staring to realize it's Christopher. Don't believe I have ever seen that man on the outside of his joint. His face looks different by daylight. Softer, maybe.

Silent we turn together and direct our steps down the sidewalk toward the two side by side houses on Christopher Street. Funny, I never have wondered where Christopher lives when he's not tending bar. Never seen him come or go. I expect he must inhabit the rooms above his joint, for nobody else seems to inhabit them. The air is chill. After a block or so, Christopher shrugs off his coat and swings it over my shivering shoulders, all without missing so much as a single step, nor speaking a single word. Just our shoes cracking brisk upon the crumbled pavement. The sun rises gradual, touches the chimneys pinky-peach. We turn the last corner. Christopher stops at my doorstep, next to his. We stare some understanding back and forth. I swing the coat off my shoulders and fold it over my arm, and he reaches inside and pulls out a stiff white envelope.

"Asked me to give this to you afterward," Christopher says gruff.
I take the envelope. "Thanks."

"I know you're sore, but you ought to read it."

"Thanks," I say again, like some machine. Turn to climb the steps.
He catches my arm.

"You need anything, you ask me, all right? Promised him I'd look
after you and the girl."

This time I just nod. He nods back and releases my arm, and the
funny thing is I don't feel it at all. So numb as I am, I can't feel a
blessed thing. Maybe I'm done drowning and now I be dead altogether.

"See you around," Christopher says.

I take the key from my pocketbook and unlock my front door.

16

INDOORS, THE house rests so quiet as a mausoleum. Soft I call
Julie's name, but she don't call back. I stand at the bottom of the
stairs and consider whether to find her. Surely she has not been so
reckless as to leave Patsy alone? Then my head turns and happens to
stop at the space between the pocket doors to the parlor, where I spy
a long bare leg sprawling exhausted from an armchair. Skin washed
in palest pink from the window that faces east.

Well. At least somebody's kept a promise to me tonight.

I descend the stairs to the kitchen, dark and empty, where I start
some coffee. Takes time to brew. Weary I settle upon a chair and
listen to the liquid whispering of the percolator. Strange I don't
feel any pain. I guess pain will come eventual, flood my nerves and
such, but for now I thank the Lord Almighty for this merciful cot-

ton wool He has draped me in. I don't comprehend a thing. A bit of dawn finds its way through the basement window and I mark the colors of its progress on the wall. Rise and pour myself a cup of coffee. When I sit back down I perceive the stiff corner of the envelope in my cardigan pocket, poking at my waist. Anson's letter. *Rip it in shreds, you fool,* somebody yells inside me. Burn it. Instead I lift the envelope free and tear open the flap. After all, Christopher did told me I should read it, and I figure Christopher's judgment is presently clearer than mine. Anyhow, might best read it now, when I can't feel anything.

My dear wife,
I may be gone some time—possibly forever. With this likelihood heavy on my mind, I have made such provision for you and Patsy as I am capable.

1. *In the desk drawer in the study, you will find the passbook to an account in your name at the Chase National Bank, registering a current balance of just over four thousand dollars.*
2. *As for my Bureau salary, I have arranged for the entire monthly sum of $120 to be deposited into the account at Chase National Bank referenced above. You may note that the name of the payee on the receipts of said disbursements is not mine, for obvious reasons.*
3. *Despite the present estrangement from my mother, I retain ownership of my portion of the Marshall family trust, valued at approximately seventy-five thousand dollars, to which I have named you as sole beneficiary and which therefore becomes yours in clear, according to the terms of said trust, once a death certificate is issued in my name.*

4. *Title to the Packard has already been transferred to your name. I have filled the gas tank and put on new tires.*

5. *The standard Bureau life insurance policy will distribute ten thousand dollars to you, also upon issuance of the death certificate. This is the condition on which I agreed to cooperate with the Bureau in this matter. You will find the policy in the desk, as above.*

6. *Finally, with my remaining assets, I have established a trust in Patsy's name in the amount of fifteen thousand dollars, naming you as trustee, which will mature on her twenty-first birthday.*

I am afraid this represents the entirety of my estate at present, but it is yours to do with as you see fit, and as you already own the house in which we lived together, I hope my absence will not cause you any pecuniary distress, at least.

As for your practical needs, I have asked our friend next door to look after you and Patsy and provide every possible service that should have fallen to my duty. I believe him to be as trustworthy as any person I have ever known, with the sole exception of yourself. In the desk drawer, you will find the name and address of my lawyer, Mr. Philip Schuyler, Esq. of the esteemed firm Willig, Williams & White, who has assisted me this past week in making these arrangements. He will advise you expertly and with utmost discretion on any legal or financial matters that may arise.

From this point, I will be unable to address any further communication to you, except by some alias. There is nothing left to say, except that you and Patsy will always carry my whole heart with you, wherever you are, and whether it is welcome there or not.

Yours,
Anson

17

I STARE MUTE at Anson's crisp, neat handwriting for I don't know how long. Long after the words have lost meaning, anyhow, and I begin to worry whether I have forgotten how to read altogether. The word *death* springs out, from time to time. Sends the faintest jolt through my chest. Possible some part of my head reflects how exactly *Anson* this letter be, stiff and downright formal even, save the one tender sentence slipping in unguarded at the last. Kind of sentiment which might make me crumple them papers up tight and throw them like a stone against some wall by the force of a fearsome rage, could I feel even the smallest emotion just now.

Coffee's gone cold. I fold the letter and slide it back into its envelope. Stand and carry it upstairs, tiptoe through the parlor so I don't wake Julie, sprawled in the paisley armchair by the fireplace. Curtains shut tight in the tiny study, where Anson made all these arrangements, his telephone calls and his diligent letters. Desk drawer be locked shut. I extract the key from the underside of the desk chair, tucked in where the upholstery tacks to the seat. Inside the drawer lies a neat stack of documents held together by an elastic cord. Oh, goddamn him. Leaving me *this* in place of himself! I toss the letter in the drawer and lock it back up before some dire wetness erupts from my eyes, some prickling of actual honest-to-God pain.

Thank the Lord Julie Schuyler chooses to wake at this exact instant and call out my name from the armchair.

"Yes, it's me."

"Everything worked out at the pokey?"

"Like a dream."

She yawns extravagant and rises from her chair. "What a night."

"I'll say."

"Not a moment's peace. First the raid, then your visitors, and—"

"Visitors! What the devil?"

She blinks like a doe, confused by the glare of day through the window. "Why, don't you know? Friends of yours from back home. Or so they said."

"Who?"

"Who? I don't know. Some woman and her hatchlings, I didn't catch the name. She spoke like you do sometimes, when you've got your mountain blood running high, and I simply *assumed*—"

"Where are they? Where did they go?"

"Why, right on upstairs. Fast asleep in one of your bedrooms, I guess, like the Three Little Bears." She covers a yawn. "I guess I'm off. No need to thank—"

But already I have swung around the newel post and galloped halfway up the stairs, mad thundering heart. Race down the landing to Patsy's room, Patsy just waking up fragrant—*Ginny, what's wrong?*—up the next flight to the third floor, spare bedrooms, one door ajar. I fling it open. Woman bolts upright in the bed.

"Geneva Rose! You about scairt me to death!"

Spots pop out in the glittery air before me. I might nearly sag to the floor, do I not grab hold of the solid wood door itself for dear life, in the last possible nick of time. Still I have breath enough to gasp, it seems—

"Ruth Mary Leary! What the *devil* you be doing here?"

ELLA

Los Angeles, 1998

THE PLANE was an hour late, something to do with the jet stream. The captain was apologetic in that deep, relaxed, aw-shucks, country-vowel voice of airline pilots everywhere. Ella used to fly all the time when she was working at Parkinson Peters, first class, whenever and wherever they needed her to parachute into some company's corpse and dissect its innards, so she considered herself an expert on all aspects of air travel. Today she flew in coach to save money and the demotion hurt her more than she thought it would. She felt *lesser,* somehow. Those businessmen up front—how she used to love sitting among them in her gray flannel suit, like an interloper—they seemed bigger, more powerful, more busy, more important. *More.* And the women, languid and luxurious, thumbing their magazines. One kid, ferociously engaged on a Game Boy every time Ella spotted him through the crack in the curtains. Ella comforted herself that the kid would grow up into a brat someday, never quite satisfied with his life.

The tires scraped the tarmac. The plane rattled. Smattering of applause from the amateur gallery behind her. Outside the window, the sky wore that eternal pale smoky blue of Los Angeles. The traffic control tower passed by like a futuristic white spider. Then a palm tree, green and brown against the concrete.

HECTOR HAD TOLD HER they would send a car to pick her up at the airport and bring her to the hotel. Ella walked off the Jetway, laptop bag slung over her shoulder, roller suitcase dragging behind her, and cast her gaze over the assembled crowd to find the cluster of men in dark suits, carrying signboards, for the one that said DOMMERICH.

"Ella?" someone called, to her right.

Before she could even turn, a pair of arms came around her waist and lifted her up—laptop bag and all—to crash against a solid chest covered by a gray T-shirt. She closed her eyes for just a second to smell him—*feel* him—then she laughed aloud and lifted her face to be kissed.

"I thought they were sending a car!" she said.

"So did I. Then I said to myself, screw it. Why wait another hour to see you? Oh man." He hugged her again. "Now I know just how much I missed you."

AS THE NAME SUGGESTED, the hotel was literally on the beach, white and rambling and pristine. Hector tossed the keys to the valet and carried her laptop bag and roller suitcase himself. As they passed through the lobby, the desk clerk and bell staff all waved and greeted him.

"You're like the mayor," Ella said.

"More like the houseguest who won't leave and plays the piano in the middle of the night." He pressed the elevator call button and turned to her. Grinned like a wolf, the way he'd grinned when she first met him, in the laundry room of the apartment building. "I can't believe it. There you are. Why haven't you been here all along?"

"You never asked."

The elevator arrived. Hector waved her inside and pressed the floor button. When the doors closed, a tide of shyness passed over Ella. Shyness! What the *hell*. She'd shared with Hector just about everything you could possibly share with another human being, a closeness so close it was like inhabiting the same body, sometimes, and now she ducked her head and stared at the panel of buttons, at the warp of her own reflection on the stainless steel.

"Hey," said Hector.

"Hmm?"

"What—"

The doors opened. Hector's room was at the end of the hall—the corner suite, he said. Ella heard the familiar crash of ocean waves, except it was a whole different ocean. He unlocked the door with one of those modern plastic cards and swung it open. Ella took in her breath. Windows all around, framing the beach, the blue ocean, the Santa Monica boardwalk to the north. Bookshelves and sofas and comfortable chairs, a fireplace, a baby grand in the middle of the room, black as ink against all the beachy pale furnishings. "They brought it in for me," Hector said, setting down the laptop bag and the suitcase. "Pretty cool, huh?"

Ella took off her cardigan and slung it over a chair. Wandered to the balcony and stared at the pummeling ocean, which seemed a thousand times larger than the ocean off Long Island. Limitless. She turned back to Hector, arms outstretched. "I love it," she said.

"Holy shit," he said.

"What?"

He stared at her stomach. "You're pregnant."

Ella looked down. "Is it that bad?"

Hector stood next to the piano, one hand resting on the top. He looked as if he wanted to say something, but he didn't know what it was. The wind from the balcony ruffled his hair.

"What's wrong?" she said.

He shook his head and walked toward her, a few quick strides. Bent and lifted her in his arms. "Should've done this on the way in," he said.

"CONFESSION," SAID ELLA, MUCH later.

"Uh-oh." Hector's arms and legs were tangled with hers; his eyes were closed. The sheets and blankets had slipped to the floor. The air smelled of flowers and ocean and sex.

Ella rolled onto her stomach and propped her chin on his chest. "All week, on the phone? I felt like something was off with you."

"Off? How?"

"I don't know. Like our connection wasn't connecting right. That thing. You know. *Us*."

Hector lifted his hand and stroked the top of her head.

"Confession," he said. "Same for me."

"Really? You felt it, too?"

"I had all these things to say to you and I couldn't say them. Hung up the phone and stared at the wall. I don't know, *hungry*. Starved for something. Not just for you. For *myself*, like I wasn't myself anymore. I wasn't feeling things right. Everything out of tune."

"Thank God." She started to laugh. "So it wasn't just me."

"Anyway, you're here now. Everything's right again."

Ella laid her hand on top of his, above his heart. "It'll get easier, won't it? It has to."

"It won't get any *easier*," he said. "Not for me, anyway. We'll just get better at it."

EVENTUALLY THEY ROSE AND showered and went downstairs for lunch. Wandered out on the beach, wandered to the boardwalk. Ella said no way was she going on a roller coaster, sorry. They ate ice cream and kissed in front of everybody. Then they went back to the hotel and made love again until dinnertime. Room service on the balcony while the sun set. Smell of the ocean and the hotel flowers. Hector put Ella's feet in his lap and rubbed them slowly, methodically, the way he did on the sofa in their apartment while some old movie played on the television. He paid special attention to her arches and the balls of her feet. She imagined she could actually die of bliss.

"So what do we do tomorrow?" Ella said drowsily.

"You're not falling asleep, are you?"

"Eastern time. I've been up since two in the morning *your* time."

"Fair. We could go to bed."

She poked her foot in his stomach. "We've been in bed half the day. And you didn't answer my question."

"Tomorrow I'm back in the studio. You can watch us if you want."

"Of *course* I want. On what planet would I not want to watch you conducting an entire symphony? Playing the music you wrote yourself? I'll be tearing your clothes off by the last measure."

He laughed. "That should keep everybody awake."

"Whatever it takes. Tuesday, though."

"What about Tuesday?"

"Well, I kind of thought I'd go down to San Diego and see my aunt and uncle."

"Ah, Frank Hardcastle's ex? You're still chasing that hare?"

"Just curious. Plus I haven't seen them in a year or two."

"But they're coming to the wedding, right?"

"Of course."

"So it can't wait until then?"

Ella opened her eyes and straightened in her chair. "What's the matter? Don't you want me to go?"

"I want you to do what makes you happy. I just love having you around, that's all."

"Every minute?"

He lifted a foot and kissed the tip of her big toe. "Waking and sleeping. What about asking her up here? Then I could meet her."

"You'll meet her at the wedding."

Hector laughed again, a warm chesty rumble. "Sounds like somebody really wants to drive down to San Diego."

Ella laughed, too, and rose from her chair to straddle him. "I *want* to be wherever you are, obviously. But I also don't want to be the kind of girlfriend who hangs around every second, watching her man do manly things."

"*Girlfriend*." He wound a bit of hair around his finger. "We need a better word for you."

"Plus there's something else I really want to talk to her about, to be honest. Not about the Hardcastles."

"And it can't wait?"

"Not really. It's about Mumma. You know she was pregnant with me that summer, when she came to stay with Aunt Tiny on Cape Cod."

"Ahhh. Now it all makes sense. You want to see if your aunt knows the dirty secret."

"Maybe."

"You know, I'm not telling you how to run your life or anything, but isn't that something you should ask your mother, straight out? Bite the bullet? Take the bull by the horns?"

"Hector, it's *Mumma*. You know Mumma. I just can't. Not without—I don't know, ammunition."

Hector unwound her hair and settled it back over her shoulder. "Look, if you want to go to San Diego, go to San Diego. You can take the rental, I'll get a ride. Just for God's sake drive carefully, okay? Remember this boyfriend of yours is dying of thirst back here."

"Dying? *Really?*"

"Ain't no sunshine when she's goooone—"

Ella buried her face in the side of his neck. "You're singing too loud."

He kept crooning.

"Oh my God, *stop*. The whole *beach* is going to hear you—"

"The whole damn beach *needs* to know that Ella's my girl, my dream girl, my forever girl. You hear that, Santa Monica? I'm *hers*! This beautiful girl right here. I belong to *Ella*."

From the sand below the balcony came the whoops of approval.

THEN THE NIGHT. TUCKED under the same sheets, sharing the same air, pillow, warmth. Same low, slow buzzing of nerves. Ella, floating between awake and asleep, a little delirious, imagined she was molten, that she was literally melting into Hector and Hector was melting into her, that there was no part of her that was not somehow touching Hector.

"Skin on skin," Ella murmured drowsily.

"Nothing else like it." He kissed the top of her head. "Now get some sleep."

EVERY TIME ELLA VISITED Aunt Tiny and Uncle Caspian, she wanted to move to San Diego. Their house wasn't big, but it had a view to die for—glorious sun-drenched cliffs tumbling into the endless Pacific, everywhere you looked, golds and whites and blues that made Ella wish she could paint. More than that, though. Every room, every corner and nook, every stick of furniture and thread of upholstery felt like it wanted you there. As soon as Ella arrived, she wished she'd brought Hector, too. She wanted him to see this place, to meet Aunt Tiny and Uncle Caspian away from the rest of the family, to spend the night with her in the guest bedroom with the breathtaking southwest view, to hang out until midnight on the stone terrace, to drink wine and laugh and go through Uncle Caspian's photograph collections while he told the stories behind each shot.

Uncle Caspian wasn't home when Ella drove Hector's rental car up the winding road to the house, but Aunt Tiny stood waiting in the driveway with a coffee cup in her hand. Her face lit up when Ella pulled in.

"Why, you're *glowing*! Look at you!" she exclaimed, folding Ella into a hug too enormous to be believed from a woman so willowy. Aunt Tiny still had the figure of a ballet dancer, hardly surprising because she actually owned a ballet studio in La Jolla and taught most of the classes herself, from the little ones to the teenagers preparing for the Royal Academy of Dance examiners who flew out every year from London. "Pregnancy must agree with you."

"Not exactly. I only just stopped barfing every two minutes."

Aunt Tiny drew back and gave her a wise look. "Then it must be this new fellow of yours. Hector, isn't it?"

"Hector, yes. We're pretty happy, considering all the drama."

Aunt Tiny linked her elbow with Ella's arm and led her toward the terrace, which was filled with sunshine pouring over the crest of the hills. The old wrought iron garden table was still there, laid for coffee. "I've been dying to hear all about it. I was never all that convinced about Patrick, to tell you the truth."

"You and everyone else. I just wish somebody thought to mention it before I married him."

"What was I supposed to do, take you aside and tell you what I really thought?" Tiny paused with her hand on the coffeepot. "Although I suppose *I* of all people . . ."

Ella was just dropping into a chair. "You of all people what?"

"Never mind. It's decaf, by the way. Cream and sugar if you want them. And I made scones fresh this morning."

OF COURSE, AUNT TINY wanted to know *all about* Hector and Patrick and the baby, and how Ella was coping with everything. She was so *proud* of Ella for standing her ground and not going back to Patrick. *A leopard doesn't change his spots,* she said. She just hoped Ella *wasn't jumping from the frying pan into the fire.*

"I don't mean to question you, darling," she said gently, "but how much do you know about this new fellow? It all seems to have happened very quickly. At a vulnerable time for you."

"Believe me, I know how it looks," said Ella. "If it happened to a friend of mine, I'd tell her to get her head out of the ground and find a good therapist."

"So why didn't you take your own advice?"

Ella stared into her coffee cup. Aunt Tiny always made the best coffee, ground the beans fresh. Even decaf tasted decent when you ground the beans fresh. The cream probably came from some local dairy. Beautiful caramel color, beautiful California morning. "I think it was the music," she said.

Aunt Tiny nodded. "You always had a gift for that. I remember I went to your piano recital when you were—I don't know, eight or nine? Believe me, I've been to enough piano recitals to know when a child actually cares about the music."

"The whole building—" Ella began.

"Yes? What building?"

"Our apartment building. It's a—well, it's a musical building. It just felt like home. And Hector and I, we just hit it off so perfectly, you know? Same taste in music, same sense of humor, same everything. It's like we know each other's thoughts."

"He's a composer or something, isn't he?"

"Oh, Aunt Tiny." Ella leaned forward. "I wish you'd been there yesterday. They're recording his score for the movie—the actual *Los Angeles Philharmonic*, playing his music—it was the most amazing thing. I mean, I knew he was good, right? I know enough about music that I could tell he wasn't some hack. But listening to a whole *symphony* play that score, when I'd only heard bits on the piano . . ."

Ella faltered. Aunt Tiny stared at her attentively.

Well, what could she say?

It was one thing to know Hector was *doing* this thing—to hear the pieces on the piano, to imagine him rehearsing, conducting. Ella had played and sung before, performed and attended performances. She knew what it was like. They drove to the studio like they might have driven out to Long Island back home, talking and laughing. Ella had been nervous about meeting Louisiana Goring, but she wasn't there. She was in the editing booth today, Hector said. Hector had introduced Ella around to the producer, the symphony director, some sound guys. *This is Ella Dommerich,* he said, hand at the small of her back, and everyone seemed to know who she was, or rather what she was to Hector, whatever that was. There was small talk and coffee and then down to business. Hector found her a comfortable place to sit, in the booth next to the symphony director. Gave her a swift kiss, but she could see he was already in the other world, the music world that existed inside his head. He bounded to the podium and took the baton. Made a joke or two, loosened everybody up, tuning and some warm-up and some more tuning.

Then he lifted the baton. Exquisite silence. A pause of eternal breath.

Then music.

Ella listened—well, of course she *listened*. You couldn't help but sink into music like that, to experience the ebb and flow of sound around you as another dimension. But all the while she stared at Hector. He was Hector, but he wasn't. He seemed two feet taller and made of electricity instead of matter. He coaxed the music free from the instruments—sometimes delicate, transparent, almost iridescent; sometimes shatteringly huge like an ocean—music that he had created himself, in his own head. He was the same Hector who had showed her the ropes in the laundry room where they met, who had poured her glasses of midnight bourbon and played and sung and laughed with her, who had held back her hair over the toilet and made sure she took her prenatal vitamin every day, who was building a whole nursery for her baby, who kissed her, made love to her, slept next to her. But he was something else, too.

The symphony director leaned to Ella and whispered, "He's a genius. You know that?"

Ella nodded. She knew. She knew now.

They took breaks every so often, a few minutes to sip water and debrief. One of these times Hector came over to Ella in the booth and asked how she was doing, hoped she wasn't bored or anything. Ella just shook her head. She might have said something, but she couldn't remember what. He kissed her again before he went back to the podium and she touched her lips with her fingers, like you might after somebody you had a crush on kissed you for the first time.

This was the last day of recording. When they finished, the musicians set down their instruments and stood and applauded. Hector looked thunderstruck. He waited for them to finish, abashed, and finally held up his hands to quiet them. Thanked everybody, singled out section leaders by name. Hoped everyone would enjoy the movie.

On the way back to the hotel, Ella didn't say much. Hector's cell phone kept ringing—the studio had given him an L.A. cell phone to use, so he wouldn't have roaming or connection issues—and although he let the calls go to voice mail, the noise prevented any conversation, even if Ella could think of something coherent to say. They went out to dinner that evening with some people from the symphony and some kind of producer. So it wasn't until they returned to the suite for the night that Ella and Hector were really alone, one-on-one, the day's business done. Hector looked at her with a worried expression, desperate for her approval. Said she'd been awfully quiet and asked her what she'd thought.

What did she *think*? Jesus. She had no idea.

The whole world had shifted on its axis. Hector stood in front of her, and he was Hector again, but he wasn't. She *knew* now. How had she not seen it before?

No, she couldn't say all that to Aunt Tiny. How could she tell her aunt when she couldn't even tell Hector?

"Anyway," Ella said, "it was incredible to hear it all finished, that's all. He's really talented."

"That's wonderful."

"And he's also the most generous man I've ever known. And we just . . . well, we just fit together, that's all. I can't really explain. Being in the room with him is like coming home."

Aunt Tiny smiled. "Ah."

"*Ah,* what? Is that how it was with you and Uncle Caspian?"

"Something like that. The trouble was, I was already engaged to somebody else. And I was young and stupid and went through with it, and it caused a lot of pain for everybody."

"Frank Hardcastle, you mean."

Aunt Tiny set down her coffee cup. "I won't have a word said against him."

"I wasn't going to. I don't know a thing about him. Aunt Julie, on the other hand."

"Julie doesn't know a thing about him, either."

"Well, she's sure got it in for the Hardcastles."

Aunt Tiny rose and poured more coffee. "Have a scone, for goodness' sake. When Caspian and the boys get home, they'll gobble them all down."

"Excuse me? The Hardcastles?"

"What about them?"

"You tell me."

Tiny sat back in her chair and propped her feet on an empty seat. "I found them unbearable, of course. But that's got nothing to do with Frank."

"Hasn't it got *everything* to do with him? They're his family!"

"He's not like them. Well, not altogether." Tiny sipped her coffee thoughtfully. "His father was vile. A terrible bully. He'd been thwarted in his own political ambitions, so he was absolutely ruthless when it came to Frank's career."

"He's still alive, isn't he?"

"Yes. But he had a terrible stroke ten years ago. I haven't seen him, of course, but I understand he can't speak properly anymore or walk by himself."

"So why *were* his ambitions thwarted? Some secret scandal or something?"

Tiny broke apart her scone and popped a piece into her mouth. "Tell me something, Ella. Why all this sudden curiosity about the Hardcastles? I don't suppose your great-aunt put you up to this?"

"Come on, Aunt Tiny. He's running for president! And you were his *wife* once! Of *course* I'm curious."

"Darling, *everyone's* curious. Do you know how many reporters Caspian had to shoo away from the house last week? It's lucky our number's unlisted. And the ballet studio! We've had two dozen new students sign up."

"But I'm *family*!" Ella wailed.

"Yes, you are. And I adore you. But what happened in *that* family is no longer any of my business, and it's not yours, either." She sat back and resumed her coffee. "Anyway, you're barking up the wrong tree. I never learned any of the family secrets. I was always an interloper. If you want to know the real dirt, you'll have to ask your uncle."

"Uncle Caspian?"

"He *is* Frank's cousin, after all. And old Granny Hardcastle is his grandmother."

HALF AN HOUR LATER, Uncle Caspian arrived home with the boys—Bobby and Mikey, still in high school but already topping six feet, lanky as a pair of storks. Tiny and Caspian had tried for years to have children naturally and eventually adopted four of them, three girls and a boy. Then Aunt Tiny had found out she was pregnant just as the adoption came through for the youngest, and Bobby was born seven months later. To make matters more absurd, Mikey followed fourteen months later. Mumma and Aunt Viv were aghast, thought it was all very unseemly and Tiny should have Caspian fixed before any further damage was done to the family prestige. Tiny just called them her miracle boys and went about raising them the same as the others. Somehow she crammed everybody into that four-bedroom house in the seaside cliffs north of San Diego. The oldest was working on her Ph.D. in molecular biology or something like that; the second had graduated from college and worked for an insurance company. The two younger girls were in college, one at Pomona and the other at UC Davis, something to do with horses. They were all very happy and noisy together and liked to greet you with hugs, which took some getting used to.

As for Uncle Caspian. Ella would never admit it aloud, or even silently to herself, but he was maybe her favorite uncle. He was so square and decent. In addition to his photography he liked to restore antique automobiles from scratch, the more terrible their condition the better. He also had a quiet, kind, terrible authority that you never even considered questioning, because he exercised it so rarely, like one summer when everyone was visiting The Dunes and the cousins had embarked on a juvenile scheme to fill the club dining room with marsh egrets.

To be clear, he didn't give a damn about the condition of the club dining room, but he did care about the poor egrets.

Now Uncle Caspian came beaming onto the terrace and kissed his wife, then pulled Ella from her chair with both hands so he could get a good look at his upcoming grand-niece or nephew.

"Look at that," he said. "Just beautiful. So where's this new fella of yours?"

"He's stuck in the editing studio today, unfortunately. But he's looking very much forward to meeting you at Lizzie's wedding."

"Hmm." Uncle Caspian didn't look impressed. He reached past Tiny for a scone and she poked him in the ribs.

"Forgive him. When it comes to judging character, he reverts to his army days. Which is why none of the kids is married yet. *I* think Hector sounds like a perfectly nice guy. And I think it's very exciting he works in Hollywood."

"He doesn't really work in Hollywood. He's a musician? A composer, actually. He's just doing the score for a movie, that's all."

"What kind of movie?" asked Uncle Caspian.

"A World War Two thing. Poland? The director is Carroll Goring's daughter. You know, the one who—"

Uncle Caspian was trading a look with Aunt Tiny. "I know who he is. His daughter, huh? Alabama or something?"

"Louisiana. Her friends call her Lulu."

"You know Goring used to be married to a cousin of yours? She was a movie star herself. Pretty big in the sixties."

Ella looked at Tiny. "Really? Who?"

"Her screen name was Miranda Thomas. I met her once or twice when I was little. She was—what was it? The daughter of Daddy's Uncle Thomas. He was a professor, I think. Killed in the war. Anyway, the mother went off and married someone else, so Miranda wasn't around when I was growing up. Lives out on Winthrop Island now, last I heard."

"She's not Louisiana's *mother*, is she?"

"Miranda? Oh goodness no. They divorced . . . I don't know, it must have been the late sixties. I'm afraid I don't keep up with all the gossip. I *do* remember hearing Goring was a very nasty piece of work, though."

Ella's coffee cup was empty, just a tiny puddle of cold liquid left in the bottom. "Wow," she said. "Just when you think you've heard everything about this family."

The French door opened and Bobby poked his shaggy head through. "Ella? Your mom's on the phone."

"MUMMA! ISN'T IT LUNCHTIME or something back there?"

"I *tried* reaching you on that cellular phone of yours but it went to the answering machine without even *ringing*." Mumma's voice was aggrieved.

"*Voice mail*, Mumma. Yeah, I turned it off. Roaming charges are insane. What's up? Everything's okay, right?"

"Everything's *fine*. The tent people are measuring out the space right now. Vivian's in a tizzy, of course. Charlie's not coming in until the day before. Apparently the Vineyard's busy this year and he can't leave that *bar* of his. And Joanie's coming all the way from Paris, although she hasn't done me the courtesy of telling me when, exactly."

"Mumma?"

"Yes, darling?"

"Out with it, okay? Long distance and everything."

Mumma made an offended noise. "Can't a mother want to hear her daughter's voice once in a while?"

"Mumma, we love each other and everything, but you have never in my whole entire *life* called me for no reason, and it's a gorgeous sunny California day outside and I'd like to be back in it. Much as I adore you."

"Well . . . it's nothing *special*, really. It's just that Aunt Julie mentioned you were going to talk to Tiny about the Hardcastles and the—well, you know. What *happened*."

"Aunt Julie *mentioned* it? Or you dragged it out of her?"

"Honey, I *wish* you wouldn't bother Tiny with all this ancient history. That was a *difficult* summer for her. And I'm sure she's had enough questions already, with Frank running for president."

"If it makes you feel any better, she wouldn't talk. She told me to ask Uncle Caspian."

"I think you should just drop it."

Ella stared through the glass to the terrace, where Uncle Caspian had taken the chair next to Tiny. He was gobbling another scone, and it looked like she was scolding him, and he was enjoying being scolded. The sun drenched his hair. Without warning, and with her whole heart, Ella wanted Hector. She wanted to sit on some sunny terrace with him after thirty years of marriage and pretend to fight over a scone, like a pair of teenagers.

"Mumma, for God's sake," Ella said. "What difference does it make to you?"

"Nothing. I'm just thinking of Tiny, that's all."

"Tiny's fine, as if you cared. Honestly, if you're worried she might drop some juicy family gossip, why don't you talk to her yourself?"

Mumma made another noise—like *hmph*, only more elegant. "Put her on."

WHILE TINY WENT INSIDE to deal with Mumma, Ella settled herself back outside with Uncle Caspian. "More coffee?" he said. "She went out and got this decaf stuff just for you."

Ella smiled and held out her empty cup. "In that case."

He refilled her cup, added the cream and sugar for her, and sat back in his chair. He moved so gracefully, Ella sometimes forgot that one of his legs was a prosthetic. Certainly, he never talked about it.

"Tiny tells me you're curious about the family," he said.

"I'm sorry. I don't mean to cause trouble or anything. It's just that Aunt Julie's been on kind of a mission lately, and it does seem like— well, some stuff has happened, that's all."

He smiled at her. "You're like Tiny, you know."

"How do you mean?"

"It's okay to cause a little trouble now and again. Don't apologize. Anyway, Julie's right. Plenty of skeletons in the closet. Which ones are you interested in?"

"Seriously? What about your cousin?"

"I don't think telling my niece about some long-ago skullduggery is going to make any difference to his campaign. He's a good man, it's not about him."

"You know what, Uncle Caspian? You're the only person I know who can say *skullduggery* and make it sound natural."

He made a half bow from a sitting position. "I take that as the highest compliment."

"The thing is, though, I'm not sure it *is* all in the past. The—you know, skullduggery stuff."

"What makes you say that?"

Ella fingered her cup. "Do you know anything about a firm called FH Trust? Based in Cambridge?"

"That's the family trust. My share is pretty small, though. I get a nice little check every month, enough to keep the kids in college. But the trust was set up to funnel most of the income to Frank. Well, Frank's father, technically. My mother was just a daughter. Much less important to the family name, right?" He winked. "So my uncles got most of the shares, and Frank's dad got the most of all of them."

"Why was that?"

"Because he was the oldest son, number one. Head of the family.

And number two, he was the one who set up the trust to begin with. Way back in the 1930s, I think."

"Right after Prohibition was repealed, maybe?"

He waggled his eyebrows. "Maybe."

"So it's true about the bootlegging, then. How the family made its money."

"Look, I honestly can't say for certain. It's not something you ask about, and the sisters—my mother among them—would've had no part at all in the family business. It was another age, right? All I know is that my grandfather lost pretty much all he had in the 1907 panic, and somehow he and Granny made it all back and then some in the 1920s, and the family never talks about how or where the money came from. Add to that the fact that my grandfather was murdered in the summer of 1924 and nobody was ever charged with the crime, and you can pretty much connect the dots. If you wanted to. Satisfied?"

Ella set down her coffee cup and leaned forward. "So what kind of man is Frank's father?"

"The worst kind. I did some reading on psychology once, and I pretty much figured he's some form of sociopath. Bad news."

"But he's incapacitated now, right? So someone else is calling the shots with the family trust?"

"It's possible."

"Like who?"

He shrugged. "Like Frank's brothers, probably. He stays above all that investment stuff. Conflict of interest."

"What about your grandmother?"

"Granny? She's as sharp as a tack, believe it or not. Still got her wits at a hundred and six. But definitely not running the family trust day to day." He looked at the French door, through which his wife's slender body swayed this way and that, on the telephone with

Mumma. "The thing about Granny, she's not like Uncle Frank. She's not some kind of sociopath, so far as I can tell. She just puts family above everything. Nothing matters more than her kids and grandkids. She would—she *has* done—just about anything to . . . well, how do I say it? Advance their interests."

"That's not a bad thing, right?"

"Sure, if you don't take it to extremes." He turned back to Ella. "She married young. Sixteen or something. Had my uncle Franklin right away. Had seven more kids, one after the other. Widowed at thirty-three. So she *had* to be a tiger."

"Kind of creepy of your grandfather, marrying a sixteen-year-old."

Uncle Caspian smiled. "He was probably under the illusion that she would be easier to control."

"So what did she think of you and Aunt Tiny? Wasn't she mad at you both for upsetting the family apple cart?"

"Oh, she was furious, all right. So was Frank's dad. But Frank put his foot down. I'll say that for him. When he saw how things were, he did the decent thing." Uncle Caspian's face turned stern. "So I don't want any of this to come back and hurt him, okay?"

"Not if I can help it. But I'll be honest, if there's stuff still going on at FH Trust, it's not going to be good. And I'm not like your grandmother. If people are getting hurt, I'm going to stand up and say something."

He looked at her for a moment and nodded. "I'd expect nothing less from you."

The door opened. "Expect what?" said Aunt Tiny, stepping back onto the terrace. Her face looked a little withered.

"Expect your niece to have the same impeccable integrity as you do," Caspian said. "What did Pepper want?"

Aunt Tiny glanced at Ella and sat down. "Oh, the usual. All this fuss over the wedding."

There was the awkward silence that follows a lie. Aunt Tiny reached for her coffee cup. Ella folded her arms.

"Look," she said, "I already know about it, okay? You don't need to hide anything from me."

"Know about what, dear?" Tiny said, hiding her face in the cup.

"That my dad isn't my real dad. I'm guessing Mumma spent that summer with you on Cape Cod because she'd just found out she was pregnant, right?"

Aunt Tiny choked on her coffee. Uncle Caspian whacked her on the back.

"I don't know what you're talking about," she gasped.

"I haven't told her I know. My dad was the one who told me. Because of me getting knocked up by Patrick and everything. He thought it would make me feel better, for some reason. Men, right? Anyway, I *know*."

"I told you so," said Uncle Caspian.

Aunt Tiny just looked helplessly at Ella. "I promised your mumma," she said, in a small voice.

"You didn't break your promise, don't worry."

Uncle Caspian rose and picked up the coffeepot. "More?"

Ella held out her cup. "So who was it? If you don't mind my asking."

"Who was what?"

"My real father. You know, my sperm donor."

Aunt Tiny coughed again and looked at Uncle Caspian, who set down the coffeepot and shrugged. "This is your deal, not mine," he said. "You make the call."

"I *will* find out eventually, you know," Ella said.

Aunt Tiny leaned forward and took her hand. "I think you're asking the wrong person, aren't you? You need to ask your mumma. It's her story to tell."

BEFORE ELLA LEFT, SHE called Hector to let him know she was heading back.

"Hey there, love of my life," he said. "I was hoping to hear from you."

"Had a good day?"

"Started out on an extremely high note with some red-hot shower sex, so it could only go downhill from there. But I think things are looking up. My girl's coming back home to me."

She laughed. "Just give me an hour or two to work my way through the traffic."

"Drive safe. Oh, and just so you know? I've got a little surprise for you when you get here. So hurry back. The sooner the better."

JUST BEFORE ELLA CLIMBED into the rental car, Uncle Caspian came out of the house to say good-bye. He held a manila envelope in his hand, which he offered to her.

"What's this?"

"Latest annual report from the family trust. But you didn't get it from me, understand?"

Ella zipped her lips. Uncle Caspian leaned forward and kissed her cheek. "Take care of yourself. And I'll see you in a week or so. Make sure this Hector fellow is good enough for my niece."

She laughed. "Now you really sound like a Hardcastle!"

She climbed in the car and started the engine.

ACT IV

I Drink My Cup
of Sorrow
(and make it a double)

GREENWICH VILLAGE, NEW YORK

March 1925

1

ON THE anniversary of the night we met, another note from my husband dropped in my lap. They used to drop regular, every couple of weeks. Patsy brung it to me on account of I didn't have much heart to waddle over to Christopher's joint myself that particular evening, exactly one year after I first set eyes on Oliver Anson Marshall right there at the bar counter. That stool he sat on, this stool me. Didn't have the heart for it. Last thirtieth of January I was so free as a sleek young bird, and never imagined in a thousand years how that wide-shouldered fellow in the gray suit had arrived to overturn my life. Now his child kicks and grows in my belly, and he himself might be anywhere on the face of the earth, and probably under it. My heart aches so hard it might break. Anyhow Patsy skipped next door for her glass of milk and to shoot the breeze with Christopher, like she did regular and still does, and when she skipped back—smear of milk on her upper lip, like always—she brung me that note.

It was written in stub pencil all smeared up and said:

Now the ice is thick enough we drive right across the lake. Last night was clear and full of stars, the moon was a slim crescent and I thought of you as I stared at the sky. I wondered whether you were asleep or lying awake and whether you have let your hair grow some more or cut it back short. I see from the newspaper that the New York weather has improved in recent days and I hope you're getting all the fresh air and sunshine you crave. I sometimes think about the way the sun always found your red hair and turned it into a fireball, and how lucky I was to bask in the glow. Next week I join the Burlington convoy. God watch over you and P.

Now I am no more superstitious than the next bastard, but it seemed to me uncanny that I should receive such a talisman one year *exactly* after I had met the sender. Like a sign from heaven, almost, even though I yet despised the man for loving so useless and diabolical a notion as *honor* more than me and Patsy, and I had no more idea of sending him some kind of answer than I had of walking down Christopher Street naked in my present interesting condition.

In the first note that Christopher passed me across the bar, which arrived only a week after Anson's departure, Anson told me that if I truly meant those last words I spoke in the precinct house, he would not reproach me nor seek to reclaim his old life when his work was done. In other words, he would stay dead, if dead I wanted him to remain. Gallant of him, I guess, and I couldn't have agreed more. Never wanted to see that faithless husband of mine again so long as I lived. But for some reason still I expected those notes to continue dropping into my lap regular, every two weeks, even though I never sought them nor replied to them.

Then February passed into March, and I began to fear that the note I received on the thirtieth of January was not a talisman at all, but just what it was—his last letter.

2

WHICH IS why I now find myself staring listless out the window of this train, rattling past swamp and smokestack and coal-streaked tumbledown shanty to Washington town. The hour's yet early, because I did promise Patsy and Ruth Mary to return home by evening. A wet, dirty snow sticks to the marsh grass and factory bricks of New Jersey, on account of March coming in like a lion, and was there ever such a thing more depressing to the spirits than a dirty March snow? And my spirits weren't at their best to begin with. For one thing, I don't relish the day before me.

For another, I'm about starving to death.

Used to be, I could rise and wash and dress and still make time for a nice cup of coffee and a fried egg or some such before I walked out my front door on whatever errand drew me to the wide world. Now my mornings whirl in a melee of hungry children and wet beds, of lost hair ribbons and spilt milk and upset tummies. Ruth Mary manages most of it, because the Lord did fashion her good for this particular task. But when a cyclone took place inside your own house you cannot help but to be drawn into the heart of it, and it happens the Lord saw fit to bestow on *me* no such trove of patience and human understanding as He did for Ruth Mary. Scarce remembered my own hat, let alone a bite of toast. Then the sight of Patsy's deserted face as I closed the door behind me. Stands to reason I should look astringent upon the world just now.

Still, there exists a remedy for one element of my distress, at least. I rise from my seat and wobble down the aisle toward the dining car, where even so weary and hardscrabble a mountain wildcat as myself might obtain a cup of coffee and an egg or two.

3

I HAVE NOT settled five minutes with my breakfast and a newspaper when a shadow falls over the columns of print.

"Why, Mrs. Marshall!" exclaims a well-bred male voice.

I allow a second or two to pass before I tear my eyes away from some interesting report of a bloodbath in Brooklyn, just to show how offended I am by the interruption. Before me stands a gentleman in a beautifully tailored suit of pale gray. His eyes are bright blue and his curling hair, newly freed from the fedora now tucked under his elbow, is of that whimsical shade they call strawberry blond, now tarnished by silver.

I lower the newspaper and fold it twice. Heart jumps straight up my throat. "Why, Mr. Schuyler. It's been ages."

He gestures to the empty seat across the table. "Would I be insufferably rude to invite myself to join you?"

"Suit yourself."

Schuyler sets his hat and newspaper on the edge of the table and sits graceful. Lifts his eyebrows at a passing waiter, who stops immediate. Addresses him respectful and asks what can he do for you.

Schuyler casts a glance at the spread of food before me—corned beef hash, couple of poached eggs, toast, fruit, coffee, sweet roll— and widens his blue eyes yet wider. Still, he's bred gallant. "Bring me the same, if you will," he says bravely, and the waiter fills his coffee cup from the silver pot in his hand and replies *right away, Mr. Schuyler.*

I watch Schuyler drop a spoonful of pure alabaster sugar in his coffee. The spoon is silver, which I figure he's used to. "I guess you ride the Pennsy pretty regular," I observe.

"I'm afraid business calls me to Washington more often than I'd like." He nods to the plate of corned beef hash. "I do hope you're not waiting for me."

I lift my fork and tuck grateful back into the hash. No point explaining to a man like Schuyler what it takes to nourish a seven-months pregnancy, to say nothing of the unspeakable luxury of eating a whole entire breakfast without fear of interruption by some ankle biter missing a chunk of hair from the head of her best dolly on account of she flushed her cousin's sergeant major down the toilet, accidental-like. "I'm not," I assure him.

He watches me eat for a moment and clears his throat. "How are you getting on these days, Mrs. Marshall? I cannot express my sorrow deeply enough."

Takes me a beat to remember what he means. "Thank you. Your note was a comfort."

"I didn't wish to disturb you at the funeral. You seemed so very distressed."

"Oh, it was a shock, all right."

The scarcest pause, and then, "May I dare to hope that your expected new arrival is some consolation to you, in this time of grief?"

"Why, yes, thanks. How kind of you to notice."

"When do you expect the happy event? If you'll pardon my asking."

"Around the middle of May, the doctor tells me."

"Your mother-in-law must be especially delighted, after all she's lost."

"Mrs. Marshall, you mean? Haven't traded so much as a how-do-you-do with my mother-in-law since she buried her husband and told the pair of us to get lost. So far as I know, she's got no idea she's going to be a grandmother."

"Do you mean to say you haven't told her?"

"As you might recollect, she wasn't bothered to attend her own son's funeral. Can't imagine she'd be interested to know he left a little something behind."

Schuyler's face turns soft and sympathetic. Kind of expression you might want to kick, if you was somebody like me and disliked sympathy on principle. Gentle he says, "I'm sure the news would gladden her, however. Theresa Marshall has borne more than her share of tragedy, though she doesn't wear her sorrow on her sleeve as most women do."

"I'll say."

"She'll come around, never fear."

"Oh, that's exactly what I *am* afraid of. If I'm lucky, the little sprout will share my sad affliction, to keep her at bay." I point to the scrap of fiery hair visible beneath my snug little hat.

He laughs. "Affliction? I happen to think it suits *you* perfectly."

The waiter saves me from replying to this intimate observation, arriving at just that second with a silver tray of food for Mr. Schuyler. By the time everything's arranged and appreciated, the words have disappeared from between us. Instead I offer him my thanks.

"Your thanks? What on earth have I done, other than send a note of sympathy, as any decent person would do?"

"The house you lent us for our honeymoon."

He might hold his breath a second or two, I don't know. The silver saltshaker hovers unshook over his hash. Without looking at me, he says, "I didn't mean for you to know about that."

"Well, I had to know, didn't I? After what happened. I hope you had insurance."

"Insurance? For God's sake. You can't imagine how distressed I was to hear what happened. How relieved there was no lasting damage."

"No lasting damage? The whole house burned down!"

Schuyler looks up for to hold my gaze. "I don't mean the house. The house is nothing."

The thing is, he appears mighty sincere. He looks as if he actually had nothing to do with any fire, honest to God, as if he was so shocked as we were, as if his world might have ended was the pair of us hurt by so much as a single lick of flame. I feel some queasiness come upon me, unrelated to the little beast kicking inside. Wasn't that I ever reckoned for certain Schuyler lent us that house only to set fire to it—for one thing, he don't look the criminal mastermind type—but then who does? And not a living soul but him and Mabel Willebrandt should have known we was nestled inside that particular mountain holler, like a pair of new-mated birds, except some bootleggers who regarded us with nothing but gratitude.

So either this kind-faced patrician Charles Schuyler is the wickedest monster I have ever known, or someone else has betrayed us.

I return to my breakfast. "Anyhow. Except for the fire, Mrs. Lincoln, that was the happiest I've ever been, and Anson, too, I believe. So I guess it's lucky we had those weeks in that paradise of yours, because that was all there was, in the end."

"My dear, I'm so sorry."

Listen to that voice of his! The scratchy undertone. Look at his face, hung with grief. The train rattles around a bend, screech of metal wheel on metal track. Dirty gray landscape whips silent past the window. Smell of good coffee hangs in the air.

"I don't guess you've ever found out who might have done it?"

Schuyler signals the waiter for more coffee. "No, I'm afraid I never did."

4

BY THE time we've eaten up all that breakfast, the train's already begun to shudder into the northern reaches of Philadelphia. Schuyler and I have chatted amiable the whole time, can hardly remember what about. They do know the fine art of conversation, these aristocrats—ask you friendly questions about your schooling and your taste in books and that kind of thing, always avoiding the dread riotous ill-mannered subjects of religion and politics, about which no two people can ever agree, still less respect each other afterward. I do recollect the way he roared with laughter when I told him the story about that girl Hyacinth at Bryn Mawr, whose lights I knocked out for the benefit of humanity. "If you're going to get yourself kicked out of college," he said, "you might as well do it right." Strikes me funny, you see, on account of men like Schuyler generally not looking benevolent on girls who hit other girls, let alone girls who get kicked out of their well-bred colleges.

"Well, my mama didn't take so charitable a view," I told him.

He wiped his eyes with the corner of his napkin and said no, he expected she didn't.

Anyway, the journey's more pleasant than it has a right to be, is what I'm telling you—surely more pleasant than I might ever have expected. When the waiter's cleared the table and there remains not a crumb but a pair of coffee cups and our newspapers, Schuyler insists he must pay for my breakfast, since he's selfishly taken up so much of my delightful company. I don't object. I get the feeling he would take offense if I did. He lifts his arm to signal for the waiter, so my gaze falls natural upon the three brass buttons at the bottom of the sleeve, and the gold link that binds together the starched white cuff of his shirt.

The cuff link looks old and worn, in the manner of these folks who prize their history and their bloodlines. I can't quite make out the shape, though it transfixes me somehow, in the short few seconds it occupies my vision. The head of some animal, I think.

5

THE OFFICE of the assistant attorney general of the United States occupies an old-fashioned building on K Street that used to be a hotel and still looks like one. Nothing grand about it, just five stories faced in brownstone and a hot, stuffy lobby that smells of cigarettes and perspiration. Painted in gold letters on the window above the door, where you might expect to see the name of the hotel, it says DEPARTMENT OF JUSTICE. I give the receptionist my name and tell her I have an appointment with Mrs. Willebrandt in ten minutes' time. She says to take a seat, please.

No doubt about it, Mrs. Willebrandt's taken right aback at the shape of me, and it requires considerable surprise to catch Mrs. Willebrandt on her back foot, believe me. She stammers some embarrassed congratulations, which I wave off. I don't have the kind of temperament to discuss babies with most women, let alone this one.

Seems Mrs. Willebrandt has aged about a decade in the months since I saw her last. Pair of bruises have took up permanent residence under eyes, and her skin droops like an elastic pulled once too many. Who can blame it, though? I don't imagine her job is easy, what with men the way they are, and having to prove yourself capable of the impossible every blessed day, all over again. As before, she wears a dark suit of no particular flavor, not so much as a lick of lipstick, hair yanked back in a convenient arrangement at the base of her wise head. She clasps her palms together on the desk before her, and I observe something I didn't trouble to notice back on the sofa of that lodge in the mountains—the woman's got herself a right lovely pair of hands.

"Well, Mrs. Marshall," she says, tinge of sympathy, "I can guess why you're here, and while of course you will always have a claim on my time and energy, I'm grieved to say I don't have much else to offer you."

"Then I figure I should start by telling you what's brought me here today, Mrs. Willebrandt, just to ensure we're properly square with each other."

She makes a graceful motion with the right hand, like a queen. "Please do."

As I sit there in the wooden chair before this woman's large wooden desk, the most powerful woman in the country, at least insofar as we can measure these things—a whole machinery of prosecution at her command, thousands of agents for the investigation of crimes, the nation's press hanging upon her words—it occurs to me how the tables are turned. She's got what she wanted from me—namely, Anson—and now Gin Kelly's no more to her than a supplicant craving for scraps of him. Hands knit together in a nice lap of respectable gabardine.

I rise from the chair and cross the room, which is not a large one, and close the door, which was left open an inch or two. Return to my seat and cross one leg over the other.

"Mrs. Willebrandt, I will confess to you, I had no great hope of seeing my husband alive again when I left that precinct house five months ago. Moreover I was plain mad at him for doing it, and he knew I was mad at him. I told him never to come back to me, and I meant it. Still he sent me notes from time to time, through a friend of ours, just for to let me know he was alive and kicking, I guess. I never sent any reply. Wouldn't have known how to reach him, anyhow, for he took care not to write anything that might give him away."

Here I pause and ask if she minds do I have a cigarette. She makes a small negative motion of her head, which I take for permission. I open my pocketbook and take out the cigarette case and light one up, more to gather my nerves than because I want one specially. As I blow out a little smoke, she regards me reflective, tilting her head a little ways to one side.

"My husband sent me just seven of these notes, Mrs. Willebrandt. The last one arrived on the thirtieth of January."

"Mrs. Marshall, if I may—"

"Now I didn't think to worry at first, because I was still plain mad, as I said, and because my house happens to be crammed with young children at the moment, which has a way of distracting your attention. The weeks do fly by, even if the days do sometimes drag. Also because his salary continued to drop into my account at the Chase National Bank, in the name of Alfred Homer, which I must say—just in passing, Mrs. Willebrandt—is not the kind of name of the kind of man I might have anything to do with." I suck on the cigarette a little and reach for the ashtray at the corner of her desk. "So it was the beginning of this month before I began to wonder if there was anything wrong with him. Not that I pretended to care, you understand, on account of I told him he should not ever come back to me after this, and maybe he figured he should take me at my word and had found some other woman to occupy his attention."

Mrs. Willebrandt clears her throat and asks delicate, "Did he know about the—er—?"

"His child? No, he did not. I had just discovered the fact myself when he told me he was leaving, and I figured I didn't want to know whether it would make any difference to him or no."

"I see."

"I guess he might could have learned it from our mutual friend, if our friend had had a way to find him, but that friend happens to be loyal to me and not to Anson, so I figure not. But that's all hypothetical, Mrs. Willebrandt, and anyhow it's not the reason I asked to meet you."

She frowns a little and looks down at the plain manila folder on the desk before her, which I guess has something to do with Anson. "Dear me," she says soft, then looks up and asks when the child will be born.

"Middle of May, I believe."

She nods as if she approves.

"I happened to notice that this Alfred Homer's salary was not paid into that account at the Chase bank as usual at the end of February, nor was it paid in March, neither. Now I have no particular need of the money itself, Mrs. Willebrandt, which I keep for our child. I have some tiny fortune of my own, besides which Anson left me, and I have no material wants at present. So I don't care whether Anson still draws a salary with the Prohibition bureau or not, under his own name or somebody else's name, but I do want to know whether this salary was stopped because of some clerical error, or because he did leave the Bureau's employment voluntary, or because he be dead."

There, I said it. The word *dead,* dropped natural from my mouth like it makes no difference to me, like the pit of my stomach's not itself dead at the sound of it.

"I see," my opponent says again.

"Oh? What do you *see*, Mrs. Willebrandt? I confess I should appreciate to know."

She picks up her fountain pen with those lovely fingers and holds it horizontal above the manila folder. Slides off the cap and on again. Off again and on again. Sets down the pen and knits her fingers together. Speaks to me in a gentle rasp, just above a whisper. "It seems there has been some miscommunication."

So harmless a word, *miscommunication*. So accidental sounding, like *misplace* or *misspoke*. A pesky error, put to rights easy.

"Has there, now?"

"I'm afraid so. I take full responsibility. You see, when Special Agent Marshall ceased communication abruptly in—" She frowns and opens the folder, sorts through the papers until she finds the right one, guides her index finger along the lines. "Ah, yes. End of January."

"You, too? How funny. You don't suppose it's a coincidence?"

"Naturally we sent a field agent to investigate, but he was unable to turn up any trace of Marshall, I'm afraid." She closes the folder and looks up. "Instead, we discovered that the liquor convoy with which he was traveling across Lake Champlain encountered a patch of thin ice and was lost. I regret to say that even without positive *proof* of death—"

"You mean a body."

"—Oliver Marshall was presumed to have been killed in the course of his duty, and his relatives should have been duly informed. Owing to the particular circumstances of Marshall's assignment, however, there seems to have been some misunderstanding."

"Because he was already supposed to be dead."

"And because only I and Mr. Hoover were aware of that fact—that

Special Agent Marshall was not already dead, his life insurance paid out, and his funeral expenses accounted—the necessary letter was not issued to you. For which I offer you my sincerest apology, Mrs. Marshall. Your husband was a valuable member of the United States Bureau of Prohibition, and his loss is deeply regretted."

6

I SIT BY the window of a second-class railroad car careering down some section of track with no clear idea how I arrived here. Likely this train is headed back to New York City, by the grace of God and habit. I don't much care, anyhow.

Let me make one thing clear, at least, for the rest is murk. I have not forgiven Anson, and never will. Should his apparition appear before me now, I would scream some foul abuse in its direction. I would beat that bull chest with my fists, though I struck but air. For the sin of forcing me and Patsy and this unborn child of his to live our lives without him, he should burn in purgatory till his soul be properly crisp. Still I love him, it seems. This is the kind of anguish that only the purest possible love can muster. Lord Almighty, I cannot even distinguish the love from the anguish at all. The edges of this wound will not close. For my wickedness, I must bleed all my days.

7

I ARRIVE HOME by the same blind means. When I open the front door, pandemonium strikes me instant, the way a slap in the face knocks you out of a trance. Ruth Mary's boys run in circles from parlor to study to hall to parlor again, one of them in some kind of an Indian headdress that sheds feathers all over the nice clean floor. The noise of Patsy's wailing comes hurtling from above in hysterical waves. I believe that acrid smell belongs to supper, burning in the oven.

Best of all, a sheet of water falls elegantly down the stairs, as the creek slips over the rocks in its way.

8

NOW IT occurs to me I have not explained about Ruth Mary Leary and how she came to stay permanent in the house on Christopher Street with me and Patsy. That *was* a surprise, wasn't it? Her turning up in the middle of the night like that. But I could no more turn away Ruth Mary than I could turn away a hound dog that needed shelter. For one thing, I owe her my life. Did she not fling me the keys to her Tin Lizzie in the woods near River Junction all those months ago, me and Patsy and Anson would surely have faced the furious justice of a mob of townsfolk deprived at once of their most necessary source of income—namely, my step-daddy, Duke Kelly.

So when she turned up at my house in the middle of that momentous night last October, enormous gravid, I sat down on the bed with her and cuddled her close and assured her she was safe with me. *They found me out*, she explained in tears, *that I done helped you to escape, and they run me out, they liketa murdered me and my babies in our beds for it.*

Ruth Mary be a widow woman, you understand, since her husband,

Eddie, passed the summer before last, and of babies she has five—
each one about a year apart from the next, regular as clockwork—
Li'l Eddie, Laura Ann, Mary Rose, Isaiah, and Petey. Petey was the
babe in her belly when she first landed on my doorstep, born under
an autumn drizzle and an unlucky star but four days later. Now he's
grown to a squalling, lusty young fellow latched to her teat most
times. Runs Ruth Mary clean off her feet, but she likes the exercise, it
seems. In exchange for her room and board and that of her children,
she undertakes to clean and to cook and keep things in some kind of
general order, though I do explain to her she owes me but nothing,
after what she done for us back in that wet woods in River Junction.
They Lord, Geneva Rose, she says to me. You think I fix to sit around
idle all the livelong day, with five children to brung up and a house to
keep tidy? My mama liketa turn in her grave.

So we have muddled on comfortably these past five months, our
menfolk all gone unnatural early to their rewards, run clean off our
feet.

9

AND NOW, the deluge. Well, I might have expected it. You turn
your back on a bathtub in order to attend to a bleeding nose,
and before you can blink that bathtub will overfill its sides and ruin
your evening.

Still, it's an awful lot of water for an overfull bathtub. I call upstairs for Ruth Mary and she calls something back, touch of panic,
so I wade up the steps and discover a terrible scene. Seems a pipe has
sprung in that brand-new bathroom. Patsy stands wailing at the edge
of the stairs while Ruth Mary holds Petey on her hip with one arm

and struggles in vain with the other to find a way to shut off the damn water in the pipe.

I turn to Patsy. "Run down and find Christopher, quick!"

She gulps and makes this amazed face like I showed her her very own page in the Book of Revelation. Turns and slides right down that flight of stairs, lands bump at the bottom, scampers to the basement steps. All I can pray is Christopher be messing about inside his bar right now, making ready for the night's revelry. I slosh across the bathroom floor and pluck Petey from Ruth Mary's left arm, first so she can better attend the plumbing, about which I know next to nothing, having been brung up with a hand pump and an outside lavatory. Through the wall I imagine I can hear the instruments warming up, the new clarinet player trying out his scales, Bruno plucking his bull fiddle contemplative, while my bathroom floor turns into a fishing hole and my staircase into a weir, and I think to myself I shall never have to do with a man again so long as I live.

10

THEN THE water stops gushing and Christopher turns up with a box of tools. Wants to know why we didn't just turn off the water at the main. I might could strangle him for that. In half a minute he's fixed the pipe and slapped on a new seal. Disappears and returns again with the mop and bucket from his own joint, along with Bruno, who sets about cheerful alongside Ruth Mary to dry up our fishing hole before bedtime. The exercise seems to bring out the pink in her cheeks.

"Why, Ruth Mary Leary," I say, handing over Petey, who's grown fretful for his milk. "I had no idea you liked music."

Ruth Mary pats down her hair. "Full-a nonsense, you are, Geneva Rose."

Over her head, Bruno winks at me and carries down the buckets, one from each sturdy arm.

Now the excitement's over, I force march the children into their pajamas and their beds and look in afterward on Ruth Mary, who rocks in her bedroom chair and nurses Petey in a glow of gold lamplight. How peaceful they be, like Madonna and child. Seems to me obvious that Eddie Leary was not the daddy of this particular baby, having been dead some time before it was planted in her belly. Still I don't ask, and Ruth Mary don't volunteer. As for Petey himself, he can hardly help who sired him, poor mite.

And just like that, my spirit scatters to dust.

Sight of Petey's eager mouth is what done it, I believe, for by some queer working of mind and body, an imaginary mouth seems to lay itself over my own teat and tug ferocious, some fatherless baby I will shortly bear into this world, its daddy frozen dead forever at the bottom of Lake Champlain, and I swan my heart stops. I cannot breathe. My brain turns white.

Anson.

So sharp is my anguish, it shoots right across the room to penetrate Ruth Mary's holy bliss. She looks up at me in the doorway and narrows her eyes. "Why, Geneva Rose! I clean forgot to ask. You learn some news out there in Warshington?"

"Bad news, I guess."

"Oh, honey. I swan, that husband-a yourn oughta be hung from his toes, is what."

"Wouldn't do any good, Ruth Mary. He's been dead since January."

"They Lord." Her voice turns reverent. "Geneva Rose, I *am* sorry."

"I guess I already knew, in my heart."

Ruth Mary looks on me with commiseration and lifts Petey to her shoulder. Pats him on his soft back. He lets loose a belch and a last shuddering sigh and settles into the hollow of her neck. "Well, you'll soon have a new babe to comfort you, Geneva Rose, and won't *that* just fill the house right up to bursting."

"Nothing but a pair of old widow women now, I guess. Sharing our burdens."

"Now, what kind-a talk is that, Geneva Rose? You's young yet. Pretty as ever. Why, I bet them gentlemen come buzzing around like flies, come summer. Have to swat them away."

With one hand, Ruth Mary buttons up her blouse and rises from her rocking chair to settle Petey in his cradle. Numb I watch her curved back, her soft hair, the side of her face as she bends over her baby. Wonder how I shall break this news to Patsy, who thinks Anson is but gone away for a visit somewhere. Baby stirs under my ribs. Merciful God, take this cup from my lips. I cannot drink.

11

FIND MYSELF in the kitchen somehow, I don't know how. Maybe I went for to get a drink. I have this urge for pickle juice. But we got no jars of pickles in the cupboard. So I stare empty-handed up through the window to the sidewalk above me. Pair of stocking legs in pretty shoes crosses the tip-top of my field of sight. Faint tinkling of laughter. Orchestra strikes up, some energetic jazz music like an echo from another time, when I was typing sheets of pristine white paper by day and painting the town red by night, when men gathered about my shapely figure and lively hair like flies round a delicious pot of sweet honey, when a photographer named Anatole paid me two hundred dollars a time to recline naked on a sofa and fill the frame of his camera with my sumptuous form, because these aching swollen teats of mine were once the kind of melons that deserved a whole series of photograph cards, selling in their thousands every month.

And all my trouble started because I had the dumb idea to entrust body and heart to one man only.

I turn away from the sink and walk out of the kitchen to the rear of the basement. Take the key from its hook on the wall and slip through door and vestibule to Christopher's larder, on the off chance he might have a jar of pickles somewhere, dill or sweet, don't matter which. But Christopher don't have any pickle juice neither and for some reason this is the last straw. I don't know why. No pickle juice! I slide down an empty patch of wall and commence to weep so silent as I can, quiet dark empty room that smells of food and the demon liquor. I don't know how long. Only the door does open eventual from Christopher's basement, rush of music and laughter, and Christopher steps in to find something for the bar, box of limes maybe, bottle of simple syrup. He searches the shelves a moment before he finds me. Doesn't startle or anything, just drops his arms by his sides and investigates me leaning against the wall of his larder. My pajama shirt is creased and damp, my eyes leak salt tears. A leaky mess, I be. He sighs and closes the door and settles down beside me, knee against knee.

"Anything I can help you with?" he asks.

"Not a thing. You best get back to your customers."

"Can't leave you here like this, though."

"Nothing you can do. My husband's dead, it seems. Baby on the way. Can't even find some damn pickle juice."

"Pickle juice? What for?"

"To drink."

In the dusky light of the larder, both doors closed, I can't see his expression so well, but I feel his surprise. Men like Christopher don't ponder much on the whims of gravid women. I never have witnessed this neighbor of mine leading any girls upstairs—him being the kind of fellow that draws a thick line betwixt work and pleasure—but I do sometimes see them steal out his front door in the early morning, and not one of them seems the matronly type. So I don't doubt I have startled and perhaps disgusted him. Not that I'm of a mind to care just now.

Our knees touch. "You sure about Marshall?" he says, after a bit.

"Went to Washington today and asked that Mrs. Willebrandt face-to-face. Turns out the Bureau ain't seen hide nor hair of him since the end of January, either, nor heard a word. They woulda declared him dead, except they already had."

Christopher nods. "He's dead, all right."

"You heard something about it?"

"Maybe I did."

"Why didn't you say anything?"

"Wasn't my place. And you know I don't pass on information, as a rule."

Funny, I'm too numb to feel a thing. Not even fury at the man beside me. How long did he know? How reliable was his snitch? Does it even matter? Have I not already grieved for Anson, so deep and dreadful as it were possible for a person to grieve? Been a-grieving since I walked out that door of the police precinct five months ago, haven't I, without so much as a pause.

"Sorry I don't have some pickle juice for you," Christopher says.

"That's all right. I guess I'll live."

"Gin, it ain't enough to just *live*. You know that. Once upon a time, you knew that better than anybody I ever met."

He don't move, and I don't, either. Some deadness fills me I can't seem to shift, a terrible loss of faith and hope that pins me to the earth. Seems to me the salt tears still track down the corners of my eyes. Christopher's thick black woolen leg props mine upright. His white cuffs glow faint in the moonlight from the square of window. After a minute or two he turns right around and takes my slipper feet in his lap. Holds my gaze for some sign of objection. God forgive me, I offer none.

He pulls off the slippers and commences to rub the sole of my right foot.

At the instant of contact, skin on skin, a spark strikes inside me and whooshes to light all my miserable bursting nerves. Starved as I am, how can I help but to give myself up? Sag shameless against the wall while Christopher's fingers work gentle but firm at their merciful task. His brusque thumbs, rising from the heel to the ball in generous strokes, so intimate an act as ever a man has performed on me. Finish the right foot, start on the left. For a minute or two or five, who knows, nothing sounds in that tiny room but the echo of music and laughter in the room adjoining, the rasp and sigh of my own breath.

At last he stops. Lifts each slipper and slides it back on each defenseless foot. Rubs the tears from my face with his two thumbs. Lord Almighty, how wrapped in sorrow have I lived these past five months, like a caterpillar in its chrysalis.

"Better?" he asks.

I nod my head yes.

He climbs to his feet and takes my hands to hoist me up. Before he lets go, he looks straight in my eyes and says, "If you need anything more from me, Geneva, you know where to find me. Understand?"

I stare back a moment and again I nod my head yes.

He lets go my hands and pulls back the shelf like a gentleman so I can step through the door to the vestibule. My legs wobble like rubber. Surely this was but a peculiar dream. Some febrile fit, born of shock and grief. I turn back swift and grab the door from closing.

"What's your real name, anyway?"

His brown eyes catch some moonlight and glitter back at me. "Joseph," he says. "Joseph Bronstein."

And though I can't be certain whether he's telling me straight or not, it seems to me I have heard that name before. Can't for the life of me remember where.

12

WHEN I stagger up the basement steps to the landing outside the parlor, some movement flickers inside—Ruth Mary, holding a book in one hand, rising from her armchair. Lamplight shadows her face.

"Geneva Rose! What in the name of the Lord you been up to?"

Speechless and shameful I stare at her, like some animal that has caught the eye of a hunter and don't know how to escape. Her eyes and mouth go round together. She claps her hand over her mouth. "You didn't!" she whispers around her fingers.

"Don't know what I did, and that's the truth."

"Well, it's about time, that's all. You been cooped up too long, Geneva Rose, and all for the sake of a man who run out on you and got what he deserved for it."

I am too astonished to answer this. Realize my hand clutches together the sides of my pajama shirt, though they are already buttoned, and make the fingers to unclench. Ruth Mary takes it all in. Now that I look upon her with new eyes, she seems a whole nother woman than the one turned up at my door at the hour of my despair, wan and scairt like a stray cat who brung in all her kittens for safe-keeping. Face filled out pink and pretty, her hair thick and shining. I think of Bruno's wide smile and deft fingers, plucking that bull fiddle of his down below.

"Might say the same of you," I tell her.

13

MIDNIGHT, ONE week later. The misery of March grows upon us. I lie aglow inside my chrysalis of sheets and listen to the music spill through the walls from the joint next door. Dead quiet sits this house of mine, not a single creak of wood.

In about three hours, Bruno will maybe tuck his double bass away in its case and steal across the vestibule and up the stairs to visit with Ruth Mary. Or maybe he won't—I don't inquire about her business. I just lie in my bed and stare at the silvery ceiling. Coal hot I burn. Fury and something else. How cold the winter, and now this heat of anger. I think what Christopher said, how I been dead so long I forgot I'm still alive. Have drunk so deep from my cup of sorrow, I don't know how to feel. And I am lately turned but twenty-three years old! I want to feel! I want to live! And I have clean forgot how. I loved a man so deep and true, my wreck was total. I can't so much as summon his image without dying all over again. Cannot recollect his lips and his arms and his grave blue eyes without slipping into some abyss. Still I want to live. I want to burn with the full white heat of this fury, every living flame of it. How could he. How could he. Me and Patsy and the babe he will never know.

How could he make us live without him.

I don't know what prompts me to rise. Why *this* night? When I have lain here aglow every blessed night this past week, since my neighbor performed his act of selfless mercy upon me. Maybe it's the moon or the coming equinox. Change of tide from winter to spring. I see myself from a distance, wicked redhead shimmies off her virtuous nightgown and puts on a plain black dress over the swell of her seven-months belly, long enough so nobody can see she don't wear stockings nor anything else underneath. Hook a pair of shoes on my fingers and start downstairs, so soft as I can on those wooden boards for not to wake the children.

Christopher spots me where I come to stand in the corner of the room. The joint is jumping as ever, music blaring every which way, men and women drinking and dancing and canoodling. Still he spots me instant. Meets my gaze for a moment or two. Wipes his hands on a dishcloth and turns to speak to one of the other bartenders. Then he walks out from behind the bar counter and takes my hand firm, for I be shook to the core. Leads me to the door in the back, which he unlocks with a key from his vest pocket, and then up four flights of stairs to the top of the house where his bedroom lies, looking out smack against the rooftops, curtains billowed to the cold metropolitan wind. He makes me to sit in the armchair while he closes the windows.

"I like a lot of fresh air, after cooping up down below all evening. You cold?"

"A little." Teeth chattering.

From the bottom of the bed he unfolds a plaid blanket and puts it over my shoulders. Sits on the footstool and stares at me. "What can I do for you, Gin?"

"I don't know," I tell him truthful.

He takes off my shoes and lifts my feet to his lap. Commences to rub them just right, not too hard and not too gentle, the exact intimate way he did before. He has short, thick fingers and broad palms. Reminds me of a bear's paw. Think I might die of ecstasy, those big thumbs stroking the soles of my poor feet.

"Used to watch my dad rub my ma's feet, when she was expecting," he says.

"What, you have a family? Not sprung from beneath a cabbage leaf?"

"*Had* one. Both dead."

"I want to hear about them."

"Not much to say. Came from Germany when they were kids, both of them. Lived in Brooklyn. Married young, had some children. I was born first."

"Sisters? Brothers?"

He works his thumbs along my arches. "Typhoid," he says.

"What, all of them?"

"My dad, too. Just me and Ma were left. I was twelve. Studying every minute, spending all my time at school or hitting the books on the kitchen table. I was supposed to go to college. Education was everything to them, see? But I had to go to work instead, after that. Ma, too. Too hard?"

"No, it's perfect."

"Started working for this fellow who owned a saloon. Friend of my dad's from the old country, strict Lutheran, eight nice blond kids. That's how I learned the business." He starts to work on my toes, each one thorough. "Then he got my ma pregnant and we had to leave. Couldn't have his wife and church find out he had a baby with some Jew. So we ended up in the Bronx. She had the baby, my little sister. Caught the pneumonia a couple of years later and left the two of us alone."

"Christopher—"

"I told you my name, didn't I?"

"Bronstein."

He nods. "All right, then. Anyway, I figured I wasn't going to let the same thing happen to my sister. Beautiful girl, my sister. Smart as hell. Never loved anything in my life like I loved that sister of mine. Made sure she went to school. Made sure nobody messed her around. Saved up what I could so I could send her to college. I wanted only the best college for her. She deserved the best. Perfect grades, top of her class, piano, sang like a bird. And none of those fancy colleges would take her. Can you believe it?"

"Why not? Because you were from the Bronx?"

He gives me a strange look. "Because her last name is Bronstein, kid. So I went up there myself. Radcliffe College, you heard of it? Just outside of Boston. I got an appointment to see the president of the college—"

"How'd you do that?"

"I just did. I went in there and I told that woman all about my sister, and why she ought to go to Radcliffe, and by the end of it, why, the president of the college agreed with me. My kid sister started at Radcliffe the next month."

"That's wonderful."

He wraps his hands around my feet, holds them flat against his black wool vest, so I can almost feel the beat of his heart. "My point in telling you this story, which I have never told to a single living soul except you, which nobody in the world knows except my sister, is I take care of what belongs to me. The money I made to raise my sister right and send her to college, it was not the kind of money that comes easy, or legal. I made it anyway. Started this joint here. Not for my health, see? Can I pour you a drink? Warm you up some."

"Sure."

He sets my feet down careful and walks to the cabinet on the opposite wall. Opens it up and takes out a bottle of fine bourbon whiskey. Pours it neat into two glasses. When he returns to me, he hands me one and sits back down on the footstool, facing my knees. I sip cautious and tell him this is awful good bourbon whiskey.

He makes a modest shrug.

"Say, I don't believe I've ever seen you touch liquor before now."

"I don't drink on the job, that's all."

The telephone rings sudden and shrill from the bedside table. Bronstein don't so much as flinch. Keeps on ringing. I ask him if he's going to get that. He shakes his head.

"Might be important. Your line of work and all."

"*This* is important. That's just business. Business can always wait, Gin." He motions his glass to my belly. "How do you feel these days?"

"Pretty miserable."

He nods. "That's why you're here with me, I guess."

I set the drink next to the lamp. "How did he die, Bronstein? Tell me something. Was it really an accident? Just drove onto thin ice like that?"

"How should I know?"

"Because you do."

Bronstein looks down at the pool of bourbon whiskey in his glass and swishes it around some. "Word is they learned who he was. Shot him through the head and dropped him through the ice. Satisfied?"

I can't speak. I can't even properly hear, like somebody stuffed cotton wool into my ears. Bronstein looks up and sets his glass on the floor. Takes up my hands.

"Look, at least it was quick, all right? Never felt a thing. Never saw it coming."

"Who?" I gasp.

"The racket up north, Gin. Don't you listen to anything?"

"But Hardcastle's dead. That Kingston woman killed him."

"So there's a new boss. Always a new boss, Gin."

"Who is he, then?"

Bronstein considers me. "In eight months he's rolled up all the other rackets in the northeast. Running them all. Shipments across the Canadian border into Lake Champlain, bonded inventory, drugstores, moonshine, running rum into shore out of Saint Pierre and Nassau and Bermuda, you name it. Not a gnat flies by one of his convoys and he doesn't know about it and kill that gnat. That's how he plays. Marshall was a fool to go out into that. A fool. Surprised he lasted as long as he did, to say the truth. Shouldn't've done it to begin with. Should never in a million years have left you like he did."

Possibly this is the longest speech of Bronstein's life. Some kind of dam broke inside him as he went. Voice turned thick and deep and urgent. Now he sits back a little on the footstool and recollects himself. Still holds my hands, though I don't believe he realizes that.

"You miss him, though," he says at last.

"Until the day I die."

Bronstein nods and lets go my fingers. Slides his hands under the hem of my dress and up my bare legs until his warm palms lay flat against the sides of my belly. Baby stirs to his touch. He stares hypnotic into my eyes.

"All you need to think about right now is *this*," he says. "You put everything else out of your mind but growing this baby. All that worry and strife. You need for anything, you come to me. Day or night. Not one whim of yours I won't sate. Not one hair of your head I won't keep safe. Understand?"

Feel I am in a trance of some kind, this man's hands on my skin and his brown eyes seeking into mine. I make so small a nod, it might be lost. But he nods back. Leans forward and kisses my stomach through the cloth, between his two hands. His lips stay there for some time. Seems the warmth of his breath spreads all across my middle. Tears run free down my cheeks to fall *kersplash* on that nice plaid blanket spread over my shoulders. And I almost never cry.

14

O N A truly breezy day in March, when the first spring zephyr strikes the tree outside my front door and sets the naked branches to shivering, I discover a plain white envelope on the tiny checkerboard tiles of the entryway, direct beneath the mail slot. When I pick it up and examine it front and back, I see it bears no postmark and no address. Just my typewritten name, Mrs. Oliver Marshall. Must have been hand delivered sometime during the past hour, when I was feeding the children their lunch in the kitchen downstairs.

I wipe my hands on my apron and tear open the flap. Single sheet of thick paper inside, folded in precise thirds, creases so sharp you might cut your finger on them. The message be written on the same typewriter as the envelope direction and says NOW I KNOW WHERE YOU LIVE, I MIGHT CALL UPON YOU AND THE KIDS SOMETIME.

That's all.

15

B RONSTEIN IS not specially bothered. He frowns as he reads both the envelope and the note inside, but then he most always frowns at everything.

"Prank of some kind," he tells me. "Some crackpot, maybe."

"How can you be sure?"

"Because anybody in the business knows you're under my protection."

It's the middle of the afternoon and I perch on the barstool at the end of the bar counter, sipping some tonic water from beneath a delicate slice of lime while Bronstein wipes his glassware methodical for the evening. The older children do their letters and numbers at one of the tables, fortified by glasses of milk and plates of cookies, while the younger fry run rampant around the room under the watchful eye of their uncle Christopher and a streak of watery sunlight through the basement window in the back. Ruth Mary be out selecting a nice beefsteak from the butcher to fry up for supper. I treat Bronstein to a frown of my own.

"Now, wait a minute. Why would anybody think such a thing?"

He shrugs his thick white shoulders. "Word gets around."

"Anyway, I'm not under your *protection*, as you're pleased to put it. Not like *that*."

"The hell you aren't. Anybody raises a finger on you, he has me to answer to. That was true before and it's damn true now."

"Why, you didn't put the word out, did you? You didn't start telling people I was your *girl* or something?"

"What I'm saying is nobody would *dare*, Gin. That's all." He turns his back to set the last glass on the shelf and folds the dishcloth in neat, careful squares. "You want another?"

"No thanks."

Bronstein looks up and rests his gaze on me. Leans forward and touches my chin with his finger. "I said don't worry, all right? I'm telling you it's a crackpot. This is New York, what do you want? Keep the door locked, like you do anyway. You see anything funny, you just let me know. I'm right next door. Not going anyplace."

"All right."

He says low, "You want me to come around tonight?"

"Sure."

"Before we open up, then." He straightens up and brushes my chin again with his index finger. "Get some rest, all right?"

16

H E ARRIVES soundless around half past nine. I don't know how he picked up the trick of walking about a house without so much as a squeak of floorboards, short thick muscled man such as that, but he does. I never know he's coming until the bedroom door glides open, no matter how I peel my ears. Tonight he settles on the end of the bed near my feet and hands me a box.

"What's this?" I ask.

"Well, open it."

The box isn't wrapped or anything. Just a small flat cardboard box in the shape of a rectangle. I admit, my heart thumps a few times. I lift the lid and discover not some diamond necklace, as I feared, but a leather book stamped in gold at the corner with my initials, GRM. The pages are creamy white and blank.

"For when the baby comes," he says. "My ma used to keep notes of us. How much we ate and slept and weighed."

"Oh!"

"A pen, too. Fountain pen."

I look back in the bottom of the box, where a beautiful red enamel fountain pen sits in cotton wool. While I pluck it out and exclaim how lovely, Bronstein takes off my slippers and commences to rub my feet. He wears his crisp white shirt rolled to the elbows and his black wool vest buttoned up, like always. Neat black bow tie. Never seen him any other way. I put the book and pen back in the box and replace the lid. What a thoughtful gift, I tell him. Thank you.

"You feeling all right? Everything good?"

"Everything's fine. Went to the doctor this morning. She likes to keep an eye on things."

He nods. "I like women doctors. They don't care so much about buying some fancy car. Waste of dough, fancy cars."

"What do you like to spend money on?"

"Nothing."

"Please. You must take in thousands, down there."

"Maybe I do. Don't mean I spend any."

"How old are you, Bronstein?"

He hesitates, like he's considering telling me a lie and decides against it. "Forty-three."

"Forty-*three*?"

"That's the truth."

"I'm twenty-three."

"I know that."

I pull my feet in and sit up cross-legged on the bed, a yard or so away from him. "What are you doing here, anyway? Ought to be out enjoying yourself."

Frowns. "I *am* enjoying myself."

"Those girls I see coming out your front door in the morning. Blinking to the sunshine. That's what you oughta be doing. Having a little fun with somebody."

He lies back crosswise on the quilt. Folds his hands across his ribs and stares at the ceiling. "When did you last see some girl coming out of my front door?"

"I don't recollect."

"Must have been some while ago. Autumn, like."

"Maybe it was."

"I don't do a thing for *fun,* Gin. I do what I need to do, and that's all."

"So you *need* to come here and rub my feet twice a week?"

"*You* need it. So I come."

I settle down awkward and heavy on my side, facing his profile. "But you don't take anything for yourself."

"Who says I don't?"

"I can't give you anything, Bronstein. I wish I could, but I can't. It's all broken and not worth having."

He turns on his side to face me. Lays his hand on the curve of my belly, where the baby rolls restless, trying to find some comfortable position, I guess.

"I told you. *This* is all you need to worry about. *I* worry about everything else."

"*Why,* though? Can't give you back a thing of me."

"That's not the question. Question is what do you need from *me,* Gin?"

Mute I be. Even could I think a single word, I couldn't say it. My whole insides rain some hurricane of despair. I lay my hand over Bronstein's hand. Baby kicks hard against the wall of my womb, just to jolt me back to life. *Oof,* I gasp.

"Shhh," Bronstein says.

I close my eyes and nod my misery against the quilt. Gentle he rolls me on my back. Draws up my nightgown like a whisper. Runs his fingertips slow over my swollen breasts, my ribs, my round smooth belly, like to study each piece of me. At last he settles his warm mouth between my legs and starts to work. How tender he be, how scrupulous. In no time my starved hands clutch for his hair, his shoulders, his ears, his hair again. Call out soft in deepest relief. At the sound of my cry, Bronstein turns still. Holds my hips and breathes upon my nethers until they quiet. Then sits up and draws my virtuous nightgown back down past my knees.

"Better?" he says.

I whisper yes.

He settles me back against the pillows and pulls up the quilt. "Don't feel bad about that, now. Like sleeping or eating. You need something to nourish you."

Then he's gone, so soundless as he came in.

17

WELL, THE next morning is the day when the trouble rolls in. A big yellow Hispano-Suiza, to be precise, which pulls to a gigantic stop outside my door without regard for the convenience of any motorists trapped behind. Chauffeur opens the back door and a woman steps out like a jungle cat and sizes up the joint. All this news Ruth Mary comes running downstairs to report, for she has watched the entire scene unfold from the window of her bedroom, where she was changing the sheets.

The next second, the doorbell rings. As it happens, I'm in the kitchen, reading the newspaper with a nice cup of coffee and a cigarette. I call back up the stairway to Ruth Mary, ask her to receive our guest for me. She patters to the door. Try as I might to return attention to this society column, in which that Julie Schuyler's up to her usual hijinks—she appears so regular, the *Post* refers to her by her first name only, in order to save ink—still I can't help but listen to the murmur of voices. Heart smacks in a curious way against my ribs. Toes commence to buzz. Sure enough, comes the step of Ruth Mary back down the stairs.

"Geneva Rose," she says, low awed desperate voice, "be your *mother-in-law*!"

"I don't have a mother-in-law."

"Says she is. Mrs. Sylvester Marshall, that's what she said."

I sit there staring into nothing. Swearing a blue streak inside my head. Then I stub out the cigarette, lift the apron over my head, hang it on the hook on the door, smooth down my unruly rufus hair, and waddle quickly out of the kitchen and up the stairs.

She sits in the exact center of the sofa in the parlor. Ruth Mary sits nervous in the chair opposite. When I enter, Mrs. Marshall rises graceful to her feet and tells Ruth Mary she can leave, and please close the pocket doors on her way out.

Now, Mrs. Marshall be a handsome woman, all right, for all she's twice as old as me. Oh, sure, that alabaster skin ain't *quite* what it was in its heyday, and maybe the face has become too bony for what we call beauty, in this frenzied new age that worships nothing but the plump bloom of extreme youth. But she arrests you, all the same. She has some height, and she keeps her figure well. She dresses beautifully in a frock the exact color of sunset. She holds out her hand to me, gloves of white kid. My hand is bare and just a mite chapped from the winter cold. We touch fingertips briefly. I ask if I can offer her some refreshment. She makes a face like I offered her one half of a lemon to suck on and declines. Won't be a minute, she tells me. I just came to return this to you.

From her pocketbook she retrieves a packet of letters, tied with ribbon.

18

O F ALL the things that honeymoon fire destroyed, what I regretted most was the packet of my daddy's letters to my mama. I hadn't read but one of them. One was enough, I thought. I don't recollect what it said, exactly, just that it was chock-full of that lovey-dovey goop I despise, that cornball sentimentality no right-thinking modern woman could properly stand. I seem to recall that my daddy had just deflowered her, and I guess he sent her this nice note to mark the occasion. Now, why she *treasured* this letter—why she kept it and all the others, and then entrusted them to her best friend Laura Ann Green to give to me when she was dead—why, I couldn't comprehend such a silly impulse, to say the truth. Why should a woman keep hold of a pack of syrupy lies such as those? Handwritten proof of her lover's monstrous betrayal? So I didn't read the others. No point in that, except to make me madder.

Still, I had kept them with me. I had left them in my dresser drawer at Windermere when I left so sudden to rescue Anson from the high seas, and I did presume Mrs. Marshall—or, more likely, one of her lackeys in a starched blue uniform—packed it all up inside the trunk of me and Patsy's things that was conveyed to Anson's Packard on the occasion of his father's funeral. Trunk which got burnt to a crisp not three months later. And though I scorned those letters while I had them, when I knew they was destroyed—the only thing I possessed that belonged to my daddy, God rot him, the only remaining trace of him except that which runs in my blood—I wished them back, the way I might wish back my own arm that had been severed.

The way I wished back Anson when he left me.

But now it seems I was mistaken. The packet of my daddy's letters to my mama did not wind up in the bottom of that poor burnt trunk, after all. Wound up instead in Mrs. Marshall's pocketbook, from which she does offer it to me now as a token of peace, I believe.

As I reach out my hand to pluck this packet from her white kid glove, my gaze happens to fall upon hers. Must be because she lays it on me so thick. She's got a large pair of peepers, all right, dark blue in color like Anson's, the kind you can't easily tear away from.

"Why, thank you kindly," I tell her. "Nice of you to drive all the way into Manhattan for little old me."

"Marie found them," she says toneless. "She was hunting around your old room and found them wedged behind the dresser. I don't know how they got there. The maids should have discovered them before. Anyway, there they are."

"Here they are."

She snaps her pocketbook shut and slings it back over her sunset-colored arm. Fidgets with her gloves, as if to straighten them, when I can see plain those gloves are so straight as leather can be.

"So you're with child," she says.

"So you've noticed."

"Is it his?"

My first impulse is to slap her face. But that would be unchristian, I guess, and anyway she does have some small grain of justice to her cause. What I let Bronstein do to me last night, not six months since my beloved left me. Not two months since he was killed. What kind of harlot am I, to allow a man to tease me to pleasure while I grow another man's child in my belly?

A man I must furthermore love until I die, howsoever cruel he departed from me.

So I just say, nice and even, "Of course it's Anson's child. Due in a few short weeks."

"Did he know?"

"I'm afraid not. Only just discovered myself on the same exact day he—he perished."

She takes a moment to gather herself, for she's only human. "After it's born, will you allow me to visit?"

"Why, I have my faults, I guess, but I am not so unnatural as to keep a granny from her only grandchild." I smile guileless, to hide the relish with which I speak the word *granny* to the stately Mrs. Marshall.

Then she looks over my shoulder and up at the ceiling, and she says something I never could imagine, so long as I lived, which just goes to show you about people.

"I don't deserve it. I have behaved unforgivably."

I run my thumb along the edge of the packet of letters in my hand.

"I guess we all behave wicked from time to time. Not one of us has never hurt another human being, whether by fault or by inattention."

"He went to his death thinking his mother despised him."

"And I might could hate you for that, some days."

"You could not possibly hate me more than I've hated myself."

"Oh, I don't know about *that.*"

We stare at each other.

"How's Marie?" I ask. "Patsy still asks about her."

"She's as well as can be expected, for a child who has lost so much."

"Same with Patsy."

"But Patsy has *you.* Marie has only Billy and me, and neither of us is fashioned to give her what she needs, I'm afraid."

"Which is?"

"Love. The ability to give and receive it, which I have lost, along with everything else I've loved."

"Seems to me all the more reason to love what you've got left."

"Yes, I'm sure that's how it seems to you. How simple, how wonderfully easy. Just *love* someone."

I crack out a dry little laugh. "I guess we're all messed up in the head, more or less. Judging each other for the sins we ourselves commit. Tormenting ourselves for the good we don't do."

"It's enough to make one envy the dead, isn't it?"

Upstairs, some child's voice pipes some question to Ruth Mary. She answers it muffled through the floorboards. Between me and Mrs. Marshall there be nothing but quiet. Few motes of dust glittering in a shaft of sun. Smell of home.

"I want you to know he was happy," I tell her. "Those weeks we spent up north. I did my best to make him happy. And I think he knew you'd come around, in his heart."

"A drunken brawl at a police station. I don't understand. It's just not like him."

What can I tell her? Too lengthy a tale for two women standing in a parlor, claws bared discreet. Maybe one day we'll sit down somewhere comfortable, clear the air. I can explain to her that while I will always remain mad as hell at her son for what he done, leaving me and Patsy when he promised never to leave again, I might yet consider him what we might have called a hero, in a previous age.

She continues. "For the longest time, I thought it was all a mistake. I thought they had the wrong man. That's why I didn't go to the funeral. I didn't believe it was true. I thought it simply *couldn't* be true, not Ollie. Why, just last week I imagined I saw him walking down Fifth Avenue. I saw the back of his head. I was so *sure* of it. A mother's instinct. I ran after him—pushed my way through the crowd, called his name. But of course it came to nothing. He's gone, isn't he?" She turns up those last words just a hint, like a question. Like she's pleading for something, and maybe it's the real reason she came, after all.

I speak firmly. "He's gone, Mrs. Marshall. Tucked safe in the bosom of the Lord Almighty. Maybe we'll find him there one day, if we mend our wicked ways."

"What a nice thought," she says. "You'll excuse me. I must be going. I've stayed far beyond my intention."

I follow her out of the parlor and into the hallway. "I'll send to tell you when the baby is properly born."

Mrs. Marshall lifts her brown velvet cape from the hook. "Why are you being so kind to me? You shouldn't. I bite, remember?"

"Because my child needs to know where he came from."

She tilts her sleek head to one side, and that's when I see the tears that brim in her eyes, because they catch the light from the window above the front door. "You'll prove a far better mother than I've been, I suspect. Rather irksome, for I don't like you at all, Geneva. Still, I'm grateful."

I reach around her and open the door. "Good-bye, Mrs. Marshall."

As she steps across the threshold, I notice her car has disappeared, and another one crawls down the street outside. I don't think anything of it, nor do I notice what kind of car it is, other than the color—black. Which I guess I will regret later, because the instant I close the door behind her, the quick familiar staccato thud of a Thompson submachine gun strikes my ears. I fall to the floor and scream for help. The sound lasts only ten or fifteen seconds—a lifetime—and the strange car zooms off noisy. Rash I spring to my feet and throw open the door, and Mrs. Marshall's body falls on my shoes. Sunset orange splattered with red. On her face, a smile of relief.

19

NIGHTFALL. WE sit pretending to eat a room service supper in a suite of rooms at some hotel uptown. The Algonquin, I think. Yes, the Algonquin. I just checked the stationery. Bronstein settled us here a few hours ago and rushed off again. Mad as a hornet he be, though he don't show it on his face. Seems he takes it personal, this murderous attack right on his own brick walls.

Well, I'm not the kind of girl to say *I told you so,* but he *was* the one who assured me nobody would dare. You heard him say it.

I don't wish to relive that scene in my whole life. Me pressing my bare palms against the holes in that sunset dress to staunch Mrs. Marshall's blood. Hollering for Ruth Mary to call the police, call an ambulance. At some point my mother-in-law's eyes flickered open, surprised and kind of disappointed to discover she wasn't dead yet. I told her help was on the way. Her lips moved but she couldn't speak, so I don't know what her last words might have been. Bronstein came bounding out the front steps next door, half dressed. Took half a second to gather it all in, then told me to get the hell indoors, please. Gathered up Mrs. Marshall in his own thick arms and carried her into the hallway. Tore off his shirt and told me to plug up the holes as best I could. Then bounded away to make his own telephone calls, do what needed to be done, I don't know. The police arrived, then the ambulance. The medics listened to her chest and said they were sorry, she was unfortunately dead already, nothing they could do, but they took her away anyhow. Police stayed quite some time, measuring the bullet holes on the wall and examining the tire tracks in the street, that kind of pointless thing. Crowd gathered, naturally. Then the newspapers arrived. Bronstein told them to get lost, but those reporters are like mosquitoes, you know. You can bat them away but they keep coming back. That's their job. Anyhow I stayed indoors through most of that. Ruth Mary took care of the children while I spoke to the police officers. Bronstein sat next to me the whole time like some kind of bodyguard. When they asked him if he was my husband, he said no, he was my neighbor. They looked at each other. Maybe a bell dinged, I don't know, because they finished up with me quick and went into the study, doors closed, to confer with Bronstein. After that—

They Lord. Rattling on, ain't I? You don't need to know any of that, and I surely don't want to recollect it. I want to eat this room service chicken that tastes like rope and dunk the children in their baths and their pajamas. We haven't told them much. Don't want to scare them. They think this is some kind of holiday. Anyhow once they're tucked in safe I might drink a glass of that excellent Scotch whiskey Bronstein left behind thoughtful, while I wait for Bronstein himself to return and ask what I need from him.

That's all I want on this earth.

20

NOT UNTIL midnight does Bronstein rattle the key in the doorknob and walk in. Ruth Mary and the kids are fast asleep in the other rooms, while I lie stunned on the bed in my dressing gown. He takes off his coat and shoes and pours himself a drink.

"Well, it's over," he says.

"What's over?"

"It's over, that's all."

I sit up against the pillow. "Did you *kill* somebody?"

Bronstein sets down the glass and turns to me. Face so grim and hard as a wall of granite. He folds his arms across his barrel chest and stares down at me on the hotel bed.

"What's the matter?" I whisper. "Was it something I did? I swan, I never figured that car would have—"

"You didn't do a thing wrong, Gin. Not a thing." He uncrosses his arms and sits on the edge of the bed. Now I see him close, he don't look so hard as I thought. Pained, almost, like some thin, deep crack opened up clear across the granite. And his eyes. Soft as caramel. He picks up my hand. "Listen. I want you to listen and not interrupt for once. All right?"

"All right," I reply, meek.

"That first second you walked through the door of my joint, three years ago, I knew you were the only girl for me. Girl I'd been waiting for all my life. But I could tell you were young and hurt. I figured you had some growing up to do first. So I stood back and kept my eye on you, on the chance you might come around one fine day. Made sure you were taken care of. Watched you fall in and out of love. Watched that lucky bastard Marshall sweep you off and figured I waited too long. Figured I was going to die alone, that was all. Still I waited. You never know, right? Meantime I saved up every dime I didn't need for food and shelter, just on the chance. And then Marshall was an idiot. And you came around. One fine day."

"Oh, Bronstein."

"I said shut up, all right? I need to finish. Now, I'm not fooling myself. I know what you feel and what you don't feel. But what happened this morning—well, I can't keep on waiting. This joint of mine is no place for you and the kids. I can't sit back one minute longer and wait around for you to feel about me the way I want you to feel. You might be dead by then. So now I lay my cards on the table, all right? Here they are. I've saved up close to two million dollars since I opened up my joint—"

"Two *million?*" I can't help but gasp.

"I said shut up. It's a cash business, that's why I'm in it, and I made a lot of dough and I put it all in United States government bonds. Two million in bearer bonds, and it's all yours, the day you marry me. I'm selling up, you understand? Maybe sooner than I thought, but I'm selling up, every last bottle, and when it's all sold up I figure to skip town for good and take you with me, you and Patsy, and look after you all your days. That's what I want. When that baby comes into this world, I want to hold it in my hands and call it my own. Maybe have some more kids with you, if you'll let me. That's all I want. Little girl with red hair like yours. Spoil her rotten. You can have anything you've ever wanted. I'll give you anything you ask for, the rest of your life. Everything I got belongs to you, understand? Honest to God. That's my deal."

I study the fear in his eyes. His fingers press hard on the skin of my knuckles, like to stop himself from shaking.

"That's it? I can talk now?"

"Go ahead."

"Just to be clear. Are you saying you want me to marry you, or else we're quits?"

"That's what I'm saying."

"This is a bad time, Bronstein. Long day. Can't think straight."

"That's why I'm asking you now."

"What about Ruth Mary? I can't just up and leave her and the kids."

"Then don't. Bring them along. One big happy family."

I look down at his wide, flat hand around mine.

"Gin, think about *this*. That baby of yours. Your sister, too. They need a father. The three of you, you need a man who sticks around. Worships nothing but his wife and children. Fights for nothing but you. I'm not asking you to love me back. Not trying to take his place. Just let me care for you, that's all."

Something drips from my eyes and splashes onto his hand, holding mine.

"Where do you want to live, Gin? Could be anywhere. The French Riviera, you name it. Mexico. Some island in the South Pacific. Build you a mansion and fill it with servants. You won't have to lift a finger, so long as you live."

"I have never wanted riches, Bronstein. Never in my life. Just enough to get by. I seen how the lust for money is what turns men into monsters."

"Then what do you want? Name it."

But I can't do that, can I? Cannot tell him the only thing in the world I want back. Would hurt his feelings, which I didn't even know he possessed until this minute. Thought he had none to speak of, which was perfectly fine with me.

Still, I have not myself alone to consider. There be Patsy. There be Ruth Mary Leary and her five innocent kids, dragged bang into the middle of this through my stupid fault. There be the child in my belly, who has lost his daddy and needs someone to rear him up responsible, safe from hurt. And I can't think straight, maybe, but I do know Bronstein is telling me the truth. Stone faithful, that Bronstein. He will provide for us all. He will take us somewhere and keep us safe from hurt, if anybody can. Take some of this dreadful burden from my shoulders, to care for my people. In my head I see that dress of sunset orange, decorated with warm scarlet blood that ought to have been mine, by rights. Mine and my baby's.

With his other hand, Bronstein fishes in his pocket and draws something out. Slides it on my finger. They Lord, must be four or five carats, single round solitary diamond on a plain gold band. Gruff as a billy goat, he says, "If you like it, you can keep it."

I wiggle that object around and Lord Almighty, I believe it winks right back at me. A perfect fit, but then of course it would be. Nothing careless about Bronstein. Three long years he has planned this, apparently.

"All right," I whisper. "I'll keep it."

21

FIVE DAYS later. Ruth Mary and I box up the contents of the house. The weather be unseasonable warm this week, March going out like a lamb, and my blouse sticks to my back. Due to wed Joseph Bronstein in two days' time and climb on board the RMS *Majestic* with all our worldly possessions crammed inside a brand-new matched set of five steamer trunks my fiancé presented to me yesterday as an engagement gift, and the truth is I don't rightly know if we're going to make it in time.

Ruth Mary lifts a wet bang from her brow and sits back on her haunches. Face all pink. Between you and me, I don't know if she's altogether best pleased about the upcoming nuptials, though Bronstein did book a pair of first-class staterooms for her and the kids. Naturally she has expressed gratitude and wonder about visiting the great sights of Europe, a turn of events she never dreamt of, her whole life. But the thing is, Bronstein has turned over his joint to Bruno—lock, stock, and bottle—and Bruno, at least so far as I know, has not mentioned any need nor desire for a consort to help him run the place.

And time be running out fast. Bronstein seems in a terrific hurry to get married and skip town, thinks he's got to seal the deal before I think twice and back out.

Why, just this morning over breakfast he was rattling on about Europe, the route he was planning for us, London and then Switzerland or something. Vienna by May, because they have the best doctors, apparently. Wasn't paying that much attention, to say the truth, but the children hung on his every word. Li'l Eddie pored over the map brochure and followed the railroad lines with his finger. We sat in the parlor of my suite, eating room service from silver domed platters. We still spend our nights at the Algonquin, because I don't care for me and the children to sleep in the same house where the eternal soul of my mother-in-law did slip its mortal bonds. To say the truth, this building unsettles me. Something out of balance ever since those ten or fifteen seconds that shut closed the book of life for Theresa Marshall. But the Algonquin ain't home, neither. Only thing familiar at that breakfast table was Bronstein's eyes seeking out mine. Eyes I have known since I first came to New York, three years before. Long before I met Anson, after all.

I reached across the eggs and toast and crisp salt bacon—the newspapers carefully folded with the screaming headlines, "No Leads Yet in Shocking Society Murder, Detectives Say"—and touched his fingers. Diamond just about blinded me.

Vienna, why not, I told him.

Now Ruth Mary gazes around the parlor, all boxed up, and says looks like we be finished here, anyhow. Time to start upstairs.

22

NOW I pack up Patsy's room. Room is a small one, all right. This was never a fancy boardinghouse, which is why I was but a boarder there in my salad days. Afternoon sunshine casts a warm spring glow on the walls. In the corner, Patsy's bed be stripped of sheets and blankets. Chest of drawers empty and wiped clean. Rug rolled up and set against the wall. Not a sign remains of all the life lived here. Just these bare floorboards on which I sit Indian style, trying not to remember how Anson once held me sobbing against his chest, right by that window through which the sunlight pours.

Inside me, the baby turns over restless. How I despised this creature at first. I can admit this now. I was terrible sick, for one thing, could scarce keep a morsel down. Even Ruth Mary knitted her brow and said she never knew a woman to take so bad. Made me to sip water bit by bit, so I wouldn't dry out. In those dark weeks, every day the sun setting earlier and earlier and rising up later and later, wind growing colder, I think I hated this troublesome kernel of humanity so much as I hated its daddy.

Then there came this thing called quickening.

When you lie in your bed alone in the dark of night, the dead of winter, tears running down the corners of your eyes and into the sheets beneath, and you are so goddamn lonely you want to die, you pray to God to take you soundless in your sleep, Ruth Mary will take care of Patsy, Ruth Mary's a better mama than you'll ever be, no joy left in the world for you, nobody and nothing to comfort you again, and right that moment, when you've sunk so low as ever in your life, this butterfly flutters by your belly button. First you think it's gas. Them baked beans at supper, maybe. Then the butterfly flutters again, brushes its tender wings against you, and you begin to understand this kernel's come alive, *alive,* and belongs to you. Belongs to the man you loved like the air you breathed. The man you couldn't do without, until you had to. Now this butterfly's here instead, all that's left of him, waving its wings against your womb. And maybe it's a sign he's not lost to you, after all. Maybe he'll find his way back to you, come the spring. Maybe that butterfly means hope.

Well, so much for hope.

But still you learned to love that butterfly, even as it grew and transmogrified into a circus acrobat, turning awkward somersaults into your solar plexus. You would do anything to keep it safe and well, even marry a man you don't happen to be in love with. Didn't my mama do the same for me? And Joseph Bronstein's the prince of the world, compared to Duke Kelly.

Surely I will learn to love him as he deserves. Surely I have chosen well.

Still I can't shake that unsettled feeling, like something's watching me, some haint that is not Mrs. Marshall but something else. Something woke by her, maybe. And as soon as the thought of my mama drifts across my head, my gaze drops to the particular wide wooden board directly in front of me. I don't know why. Like the others, it's polished new, made fine again by the man who bestowed it on me. Except that it seems to me to stick up a little above its neighbors. Just a fraction of an inch, mind. No more than that.

I reach out to run my thumb along that edge of floorboard. When my skin makes contact with wood, a familiar buzz jolts up my nerves like electricity.

My hand snaps back. My heart thumps.

Oh no you don't, I think. Don't you do this to me. Not now, just when I'm leaving this land of sorrow behind me forevermore.

Yet I cannot stop my hand from reaching back. God help me. I cannot help fingering the edge of that floorboard, to discover the curious fact that it ain't nailed down like its neighbors, but laid in place. Buzzing passes gentle through the fibers of wood, more to soothe than to pain me. I dig my fingers down the edges and pry them upward. Board pops out with a noise that sounds like a woman's faint cry. Buzzing quits altogether. I rise on my knees and put my hand into the space underneath, where it finds a piece of smooth polished wood, the lid of a box that once sat on my mama's own drawer chest, and now belongs to me.

23

I ALREADY KNOW what this box contains. Did I not open it last year when my mama died, and sift through the contents? Buttons, nothing but buttons. The kind of buttons a man might wear on his coat or his jacket, and what is more, these be quality buttons, not the kind you find lying unattended upon the streets and sidewalks—such as they are—of River Junction, Maryland. Handmade buttons, expensive buttons, fashioned from ivory and polished bone and mother-of-pearl and shining brass. Goes without saying, I have always reckoned they once belonged to my daddy. Can't you just see it? Every time he visits her, he leaves behind one of his buttons for a keepsake. Wouldn't be the first gentleman to think himself so clever, I imagine. How I did hate those buttons once, and still I could never just bring myself to throw them out with the refuse.

Funny, though, that this box should have been tucked beneath a floorboard in this particular room. Wasn't me who left it there, I assure you. When I departed this room a year ago, I departed it hasty, to say the least. No time to pack my things. Didn't realize I was gone for good. Afterward, if I thought about this box at all, I just presumed it was thrown out with the rest of my things, which I never saw again. Not hid safe in the floor, for to discover all over again. And now I lift that box free, the exact same as it was before, beautifully painted in climbing vines upon a shiny black lacquer, and I come to realize I don't hate those buttons anymore, if I ever did. I feel something else, something else that charges up my heart until it overfills, and that thing is pity. We are but human, after all, made of base clay, and does not the Good Book remind us how man is inclined to evil as the sparks fly upward? We cannot help but to stumble and fall. We cannot help but to hurt each other, by fault and by accident, all the days of our lives, and the charge laid upon us is to forgive one another as we ourselves hope to be forgiven. There is no other way.

So I lift the lid of that box and take out each button, one by one. Did my mama snip them from his sleeve with her sewing scissors, maybe? Did he do it for her, just leave it behind on the pillow while she was still sleeping? Did he love her for a little while, maybe? Does it matter whether he did? He must have felt *something*, or he would not have looked after me as he has. My education. This house. Who knows what else, that I never knew.

I don't know just how long I sit there, sorting those buttons. The sunlight fades and vanishes. Ruth Mary's voice calls up the stairway. Near six o'clock, Geneva Rose. Time to collect the kids for their supper.

Kids. Supper. The children have been playing next door all this time, under the careless supervision of Bruno and Bronstein and mostly each other, probably, while the two men haggle over the complicated details of running one of New York City's most popular speakeasies. If the poor mites still be alive, by the grace of God, they will need whisking uptown immediate for a room service supper at the Algonquin. Time to set aside whimsy and address the practical matters of life.

Quickly I pile the buttons back in the box, and as the last one goes in, some detail catches my eye. I pinch the edges between finger and thumb and hold it to what dusky light remains through the window.

A beautiful round brass button, like a coin, embossed with the head of a tiger.

24

I DISCOVER RUTH Mary in the kitchen, checking the cupboards one last time for anything left behind accidental. "Ruth Mary," I ask her, casual-like, "when you was packing up that parlor, you didn't happen to catch sight of a packet of letters, did you?"

"Why, no. I surely didn't. What kind-a letters you mean?"

"Just some old letters. Can't remember where I left them. You sure you didn't pack them?"

"I guess I might have, without knowing. But I don't recollect seeing any. I'm sorry, Geneva Rose. Was they important?"

She looks up at me harassed. Petey fusses on her hip, scrabbles at the buttons of her blouse. Sometimes when I catch sight of a certain look on his round, red face, I see the look of my step-daddy so plain I have to stop myself from recoiling away. I wonder did Ruth Mary take him willing, or did he force her. Or maybe when a man like Duke Kelly prowled to your bed, him bulging dollar bills and power and you a widow with four little mouths to feed, why, you didn't think to say yea or nay, you just lay back and gave him what he come for. But none of that is poor Petey's fault, is it? We can't help who sired us. I caress his silky head and say to Ruth Mary, "Don't you worry, it'll turn up, I'm sure. Always does."

25

BRONSTEIN HAS been so good as to secure us several rooms in that hotel, so there be plenty of space for everybody—two bedrooms for the kids to share, a small bedroom for Ruth Mary that has a door to one of the kids' rooms, and a large, luxurious parlor and bedroom for me that connects to the other bedroom, where Patsy and Laura Ann curl up in their flowing white nightgowns like angels. Like two sisters they be, near inseparable. Meanwhile Bronstein himself keeps but a small bachelor bedroom across the hall, for he spends most of his time on Christopher Street—tying up all the loose ends, he says. So when the children have gone to sleep and Ruth Mary retires grateful for some peace and quiet, leaves me nothing to do but pace the handsome burgundy carpet in my parlor and consider where on earth I have left that packet of letters Mrs. Marshall gave me, in the minutes before she was shot to pieces.

I figure I must have dropped it, don't you think? When she fell back dying in my arms from the doorway, bleeding like a pig at butchering time, I surely dropped that thing in my hand, without even noticing what I done.

But if I had dropped that packet on the rug in the entryway, where was it now? Never saw it lying there, when me and Ruth Mary cleaned up afterward. Maybe one of them police detectives picked it up for evidence? But I do imagine he must've had to said something to me about it, on account of it being my property. If it was kicked under the sofa or something, Ruth Mary would've found it when she packed up the parlor, because she moved around the furniture for that reason. And every stick of everything has been sorted through by now, packed or given away or spoken for.

Did I brung it with me to the hotel somehow? Slipped it inside the pocket of my skirt without realizing what I done? But I have worn that skirt since and never found a thing in the pockets.

Still I search the parlor, the desk drawers and the cabinet and so on, just on the chance. Maybe some hotel maid discovered it and put it away. Maybe some hotel maid discovered it and kept it for herself, come to that, though I can't imagine why. No money inside, nothing valuable to anyone save myself.

When I have scoured the parlor, I move to the bedroom. Chest of drawers, bedside table. Check the pocket of that skirt in the wardrobe, just in case. Empty. I sit on the bed and stare at the window, cracked open because it's been so warm these past days of untoward sun. Now the breeze grows chill again. Tang of winter still. In your bones you feel the weather change, currents of air shifting and roiling outside.

I rise, not to close the window but to open it more—to allow that good fresh air to disturb the still warmth in my bedroom. I yank up the sash and stick my head out into Manhattan. This dear, wicked city that did shelter me in my sorrows. The air runs colder than I thought, the wind pulling strong from the north. Seems I might have to wear my coat tomorrow.

My coat.

I turn back to the wardrobe, where my coat has hung unworn for the past five days, on account of the warm air blowing up from the south the day after Mrs. Marshall was killed. Of course, I know for a fact I never put the letters in the pocket of my coat. Why should I? Mrs. Marshall had been dead for hours before Bronstein helped my numb arms into that garment and loaded us into a taxi uptown for the Algonquin Hotel.

Nevertheless, I make my way around the corner of the wide hotel bed and open the door of the wardrobe to contemplate my coat on its hanger. Just an ordinary coat of dark wool, not quite black but not brown, neither. Bronstein talks with pleasure about acquiring me a whole new wardrobe in Paris, take over some suite at the Hotel Ritz or someplace and order those fashion houses to adorn his bride in the finest feathers money can buy. I guess this old coat will have to go in that case. Still, it's seen me through many a shabby New York winter. I shall surely be sorry to see it given away. I ease my hand into the left side pocket and draw it out again, packet of letters snug between my fingers as I knew it would be.

I read them all one by one, weeping as I go, and when I'm done I fold them back together and tie the ribbon and tuck the whole packet back in the pocket of my coat, which I slide over my shoulders. I check on the children in their bedrooms, sleeping sound, and slip out the door, down the elevator, and into the windy Manhattan street.

26

WHEN I return to my rooms an hour later, the first thing I notice is Bronstein. Hard to miss him, standing there in the middle of the parlor, bristling with worry though his face wears no particular expression.

"Where have you been?" he asks, nice and reasonable.

I shut the door and pull off my gloves. "Went to see a friend."

He steps forward and helps me with my coat. Lays it over a chair. "Anyone in particular?"

"He wasn't home."

"That's not what I asked."

"Say, you're not jealous, are you?"

"If I was jealous, Gin, I'd have had a man out following you, wouldn't I? I would already know the answer."

"Well, do you?"

He runs a swift hand through his hair. "Listen. For three years I watched you step out of my joint, arm in arm with some fellow or another. Feeling the exact same way about you then as I feel now. Like a punch to the gut, each time. Did I once step in? Then when Marshall came in the picture, did I try to get in the way of that? You were happy. Who was I to think I could've made you happier? Honest to God, the only time in my life I have ever felt jealous of another man was this winter when I watched his child growing in you, and him upstate somewhere, and you near dead with grief. Thought I might kill him if he was in the room with me. The only time. So if you think you might be in love with some other man, tell me now. We'll call it off. I'll give you away at the wedding, I swear I would."

For a moment, I'm too stunned to speak. Then: "You're sure about that?"

He frowns at me and walks to the cabinet. A bottle sits on top, half-empty, and a glass next to it. I think how I never used to see him drink a drop, figured he was teetotal himself—you'd be surprised how many teetotal bartenders and bootleggers inhabit this peculiar country of ours—but it turned out he's got a whole nother side to him, outside of his joint. Next to the bottle and the glass sits a plain wooden box, polished high. He picks it up and hands it to me. Says to open it. I sit down on the sofa and open the lid. Inside there lies a king's ransom of jewels, mostly diamonds but some colored stones, too, all worked into necklaces and bracelets jumbled together careless, some fat bright rings and earrings in a felt compartment, so many enormous dazzling gems you would think they must surely be paste, though I know right well they aren't. I just know.

"You can keep that, if you want," Bronstein says. "Even if you walk out that door and leave me, you can take that with you, no hard feelings. Been saving them up for you for years, on the chance."

I set down the box and pat the cushion next to me. He sits stiff. I reach out and take his hand. "I have but one virtue, Bronstein, and that is I don't break my word. I said I would marry you at ten o'clock tomorrow morning, and at ten thirty I swear to God I will be your wedded wife. Better or worse."

Bronstein don't move. Jaw locked tight.

"This man I went to visit, it wasn't that kind of visit. It's something else. I'll tell you later, once I speak to him. I'll tell you the whole story, all right? I just don't know exactly what the story is yet."

"You don't need to tell me. Don't owe me anything."

"Are you kidding? I owe you everything. You're a prince, Bronstein. A prince. Do you even understand what a prince you are?" I rise to my feet and hold out my hand. "Come to bed."

He stares amazed at my hand, at my face, at my hand again. Shakes his head. "No."

"Why not?"

"It's bad luck, doing it right before the wedding."

"Who says?"

"Everyone says."

"Well, it so happens I don't believe in luck."

"Then what the hell do you believe in?"

"I'll show you if you let me."

He stands. Honest to God, I don't know what he means to do. I am

not what I was, after all. Dumpy and gravid, swollen in every joint.
Worn old dress. Why, the Gin Kelly of old has all but disappeared
inside, leaving nothing behind but a thatch of flame on top of her
head. He is my exact height, so we meet eye to eye. Belly protrudes
between us. I guess I have called his bluff and he'll walk away now,
but instead he takes my hand firm and leads me to the bedroom like
a bridegroom. Steals away the next morning but half an hour before
Patsy toddles in, trailing her blanket, to say there is a bellman at the
door who insists he has an urgent message he must deliver directly
into the hands of Mrs. Oliver Marshall, from her father.

27

BY NINE o'clock the trunks be packed full and the bellman called
to transport them to the west side of town, where the magnificent *Majestic* reclines against Pier 50 and loads in coal and provisions
for her journey across the Atlantic. Bronstein keeps hold of our tick-
ets and passports. He sent word with breakfast how he's terrified of
bad luck, what with fate sore tempted and all, and so long as I am
feeling well (double underline his) he will meet me at the registry office for the ceremony at a quarter to ten, while Ruth Mary wrangles
the children to the docks.

I scribble back a reply that I happen to feel exceptionally well this
morning, thank you, though I might require to nap later that afternoon, once our ship is underway, and send Patsy to carry it to him,
for she does love to play messenger between us.

When she returns, she carries a leather portfolio, of the kind in
which you keep your important documents. Hands it to me solemn

where I sit at the room service breakfast table and says it be from Bronstein, with his compliments. I untie the leather strings and look inside to find a thick stack of United States government bonds in ten-thousand-dollar certificates. I don't bother to count them. Just close up the portfolio and tie the strings snug.

Then I notice Patsy. She stands still nearby, staring at all the trunks stacked by the corner for the bellman to take down. Her pretty face hangs forlorn. I ask her what's the matter and she comes up to me in my chair and leans into my shoulder.

"Ginny, how will Anson find us in Europe?"

Ruth Mary's head shoots up. Her eyes reproach me. She did tell me I should break the news to Patsy, after all. Should tell my sister that her beloved Anson has not just gone away on a business trip but is gone forevermore, and now Bronstein will be her daddy and love and raise her. But how could I tell Patsy a thing like that? Already she has lost so much. All last autumn and winter I guarded her careful from the mock funeral, from any whisper of Anson's so-called demise, because in my deepest heart I always figured he would come back home. Now I know I was wrong. Her adored Anson never will return to her. These past weeks, I knew I should take her aside and say the awful truth, explain what's really happened. But every time I gathered myself to do it, I lost heart. How do I hand yet another terrible measure of grief to her, when she has had to grieve her mama and papa and brother, too? For now, Patsy believes Bronstein is our friend who's taking us on a vacation across the ocean. She don't know about the errand to City Hall this morning, nor what will come of it. I figure I will find some moment in Paris or Vienna, some sunny morning before the baby is born, to explain why I wear a new ring on my finger, on top of the one Anson gave me, which I swore never to take off and never shall.

Ruth Mary looks away. I cuddle Patsy close and tell her that wherever Anson be, he's happy and well, and his heart will always journey with us, wherever we go.

At half past nine I finish the last of my coffee, gather my pocketbook and my small valise that contains that leather portfolio and the jewelry, for I don't quite trust that kind of thing to the tender care of bellboys and cabbies. Then I take the elevator downstairs to catch a taxi to City Hall, for the second time in a single year.

The morning rush has already died, and the drive downtown takes no time at all. Bronstein stands waiting by the curb in a black funeral suit that strains across his shoulders. Hustles me upstairs to some judge's chambers where we repeat the necessary statements in front of some witnesses I've never seen in my life. I walk out ten minutes later as Mrs. Joseph Bronstein, though I confess I don't feel a bit different.

28

NOW COMES the hard part.

"Bronstein," I say, turning to face him, holding his hand nice and snug, "I have an errand to run, I'm afraid. You go on ahead and meet the children at the ship."

The light dies in his eyes. "What kind of errand?"

"That fellow from yesterday. He's waiting for me at a coffee shop nearby. I have to see him before I leave town for good."

With his thumb and forefinger Bronstein grasps the three rings snug on the fourth finger of my left hand, the plain slender band Anson once put there and the enormous diamond engagement ring and the brand-new wedding band encrusted with tiny diamonds. He wiggles them gentle, so as to ensure himself they rest exactly where he put them. Looks at me opaque and unblinking.

"All right," he says. He leans forward and kisses me, then turns to hail me a taxi.

"Don't trouble yourself," I tell him. "I'll just walk. It's only a little ways."

29

WHEN I walk through the door of the De-Lite Coffee Shop on Reade Street, Charles Schuyler stands up immediate, because he's a gentleman, don't you know. He pulls out a chair for me and motions for the waitress to bring me coffee. I don't tell him I've already drunk four cups this morning. I figure I need all the coffee I can get.

Schuyler looks down at the rings glittering like bejesus on my finger and offers his bewildered congratulations.

"Thank you. I guess you can say it's been a whirlwind."

"But he's a good man? He'll take care of you and the children?"

"Of course he is. He's a prince. Taking us all to Europe in just a few hours. First class on the *Majestic*. Leave all this misery behind us and start again."

"You'll miss the funeral, then."

"I wasn't invited, I'm afraid. In fact, Billy took the trouble to wrote me himself, just to disinvite me proper."

"I'm sorry to hear that. Billy's a decent boy. I'm sure it was just the shock—"

I wave away his concern. "I don't care much for funerals, to be honest. Seems to me a lot of crocodile tears and morbid curiosity.

Much ruther do my mourning in private. Anyhow, I guess I won't be missed. Biggest society funeral since—well, since we buried her husband last year."

"It's a terrible loss. She was a pillar, a giant. I still can't quite believe it."

"Oh, you can believe it, all right. Held her in my arms while the life passed right out of her."

"Geneva," he says softly.

The waitress arrives with my coffee. My fingers shake as I add the sugar. Left hand can't get used to this unnatural weight. I ask Schuyler if he minds do I smoke. He says not at all. When my fingers fumble with the pocketbook and the cigarette case, he takes away the cigarette and lights me up.

"There we are," he says, handing it back.

"Thank you."

"I'm the one who should be nervous, you know. I'm the one who's asking for forgiveness."

I sip the coffee and blow out a little anxious smoke. "My mama left me the letters you sent her, when you was courting. I read them last night."

For a second or two, he seems to lose breath. "She kept them?"

"In her drawer chest. Then she gave them to her best friend for safekeeping. They came to me after she died."

He turns his head swift and looks out the window. My wedding day dawned chill and gray, alas. Wind blows heartless over the store awnings to whipsaw the New Yorkers scrambling past. "I want you to know how much I loved your mother," he says.

"But not enough, right? Not enough to keep her with you when the time came to make good. When she needed you most."

"I didn't give her up, Geneva. She gave *me* up. She left me."

"Left *you?* Go tell it to the Marines. Leave you for a life of misery and want as the footstool of Duke Kelly? With a little helpless baby that was yours?"

He turns back his head. Blue eyes glimmer in the overbright electric light. Skin worn and pallid. "We were living in a little apartment off West Fourth. It was all I could afford. I'd quit college, my father had cut me off. I begged her to marry me, but she wouldn't do it. She didn't want to trap me, she said. I was only nineteen. Then you were born. I thought I might burst with happiness." He stops to draw a starched white handkerchief from his pocket, which he hands to me. "After about a year, my father paid her a visit, while I was out working. I had taken a job as a runner at one of the stockbrokers, to support the two of you. When I came back she was gone, and you, too. Father told me he had paid her ten thousand dollars to leave me."

"Ten thousand dollars? Baloney. Mama wouldn't have taken a dime. Anyhow, where *was* all that money, if she took it?"

"Well, I was young and hurt. I believed him. For a while I thought I hated her. And then he died. That was when you were about seven. On his deathbed he confessed to me that she hadn't taken his money, after all. She refused him, no matter how much he offered. So he tried another tack. Her conscience, Geneva. She always did have the softest heart in the world. He told her I was too young. I had already left Harvard. I had ruined myself, and what was more, he said, I had ruined the family. The scandal had brought shame upon my parents and especially my sisters. My innocent sister Julie, he said to her, was tainted by disgrace."

"Well, *that's* rich. Julie *innocent*—" I clap my hand over my mouth. "*They Lord.*"

He smiles a little. "Your aunt."

"Does she *know?*"

"When did my sister Julie *ever* leave a secret undiscovered?"

I spread out my hands, palms down, and stare at the backs of my knuckles. The enormous ring to the left, the stub of cigarette clenched to the right. Brain starts to spin. I might be sick. *What an idiot*, I think. What an idiot you are, Gin Kelly. Right there in front of you.

Schuyler looks up and signals the waitress for more coffee. Not a word, not a sound but the hooting and hollering outside, New York City going about its wicked business, the underwriting of company stock and the seduction of showgirls. Families rising and falling, fortunes gathered and spent. Art created and hung on walls for the delectation of others. People married. Babies born. Blood spilt. Liquor drunk. Ships arrived and departed, dumping additional people into the avenues and alleys, taking a few back away. Waitress pours more coffee and walks away silent, like she understands how something important brews at this small table in the corner, this man with the waving strawberry blond hair and the redheaded, red-eyed floozy smoking the cigarette with her trembling bejeweled fingers.

"He worked on her with all he had," Schuyler says, "all the rhetoric at his command, which was considerable, I assure you. Eventually he wore her down. When I came home from work that evening, she had taken you and disappeared, and all she left of you both was a note and a snapshot."

He reaches into his pocket and removes a small leather wallet. No money inside, just a square of photographic paper he draws out and hands to me. Might be any baby, I think. Gurgling smile, round cheeks. You can't tell the color of its hair, from that faded sepia. On the back, in elegant purpling script, it says *Geneva Rose Schuyler, 8½ mos.*

"By the time my father told me this, of course, she had long since gone back to Maryland and married your stepfather, and I had married Harriet. Still, I tracked her down and wrote to her. She made it clear I was not welcome to interfere. Eventually I convinced her to allow me to arrange for your education, at least. When you arrived in Manhattan after that *disgraceful* incident at Bryn Mawr, she wrote again and begged me to look after you. Unfortunately, my wife discovered the letter in my desk drawer."

"Ah."

"She responded badly, I'm afraid. Threatened to divorce me, and then to kill herself if I were to take you in, or to claim you publicly."

"Well, we couldn't have that, could we."

"I would have done it, Geneva. God knows I wanted to know you, to call you my daughter, as I've never wanted anything in my life. But your mother made me promise. She had this idea you might feel like some kind of poor relation. She wrote that she knew how such a thing ate into the soul, and she didn't want that for you."

"Mama was proud. You wouldn't think it, but she was. That's why she stayed with that bastard so long. Kept on whelping his children, one after another. She was too proud to admit she had made such a terrible mistake. Too afeared, too, for what he might do to her and to me if she tried to go."

He leans forward. "If I'd known, Geneva—"

"You couldn't have known. Anyway, if you had turned up in River Junction, why, Duke would've murdered you sure, then beat hell out of her and me. No, that man burns in eternal purgatory for what he done, and good riddance."

"I wish I had killed him myself."

I stub out the remnants of the cigarette and light another. "He weren't yours to kill."

Seems I have the same trouble lighting my cigarette as before, and Schuyler reaches across the table to take the match from my fingers and do me the service. When he sits back again, his face be terrible grave.

"I have done my best, Geneva, though it seems to me I haven't done nearly enough."

"You gave me plenty. Sent me to school, so I learned how to speak proper, even when I don't see fit to bother. Why, you bought me a whole house, didn't you? Furnished it nice. Stood by me and Anson in Halifax, ungrateful though I was. Gave us a place for our honeymoon."

"But you never knew."

"I knew it was you, all right. I just didn't know *who* you were."

He leans forward earnest. "Forgive me. But I think your mother was wrong to make me promise what I did."

"You think so?"

"My darling girl, you have walked the streets of this city every day and never known what a mantle of love rests on your shoulders. How much I have admired your strength and nerve and beauty. All these years, you should have had a father to love and support you. You should have had a father to give you away this morning. So I hope—I hope you'll allow me the—the very great privilege . . ." At last, his voice cracks. He looks down at his hands. "When you're settled in Europe, perhaps you'll allow me to visit you and—and my grandchild."

Maybe Schuyler was wise to suggest we meet here, in this public place. Whatever I did expect from meeting him, I didn't expect this. Did not expect him to care so much. To be human and not a monster. Did not expect to be rent open and my guts spilt all over the floor, my whole soul wound up too tight to breathe, while the magnificent *Majestic* fires her boilers on the other side of town and waits to take me across the ocean.

"Sure," I tell him.

"My son, too. Your brother."

"Mrs. Schuyler won't be best pleased."

"I don't give a damn."

I look up the instant he looks up. We smile at each other, and that's when I understand I have my own daddy's smile, reflected back upon me, which must have been either a dagger to my mama's heart or her only single comfort. I wonder which.

30

W E SPEAK a little more—careful sentences that don't say nearly enough. Figure when he comes to visit me this summer, we will learn to be more comfortable with each other. At least some of my guts are cleaned off the floor. I can properly breathe. For the first time in my life, I feel my daddy's love like a mantle on my shoulders. The minutes tick. I want to stop them. I want to climb up on that bar counter and hold back the hands on that clock with my two hands, but you cannot ever do such a thing. They will just keep on ticking, whether you hear them or no. This moment will pass, and the next, and I won't ever be able to live them again, sitting here drinking coffee with my daddy for the first time, while his blue eyes gaze naked adoring upon me. Finally I stub out my last cigarette and tell him I'm going to miss the boat if I don't skedaddle.

"Let me give you a ride," he says.

"No, I don't think I could stand it. Saying good-bye in front of everybody."

"Write to me when you arrive safely. Let me know everything

you're doing. Cable me if you have any trouble. I know a few men on the consular staffs in London and Paris, they'll be happy to help."

"I will do that, if I need."

I rise from the chair. He rises, too, and takes my hands. Asks humble if he may kiss me good-bye. I throw my arms around him instead, like we do in River Junction, and I guess the two of us stand like that for a minute or so, not saying anything. Father and daughter. Finally he pulls away, though his hands clutch my shoulders yet.

"I forgot to ask. Which hotel should I write? And which name shall I address you?"

"Oh! The Dorchester, I think. Bronstein made all the arrangements."

He frowns. "Bronstein?"

"Mr. and Mrs. Joseph Bronstein." I look at him mischievous. "That ought to give the home folks an apoplexy, I guess."

"Geneva, I don't give a damn *whom* you've married, so long as he loves you. I just—well, it must be a coincidence, that's all. Bronstein. You know she had a brother by that name. Joseph Bronstein."

Some slight chill invades my bones. Seems I forgot how I thought the name was familiar, when Bronstein told it to me, though I couldn't recollect where I might have heard it. Now I hear the word *Bronstein* again in Schuyler's voice, and the familiarity rushes back. Something he said to me on the high seas, looking for Anson before the ambush closed in. Some person. Another name, not the one I knew her by.

Some terrible truth opens itself upon me. Still I ask, "Who had a brother?"

"Why, Hardcastle's mistress—"

"*Luella?*"

"You must remember. She was the Prohibition agent, the one you thought had betrayed poor Marshall, except it turned out she was betraying—" He snaps his fingers. "Of course, she gave you another name."

I sit back down hard. "Luella Kingston," I whisper.

31

I TELL SCHUYLER I want the whole story, every word. He says I'll miss my boat. I tell him he'd better talk fast, then. Starting with Louis Hardcastle. Now he looks uneasy.

"You knew all along, didn't you?" I said. "You knew who he was."

"There are more lives entangled in this than you know, Geneva. How do you think he operated his business without interference for so long? If I told you who was in his pocket, your hair would curl."

"You should have said something. You should have reported him."

"Yes, I expect I should. God knows I've reproached myself enough. Sylvo Marshall might be alive today. But if I *had* exposed him, I should have exposed others—friends of mine—whose lives would have been ruined. And we are all complicit in this. Aren't we all drinking the liquor supplied by these rackets? You yourself, Geneva."

"But Hardcastle was different. He was ruthless, you know he was."

Schuyler looks away. The adoration has fallen clean off his face, so he looks like what he be—a man who has made mistakes and regrets them, who has not quite lived up to his own ideals. "There are some men, Geneva," he says, picking his words, "who are simply born without what we call a conscience, and he was one of them. I knew it when we were still young, and God knows I kept my distance. But others didn't. He had a way of casting a spell on you, as such men do. He gathered around him a group of boys who did all his bidding, whether they wanted to or not. I saw it with my own eyes. When I heard he was murdered, I was glad someone had the nerve."

"It was Luella. Luella killed him."

"I'm not surprised. She was closest to him. He trusted her, I believe, so much as it was possible for him to trust anyone."

I stare at his haggard face. I tell myself I should just rise from my chair and hail a taxi for the Hudson River docks, climb on board that ship with my prince of a new husband and forget I have ever heard any of this. But I cannot. Shocked stiff in my chair. Charged to pick at this scab until I have picked it clean off. I taste the words on my tongue—*Luella Bronstein*.

Schuyler puts his hand on top of mine. "It's just a coincidence, I'm sure."

"They knew each other. I saw them together at Christopher's. At Bronstein's joint, I mean. You could see they had a bond between them. Everyone figured they were intimate. Everyone figured—it's not possible—"

"Has he told you anything of himself? His background, his family?"

"He did say he had a sister. He raised her up himself, after his parents died. But it can't be Luella. He would have said something if it was."

"I'm sure he would. I'm sure you're right."

"No, you're not. I can see it in your face. What are you getting at? What do you know about him? About this—about Luella and her brother?"

"I only know Luella because of Louis. As I said, I kept my distance, but we saw each other from time to time. We moved in the same circles."

I lean forward. "But where did he find her? How did they meet?"

"I don't know exactly, just that she dropped out of college to become his mistress. You must understand what a personality he had, how magnetic he was. He told her right off he couldn't marry her, because she was a Jew, but he gave her everything else. She was like a consort. I'm sure she had a hand in his operations."

My mouth is almost too dry to speak. "What college?" I rasp out.

"I beg your pardon?"

"What college did she drop out of?"

"Why, it was Radcliffe, I believe. Cambridge, Massachusetts."

32

EVER SINCE I walked out of that police precinct house, I have felt as if I was walking through a fog. Sometimes the mist thins some, and sometimes it thickens so I can't see but a thing. Even last night in the heat of bed, determined to dedicate myself faithful to a new life with Bronstein, I felt I was pushing away the tendrils of cloud with my own bare hands, and still they kept closing back around me like they meant to stay forever.

And now—*poof*. The fog's gone. Vanished into the crystal air. I see my father's face in crisp, multitudinous detail, each tiny capillary like a map beneath his skin, each fair hair that rises from the edge of his scalp. Each striation of those blue irises the exact shade of my own.

I reach for Schuyler's hand and close my fingers around it. "I need your help."

"It's yours."

"You need to go down to the pier for me and tell them I'm took sick. Gone to the hospital. Take Ruth Mary and the children some-place safe. Send Bronstein to some hospital. Don't matter which, any hospital, so long as it's going to take him a while to get there. Should buy me some time, anyway."

"To do what?"

"Don't know exactly yet. Seems I have unfinished business up north, that's all."

"But you can't do that! In your condition!"

I smile and pat his hand. "Don't you recollect, Schuyler? I was bred up hardscrabble. Can I walk straight and shoot straight, that's all I require. You just look after Patsy for me. Ruth Mary and hers. I'll send word, I promise. Let you know if I require help."

"Send any message to Julie. Safer that way. She'll pass it on."

"She better."

He helps me to rise again. I lean forward and kiss his dry cheek. "Now, I'm trusting you, Daddy."

How pink his face turns at that word! His eyes shine. His hand comes up instinctive to brush the ends of my hair. He nods.

"You better."

ELLA

Los Angeles, 1998

B Y THE time Ella drove the rental car up to the front portico of the hotel, the golden California sun had sunk low in the western sky. The traffic was awful, and her brain was crammed with everything Uncle Caspian had told her. She gave the keys to the valet and hurried through the lobby.

A surprise, Hector had said.

No. It couldn't be *that*. Hector had all but said that he didn't want to make things official until the divorce came through. You couldn't be engaged to a married woman, right? Besides, Ella didn't need a ring on her finger as proof of Hector's commitment to her. She trusted him!

Anyway, it was too soon. Too soon, too much. Why hurry?

Ella took the stairs instead of the elevator. The morning sickness had put a stop to her running, and she missed the exercise. When she reached the third floor, she stopped for an instant, disoriented, before she remembered which way to turn. As she walked down the hallway, some noise reached her. Noise of a bunch of people having a good time. A piano playing something bluesy. By the time she stood at Hector's door, it was clear the noise came from within, and the piano player was Hector, and the people inside were having a good time, all right.

Ella leaned her forehead against the door. Not the right surprise, she thought.

Still, she was a good sport. She reached into her handbag for the plastic card key and drew it out. Just as she was about to stick the card into the slot, the door flew open. A woman stood there, strikingly attractive, high slash cheekbones and dark doe eyes. She parted her straight, dark hair down the middle, a half-smoked cigarette trailing from one hand—a *cigarette*! Her lips were red and round with surprise.

"Oh!" she exclaimed. "You must be Eloise! I'm *dying* to meet you!" The woman grabbed Ella by the shoulders and kissed both cheeks, then drew her through the doorway. "Everybody! Everybody!"

The piano stopped. The room hushed. Everybody turned to look at them, twenty or thirty people at least, holding drinks and pleased with themselves.

"Everybody! Say hello to Eloise!" the woman said.

Hello, Eloise! came the chorus.

"Ella," said Ella, but nobody heard her among all those voices, not even Hector.

HECTOR BOUNDED RIGHT UP the next second and kissed Ella on the lips. "Hey, sweetheart! I see you've met Lulu!"

"Not officially."

The woman laughed and held out her hand. "Lulu Goring. I've heard *so* much about you, I forget you don't even *know* me!"

"Oh, I've heard a lot about you, too," Ella said. "Just not from Hector."

Lulu looked sideways at Hector. "Men, right?"

Hector grinned and shrugged. "Hey, I figured you could speak for yourself. Modern woman and all."

"It's Ella, by the way," said Ella. "Not Eloise. My full name is actually Eleanor."

"Oh, fuck it, I'm sorry. Bad with names. Hey there, buddy! Lost your piano pal?"

Ella looked down. A toddler wearing an exquisite blue jumper came running up through the thicket of legs and wrapped his arms around Lulu's legs. She lifted him up on her hip. "Say hello to Ella, Harry!"

"Hi, Harry!" Ella said.

"My buddy here and I were playing the piano," said Hector.

"He's a cutie, all right."

Lulu sniffed. "Stinky, too. Excuse me a minute. Oh, wait! Monty! There you are. Can you change Harry for me? Ella, this is my husband. Monty Abbott?"

A man appeared through the shifting bodies, handsome, balding, lean as a whippet, about forty-five, wearing a pair of sleek, creative eyeglasses. He held out his arms for the wriggling boy. "Ella! You must be Hector's main squeeze. We've heard a lot about you, around here. I'd shake your hand, but . . ."

"Not at all. Nice to meet you."

"I hear you'll be on diaper duty yourself in a few months."

"November, actually."

"Well, enjoy your last months of freedom, that's all I can say! Seriously, though, it's the best thing that ever happened to me. Except for this woman here, of course." Monty laughed, all fatherly and salt-and-pepper and businesslike, the kind of man Ella recognized from her accounting days. She remembered this now. Something about Louisiana Goring marrying some studio executive a few years ago, older guy, Hollywood power player type. Everybody snickering that it was a career move. But Louisiana laughed and kissed Monty's cheek with wifely affection. Ruffled their son's fine hair.

Ella's shoulders loosened. Her stomach settled. Hector's arm lay snug around her waist; she leaned into his shoulder.

"Sorry for spilling the beans," Hector said.

"No, he's not," said Lulu. "He couldn't wait to tell us the news."

"Look, can you blame me?"

"Nope. She's a catch, all right." Lulu reached out and took Ella by the arm. "Now come along with me. I've got all kinds of people to introduce you to."

"Can I have a quick minute first? Just drove up from San Diego."

"Oh, of course! Preggo bladder, I know it. Come find me when you're done." Lulu turned to Hector and winked. "Now I see what you mean."

HECTOR FOLLOWED HER TO the bedroom and closed the door behind them. "Everything okay? Good drive?"

Ella tossed Uncle Caspian's envelope and her handbag on the bed and turned to face him. "Fine. I—"

But her reply was swallowed up in his kiss. "What?" she gasped, laughing.

"You. Just *you*."

His hands went under her shirt, unhooked her bra. He tasted like bourbon, like when they had first slept together. The memory made her drunk. They stumbled against the wall, kissing, tearing at buttons and zippers. She clutched his shoulders, his ribs, his head. She was in shock—this wasn't like Hector at all—Hector took his time, Hector kissed every inch of her. Now some stranger who smelled and tasted and felt like Hector humped her furiously against a wall, muttering dirty erotic words—she couldn't think, she couldn't see or hear—delirious.

"What in the hell," she said, when she could catch her breath, "was *that*?"

Hector kissed her jaw and cheek and neck and leaned his forehead against the wall next to her ear. "Heck if I know."

"You don't even *like* quickies."

"I liked *that* one." He lifted his head and grinned his wolfish grin. "Any way in the world, as long as it's with you."

She laughed. "You realize someone's going to walk in here any second, looking for the bathroom."

"Do I look like I care?"

"Seriously, let me go, you sex maniac. I have to clean up."

"I could chase everyone out of here and we could start all over again."

"On the bed this time?"

"Bed, floor, desk. Hanging from the ceiling. Anywhere you want it."

"Bed's fine, actually. Although I could handle a little dinner first."

He planted his hands on the wall on either side of her ears and pulled out slowly, kissing her as he went. "Your wish is my command, dream girl."

ELLA'S NERVES STILL BUZZED when she slipped out of the bedroom a moment later, having cleaned herself up in the master bath and finger-combed her hair back into something that didn't look exactly as if she'd just had wild sex against the wall of a hotel bedroom.

Hector hadn't chased everybody out of the suite, after all—he was sitting on the piano bench next to little Harry, showing him how to plunk out "Twinkle, Twinkle, Little Star."

"Cute, aren't they? You two are going to have a ball with yours. All-star dad material, right there."

Ella turned to find Lulu at her elbow. "I have to say, he's pretty excited about everything."

"Lucky girl. He's such a catch. You heard the music today, right? Insane, right? I always knew he was a sick genius."

There was something intimate, something possessive about the way she said the word *always*. Ella's stomach turned over. Her fingertips felt cold. "How long have you known each other?" she asked.

Lulu laughed. "Wait. He didn't *tell* you about us?"

They stood near the open balcony. A breeze ruffled in from the beach. Behind it, the Pacific sunset lit the ocean to shimmering color.

"Not everything," Ella said.

"What a gentleman. I still feel bad about how it ended." Lulu started to light a cigarette and stopped. "Sorry. Can we go on the balcony? I really need a smoke."

Ella didn't really want to step on the balcony with Louisiana Goring, who needed to smoke a cigarette, but she found herself doing it anyway. She couldn't stop herself. Like you kept eating the potato chips, even though you knew they were bad for you. Outside, the air was beginning to cool. The boardwalk was lighting up. You could almost smell the cotton candy in the air, the briny ocean, except that Lulu was lighting her cigarette, which obliterated all the other scents.

She sucked deep and blew the smoke carefully away from Ella. Put her elbows on the railing. "We met through some musician friends of mine, that's all. Five years ago, maybe? We went out for a couple of years. I should have ended it sooner, but . . . my *God*, right?" She laughed, and Ella laughed, too, like hollow tin. "You should thank me, by the way. I was the one who taught him all that kama sutra shit. The tantric rhythms. By the time I was done with him he could go all fucking night. Hottest sex of my life." She drew again on the cigarette. "I made him do all kinds of bad shit. We once had this threesome with Johnny—"

"Johnny *Depp*?"

"I didn't say that, did I?" She flicked ash from her cigarette to the sand below. "God, all that seems like ages ago. Let's just say life's a lot more boring now that I'm such a nice square married chick. *Good*, don't get me wrong. But not exactly lighting my world on fire at night. Or the middle of the day."

The sound of voices drifted from the hotel room. Ella couldn't hear the piano anymore.

"So why did you break up?" Ella asked, in a calm and rational voice.

"Oh, you know. I was stringing along Monty and everything and the guilt was killing me." She turned around and leaned back against the railing, smoking her cigarette in quick, jerky strokes. "And I was bad for him. He's such a good little puppy, you know? He was starting to be all, *let's get married and shit, settle down,* and I couldn't do that to him. I mean, we would never have lasted. I have to be in L.A. because of work, and he would hate L.A. after a couple of months, you know? He's a New Yorker all through. Plus Monty *gets* this business. He understands me. Hector—all that screwing around, it was kind of killing him inside. You know."

"I know."

"But I always felt like shit, you know, dumping him out of the blue.

That's why I asked him to score this movie, right? Give him his start and everything? Not that he doesn't have the sheer fucking talent, all on his own. But still, someone needs to bankroll you." She stubbed the cigarette out against the railing and tossed it over the side, into the sand. "Monty doesn't know about all that, by the way. I'd appreciate if you didn't say anything. He's the one who got the movie deal made, so . . . you see what I mean?"

"Absolutely."

Lulu turned to look at her. "You okay? You seem a little pale."

"Me? Gosh. No. Fine."

"You want to go inside?"

"Sure. I could use a drink. Water, I mean. Super thirsty after that drive."

Lulu laughed again, that rich pealing laugh from deep in her throat. "Oh, the *drive*. For *sure*. I *saw* you two sneak out of the bedroom a minute ago. Little nooky-nooky when no one's watching?"

"Oh, that? We just—I was just—"

"Nothing to be ashamed of. God, I was horny as fuck my second trimester. Poor Monty, he was like, *what the hell, Lulu*. One time we—oh, hey there, hunkosaurus. We were just talking about you."

But it wasn't Monty who ducked onto the balcony, carrying Harry on his shoulders. It was Hector. He looked at Lulu and then at Ella. A little warily, she thought.

"Sorry to bug you two. This little guy was wondering where his mommy went."

Lulu held out her arms. "Aw, sorry about that, buddy. How's my main man?"

Hector transferred the boy carefully to Lulu, a brief but intimate act. Harry squealed with joy and sprawled over his mother's shoulder to stare at Ella, stock-still for an instant, and for that instant, as Ella met his round brown eyes, she had the strange feeling that she was looking at Hector.

HECTOR LOOKED UP AS Ella came out of the bathroom. He put his hand over the telephone mouthpiece. "Feeling better?" he said.

Ella nodded.

"Just ordering some room service for dinner. Plain pasta and chicken okay for you? Some ginger ale?"

"Fine," she said. She went to the sofa and sat down. Her stomach still simmered inside her, her head was still dizzy. The rest of her just felt like a truck had run her down. All the old familiar sensations. Those days during the worst of it, when it was all she could do to haul herself out of bed just to vomit again. Hector's voice floated over her head with the dinner order. She picked up a throw pillow and laid it over her middle. Heard Hector finish the call, hang up the phone. He came around the corner of the sofa and sat next to her.

"You sure you're okay? You're really pale." He reached to stroke her hair. "It just came on suddenly? You seemed fine earlier."

"The doctor said it would come and go, remember?"

"You don't think anything's wrong, do you? Should I call someone?"

"I told you, I'm fine. Besides, I don't know any doctors out here."

"I'm sure Lulu could—"

"No. Nope. Really do *not* want to see Lulu Goring's ob-gyn, thanks."

Hector didn't ask why not. He removed his hand from her hair and linked it with his other hand, between his knees. "So I guess she must have said something?"

"Of *course* she said something. What did you *think* she would do? Keep all those juicy details to *herself*?"

"I guess I thought she would—look, I'm sorry. I should have told you about us."

"Yes. You should have told me. She *ambushed* me, Hector. Ambushed me. And enjoyed every second, I must say."

He swore. Leaned his head forward and spiked his hands into his hair. "What did she say?"

"Oh, good Lord, what *didn't* she say? Hottest sex she ever had? Taught you the tantric rhythms until you could go all night? Threesomes with someone named Johnny, which I can only guess, right? You asked her to marry you—"

"I did *not* ask her to marry me!"

"So the rest is true?"

He stood up. "Without denying that I have behaved like a total jerk here, I just want to point out that you had a serious relationship, too, Ella. You were *married*. You still *are* married. I think I'm allowed to have some baggage, too, all right?"

"Of course you are. But you *knew* about me and Patrick. I never hid it from you."

"I wasn't *hiding*—all right. Yes. I was. I didn't tell you that I had history with Lulu because I didn't want you to worry. I didn't want you to know I was—you know, out here in L.A. with a woman I once had a relationship with, because of what happened to you with Patrick. I knew you were still getting over that. You've got enough on your plate right now. I just didn't want you to worry for one second that I would ever, *ever* betray you. In any possible way."

He stood with his back to the balcony, looking at her, arms folded defensively across his chest. The curtains were shut, like an empty screen behind him. His face was stricken. Ella couldn't speak. She couldn't think of a single thing to say. She was still shocked, still queasy. She hugged the pillow tight to her middle.

"I was wrong about that, obviously," he said. "I'm sorry."

"Did you love her?"

He hesitated. "Yes. I did. For a while. Or what I *thought* was love, at the time. I was just out of conservatory when we met. She was pretty dazzling. She came on strong. I was head over heels, I admit it. It was the most intense relationship I'd ever had, until you."

"And when did it end?"

"About two years ago, I guess. Two and a half? By then, things were going downhill in a weird spiral. I mean, it wasn't love at all at that point. It was just—I don't know what it was. More like a habit you couldn't break. She had this loft in Tribeca, so she would fly back and forth between New York and L.A., and one time she just stayed in L.A. Stopped answering my phone calls. Eventually I found out she'd gotten married. All that time she'd been seeing me in New York, she was actually engaged to Monty in L.A. I was just the piece on the side. So, yeah. That was rough. Especially when they had a baby. But I got over it. Figured out that I was actually pretty miserable with her, most of the time. She had this mean streak that would just appear out of nowhere."

"No kidding."

"So, yeah. Good riddance. After a while I started dating Claire, which was a relief. Nice girl, low maintenance, no big emotional attachments. Then about a year ago, Lulu called me up out of the blue and asked if I would score this movie for her. I was going to say no."

"But you didn't."

"It was my *dream*, Ella. And she was married with a baby. We'd both moved on. We were grown-ups, we could make it work. And I was right. The first meeting was a little weird, but when I walked away, I felt free as a bird. All done. I was dating Claire, it was all cool. And then I met you. Case closed."

"Okay, fine. Case closed."

"Don't you believe me?"

"I mean, I guess this explains why you were so horny when I got back today."

"What's that supposed to mean?"

"That funny feeling I got, the past two weeks. Whenever we were on the phone together. Like you didn't know what to say to me. And then, wow, suddenly you were so *desperate* for me to come out here."

"You're saying all that was because of *Lulu? Seriously?*"

"I'm just saying you maybe had something to prove to yourself. And to her."

He threw up his hands. "What am I supposed to do, Ella? How am I supposed to make you believe in me? *This* is why I didn't want you to know about it. This is *exactly* why."

"That makes no sense. If you had trusted me enough to tell me before, I wouldn't be sitting here right now, like I was hit by a truck."

"I'm sorry, all right? I made a mistake! *Yes,* I should have told you. It's obvious now."

"It's obvious because I found out, not because it was the right thing to do."

"What would you have done, in my place? Not wanting to cause you any anxiety?"

Ella threw down the pillow and stood up. "I would have *told* you! It would have been hard, yes, but I would have told you, I would have sat you down before I left and told you I once had this crazy intense sexual relationship with the director of this film I'm working on, three thousand miles away from you, but it's over and I love you and nothing's going to happen."

"All right, Ella. Yes. I once had this crazy intense sexual relationship with the director of this film, but it's completely, one thousand percent over and I love you with all my heart, all of it, and I swear to God, I would never in my life do anything to hurt you."

"The thing is, Hector," Ella said softly, "I'm actually pretty hurt right now."

He stared at her helplessly. She stared back, waiting for him to speak. But he didn't.

She said, "I'm sorry, but it's true. I don't know what else to say. I don't know where I fit anymore. Like, is our relationship so intense because it's intense, or because he's trying to get back what he had with *her*? Did he want me to come out to L.A. because he missed me, or because he wanted to make her jealous? Did he just screw me against a wall out of *nowhere* because *I* drive him crazy with lust, or because *she* drives him crazy with lust? Is he excited about this baby because he wants to raise a child with me, or because *she* had a baby?"

"This is complete bullshit. I can't believe I'm even hearing this. I can't believe you're saying that. I can't believe you're *doubting* me, after everything, after all we've done together."

"I'm not *doubting* you. Good grief. I know you didn't *cheat* on me. I know you wouldn't ever *physically* cheat on me. What hurts is that you didn't trust me to trust you."

"I *do* trust you."

"You didn't trust me with all of you. You left out this incredibly important part of your life. All this time, all this was going on in your head, and I had no idea."

"Because it has nothing to do with how I feel about you. It's done. It was over *years* ago. The only reason I—"

The telephone rang. Hector didn't move.

"Aren't you going to get that?" Ella said.

"Only if you want me to."

"It might be something important."

"*This* is more important."

The phone kept ringing. Hector sighed and went to answer it. Ella sat back down on the sofa.

"Hello," said Hector. "Yes, speaking. Who's this? *What?* Yes, she's right here."

Ella turned. Hector lifted the telephone from the table and brought it as far as it could go, to the top edge of the sofa. He handed her the receiver. Quizzical frown.

"This is Ella," she said.

"Ella Gilbert?"

"That's my married name, yes."

"And your husband is Patrick Gilbert of Prince Street, New York City?"

A chill went down her spine. "Yes. Is something wrong?"

"My name is Hannah Brisbane. I'm a nurse in the ICU at Lenox Hill Hospital? We've been trying to reach you on your cell phone. I'm sorry to tell you that your husband has been in an accident."

ACT V

We Are All
Desperate Wicked

1

W HEN ANSON and I drove away from this valley on the shore of Lake Champlain, the green leaves that witnessed our first weeks of marriage contained not a whisper of autumn. Now our leaves have all died and fallen to earth. The snow did bury them, did come and go, left behind mud and meltpools that turned those leaves to rot. Tiny new buds of green now erupt on the skeletons of our darling trees, but you have to bend close to see them. In the middle of April, spring's just a promise so far north as this. The wind still blows off that great icy lake to chill your bones.

I stand against the car door and smoke a cigarette, like I have done the past five nights. The moon hangs delicate as a fingernail in the western sky, shedding no light to speak of. Nobody has come to claim the scorched ruins of Charles Schuyler's house. Them timbers just lie there in a black pile and stink of damp smoke. Don't know if you could ever get the smell of smoke out of this valley, not for a hundred years. But maybe I'm wrong. Maybe next year that pile of charcoal wood will fertilize the soil nice and rich, and all kinds of things will begin to grow from it, and nobody will remember this verdant mound was a house once, and three people spent a summer there that was as near a glimpse of heaven as the Lord Almighty ever allows His blind and sinful children, and sometime right before this house went up in flames the man and woman inside it created a brand-new life for to carry on the human race. Nobody but me to remember that.

But I am grown maudlin. These raw, dark nights will do that to a body.

Now I have stood here for a time, the dark has lightened some. The scudding clouds open and close over the million tiny stars. I recollect how Anson and I sometimes came outside at night to marvel at the multiplicity of them, how profuse the rest of the universe really was, once you got outside Manhattan Island for a minute. The lake shimmers every so often between the black sides of the black hills. The boathouse is a smudge against a smudge. What I'm looking for, I don't rightly know. A flash of light? I don't know the habits of these men. How they do their work. The cigarette's a stub between my fingers. I drop it to the muddy ground and grind it with the toe of my shoe. Wrap my wool coat snug about my shoulders. I would die to sit, but if I sat I would sleep.

I'm here on a hunch, that's all. Five nights running I have stood here next to Anson's old Packard roadster, smoking and staring at the water. Five nights running I have seen the dawn turn the water gray then pink and driven back into town ten miles away, where I stay at a plain boardinghouse and claim to be a widow woman painting landscapes for my own amusement. Not that the landlady believes me, but she's the type that takes the money and don't ask questions.

When I arrived here tonight at nine o'clock, I first searched the boathouse, like I do every night. Took my flashlight and ran it over all the nooks and crannies. Looks different by night, thank God. I don't think I could bear to see it by day, even now in early spring when the place seems a different country altogether. Anyhow there was no crates of liquor stacked in the back or anyplace else, but when I hauled the air deep in my lungs I found the smell still left behind.

You know that peculiar spice of good Canadian whiskey. Delicate but present. Like you might smell the perfume left behind by your husband's mistress.

A year ago I might have put that different. Might have *been* the mistress.

My wristwatch has a luminous dial. Tells me it's eight minutes past two o'clock in the morning, and why aren't I in bed. I drop the sleeve of my coat back over the watch and stifle a yawn. Cold makes me sleepy. Everything makes me sleepy. Baby stirs restless inside me. Waiting for what, mama? Trying to prove *what*, mama? Go back to bed and get some rest. You'll wish you had, believe me.

As this lecture takes place inside my head, I nearly miss the prick of light that flashes just off the western headland.

Straighten up from the car door. Squint my eyes at the water. Nothing. My imagination, that's all, or else some trick of optics. That sliver of moon catching a ripple just so.

Still.

I parked the car on the other side of the old carriage house, so nobody could see it from the drive or from the lake. Nice shadowy hiding place for us both. You recollect I was bred up in the mountain woods, stalking rabbit and deer with my kid brothers. I know how to fashion some lair in which to lie patient for my prey. Still I have never wanted any old hare so desperate as I want this. When the flash of light don't appear again, my legs are drawn inexorable from the shelter of the carriage house, down along the line of trees at the edge of the lawn. Slides that old picnic pavilion just yards to my left, where Anson and I did consummate our marriage vows one sacred June morning and afterward sheltered occasional from squalls and such. I don't dare look. Yet I can't help but to notice its gravitational mass while I creep heavy toward the lakeshore. Pulls my heart right from between my ribs.

Now my view is straight and clear, the whole cove spread before me, dark and restless. Baby's gone still to the terrific thump of my heart. Moon has disappeared altogether behind some cloud. Be fallen soon anyhow. But each day it will grow brighter and bigger, rise earlier and set later, and this hope of mine—if you can call the dead cold desperation in my chest by such a name as *hope*—will flatten under the weight of that dumb luminous rock. So where is that goddamn flash of light? Where are my wicked smugglers with their load of Canadian contraband? Seems to me—

Flash.

And again.

I push back against the tremor of nerves under my skin. Nothing to fear, Gin Kelly. You constitute no threat at all to a boatful of bootleggers, once they perceive your wan female face and your thick belly and understand what you want from them. Don't they owe you a favor? Brazen it out like you always do. That old spirit of yours. Trampled on, maybe, but not yet altogether crushed.

The flash of light has turned clear now and steady, a plain lantern on the bow of a sailboat. Can about make out the lines of that vessel as it bobs silent toward me, a small fishing craft of no account. Soft call of a man floats across the black water. Careful I tread closer. Mud's begun to seep through my shoes and stockings. More voices, men calling quiet to each other, angling the boat to shore. Might could be the very men who murdered my beloved. Might could be their friends. Beneath my coat and hat I start to shiver in small, violent tremors. Now I stand by the very shore, maybe ten yards away from the boathouse, shrouded in dark. Closer and closer that sailboat bobs. Gather my courage to open my mouth and hail it when a hand clamps over my mouth, a big arm belts my middle and throws me to the mud while the muzzle of a gun stares me in the teeth.

2

Now it seems to me a certain small fraction of the population be natural villains, drawn to cruelty for its own sake, and maybe bootlegging has more than its share. But your average smuggler of the demon liquor, whether by land or sea, only cares about the dough. They be rough, and they be hard, but most won't kill indiscriminate unless provoked. And I am but a wan, exhausted, mud-splattered redhead in her eighth month of pregnancy, and they have sisters and mothers and wives and daughters and mistresses—sometimes all five at once—and what I mean to say is you should hear the cussing when they shine a torch on their prey and discover what kind of bird she be.

Somebody gags me with his stinking handkerchief—makes me to gag, all right—while another takes me by the shoulders and drags me kicking to the boathouse. Lays me out like a sack of flour. Around that wadded handkerchief I yell that I might could tell them what I'm here about, if someone took this stinking cloth out of my mouth. My words aren't clear but I guess my meaning is. One of the men holds a gun to my temple and says if I scream, he'll blow my head off. Nod if I understand he means business. I nod vigorous. He signals to the other fellow, who unties the gag. Safety goes click, just to make his point clear. I spit out the cloth and work my numb mouth. Pistol nudges my temple.

"So talk," he says.

I sit up and glare at him good. "Ginger Marshall. You burnt down my house and murdered my husband, and I don't have no quarrel with you, but I want to know who gave you those orders."

"Jesus H. fucking Christ," says the other man. "She's pregnant."

"You just *noticed,* you dumb cluck?" says the first.

"Watch it! Rabid crazy, them pregnant women."

"Oh, I'm crazy, all right," I tell them. "Drove all the way up here from New York City and believe me, I ain't going nowhere until you explain to me why my baby has no father to speak of. And you had better point that pistol somewhere else, brother, on account of my haint will surely follow you the end of your days, if you kill me and my child. Accidental or otherwise."

Reluctant he lowers the gun.

"That's better. Like I said, I got no quarrel with you. It's business, I know. Nothing personal. What's personal is between me and the man who wanted me and my husband dead."

The two men look at each other. I can't see their faces much, because the flashlight blinds me some, but I don't recognize either one from last summer, when me and Anson rescued those fellows from the shipwreck. Smell of perspiration and wool. Voices call out from the dock.

"You better get that boat," I tell them.

The one with the gun stands up from his crouch and tucks his pistol in his jacket pocket. "You stay here with the bird. *You* don't move an inch, lady, or that baby's getting born underwater, see?"

He ducks out the opening of the boathouse and strides down the dock, where someone on the sailboat throws him a rope.

"Crazy bird," says the man next to me. "You shoulda stayed in the city. Why you gotta come up here and make trouble?"

"Did I *make* this trouble? Last thing I *want* is more trouble. That's why I'm here."

"You want to stay out of trouble? Go back home and forget you ever saw this place. Find some nice fellow in a different line of work. Insurance, maybe."

Out on the dock, the conversation trades hushed and serious. Noises of incredulity.

"Don't need this," he mutters. "Came out to take in a shipment. Go home to my ma. Don't need this. When're you having that baby, anyhow?"

"Next month."

"Crazy bird. Can't you find some fellow to take care of you right?"

"Seems I can't. Seems the only one to take care of me is me."

"You ain't going to get what you want, see. Nobody's going to rat anybody out around here. We don't want that kind of trouble. All we want—goddamn."

From the end of the dock, the first man whistles between his fingers and motions us toward him. The young fellow with me takes me by the elbow and hauls me to my feet. About drags me down the dock to stand in the dark between the two of them. Couple of men stand on the deck of the sailboat. In the dim lantern glow, I see one of them is my old friend Standish.

What do you know.

"*You*," he says harsh, then his gaze drops to my stomach. "Jesus Christ."

"I *told* you."

Standish jumps from boat to dock and looms right over me. "You get the hell back where you came from, you hear me? For all I know you're a damn snitch like your husband—"

"He wasn't a snitch—"

"Hell he wasn't! Shot him with my own hand, like the rat he was!"

I haul my arm and knock him in the jaw. He staggers backward and wavers precarious over the edge of the dock. Catches himself on the bollard and rubs his jaw. The first man grabs my arms from behind and yanks me against his chest.

Standish checks his fingers for blood and swears. "'Sall right, Davis. Let her go."

"Hell I will!"

"Murdered her husband, didn't I? She's got a right."

"You murdered a rat, like the rat he was."

"Still he was her husband. Doing his job, that's all. Let her go."

In my ear Davis snarls, "You lay another finger on him, that's it." Shoves me free so I fall on my knees at Standish's feet. Brace myself on the boards to rise, but Standish hauls me up first. Sets me on my feet.

"Now, you listen," he says, nice and quiet. "I don't forget what you did for me. Don't forget what I did to that goddamn fool husband of yours, either. I hated to do it, ma'am. Killed him quick. Didn't know what hit him. But orders is orders, you know that. If I hadna done it, some other man would."

"Orders from who?" I whisper.

"Now, you know I can't say that."

"I'll pay."

He scratches his head. "How much?"

"How much do you make in one shipment?"

"None of your goddamn business, ma'am."

"I'll double it."

Standish stares at me. Flicks a glance at Davis and the other fellow. "No deal."

"Triple."

"Just shut your mouth, you hear me? I said no deal and I mean no deal. What do you think happens to me and my boys if I snitch on the boss? Even it won't help nothing. My boss has a boss, right? You think I know who that is?"

"I'll find out if you give me a single damn name. That's all I need, one name."

"You're crazy." He signals behind me. "McCracken. You drive the lady back into town. You staying in town, lady?"

"I might be."

"So you go back in the car with McCracken—"

"I brought my own car."

"Shut up while I finish. McCracken drives you into town, see, while Davis here follows with the shipment. You take her straight back to where she's staying, right? Not a hair on her head, right? You understand me?"

"Yes, sir."

Standish stabs a finger at my chest. "*You.* You go back where you came from and forget any of this ever happened. I said I owed you a favor, and this is it."

"But—"

"Don't push your luck, all right? You think the four of us wouldn't ruther just toss you in the lake for the fish to get rid of? Count yourself lucky and scram. Go back where you came from. Get some sleep."

"Goddamn it, Standish—"

"You deaf or something? I said, go *back* where you *came from* and get some *sleep. Trust* me, lady."

He stares at me square, and I stare right back, and we stay locked like that for a few long seconds. Then I nod.

"You can go to hell where you stand, Standish," I snarl, and I snap around back down the dock, followed by McCracken and Davis, who don't relish this night, believe me.

3

GET SOME sleep, Standish ordered me. What a gas. Near three weeks now I have scarce slept, not since my wedding day. Drove all day and all night by the full fierce light of the moon, stopped only for gas and something to eat when I knew I must, though I could no more eat than sleep, then or now. Think of the baby, I tell myself, and obedient I force some eggs or some bread or chicken or restaurant hash down my throat. But my stomach don't want it. I must chew slow, swallow careful, or it comes back up. Skin and bones and breasts and baby child, that's all I be.

And that clarity of vision that came upon me in that coffee shop with Schuyler? Has become my nemesis. Head aches with it. Chest hurts with it. I lie on my bed in that boardinghouse and close my eyes to sleep, but my vision's replaced only by imagination and vile memory. When I do find some hour of fitful sleep, the dreams are yet worse.

I never did like that Luella, you recall, though Anson always laid down my dislike to feminine rivalry. He never could see what I saw, that she was hopeless in love with him—and what I *felt*, though I couldn't put my finger on, was how this passion for Anson pitched Luella's soul into mortal conflict with what she was bound to, which was Hardcastle. You could see her torment when you looked close. Those nervy cigarettes and brittle laughs. The venom she spat to me. But it was like looking through one of them stereoscopic cameras with one side missing. You didn't see the full dimension. Then the other picture popped into place and it all took shape.

Not just Hardcastle's mistress. Luella's also Bronstein's *sister*. The precious, precocious sister he raised by his own hand, the darling he gave everything she wanted, until she felt like she was just entitled to a thing because she wanted it. Sister he loves beyond all things.

Loves. Yes.

For there is one other thing I know in my heart about Luella Bronstein, as sure as I know the beat of my baby's heart under my ribs.

Alive she still be.

4

SOMETIMES, WHEN I be particular inclined to torture myself, such as now, I recall that night before we married. Me and Bronstein, I mean. In order to inflict the maximum anguish upon myself, I will recollect each minute so clear and precise, I might be doing it again. How he sat me on the bed like a princess and took off his clothes for me, piece by piece, folding each one neat on the dresser. Exact warm shade of his naked skin in the light from the single lamp next to the bed. How he went on his knees, how he laid his hands reverent on the ungainly womb and swore his allegiance to us both. How tender he was of my condition. How patient and measured compared to Anson, who tended to lose himself delirious in the act of love. Gentle way he tucked me into bed after and cuddled me spoon fashion, on our sides. Then him waking full libidinous some hours later so we did it again, as sure and inevitable as before. Hard cruel I torture myself. Grind my mind over and over the carnal details until my flesh curls inside itself. Until my shame curdles my very blood. This body I once consecrated to my beloved. How could I let Bronstein make free with it? Him who conspired to rob me of my heart's desire.

Did they plot it all out, Bronstein and Luella? She got her prize, he got his? Whose idea to begin with? Mad as I am at Bronstein, I feel sure it was Luella. Her greed for Anson was like a mania. Only a woman schemes so deep. But she overplayed her hand, didn't she? Someone discovered what Anson was up to and swatted him down like one of them pesky black flies you find up north. Now she has got nothing left to her, not her protector nor her true love. Why, even her loyal brother meant to leave the country with his money and his prize.

So where is Luella?

That's all I want. I don't give a damn about breaking up this racket, about the sanctity of the Constitution in a democratic republic. I don't care if people have a right to drink whatever they want or not. Don't care how many more people get themselves killed over that particular principle. Don't care about a single one of the million ways the law is broken in this broken land, stuffed with hypocrites top to bottom who deserve what comes to them. All I want is Luella.

As for Bronstein, I have two million dollars of his money and his jewels in my satchel. I reckon he'll be coming after me.

5

GUESS I do sleep some. Wake sudden from a dream I've been having lately, when I am apt to dream at all. You might say it's the mirror opposite of the memories I conjure awake. In this dream I stare through a dirty window at a kitchen. Plain country kitchen like I grew up in, the kind you see in River Junction, some small house in the mountains or woods somewhere. Wallpaper peels from a sepia corner. Dull Welsh dresser against a wall. Wooden table set for breakfast. Tall blond pink-skinned woman fries some bacon or sausage or something on a coal stove. Hums to herself. She wears a man's white shirt and nothing else. Bobbed platinum hair tousled every which way. Her fine long slender bones are too elegant for this room, like a bowl of Meissen china left unaccountable on a tack room shelf. Door opens. From some rumpled bed in the back room comes a man about six feet tall. Stark naked he be, brown hair, fresh purpling bruise on his left eye. Pale wasted flesh on a wide bony frame, like somebody starved him almost to death. Still he prowls into that kitchen like a jungle cat. Comes up behind the woman at the cookstove and kisses her neck. Slides his big hands under her shirt and rucks it up so you can see she wears not a stitch beneath. Fondles her breasts while he nibbles away at that creamy throat. Woman closes her eyes and leans back sighing against his ribs. She reaches almost the same height as him, a perfect match. When she can't stand it no more, she abandons that bacon and turns around to hang her arms from his neck. They kiss frantic. He unbuttons her shirt that really belongs to him—shirt he discarded in a hurry on the bedroom floor last night—and feasts himself on her bosom. All the while I stare mute and frozen through my dirty old window. Can't do a thing about it. Can't look away, neither—it's a dream, after all, meant to torture me. Dainty breasts she has, firm and elegant as peaches, and my goodness if he can't get enough of their sweet taste. She arches back in his arms. Hooks one leg around his stark-naked buttocks. He hoists her up and carries her to the kitchen table. Knocks some dishes aside. Lays her out flat. My throat be too choked to breathe. Smothered in grief. When he has buried himself full deep, he slings her antelope legs over his shoulders and commences the rhythm of intercourse. Like animals they mate. Because it's a dream, as I said, I am required to perceive every detail, howsoever it kills me, and so must you, by God. How she sobs. How he growls. Bacon starts to burn, smoke drifts from the pan. Through the window glass I hear her call to him, dirty as hell, how big he is and how good he feels. Goes on for hours, it seems. All I learned this man he lavishes on his lover. At last she grabs hold of the table edges and steels herself. Arches her back and screams out her last final rapture. He comes roaring. Both of them arching and straining and roaring and spending until every last drop be milked from their bones and the sweet lull steals over. Panting and sweating and dead spent. Smell of burnt bacon and the salt of human ecstasy. He releases her legs, which she wraps around his waist to hold him fast. Sets down his palms on the smooth table wood and leans to suckle each small, flushed breast. Her fingers burrow into his hair. She murmurs nonsense to him. He murmurs back. Lifts his head and kisses her mouth. Joined still. Endless decadent minutes they kiss each other while smoke billows unheeded from the iron frying pan. Burn that kitchen to a crisp in a second or two, and neither gives a damn. At last the man straightens and unhooks her ankles from the small of his back. Pulls out so slow and rigid as he went in. Drags her thighs lovingly with his fingertips. Looks laconic to the window and stares his navy-blue eyes triumphant on my face, like he knew I was there all along, and how I suffered.

That's when I wake up gasping.

Cold gray dawn creeps through the window. Cold gray boardinghouse room. Heart thuds so hard, I might die. Reflexive I put my hands on my belly and wait for the reassuring kick within. Close my eyes again and squeeze out a pair of salt tears. Every night that dream gets worse. Each time more lurid, each time some new detail more obscene than the last. Each time they do it hotter and harder, they spend with more relish, they devour each other more lustful and dirty and mindless. And I stand at my helpless window and watch it all. Any wonder I don't dare to sleep? My hands shake. My brain has taken up a permanent ache of fatigue and want. I force myself out of bed and light a cigarette. Check my wristwatch on the bedside table, it's a quarter to six.

Just a dream, I say to myself. Just your febrile subconscious emitting some sacrilegious nightmare. Making out Anson so wicked as you be. Your penance, to imagine him doing to her what Bronstein did to you. Still just a dream.

This is real. Cold gray dawn. Cold gray room. Cigarette burns between your fingers. Baby stirs in your womb. Sole living relic of your faithful beloved. His parting gift. Yours to protect so ferocious as only the wicked can.

Standish was right. Go back home and forget you ever came. Find shelter among your people and deliver this innocent infant safe into the world. Why risk a thing so precious and fragile and irreplaceable as Oliver Marshall's only begotten child?

With one hand I reach to part the calico curtains an inch or two. Outside the world's half-dark, the nearby trees obscured by fog. Some movement in the shadows. Man in a cap and wool coat, collar pulled up around his ears. Cigarette hangs from the corner of his mouth, like he's waiting for something.

I let the curtain fall and stub out the cigarette. Pull on my dress and stockings. Coat and hat and gloves. Shoes, still wet and mud crusted. Quiet as an Indian I steal down the stairs and out the back door.

6

FOR A man accustomed to keep watch vigilant, Standish don't hear me coming. Spins so fast when I whisper his name, he near falls over. Eyes ferocious wild. Whole red-cold face sags relief as he makes out my figure in the mist that might turn to drizzle any second. He chucks his cigarette to the grass and motions me to follow him.

His car is a regular black flivver, five or six years old. He opens the door for me and I climb inside. Smells of tobacco and booze and male sweat. He gets in the other side and offers me a cigarette. Lights me up. For a minute or two we smoke companionable. Share a gulp or two of whiskey from a bottle he passes to me. He asks what'll I give for this information. I say I'm willing to pay whatever he asks. He says he don't want money from me, which I guess I expected. So I balance my cigarette careful on the dash and lumber down awkward to my knees. Unbutton his trousers. Stiff as a foremast he pops free. Cups his hands round the back of my head and we settle to rhythm. I pick up his beat right easy, the way my step-daddy learned me when I was but small. Fly away somewhere else so I don't think on what I do. In no time he's spending hard. Groans like he might could die of it. Once he's finished I allow him a moment to catch his breath. They do appreciate that. He swears some gratitude to Almighty God and tucks his wet tool back into his trousers. Helps me to flop on the seat again. Thanks me courteous. Apologizes for my trouble and says he needed that pretty bad, hasn't seen his wife in five weeks and this job winds you up tight as a steel spring.

I swish my mouth with whiskey and wipe my handkerchief across my lips. Pick up my cigarette from the dashboard. Rest my hand on my belly. Ask him what he's got for me.

He smokes his cigarette in quick, nervy movements that remind me of Luella. "I might quit," he says, and at first I think he means the cigarettes. Then he adds, "This business, used to be we brought over some good whiskey and took our dough and did the same again next month. Nobody got hurt. But this new boss."

"You mean the one who took over last summer?"

"Look, I'm no snitch. First of all I seen what happens to rats around here. But I'm square with those that are square with me, see? You scratch my back, I scratch yours. This new boss ain't for scratching nobody, though. I started hearing how they took my good whiskey and mixed it up with that industrial alcohol, denatured like, so if you drank enough you died. All for more profit, see, like they wasn't making barrows full already. So I said look, you mix up my booze with poison to kill people, you pay me more. What happens? One of my men turns up dead. Hands cut off. Balls cut off and stuffed in his mouth with his pizzle."

"They Lord," I whisper.

"So I keep my mouth shut, right? I keep my mouth shut when this fellow of yours turns up. I know what side he's on, all right. Figure I'll just play dumb and let him do what he needs. He wants to work his way up slow, find out how the new boss—"

"What's his name? The new boss?"

"You think I know that? Nobody knows that but maybe a handful of men. All I know is your husband—tells us his name is Black, Caleb Black—aims to take him out, and I say to myself, God help him if he can do it. He takes over convoys across Vermont into Massachusetts. You know, meets me at the dock here and drives my crates to wherever he goes. Then one day the car meets us at the dock here, and who do you think they have inside? Caleb Black, all bound up like a hog."

I stub out my cigarette on the floorboards and bend my head over my knees as best I can.

"You all right?" Standish asks me, patting my back.

"Go on."

"Nothing more to say, right? Fellow gives us our orders. We take him out on the lake and—well, I guess I don't need to spell it out for you."

"Did he—did he say anything first? Before he died?"

"Sweetheart, he was already passed out cold. I'm sorry. You want a drink?"

"No thanks."

"Smoke?"

I shake my head. "That's all, then? That's all you have for me?"

Standish hesitates a second. "That's all."

"Because there's one thing I need to know. You have to tell me the truth. Was there ever a woman with him? Tall blond woman. Beautiful."

"With Black? No, ma'am."

"You're sure about that?"

"Absolutely."

"On the level, now? Square like you say you are? After what I just done for you?"

Standish wraps both his hands around the top of the steering wheel and swears.

"Look. I never seen her with Black, and that's the truth. Only met her once."

"*Who?* I need her name."

"I don't got a name. All I know is who she is. Called me in to do a job for her once."

"A job? What kind of job?"

"The dirty kind, what do you think?" He turns to me, bleak honest face. "She was the boss's bird once, see? Before they murdered him. Now she runs the convoys out of Canada for whoever's in charge. And she don't need no lessons from nobody."

7

TWELVE MILES away from Sharon, I pull the Packard over at the sight of a dingy post office. Signboard says I am in Randolph, Vermont, though it don't seem much of a town, frankly. Dry goods and what used to be a saloon. Feed store next to a clean white church. It's ten o'clock in the morning and the April drizzle beats down on my hat. I scurry inside and ask for a telegram slip.

```
MISS JULIE SCHUYLER
THE DUNES
EAST HAMPTON NEW YORK
FOR MY FATHER STOP ALL WELL STOP ON MY WAY TO
SHARON VT ON URGENT BUSINESS STOP HOME SOON STOP
THOUSAND KISSES TO PATSY STOP DEAREST LOVE FROM
YOUR GENEVA
```

I pay for the telegram and wait while the silent clerk taps it out on the telegraph machine in the corner. You know the sound, the irregular click of Morse code, which I never learned. As I stand there and listen, the muscles of my belly seize up. Happens from time to time. False labor, the doctor called it. Just the womb getting some practice. I lean one elbow on the counter until it passes. Clerk finishes her tapping and looks up. Asks if I'm all right. I say of course. Then I ask if the office happens to have a public telephone. She points to the corner, where a dusty black Western Electric box hangs from the wall. I lift the earpiece and insert a nickel into the slot. Have to wait some time for an operator. She introduces herself with this fierce

Yankee twang to her vowels. I tell her I wish to make a collect call
to the Department of Justice building in Washington, Mabel Willebrandt's office.

8

WHAT STANDISH gave me in exchange for my expert ser-
vices is a square of dirty notepaper, *Hardscrabble Lane*, *Sharon* written in pencil. That's Vermont, he told me. And it didn't come
from me, right? You chew up that paper and swallow it soon as you
get there. House is at the end of the lane. Old dirt road. You can't
miss it.

Outside of Sharon, the hills rise and fall. Stubble fields waiting for
the plow, soon as the time for frost has properly passed. Some pas-
tures starting to green, crisscrossed by crumbly stone walls, popu-
lated by black-and-white cows. Here and there, a thicket of woods. A
big barn painted in peeling red. The road's unpaved and soft with
mud. Every so often the Packard loses its grip and slides its rear end
back and forth. The last mist lifts, the sky clears. I stop and take down
the top so I can breathe some fresh air. Slide back into my seat just
as the muscles of my womb seize up again, harder than the last time.
Grip the steering wheel a little. False labor, I assure myself. Baby's
not due for another four weeks. After a bit the tension gives way and I
start the engine again. Pull back out on the road. A short while later I
pass the signboard for Sharon. Another mile and Hardscrabble Lane
appears on the left.

Now this road's even worse than the one I left behind me. Twice
the mud sticks the Packard good. I have to slide some twigs around
the wheels to get myself out. Drive mostly on the wakening grass

next to the road. Up and down the hills I trundle in Anson's spruce-green roadster. Satchel in the trunk worth two million. Brown fields unroll beside me. Finally I come to a copse, thick with trees and shrubs. Standish said the house was inside the woods there. I bring the Packard to a stop behind a tangle of pricklebush and light a cigarette to calm my nerves. Tiny new stiff leaves just coming out on those untamed branches. Sweet spring unfurling. There will be summer again, as sure as sunrise.

Belly tightens again, so hard I wince. Arch my back a bit to relieve the strain. Now that I notice, a faint dull pain seems to have wrapped around the lower half of my spine. Surely must be all the driving. Sitting around stiff like this. Or else I need some sleep. Close my eyes and wait for the tension to ease. Wait and wait. Finally it lets go, but the ache in my back remains.

That's what happens when you notice an ache, after all. All you need to do is ignore it and it goes away.

As I open the window to release my cigarette, a noise reaches me. Rattle-roar of a fast engine. I make myself small and pray my spruce-green Packard's well camouflaged behind this shadow-speckled pricklebush, at least to somebody not looking for it. Over the top I catch glimpse of a car headed back the way I came in. Flashes in and out between the vegetation. Driving fast along the sure grass beside the road, same trick as I used. Roars past the pricklebush without slowing. I turn around in my seat in just enough time to catch sight of a pale blond head at the wheel.

My heart pounds so fast, a dizzy spell comes on me. Baby kicks and pokes, wonders what the hell is going on with Mama these days. I never did eat any breakfast this morning, poor thing. Drank a quick cup of coffee at the filling station while I took in gas for the Packard, that's all. Well, once this is over with, I'll start to eating again.

Beefsteak and spinach and milk to make me strong. For now I take out the square of paper Standish gave me and rip it into tiny pieces. Open the door and climb out of the car. Shoes sink into the soft turf. Pat my jacket pocket to make sure of my pistol. When she comes back, I'll be waiting for her.

I drag some branches around the Packard to hide it better still. God praise Anson for choosing such a color, or maybe it wasn't accident at all. Warm sun sifts through the trees. I start down the lane, toward the house that sits at the end of it. Birds sing out joyful above me. Clouds hurry past a blue sky. Through the treetops I spot a chimney, the peak of a roof. Then the clapboard side of a building. Few steps more and the whole house appears before me, small and square, unpainted, two dormer windows popped out from the attic. Kind of a sweet symmetry to the place, though it be but humble. To one side is some kind of kitchen extension, stovepipe trailing a faint gray smudge of smoke.

Seems a craven thing to slip inside and lie in wait for her, don't it? What I ought to do is settle myself on her front stoop. Yet she might not return for some time. Maybe days. She tore off in a terrible hurry, after all. Some kind of business to attend to, maybe. What will I do until she returns? Can't sleep under her roof. Can't steal her own bread to eat, for I have some scrap of honor remaining to me. But if I leave, I won't know when she returns.

That thin smudge of smoke from the stovepipe, though. Surely she would have made sure the fire was out, if she meant to be away for days?

I start forward toward the front door, set betwixt two prim windows. No porch, just a couple of stone steps. I try it careful and find the knob unlocked but the door bolted shut. Around to the kitchen door. Knob turns easy under my hand. Door swings open.

I step inside.

But surely I dream.

Surely I have fallen somehow to sleep in Anson's old spruce-green Packard and begun to dream that terrible lewd dream again. Same kitchen. Same Welsh dresser. Same wood table. Same cookstove, except there be no tall blond goddess frying bacon, nor anybody at all. I stand paralytic. Dizzy, maybe. Belly starts to tighten again, like a screw winding downward, turn by turn. Hear a noise from somewhere. Door swings open.

"Lu? Forget something?"

Familiar honey baritone voice. My own breathing husband, brought back to life, six feet tall and starved thin, brown hair damp and disordered, buttoning up his crumpled white shirt above a pair of wool trousers. Fresh purple bruise on his left orbital socket. Cigarette dangling between two fingers. Looks up laconic and meets my gaze.

I turn away so swift, I don't even know his reaction. Like a reflex, like you pull your hand from a hot stove. Stumble back out the door and lumber down the drive. Black spots before my eyes. I'm going down, I realize. Going to pass out. Hear my name shouted out behind me as I fall to my hands and knees. Rush of heat and nausea. Belly seizes up so hard I can't see. Still I cling to consciousness. Only last thing I own. Then not even that.

9

COME TO in the drive still, cradled in a man's arms. I roll away and vomit onto the dirt. He sobs, actually sobs my name. Am I all right, does it hurt, what do I need.

Need you to leave me be, I whisper out. Vomit some more, but there's nothing to vomit. Bile. Next thing I know he lifts me in the air. Carries me into the kitchen, the goddamn kitchen. *Take me somewhere else,* I tell him. *Somewhere you haven't done it with her.*

Shut up, he says, like I stabbed him through the gut. We pass through the door into some kind of front room parlor. He sets me on a fat chintz sofa. Realize I'm gripping my belly with both hands. Can't breathe for the pain. He looks on me horrified.

"Is it—are you—"

"No! All I need is a glass of water and I'm gone for good. Promise you that. Gone. Didn't never mean to spoil your secret."

He runs to the kitchen. Creak of a pump handle. By the time he returns I have sat up groggy, eyes shut closed so I can't look around me and see all the furniture, the rugs, the places they might have done it together like in my dream. Dream that was not a dream after all. Glass presses against my lips. I swish and spit on the rug and sip more. Push it back to him and try to stand up. He won't let me.

"When? How much longer?"

"Weeks yet, don't worry."

"I never *knew*. I never *knew*."

"Only just found out the day you left."

Hands shaking so bad, I must knot them together. Head so dizzy I can't scarce think.

At least he didn't ask was it his. Might have murdered him right there if he had. Might murder him yet.

"You were in Europe," he whispers. "I thought you were in Europe with him."

"*Europe?* Who told you that?"

"The newspaper. In the newspaper."

"I thought you was *dead*, Anson. *Dead!* All the time shacking up with Luella!"

"I was shot! She rescued me—fought them off—brought me here—"

"*Rescued* you!"

"Someone found me out. Tried to kill me. She *saved* me, Gin."

"You're a liar or else an idiot. A goddamn idiot. She set it all up, don't you see? She runs the whole racket! My God, I should have *known*!"

He sits back on his heels. Still I can't look at his face. After a moment he says, nice and reasonable, "That's nonsense. I don't know who told you that. It's the widow who runs it now. Hardcastle's widow. She took over after he died. Runs that racket ruthlessly. You heard about those people who died. That's what we're doing here, Luella and me, preparing to take her down as soon as I'm on my feet—"

"Who served you all that baloney? Luella? *She* told you that?"

No answer.

"I heard from *Standish*," I tell him, "that Luella called him here to this house in the middle of January to give him a job. A dirty job. He was to drag Caleb Black out on the ice and shoot him through the shoulder. Leave him there bleeding for dead and tell the others he'd killed Black for a rat and dumped his body down a fishing hole."

"That's not true!" he yells.

"You don't have to believe me. I don't care if you do."

At the word *care* comes another labor pain. Lucky Anson's just turned away, face to the ceiling, hands in his hair. Grind my teeth to keep from making a sound. Time winds out agonizing. Old terror takes over me. Mama screaming for mercy as my brother Angus tore out of her. Realize I need to leave this place right now. This pointless argumentation. Need to get back to that town and ask for help. I brace my hand on the sofa arm and climb to my feet. "Thanks for the water. I'll show myself out."

He turns back and stops me. "I saw the *wedding announcement,* Gin. I went out of my mind. Mrs. Oliver Marshall to Mr. Joseph Christopher. I thought you were in *Europe* right now. You were sailing to *Europe* together."

"That's true. I went to Washington in March and Mabel Willebrandt told me you was dead, Anson. Dead since January, and I was having your baby in May. Then somebody tried to kill me. So Bronstein offered to marry me and take me and Patsy somewhere safe."

"Bronstein?"

"Yes, Bronstein. Her *brother,* Anson. He's her brother. Joseph Bronstein. Raised her himself. Set her up in business with Hardcastle. A real team, they were."

He takes a step back and shakes his head. "That's not true."

"Whatever you want. I'm leaving."

"It's not possible. Her *brother?* She never said."

"Well, she wouldn't, would she? You were just the patsy she worked with at the Bureau. All along it was her and Bronstein milking old Hardcastle. No more than he deserved, I guess. Then—well, with Hardcastle gone, that left an empty space in her bed, didn't it?"

Anson spins around and hits the wall with his fist. "It's not *true!* It's not *possible!*"

"What am I, lying to you? You think I'd *lie?*"

"But you *married* him—"

"That was before. Before my father told me all this. Right on my wedding day. Right before I went to board that ship for Europe. So what did I do instead of a honeymoon, I drove straight up north to find out what had happened to you. My dear departed husband. I was going to kill whoever was responsible for killing you, just so I could sleep at night."

"But you *knew* I was alive! I sent *messages*, Gin. Every *week*! Where to find me!"

"Gave them to Luella to send, didn't you? While you was flat on your back and helpless? Because I never got one. Bronstein himself told me exactly how you died."

Another cramp commences to seize me. I sit back on the sofa and clench my jaw. Grip the arm with my hand. Anson stands braced against the wall, head down.

"Pneumonia," he says. "I had pneumonia."

I don't answer because I can't. Pain like a hot iron pressing on my lower back. White light on my eyes. Leave, Gin. Split. Why can't you just *leave*? Require to torture yourself first?

"Went on for weeks. Only just got out of bed. I swear it, Gin. Look at me. Couldn't even stand, even after the fever left. All that time I figured you might come. Waited and waited for you. Prayed you might forgive me. And Lu was devoted, she never once—I don't understand, she never—not until after I saw that goddamn announcement in the paper . . ."

I open my eyes. "Don't call her Lu."

"I'm just saying it wasn't what you think."

He turns to cast his eyes around the room, everywhere except me. Like he's looking for something. Spots it on the sofa table—a pack of cigarettes, a box of matches. I watch dumbfounded as he shakes a smoke out of the pack and lights it with trembling fingers.

"What in God's creation are you doing?" I ask.

He sucks in some smoke. Then looks down at the cigarette like he's not sure how it got there. Voice rasps like a saw. "Doctor prescribed them for the pneumonia."

"They Lord."

He holds out the pack to me. I shake my head. Just stare at him.

Bony, stricken face like he has near starved to death. Bruised left eye. Shirt hangs from his wasted shoulders, halfway buttoned, not yet tucked. Concave stomach beneath. Skin so pale as a ghost's. Eyes wide and wild and anguished. Stunned and stricken and utterly lost, because his world has heaved beneath him, and what was up is down, and then he was blind and now he begins to see through a glass but terrible dark. Still my heart lurches at the sight of him. Living, breathing, fallen beloved. Alive. *Alive!* Smoking a goddamn cigarette because the doctor told him to. What doctor? Just how sick has he been these past weeks?

"Which shoulder?" I ask.

He shakes his head like he don't understand.

"Which shoulder did Standish shoot you?"

"The left," he whispers.

"And you woke up here, didn't you? All bandaged up. Lost a lot of blood, I'll bet."

"Gin—"

"Then you got the pneumonia, lying flat on your back in the middle of winter. And she took care of you faithful. Like an angel, she was. Offered to send your messages to me. Held back the news of my betrayal till you was strong enough to take it. A real heroine."

"Don't *say* those things! It wasn't like that. She kept me *alive*, Gin. She brought in a doctor. Had a nurse come to stay when she was gone!"

"What about that black eye? Did she give you that?"

He touches it with his thumb. "It's nothing. An accident."

"Accident? How do you give someone a black eye by accident? She likes it rough or something?"

"I said, it's *nothing*!"

"My God. What's she done to you? Why can't you see it?"

"There's nothing to see! You've got it all wrong! Something—something must have gone wrong with the messages—she would never have . . ." He looks at me. "She'll be back soon. Just went out for food and news. She'll tell you herself what—"

"I don't need to hear it! I *know* what she is, Anson! I've always known—"

Screw starts to tighten down below. Goddamn. Goddamn. Grip the sofa arm.

"What's the matter? Is something wrong?"

"It's nothing!"

Anson's head snaps to the front window. Hurries to squint through the glass. "Who the hell is that? Someone follow you?"

"No!" I gasp out.

He crushes out the cigarette and hurries to the cabinet in the corner. Opens it and pulls out a pistol. "Stay here."

Well, I can't move anyway. Can't hardly open my eyes. From some distant point outside the room, I hear somebody roar out *Lu! Lu, where are you? It's Joseph! Open the door!*

Eyes flash open in time to see Anson throw open the bolt on the front door. Bronstein staggers in and stops at the sight of Anson with the pistol.

"Dammit, Marshall! Put the gun down! Where is she? Where's Luella?"

"Out," says Anson.

Then Bronstein spots me on the sofa. Starts toward me but Anson grabs him by the arm. I have the dumb idea to try to stand. End up on my hands and knees, gasping for breath. Dim I hear Bronstein ask what's wrong with me. Anson says he's going for the telephone, going to get the doctor, and I swear fluent at him, tell him it's passing already, I'm leaving. Stagger to my feet. Anson lurches forward to take my weight, though he be terrible thin. For an instant I feel the shock of his emaciation, because my nerves somehow expected the old solid prizefighter heft of his chest and arms. Then I push him away and tell him I can stand, all right. Turn to Bronstein and ask what the hell he's doing here.

He reaches for my shoulders. "Taking you out of here, that's what. Come on."

"You're not taking her anywhere!" shouts Anson.

"I'm not leaving her here for my sister to maul, that's for sure!"

Anson falls back a step. Face drains of what color is left. "*Sister?*"

"That's right. Come on, Gin. He's not worth it, I swear."

I throw off Bronstein's hand. "Don't touch me! The two of you! I can leave on my own, all right. Just—"

"Gin, I can't stand here and argue with you, not when—"

"Don't you *touch* my wife!" Anson roars.

Bronstein spins. "Your *wife?* When you been up here with Lu for weeks? Not anymore, Marshall. She's mine now."

"I am not *yours*! Don't belong to nobody! Neither-a you!"

"Gin, I don't care *what* you think of me right now. All I know is if Lu finds you here, you'll wish you were anywhere else. Already tried to murder you once—"

"*Murder* me?"

"That's right. Who do you *think* that was outside your front door? Couple of her boys. She sent her own men down to take you out of the picture for good, and it was only God's own luck she got Marshall's mother instead of his—"

"*What?*"

The two of us turn to Anson. Pistol falls from his hand to clatter on the floor.

"*What* did you say?" he whispers.

Bronstein swears. "You didn't know? She didn't tell you?"

Anson just stands there, shaking his head back and forth.

"Outside the house," I say softly. "Three weeks ago. The end of March. She came to visit, she was just leaving, and a car pulled up—happened so fast—"

Anson falls back on the sofa and puts his head in his hands.

"I'm sorry, Anson. I'm so sorry. She came to visit me. I told her about the baby, that she was going to be a grandmother, and she—she—"

"Opened the door just in time for Lu's boys to spray her down. Gin was standing right behind her, it's a miracle she didn't get hit. That's when I gave up. *Swore* to me she wouldn't touch Gin—"

Anson stands up, draws back his hand, and slugs Bronstein in the jaw. And I guess our merciful Lord grants to His frail servant Oliver Marshall some kind of unnatural strength in that moment, for Bronstein's knocked clear on his backside like a bowling pin. Anson stands over him, fists raised. "Now get back up on your feet so I can do that again," he says.

Bronstein shakes his head, roars in fury, and throws himself at Anson. Knocks him down flat on the floor and pulls back his fist. I start to screaming. Lunge forward and grab that fist.

"Don't you dare! Don't you dare! Can't you see how sick he is?"

"His own goddamn fault! Leaving you like that! Would I ever have left you like that in a million years, if you were mine? All I ever did was *protect* you!"

"Get off him! Get off him!"

Bronstein rolls away. I take Anson by the shoulders and help him to sit up. Bruised but not bad hurt. I ask him if he's all right, can he talk. He shakes his head like to clear it and stares past my shoulder at Bronstein, who rises to his feet and rubs his jaw. Stares a bit. I recollect that moment with my father, when the scales fell from my eyes, and the world became so icy clear as to hurt my head. Anson brushes my hands away and braces his hand on the sofa arm. Gets on his feet and dusts his trousers slow and methodical.

"What you're saying," Anson says, dead cold, "is you and Lu planned this out together?"

"That's what I'm saying."

"From the beginning?"

"Soon as you got back from upstate, end of August."

"And it was your idea?"

"It was Lu's idea. She said she was rolling up Hardcastle's racket and wanted you for a partner, someone she could count on with no strings attached to him. I'm no idiot, I knew she also wanted you out of Gin's bed and into hers. I went along with it because she's my sister and blood comes before everything else in this world. But also I figured she might try to get rid of Gin herself if I didn't step in with something. I never asked her about that fire—didn't want to know— but I had my ideas. You know she went clear out of her head when the two of you got married. So I made her swear she would leave Gin alone if I did what she wanted."

"Which was?"

"Spread the story she'd been murdered for revenge by Hardcastle's men. Give you the idea to make it look like you were killed, so you could go back in undercover. Set it all up. Make sure Gin didn't find out. That was all, Lu did the rest herself. She gave me two million of Hardcastle's money to do it, so long as I kept Gin out of the way."

"Which you did."

Bronstein folds his arms. "Which I did. Kept her safe. Cared for her every way I could. Gave her your letters, even, until they stopped coming at the end of January. Then I guess Lu got impatient, maybe found out Gin was having that baby—I don't know how, I made sure not to tell her, knowing Lu. But word gets around sometimes. Must've uncorked her. She broke her promise. Sent out her boys."

"My mother. Killed my mother. My mother is dead."

"Look, I never in a million years meant for that—"

"Lu who ordered it? No question at all?"

"Would I be standing here telling you my own sister did such a thing if she didn't? I'm sure, all right. So I did what I had to do to keep Gin safe."

To look at Anson, you wouldn't think he was mad at all. Just balances there light on his feet like a skeleton and stares at Bronstein, who stands four or five inches shorter yet must weigh fifty pounds more, thick and barrel-chested and powerful. Still I know the coldness in those navy eyes. Have seen it before. Like a tiger before it strikes.

"I *trusted* you, Christopher," he says. "I trusted you with my *wife*. With my *life*. Remember what I said to you that night?"

"I remember."

"We shook hands. *We shook hands.*"

"I swore to look after *Gin*, Marshall. Not you. If a man won't look after his wife first before everything else, he's got no business marrying her to start with."

Like a flash, Anson turns and scoops up the pistol lying on the floor. Points it at Bronstein, who only has time to start forward before that gun barrel stops him cold. Slowly he puts his hands up.

"Give me the keys to your car," says Anson.

"In my pocket."

"Gin, take the keys from his—*Gin!*"

For I'm back in the grip of another pain now, staggering to my hands and knees, smashing my teeth together to hold back the screaming.

Anson drops next to me. "Call the doctor! *Now!* She's having the baby!"

I hear Bronstein's footsteps, the ding of the telephone bell as he lifts the earpiece, rattles the arm. Tells the operator he needs the doctor now—the town doctor, right now—his wife's having a baby. Meanwhile Anson pulls me back against his chest and tells me to breathe slow, that's it, he's got me. Bronstein's shouting into the receiver. Some trouble with finding the doctor. Bronstein barks me some questions, like how long have I been having pains, how long since the last one, and I just shake my head because I can't speak and anyhow can't think of the answers. Bronstein slams down the earpiece just as the pain begins to flatten out. Says the doctor's not in his office. He's driving me to the hospital instead.

"The hell you are," Anson says. "I'm driving her."

"In *my car,* you think? Who's taken care of her all these months? Rubbed her poor feet? Who, Marshall?"

"For God's sake!" I grind out. "Just help me up."

Anson's arm slips around my waist. Gentle he supports me to my feet. "Help me get her to the car," he says to Bronstein. "Do *that* for me, all right?"

Bronstein runs to the front door and pulls it open. But the doorway's not empty. Woman stands there, tall and gold in the afternoon sun.

10

Y OU WILL recollect I last met Luella Bronstein all the way back in that hotel lobby in Brooklyn, almost a year ago. What she's done since, I know by hearsay. In my head she remains pristine, beautiful, made of porcelain. Even rutting atop the kitchen table in my dream, she contrived somehow to exude this same exquisite quality. So I'm right surprised to see how haggard she be, as she steps into the house and takes us in. Faint lavender shadows beneath her eyes. Pale hair lank. Expression pulled into shock, concern.

"Oh no! What's happened? Is she hurt?"

Anson growls, "Get out of the way. I'm taking her to the doctor."

"Darling, what's wrong? What's the matter?"

He turns his head to me. "Can you walk?"

"Yes, dammit!"

Blood runs fast and light just now. Vision narrows to the ground right in front of me. All my body's in thrall to this one emergency, this single urge taking over my head and limbs and everything—to find some shelter fast, find some safe place, don't matter where so long as this woman is away from it.

Luella's voice rings clear. "You'll have some trouble getting out, I'm afraid. The police are on their way."

"*Police?*"

"I saw them in town. Gathering at the county jail. We've got to get out of here, Marshall. I—"

"I said, get away. I'm taking my wife to a hospital."

"Your *wife*! Don't be an idiot. She's not—"

"*She is my wife!*"

Luella speaks like to a child, hard of understanding. "She's not. She's married to Joseph, she's having his child, don't you know? And you and me—"

"There's no *you and me*!"

"You're *mine* now, you said so *yourself*, when we—"

"Bronstein, give me the keys to that car. *Now*."

"You're mine. I saved you, I nursed you, you're *mine*. She's been lying to you, Marshall—"

"My wife does not *lie*."

"*Your wife*. That's rich. Was she your wife last night, when we were doing it on the rug?"

"Shut *up*, Lu!"

"What about this morning? Did you tell her all about *that*? Why, hardly an hour ago, right there on the kitchen table while the bacon burned on the stove. He was an *animal*, Gin. I can hardly *walk*."

"Put your arms around my neck," Anson says to me, low-voiced, and I obey him because I got no choice, can't stand no more on these exhausted legs, overcome with mortal dread at this *thing* rushing on to me, poor Mama's screams ringing in my ears, do anything to unwind this infinite screw that tightens on my back and my insides. Don't give a good goddamn right now who did what on a rug or a table or up against a goddamn wall. With some mighty, miraculous effort Anson lifts me in his wasted arms and carries me past Luella. Bronstein yanks the door open and hands Anson the car key.

"Get her out of here," he says. "I'll deal with Lu."

"Stop," says Luella.

Bronstein swears. "Put that down, Lu. Dammit. Just let them go."

"I couldn't possibly. Anson, set her back on the sofa. My brother will take her to the hospital."

"Go to hell."

"Darling, I'll shoot her. I will."

Can't see what's happening on the other side of Anson's chest. Brain now white hot with the heat of this tightening vise. This instrument of natural torture. From my mama's travails I understand in my bones that my time's coming hard upon me, won't be one of those long drawn-out affairs, no. My insides are fixing fast to rid themselves of their parasite nuisance, and they have got no time to worry about jealous husbands—past or present—and women with guns. That pistol Anson left on the floor by the sofa. Dim I hear some voices on the other side of that front door, out on the drive, men's voices. Rock and a hard place. And I will be laboring a baby out into the world betwixt them somehow, someway, any moment.

Anson stands stock-still with his back toward Luella, his own body in the way of me and the barrel of that gun. She tells him to turn around slow and put me on the sofa.

"No," he says.

"Lu, the police are here. Give up."

She moves behind us. Gun fires off. Anson staggers and spins against the wall so he don't fall forward on top of me. Tries to take the impact on his arms, I think, but still the crash shudders through me. Hear the noise of my own howling. Footsteps hammering up the steps and through the door.

Hands in the air!

Don't shoot! Don't shoot!

Gun cracks out again. Screaming.

We need a doctor! A doctor! yells Anson.

Lift my head from his arm. Stars pop out. Still I glimpse some stocky figure prone on the floor, Luella dragging herself out from under her brother's body.

Then my head won't hold up no more. I'm done.

ELLA

Funny how quickly your life could settle into a whole new routine.

For a week now, Ella had risen at six, showered and dressed and made her way north on the subway to Lenox Hill Hospital. She bought a decaf coffee and a yogurt parfait from the Starbucks at the Seventy-Seventh Street subway exit and ate her breakfast during the short walk to the hospital visitors' entrance. By now the nurses recognized her. Took her through to Patrick's room, where she would sit next to the bed and talk to him, read the sports page, so his mother—who kept vigil at night—could go back to Patrick's apartment in Soho and rest.

THEY HADN'T BEEN ABLE to save his left leg. Ella still heard the doctor's voice in her head, that first day, kind and grave at the same time. *We weren't able to save the left leg, I'm afraid, but the right one should heal so he can walk again with a prosthetic, after physical therapy.* Apparently, when you were hit by a car, the legs took the worst of it. In fact, the bone trauma from a car-pedestrian collision was so characteristic that emergency physicians and surgeons in New York

City were practically the best in the world at screwing and bolting legs back together again, so it was lucky for Patrick that the accident happened in downtown Manhattan.

Ella's uncle Paul, who was a pediatric surgeon himself, explained all this to her. Uncle Paul had been an absolute rock. He was actually on call at Lenox Hill when Patrick came in, so he was the one who was able to connect the nurses in the ICU with Hector's hotel room in Santa Monica. He'd made sure Patrick had the best doctors, the best treatment. Reviewed every chart himself, just to reassure Ella and Patrick's mother, who had driven thirteen hours straight from Indiana to stay by her son's side. From what Ella could tell, Patrick had never worked up the nerve to tell his mother what had happened between him and Ella, about the divorce proceedings or anything. *Thank goodness for you and the baby,* Mrs. Gilbert kept saying. *You'll give him something to live for.*

Ella didn't have the heart to tell her the truth. Not about the divorce, or how Patrick had cheated on her with dozens of women over the course of their marriage. That would all come out eventually. She didn't have the heart to tell Mrs. Gilbert that this was all Ella's fault. The accident happened because of Ella. Of course, there was no way to prove that the accident was no accident. But the pieces fit together, once Ella listened to the voice mail messages that Patrick had left on her cell phone, which she'd left switched off in Los Angeles because of roaming charges, and because she was too busy having sex with Hector.

Hi, honey, he'd said on Monday morning. *I hear you're in L.A. for a few days. That's cool, you deserve some time away. So I figured out where to find the Bronstein stuff you were asking about. Buddy of mine in the Manhattan DA's office says the investigation records should be available on request at the FBI archives in D.C. Put in a call there. I'll let you know what I hear. Could take a while, though. You know how government works, right? Anyway, I guess I'll see you when you get back. Hope you're having a nice time.* (Short pause.) *I mean that, Ella. Wish you the best. Love you.*

Late on Monday, Patrick left another message. *Hi, honey. Me again. So this is weird. Or not so weird, knowing what we know, right? Guy called me back from the FBI today and said they have no records on the Bronstein investigation. Said those files went missing from the archives sometime in the late 1920s. Case never went to trial. So I'm going to call up the* Boston Globe *and the* New York Times *and see what they've got in the news vault. Figure there must have been something in the papers about it, right? This is actually getting pretty interesting. Kind of jazzed up now, I have to say. I'll let you know what I find. I guess you're probably in bed by now. Sleep tight. Take care of that baby, all right? And yourself. Love you. Bye.*

And the last message, early Tuesday morning—*Goooood morning, you. Sorry to buzz you so early out there in La La Land. Just wanted to keep you in the loop for when you finally rise to the surface, ha ha. Got some stuff to do in the city today so I thought I might swing by and see my buddy in the DA's office, see if he can shed some light for me. Maybe the* Times *building, too, check out the archives. Just call me Dick Tracy or whatever. Hope you're well and happy. Enjoying the California sunshine. Wear your sunscreen, right? Gotta hop and catch the train. Talk to you later.*

A few hours later, just after lunchtime, as Patrick walked down Broadway toward City Hall, a plain black sedan ran a red light and plowed into him where he crossed the street, then drove off and left him for dead.

The police never found the car or the driver.

ACCORDING TO DR. DOYLE, Patrick's lead physician, the latest surgery yesterday had been a complete success and they were going to start weaning him off the medication to see if he woke up naturally.

"What if he doesn't wake up naturally?" Ella said.

"Then we'll see. But there's no reason why he shouldn't. The MRIs revealed no significant brain trauma. The rest of his injuries are healing well. Of course, he'll be confused. He'll be in a lot of pain. The loss of his leg is going to take time to deal with."

Ella nodded vigorously. "I have an uncle who lost a leg in Vietnam. I know he'd be more than happy to talk to Patrick, as soon as he's ready."

"Good. Good, that's excellent. He's going to need a lot of love and support. Although I can see he's in good hands in that department." Dr. Doyle smiled and glanced at Patrick, who lay on his bed, white and still, hooked up to all the machines and the IV drip, blanket draped discreetly over the tented right leg and the left leg bandaged at the stump.

The *stump*. That was the only thing that did it for Ella—the word *stump*. She could keep her composure through everything else, the long technical discussions about blood vessels and bone tissue. But *stump*. The word made her shake inside, made the panic boil from her middle to her toes and fingertips and scalp. They'd amputated just above the knee. So now Patrick didn't have a left leg, he had a stump. If he were lucky, and worked diligently at the physical therapy, he might be able to walk and even run again. But that leg he once took for granted would never come back. Foot and ankle and calf, shin and knee, the tendons and skin and muscle that held it together—gone.

Dr. Doyle rose and gathered her clipboard and papers. "Oh, one more thing," she said. "There was a bit of an incident last night I thought I should tell you about."

"Incident? What kind of incident?"

"I wasn't on duty. The attending passed it on to me. Apparently someone tried to enter Mr. Gilbert's room around two in the morning. There was a nurse inside at the time, fortunately. She challenged him. Security escorted him out. He gave his name as"—Dr. Doyle looked back at her clipboard, flipped through a few papers—"Caleb Black? Does that ring a bell?"

Ella shook her head. "Not even a little one."

"Hmm. Well, we've given word to security to keep a close lookout. Sometimes we get reporters trying to get inside patients' rooms, although there's been surprisingly little press about this one. Usually when someone like Mr. Gilbert—high-profile investment banker type—gets involved in an accident like this, the New York tabloids are all over it."

"Maybe it was a busy news day?"

"Well, we can count that blessing, anyway. We'll let you know if anything else occurs." She checked her watch. "I'm off. I'll be back later to see how our boy's doing. The button's right there if you need a nurse."

"I know that button very well. Thanks, doctor."

Dr. Doyle turned to leave, nearly colliding with the nurse entering the room.

"Oh, I'm sorry, doctor," said the nurse. He looked at Ella. "Mrs. Gilbert? You have a couple of visitors in the waiting room."

FOR THE MOST PART, Ella's friends and family had left her alone, at her request. She was busy enough dealing with Patrick and all the paperwork and insurance, with Patrick's mother and his treatment and all the million and one little things that went along with an accident like this one. Uncle Paul passed along any family messages of support and love. Either Dad or Mumma called every day to make sure she was taking care of herself. Dad was supposed to swing by tomorrow on his way from D.C., to take her out to the Hamptons for Lizzie's wedding on Saturday. Then Dad would spend two weeks at The Dunes before he had to return to his law practice, bringing Mumma back home with him. Ella had insisted that everyone carry on as usual with their summer plans and not to worry about her. She was absolutely, totally fine.

So Ella couldn't imagine who might have come to visit her, here at the hospital. As she walked down the corridor to the waiting room, she thought about what Dr. Doyle had said. This Caleb Black person who had tried to visit Patrick in the middle of the night. But surely nobody would try any funny stuff in the middle of Lenox Hill Hospital in the middle of the day, right? Far better to catch Ella on the subway at eight in the evening, when she was on her way home by herself.

She crossed the threshold into the waiting room and looked around.

"Ella? Oh my God."

Ella turned toward the woman's voice just in time to see Lizzie hurtling toward her, arms outstretched. She tried not to say *oof* as her cousin caught her in an embrace like a boa constrictor.

"Ella! I'm so sorry! *We're* so sorry! How is he? Has he woken up yet? Mom said they were going to wake him up today."

Ella peeled herself from Lizzie's arms and smiled at Owen, who'd appeared at Lizzie's shoulder, pale and grave. "Not yet," she said. "But they've started the process. It takes a little while. He's been under for more than a week now."

"His leg." Lizzie's lip trembled. "I can't believe it."

"I'll take his leg in exchange for his life, right? It was a close call for a while there. The blood loss alone."

Lizzie covered her face with her hands. Owen put his palm on her shoulder. "She's pretty broken up about it," he said apologetically. "With the wedding and everything. She thinks it's her fault."

Ella looked at Lizzie in amazement. "Your *fault*? Of course not, honey! What are you thinking? It was an accident."

"But if it wasn't for the wedding—*hiccup*—you wouldn't have been out at The Dunes. And he wouldn't have—wouldn't have . . ."

Ella looked at Owen, who shrugged. "It's kind of a twisted line of logic," he said. "I've tried to tell her. She's been talking about calling off the wedding."

"I just don't see how we can have a wedding when poor Patrick is *lying there*," said Lizzie. "Without a *leg*."

Ella took her by the arm and led her to one of the plastic chairs. Sat down beside her and laid her arm around Lizzie's thin shoulders. "You absolutely *have* to have this wedding, Lizzie," she said. "I *command* it. Patrick would never in a million years want you to postpone your own happiness. This was just a random, terrible accident. It happens. Terrible things happen. It's not your fault, not even remotely. Look, *I'm* coming, right? I'll be there. Everything's going to be fine. Patrick will be okay."

"He lost a leg, Ella. He's not okay."

"So did Uncle Caspian, and I guess he's happier than most people I know."

Lizzie hiccupped.

"Listen, honey. I have to go. Keep an eye on things while they're waking him up. I'll see you in a few days, all right? Joanie's due in tomorrow from Paris, she'll keep you company. Your mom and dad and all the uncles and aunts and cousins. We're all here for you. We all want to see you married and happy. Your special day. Don't worry about a thing." Ella looked up at Owen. "She'll be all right. Just be gentle with her, okay?"

"Of course."

Ella felt a vibration in her pants pocket and swore. She'd forgotten to switch off her cell phone when she arrived at the hospital. She slipped it out to turn it off, and as she did so, she caught sight of the number on the screen. The area code belonged to a Los Angeles phone.

WHOEVER IT WAS, HE or she didn't leave a voice mail. As soon as Lizzie and Owen had bustled off, Ella went outside and called the number back.

"Hello?" said a woman's voice. "Is this Ella?"

"Speaking. Who's this?"

A soft sigh. "It's Louisiana Goring. I'm here in New York. I thought we might have a coffee or something."

THEY MET AT THE Starbucks on the corner of Seventy-Seventh and Lexington, where Ella picked up her coffee and yogurt every morning. When she arrived, Louisiana was already there, nursing a cappuccino. She didn't look as if she'd had much sleep. "I took the red-eye," she explained, as Ella dragged out a stool at the bar of pale wood that fronted the street. "So please excuse me if I'm not totally coherent. You want something?"

"No thanks. I can't stay long. My husband's in ICU at the moment."

Lulu glanced down at Ella's belly and back again. "So I heard. Sounds like your life is even more complicated than mine."

"It's been a crazy year. So. To what do I owe the honor?"

"Good question. My conscience?" Lulu paused with the cappuccino at her lips. "Or the fact that my composer is about the most miserable person in Los Angeles at the moment."

"He does have both his *legs* at the moment, though? So I don't have a lot of pity to spare, actually."

"Oh, he doesn't want your pity, believe me. Whatever happened after I left that party, he knows he was the ass. Have you talked to him at all?"

"That's not really any of your business."

"So you haven't."

Ella turned to look through the window. Manhattan bustled by— moms propelling strollers to playgroups and music classes, seniors getting their medications and walking their dogs, actress-waitresses heading out for bagels and coffee. The day was warm and muggy, typical end of June weather, faint subway stink in the air. Behind them, the coffee grinder whirred and whirred. The milk frother sloshed. Ella faced west, across Lexington Avenue, toward California, across miles and miles of America to where Hector lay or sat or showered in his hotel room, perched on the edge of the giant Pacific. Far away now.

She'd taken the red-eye back to New York, had started packing as soon as she hung up the phone, shoved everything into her roller suitcase in a blind panic. Hector hadn't said a single unnecessary word. Had driven her to the airport. She didn't even remember if he'd kissed her good-bye. He asked her humbly to please call him when she got in safely, let him know what had happened, and she did. A short, utilitarian conversation. But she hadn't spoken to him since. She couldn't even begin to focus her mind on Hector. Even to *think* about Hector seemed like a colossal betrayal. Of what, she wasn't sure. Her heart ached now. But her heart had ached all week, had ached for Patrick and for her own guilt. She didn't know what she felt anymore. She didn't even know how to feel.

"Look," said Louisiana Goring, "first off, I was way out of line last week. I was out of my head with jealousy. I admit it. My therapist says I need to be more self-aware, like when I'm doing shit my dad taught me. You waltzed into the room all graceful and gorgeous and genuine, like right out of a J. Crew catalog or something, and Hector lit up for you, and you disappeared into the bedroom together, and I lost it. So I'm sorry. If what I said caused any trouble between the two of you, you know, mea culpa. Don't let me ruin anything, okay? I'm not worth it."

Ella turned to her. "I don't get it. You're rich, you're powerful. You're beautiful. You have a husband who adores you, an adorable kid. Why?"

"Honey, we are all *mean*. We're all bad, right? We all have the wicked thoughts. Even Hector, right? He liked him some kinky shit sometimes. He didn't always *want* to like it, but he did."

"But that's different. Sex is different."

"You think so? Because I think sex shows us who we really are. Tells you everything you need to know about a person. Me, I like to push it to the limit. Go to the dark corners and see what's there." She paused to swish her drink. "It's what makes me so good at what I do, by the way. Like my dad. This movie? Did Hector tell you about it?"

"Just the bare bones. The Nazis in Poland."

"Yeah, so believe me, you know human nature well enough, see how fine that line is"—she held up two fingers and pressed them close—"between the hunter and the prey. Just pure luck that you were born on one side and not the other. Was every single Nazi a fucking psychopath? No, he wasn't. They just let him do the bad things and it made him bad. We could all do it. We could. Like the Resistance? Everybody said he was Resistance *after* the war, right? But honestly, maybe one percent of people actually have the guts to resist a true police state. A real one, you know, when speaking up means you get your brains blown out? One percent have the guts. The rest just do what their friends do. Think what their friends think. That's human nature. But here's the thing, Ella. We all want to *believe* we're the hero. The plucky hero standing up for truth and justice and shit. Oh yeah. We all want to think we're on the right side. I mean, the Nazis sure thought they were. So did the Soviets. Every fucking totalitarian ever just *knows* he's on the right side of history. That's how he justifies all the totalitarian shit, right? Fuck. I could really use a cigarette right now. I swear to God, New York is getting as bad as L.A."

"We could go outside, if you want."

"I'll live. I went without fags for *months* when I was pregnant with Harry. Well, almost."

Ella ran her thumb along the edge of the counter. "Does Hector know he's Harry's father?"

"What makes you say that?"

"Just a hunch."

"You clever thing. Well, he doesn't. He doesn't even suspect, isn't that weird? Nor will he. I don't need that level of complication in my life."

"You don't think he has a right to know?"

"Of course he does. But I'm too selfish to give it to him. So there." She paused. "I got pregnant on purpose. I admit it. I mean, I knew the end was near. Every relationship has a natural life span, right? And I literally had no future with a broke and fatally virtuous New York musician who, for example, refused to move out of the shitty dump he was living in because it had *atmosphere*." She put the word in finger quotes. "But I couldn't just quit him cold turkey. God, his fucking *genius*, I mean I could come just *listening* to him, right? And I couldn't let that go. I needed a piece of that to keep with me forever. So I stopped taking the pill. Spent six weeks in New York humping his poor brains out, I mean when we weren't trying to kill each other. I was such a bitch to him, I really was. Sick, sick times. When I missed my period, it was like a relief. Flew back to L.A. and told Monty let's elope to Vegas, like *now*. But I won't ever regret it. Harry's the best thing that ever happened to me. Sweet, beautiful kid, just like his dad."

"That's why you gave Hector the job on the movie, isn't it?"

"Partly. But mostly because I wanted the best, and he's the best. *Also*, if I'm honest, so I could sleep with him again. Which did *not* happen, for the record. But yes. I wanted to introduce him to his son. I just really *needed* to see them together. Harry loves music, you know? It's amazing, DNA."

"And you're happy now?"

Louisiana laughed. "I mean, what's happy? I'll tell you what. You know what's the weirdest thing about this whole shitty bubble I live in? You meet somebody for the first time and they already know everything about you. The whole story. Like, how I was born to this bit actress my dad had a fling with on set in New Orleans, spent my childhood back and forth between them, all of it. Wild child, years of therapy, blah blah."

"If it makes you feel any better, *I* didn't know all that. Or I didn't remember."

"Good for you. Anyway, I treat men like shit, because of my dad, apparently, and about the best thing I've ever done in my life was to leave Hector before I could wreck him. And now I'm going to give you a big fat present, courtesy of my therapist, and tell you how *lost* he is without you. I mean, his heart is *broken*. I really hope you forgive him. I really hope you're as kind as I think you are. I really hope you love him as much as he loves you. I don't know what the deal is with your husband and everything—all Hector would say was that you were separated, wouldn't say why, I'm guessing the guy was a cheating pig, they all are, except Hector—anyway, I hope you do the right thing here. I hope you find it in your heart to make that darling man happy, because he deserves it. He deserves someone like you. That's all." She set down her empty cappuccino cup and rose from her stool. "That's all I flew out here to say. Now I'm going to go smoke a cigarette and polish my fucking halo."

PATRICK WAS THE YOUNGEST of four children, and his father had died of pancreatic cancer when he was twelve, so his mother poured all her love into him like he was a vessel with no bottom. When Ella returned to the hospital room after having coffee—well, *not* having coffee—with Louisiana Goring, Mrs. Gilbert sat in the chair by Patrick's prone body, reading aloud from a Tom Clancy novel.

"I couldn't sleep," she said, folding the book over her finger, "so I came back. You should go home and get some rest, honey. You're looking tired. You need to take care of yourself, because of the baby."

"I'm fine."

"Now, honey." Mrs. Gilbert rose and patted Ella's arm. "The most important thing in the world is that baby, you hear me? I'll keep watch here. I'll let you know when he starts to wake up. Everything's going to be fine now."

Ella looked into her soft blue eyes and thought, *You have no idea.*

HOME WAS NOT THE apartment building on Christopher Street, at least for now. Because of Mrs. Gilbert, Ella had been staying at Patrick's loft in Soho, which she'd never imagined she would ever enter again. Yet here she was. Inhabiting her old apartment, sleeping in her old bed. Partly to be there for Mrs. Gilbert, who didn't know how to work all the modern appliances, let alone navigate a New York grocery store—and furthermore wasn't aware that her son and pregnant daughter-in-law were, in fact, separated—but also because the building stood right on the Lexington Avenue subway line, so Ella could be at the hospital in twenty minutes door-to-door. The day after she arrived, she'd gone to Hector's apartment in the Village to gather a few things. She had done this quickly, efficiently, allowing not a single scrap of sentiment to gather about her. She'd needed all her emotional strength for the ordeal in front of her.

But now Patrick was going to live. Minus a leg, but he was going to live, so at least *that* burden was lifted from Ella's paralyzed shoulders. She found herself getting off the 6 train at Grand Central, taking the shuttle across to Times Square, the 1 train to the Christopher Street station. The familiar walk down the leafy, cobbled Village streets to 11 Christopher.

Upstairs, the apartment smelled like wood and sunlight, abandoned. She set her pocketbook on the kitchen counter and stared for a moment at the piano. The window beyond it, overlooking the street. It was two o'clock in the afternoon at the tail end of June, and the air was hot and stale, and Ella's heart swelled so it might explode from between her ribs. These dear walls, packed with memory. Was it only a couple of weeks ago Hector had kissed her good-bye and flown to L.A., and she and Nellie had left for The Dunes? Now the dog was happily romping the beaches with her Labrador cousins, and Ella . . . and Ella . . . what?

Don't go.

Ella started and looked at the bedroom door. Had she actually heard the words, or did they echo from her memory? Except she'd almost forgot about that strange, ghostly voice altogether. The night before Hector left.

Don't go.

Well, you got that right, Redhead. Any more news I could use?

But the air was silent and dense. Ella went to the fridge and got out a bottle of water. As she did so, she saw the jar of prenatal vitamins on the counter, Hector's note still attached. Oops. She opened the jar and swallowed one with her water. Finished the bottle—she was thirsty—tossed it in the recycling bin and went into the bedroom.

They were still there in the bottom drawer—her enamel box of buttons, hidden under the floorboards of her old apartment downstairs, and the shoebox filled with old photographic plates. The Redhead, in her naked and delectable bounty. Ella sat on the floor and laid them out, one by one. All in black and white, except for the red-tinted hair. *Redhead Takes the Bait. Redhead Rides Again. Bon Voyage, Redhead.* In each one, whatever her pose, the Redhead's face was coyly hidden. That was part of the appeal—you couldn't tell who she was.

Except . . .

Ella picked up one of the plates, labeled *Redhead Meets Her Match.* The Redhead reclined on one of those Victorian fainting couches, miraculous breasts pointing to the ceiling, tiny waist and curving hips and long, slender, creamy legs arranged against the upholstery for maximum erotic effect. Short, curling red hair. One arm stretched out from her divine torso and held a large, ornate hand mirror, in which the Redhead was admiring her reflection. As in the other photographs, her face was turned away from the camera. But if you looked carefully at the mirror, you could just make out what seemed to be the tiny shape of a woman's head at a three-quarters angle.

Ella got up from the floor and went back into the living room. She rummaged in the drawer of the rolltop desk until she found the old-fashioned magnifying glass in its soft red leather case, which Hector had found in a junk shop and gave to her when she started looking for a job a few weeks ago—*For my Sherlock*, he said, hunting for clues in spreadsheets. She carried it back into the bedroom, held the plate up to the light, and examined the mirror through the magnifying glass.

Blurred like a ghost. Overexposed. The lines and shadows of a face looked back at her, almost alive.

Her own face.

Ella jumped back. Dropped the magnifying glass. Turned by some kind of instinct to the mirror on the chest of drawers that Hector had made for her, the Art Deco mirror he'd found in another junk shop, refinished the wood, left the old silvering as it was, speckled with age.

Her face glimmered back at her—the same angle, the same face as in the photograph.

WHEN THE FRONT DOOR opened, Ella was sitting in the middle of the bedroom floor with a pair of scissors, cutting the FH Trust annual report into tiny pieces.

Hector's voice called, "Ella? Is that you?"

She heard a soft thump, like a suitcase landing on the floor. Her fingers went still. Her pulse jacked in her throat.

"In the bedroom," she called back softly.

His footsteps came quiet on the wood floor. There were so many of them. How long did it take for one long-legged man to cross a room? Then he appeared in the doorway. His surprised eyes found her on the rug, surrounded by scraps of paper.

"What are you doing?" he said.

"Nothing."

"Doesn't look like nothing."

"Getting rid of some old papers I don't need anymore, that's all." She realized she was out of breath at the sight of his strong, lean body in chinos and a T-shirt. Tanned face and ruffled golden-brown hair and puzzled caramel eyes.

She drew some air into her lungs. "You're home," she said.

"I'm home." He sat down on the floor next to her. "How's Patrick?"

"Stable. They're taking him off the medication so he starts to wake up. He'll be in the hospital another week or two, if all goes well, and then rehab upstate."

"So I guess you'll be going with him?"

"I'll get him settled in, definitely. The rest depends on him."

Hector nodded and picked up one of the scraps of paper. Tore it in half. "I'm so sorry, Ella. I really am. For both of you. It's a shitty, shitty deal for you both."

"He was in the city because of me," Ella said. "I asked him to look into some of this FH Trust stuff for me."

"You *what*?"

"There was this big bootlegging trial in the summer of 1925, and I thought there might be some connection to the Hardcastles. So Patrick went downtown that day to visit this friend of his in the DA's office and find out more."

Hector stared at her. "He was doing all that for you?"

"It kind of snowballed quickly. While I was in L.A. with you."

"Okay," he said slowly.

"Okay, what?"

"Nothing. I just—I didn't realize you two were—never mind. Doesn't matter."

"It *does* matter, actually. I shouldn't have asked him to do it. I took advantage of him, I *used* him—"

"Stop. You're feeling *guilty* because he was sleuthing for you while you were in L.A. with me? Ella, it could have happened to anyone. It was a random act. It's not your fault."

She shook her head. "Before I left, Patrick tracked down the Sterling Bates trader who handled the FH Trust account. Turns out he'd just been killed. Fell out of his eighteenth-floor window." She put finger quotes around *fell,* the way Louisiana had. "Patrick wanted to let the whole thing go. Said it was too dangerous. But I asked him to keep investigating anyway. Even though people were getting killed over this."

"Hold on a second. You're saying this *wasn't* an accident? Someone tried to *kill* Patrick?"

"I'm sure of it."

"Holy shit."

"I thought I was doing the right thing. I thought I was standing up against those crooked Hardcastles and everything. I was just so proud of myself. Standing up for truth and justice. What a hero. Honorable, principled Ella."

"You *are* honorable. You *are* principled. That's why I love you."

Ella picked up the remains of the FH Trust report and sliced off a corner. "I've been living with you, having *sex* with you, while I was still married to someone else. Pregnant with his baby. Then I asked him to do something dangerous for me, knowing he would do it because he still loved me."

"To be *fair,* Ella—"

"Do you know where I've been staying this week? Patrick's apartment. Do you know why? So his mother won't know I've been sleeping with someone else since April."

"You're saying it was a mistake? We were a mistake?"

"I'm saying an *honorable* person would have waited to start a new relationship until after her divorce came through. After her baby was born."

"And if *I* was honorable, I wouldn't have seduced you into it."

"You didn't seduce me. You gave me a choice."

Hector looked down at the scraps of paper, scattered around her like snowflakes. He gathered a few of them into a pile. "Can I tell you a story, Ella?"

"A *story*?"

"It's about a guy taking stock of his life a couple of years ago. Lonely guy. His mom was dying. He'd just got out of a bad relationship. He got to thinking that maybe it was time to put away childish things. Stop feeling sorry for himself. Stop taking stuff out of life and start making stuff. After a while, he got up and went to his piano and started composing music, different music than he'd been writing before. He learned some carpentry and started building things, furniture and cabinets and objects, as well and as beautiful as he could. He stayed up all night and thought about everything. Listened to the music in the walls around him. After a while it seemed to him that the house was trying to tell him something. He started remembering things his mom had told him when he was a kid. Sometimes, during those long hours in the hospital room, he asked his mom about them. She told him about his family, about the house and what had happened there a long time ago. All these stories. Then she died. The guy took her dog home with him to live. He found a girlfriend. Still there was something missing. He didn't know what it was. He talked to the people in the building, his family. Asked them some of the things he'd asked his mom. Then one morning he woke up and wrote a classified advertisement for the studio apartment on the fourth floor, the one none of the other cousins wanted to live in, because *she* had lived in that room once."

"Hector—"

"Just listen to me. Please. He put this ad in the paper and nobody answered it. Not one person. It was like nobody even saw it, nobody in the whole damn city. Until one morning this woman calls the super and asks if she can look at the apartment. She comes and looks at the apartment. Super says she loved the building, she wants the apartment, it feels like home to her. Wants to move in right away. And this guy who lives upstairs, it's all he can think about. Who is this woman. What's she like. He's got this feeling he can't explain, like the building *wants* her there, *he* wants her there. Like nothing he's ever wanted before. She moves in a few days later. He catches glimpses of her on the stairs, through the window on the sidewalk outside. She takes his breath away. *It's her,* he thinks. He knows it's her. Finally he hears her head down to the laundry room early one morning. He screws up his courage and follows her."

"And?"

"And you know the rest of the story."

Ella stood up and walked past him to the kitchen. She came back with the brush and dustpan. He still sat in the same place, the same position. She brushed the scraps of paper into the dustpan and threw them in the garbage. When she was done, she sat on the piano bench and stared at the keys. Hector came up behind her and sat on the extreme edge of the bench, not touching her.

"I kissed her," he said.

"Louisiana?"

"I didn't want to, obviously. She came by after lunch that Saturday, the day before you flew out, and she sat down next to me on the piano bench and started to kiss me. I froze up at first. I didn't know what to do. Just shock. I couldn't even believe it was happening. That she would ever do something like that, married with a kid and everything. *Knowing* I was with you. And—this is what's hard to explain without—I mean, obviously we'd kissed a million times before, and just for a moment—I'm in shock, right—it was like autopilot or something. Lasted about—I don't know, four or five seconds before I woke up and pulled away. Then I stood up and said she had to leave. She asked if I was sure about that, and I said I was never more sure of anything in my life. And I reached for the phone and called you up and asked you to come to California. She was still there, listening to the whole thing. I felt physically sick about it."

Ella put her finger on middle C and pressed the key gently down. A soft note tickled the air.

"I'm so sorry," he said. "I never in my life meant to kiss another woman but you."

"It's all right. It doesn't matter."

"Do you mean it doesn't matter, or you don't care?"

She turned to him. "Of course I *care*. But you letting an old girlfriend kiss you for a few seconds? That's nothing. I've committed *adultery*. I almost *killed* my husband out of—I don't know, selfishness or arrogance or whatever it was."

"My God," he said. "Do you really believe that?"

"It's true."

"No, it's not. What Patrick did to *you*, that was wrong. You had a marriage together, you had trust. What happened to him last week, you didn't *do* that. You wouldn't hurt anybody."

"We all do bad things," she said. "We all hurt each other, whether we mean to or not. Do you remember the night before you left? How I got up in the night because I heard a woman crying?"

"I forgot about that. Did you hear it again?"

"I didn't tell you the other part. I didn't tell you what she said."

Hector leaned toward her. His eyes turned sharp. "What did she say?"

"*Don't go.* She said it a few times. *Don't go.*"

"But you let me go anyway."

"What else was I supposed to do?"

Hector frowned at her a moment. Rose from the bench and held out his hand. Ella looked at his palm and put her fingers there. He drew her up and led her to the sofa. Sat down and gathered her close.

"I need to tell you some things," he said.

"Another story?"

"Not a story, exactly. Things I want you to know, because I want you to know everything. I don't want to feel like I'm hiding anything from you, ever again. So listen. She was my mother's godmother."

"The *Redhead*?"

Hector stroked her arm with his thumb. "My grandmother was a friend of hers. They all lived together in this house. She had a bunch of kids, and Gin Kelly took them in, and her own kids, too, like one big happy family. Eventually my grandmother got together with the guy who played the bull fiddle in the speakeasy next door."

"Bruno!"

"And they had my mother, and Gin Kelly was her godmother."

"So what happened?"

"They had to leave. Gin and her family. Something to do with a bootlegging syndicate that was after them. But she left behind the box of buttons that was a keepsake from her father, and she asked my grandmother to hide them for her. When I was little, Grandma would tell me this story. All of us cousins would ask her where she hid it, and she wouldn't tell us. She said the rightful owner would find them one day."

"Me."

"You." He kissed her hair. "When I said I belonged to you. *That's* what I meant."

There was no understanding this. There was no wrapping her head around any of it. Ella thought her fingers should be shaking, she should be trembling or something. But she wasn't. She lay against Hector's chest and smelled the familiar smell of his skin and his shirt and let everything settle around her, let it just sit there and *be* without comprehending any of it. Without even feeling any of it. She just wanted to rest now. His thumb stroking the bare skin of her arm.

And the thing about Hector was, he let her rest. Didn't demand any declarations or reassurance from her. Just gave her everything he had—his love, his strength, his warm, solid body—and didn't ask for anything back.

She closed her eyes and realized her belly was rippling after all. Like a butterfly fluttering by, beating its wings softly in her middle.

Her eyes flew open.

"The baby," she whispered.

"What's the matter?"

Ella took his hand and drew it under her shirt. Laid his palm against the knob that rose beneath her belly button. "Close your eyes," she said.

All was quiet. Still and sacred as night. Then—

Flutter, flutter.

"No way," said Hector.

"Way."

"That's our *baby*."

"That's our baby," Ella said.

She went to sleep like that, lying against Hector's chest, while his hand lay warm against her womb. *Skin on skin,* she said to herself, last words before she slipped away.

ELLA SLEPT RIGHT THROUGH her cell phone ringing, until Hector nudged her gently awake and handed it to her.

Sorry to wake you, he said. *I thought it might be from the hospital.*

She answered groggily. It was Mrs. Gilbert. Patrick had woken up. He was asking for her.

FINALE

Now We Are Found

(mea maxima culpa)

CAPE COD, MASSACHUSETTS

April 1925

1

I NAMED HIM John Oliver Marshall, for his dead uncle and for his father. Call him Johnnie for every day. He was awful big for an early baby, eight pounds exactly. Near enough split me apart. Has nobody's face or hair or eyes that I can tell, and his voice bawls loud and lusty when he wants for milk. Born on the rug in Luella's front parlor. One of the sheriff's deputies was the town doctor—that's why Bronstein couldn't reach him on the telephone, he was saddling up to secure Luella's place on orders from no less than the Bureau of Prohibition headquarters in Washington—so I guess maybe the Lord Almighty kept an eye out for me that day after all. Near enough split me apart, as I said, yet the doctor told me he never seen such an easy birth for a first time.

Mind you, this be the same physician who prescribed Anson tobacco cigarettes for his pneumonia, so you may take his opinion with howsoever much salt you can hold in your hand. Still, now I have the chance to reflect more objective, I admit I have recovered from my travails disgraceful quick, according to my mountain breeding.

Where was I? Brain's apt to scatter these days, which Ruth Mary says I will have to get used to. Scarce a week passed since that remarkable day my son came squalling to mortal life and his daddy resurrected from the dead. Now I sit tranquil in a fine wooden rocking chair in a fine ocean cottage, sun streaming through the window-panes, Johnnie nursing ferocious at my left teat. The right he has already emptied. Gained nearly a pound already, Ruth Mary tells me. Thank the good Lord for Ruth Mary. Window sash hangs open an inch or two to let in the good sea air. My daddy found us this place, facing due east over the unruly Atlantic. Drove the pair of us there himself, once I threatened to tear the hospital down if they didn't let me out. Told them nurses if I was strong enough to born a baby on a rug in Luella Bronstein's front parlor, attended by a sheriff's deputy and a frantic skeleton husband, I was strong enough to recline luxurious in the back seat of Charles Schuyler's stately Duesenberg for the eight hours it took us to reach Cape Cod.

Johnnie's mouth has just begun to slow from its desperate pace when a knock sounds on the door. *Ruth Mary?* I call. *That you?*

"It's your father."

"Well, come on in."

Schuyler, who has just swung jaunty through the door, turns a remarkable shade of puce and spins back round. Poor fellow, he can't quite get used to the sight of his grandson taking nourishment, even though I take care to lay a linen cloth over the relevant parts to save his embarrassment. Seems most of them blue-blooded *Social Register* types never dream of nursing their young when good scientific milk is available for purchase, whereas I was bred up hardscrabble, not knowing one end of a hygienic glass bottle from another, except for the rubber nipple at the end.

Schuyler clears his throat and says to the wall, "You have a visitor."

"Visitor? Who on earth?"

Clears that throat again. "Your husband."

Heart makes a peculiar lurch, which I disguise by pretending to adjust the linen cloth veiling Johnnie's busy wee head, not that Schuyler looks in my direction. "Turned up, has he?"

"Downstairs this minute. Drove all the way from Washington during the night, he says."

"My goodness. Hope you offered him a glass of something."

"He wouldn't take it. Wants to see you."

"Why, then I guess you'd better show him up."

Schuyler slips grateful back out the door, just as Johnnie starts to fuss. I lift him to my shoulder to pass some air. Wee fellow reminds me of a prairie dog the way he bobs his head around. Never think he came early, to look at him now. I don't know, maybe he wasn't. Maybe we got our dates wrong. Can't say I was paying all that much attention to the natural rhythms at the time, being on my honeymoon and all. All this I tell you so I don't have to think too careful about the man who hurries up the stairs right now. That bridegroom I spoke of. Haven't seen him since early morning after Johnnie was born, when he joined the Prohibition bureau boys to hunt for Luella, who ran off in all the confusion, the sheriff's deputies of Sharon, Vermont, not being much accustomed to the cunning ways of—

Door cracks open. Johnnie chooses this instant to belch up some milk on my shoulder. I make busy cleaning the sour spit from my blouse while my prodigal husband stands awkward in the doorway.

"Well, come in," I say.

From the far edge of my vision, Anson steps forward. Wears some kind of brown wool suit, tweed or something. Hat in hands. Rasps out a respectful, "How is he?"

"Why, your son's the very bee's knees, Oliver Marshall. What did you expect?"

"May I see him?"

"They Lord. He's your own child, isn't he?"

In a couple of giant strides Anson reaches the chair and drops to one knee at my side, where Johnnie bobs his fuzzy head from the height of my shoulder.

"Did you find her?" I ask.

He catches his breath. "Yes. Outside of Saint Albans. Headed for the border. She's in the federal prison in Boston, awaiting arraignment. Drove to Washington to file the paperwork and then straight here."

"What about Bronstein?"

"No sign of him. Walked out of the hospital and disappeared into thin air."

"The good Lord protect him, wherever he be." I lower Johnnie from my shoulder and hold him out. "Here you are, then. All full up with milk."

Anson gathers up his baby son in his arms and stares down amazed. Johnnie stares back in equal amazement. Shudder passes through Anson. He smells of car exhaust and ozone and perspiration. Black eye's healed to yellow dun. "I should have cleaned up first," he whispers.

"Oh, he won't notice. Take him for a walk around the room."

Poor Anson can't seem to look away from his son's wee squished face. Rises slow and careful to his feet and walks to the window. The sight of them together starts my breath to catch in my throat. Still I can't look away, any more than Anson can look away from Johnnie's new eyes. Holds him secure and natural, like a man accustomed to babies. I recollect how Mrs. Marshall bore little Marie as a kind of afterthought, when Anson was already grown, and my heart hurts all over again.

Poor man, I don't believe he's gained so much as an ounce of weight this past week. Clothes just hang from his thin, starved bones. Yet those bones be sturdy still, and Johnnie fits right into the nook of his elbow like a football. Waves his wee fingers. Makes those funny cooing noises, for to make a fine impression on his daddy.

I button up my blouse and fiddle with my sleeves. "Growing like crabgrass. Every three hours he's howling for more. Sleeps all right, though."

Anson moves on from the window, bouncing Johnnie gentle in his arm. Opposite side of the room and back while I twiddle my sleeve some more. Just stares and stares in that baby's face, like nothing else exists in the wide world. Johnnie waves his hand and grabs hold of his daddy's fingerbone. Anson catches his breath and comes to a stop. Stands a moment, holding hands together. Turns his son onto his chest and stares out the window while Johnnie kind of burrows into him.

"What are you thinking?" I ask.

"Just remembering how I used to hold my sister, after she was born. I'd forgotten that smell." He puts his nose to Johnnie's soft hair. "Like a new puppy, almost."

"And for the same reason, I'm sure. Makes them so irresistible you don't mind crawling out of bed in the middle of the night to feed and cuddle them."

"Are you getting enough rest?"

"I'm all right. Used to help my mama take care of her little ones, when she was sick abed afterward, so I guess I know what to do with them. And Ruth Mary holds us all together. Sent by the Lord, she was."

"She's a fine woman."

"She's a wonder with Patsy. Keeps her clear while I see to Johnnie." He turns. "Where *is* Patsy?"

"Ruth Mary took the children into town for ice cream. Be back soon, I guess. Patsy'll be over the moon to see you. Keeps asking for you."

He nods and turns his head back. Dressed for travel in brown tweeds and vest and wilted white shirt. Must have left his jacket downstairs. Needs a haircut and a shave and maybe a bath. Dark stubble dusts his jaw like a shadow. Hand spreads big over the white swaddle blanket that covers Johnnie's back. "Thank you," he says, so soft I almost don't catch the words.

"For what?"

"For having him. For taking care of him so well."

"What else was I going to do?"

"I should have been with you. I should never have left to begin with. And I'm due to leave again this afternoon. Gather up evidence, interview witnesses. Willebrandt wants to bring her to trial by September."

"You do what you must. Don't worry about us."

"That's not what I mean."

"What do you mean, then?"

"I mean he's my son. I don't *want* to leave him."

How the light falls upon the two of them. Anson and Johnnie in a nimbus together. My heart might burst. I ask if he's asleep.

"Yes, I think so."

"Give him back to me, then, and go wash up. Bathroom's down the hall. When you're done we'll leave this cherub with his granddad and go out on the beach."

2

OUTDOORS, THE air is mild and true, uncommon warm for the tail end of April. Breeze blows kind on us both. Schuyler was happy to take Johnnie for a bit. How he dotes on that child, I tell

Anson, as we take off our shoes and stockings and stick our feet in the cool sand. Anson rolls up his trouser legs an inch or two and says he's not surprised, it's all a parent can hope for, isn't it? To hold a grand-child one day. He's thinking of his own parents, I guess. He takes my arm to help me down the beach. The hand is warm and hard, just bones. He wears the same tweed suit with a fresh shirt. Smells of sweet soap and cleanliness. Sleek pink cheeks. Just before we reach the line of high tide, he shrugs off his jacket and spreads it on the sand for me to sit. Helps me down. Takes a pack of cigarettes from his vest pocket and offers me one. Lights us both up.

"Picked up the habit, have you?"

"I should stop. I *will* stop, once the trial's over and done."

We smoke in silence. It hurts me to see Anson inhale that ciga-rette, I don't know why. Waves rush upward on a rising tide. It's just mild enough to sit in our shirtsleeves, with the sun warm upon our shoulders. Smell of salt and old seaweed and tobacco. I feel like Anson has got something to say to me, and he's working out how to begin.

"I telephoned Billy," he says, "about Marie."

"How is she?"

"She's fine, according to him. Doesn't really understand what hap-pened. She's so young, you know. Billy says he'll raise her. He was pretty firm about it."

"Billy? He's just a kid himself!"

"He's got a new fiancée. Thinks she won't mind."

"*Thinks?*"

Anson pauses to smoke. "He blames me. He wasn't cruel about it, but he made it clear he wants no part of me. And he's right."

"No, he's not. It's not your fault. You didn't kill them."

"I might as well have."

"Listen to you. Was it *you* who drug your father out on the high seas in search of you? Was it *you* your mother came to visit that morning? No, it was *me*, Anson. Me. You was the most upright fellow in the world until I walked into your life. Not a sinful bone in your body."

Anson makes an angry noise and crushes out his cigarette. Stands up to face the surf with his hands stuffed in his pockets. "I wasn't keeping track," he says, "but I'm pretty sure it was about the middle of March by the time I was strong enough to get out of bed for longer spells. Snow'd melted some, anyway. Lu brought clothes and shoes so I could walk outside, build up my strength—"

"I said not to call her that."

He hollows out some sand with his heel. "When I could walk a mile or so without losing breath, I asked her to drive me to the nearest train station so I could go back home to you. I said I couldn't stand another day. I hadn't heard a word from you, even when I was sick. All I wanted was to get back before I lost you forever. She got upset. She said I wasn't well enough yet, I'd have a relapse. Said she'd send down another message. We argued all day about it. I said I'd walk to Manhattan on my bare feet if I had to. Finally she agreed to drive me down to Brattleboro in the morning, if I felt that strongly about it. And the next morning I woke up sick as a dog. Couldn't keep anything down for a week, almost. Another week before I could get out of bed for longer than a few minutes."

"You think she made you sick?"

"I think that was about the time she sent those men to kill you."

"They Lord." I make to stand up next to him, so I can hear him better with all that noise of wind and surf rushing past my ears. He reaches down his hand to help me. Soon as I have my footing, he withdraws the hand and lights another cigarette.

"The more I think about it," he says, "the more I figure I knew something was wrong, deep down. Just wasn't right. But I couldn't summon the will. There was nothing left of me." He turns up his palms and stares at them. "Anyway, she went away for a few days. She'd leave like that, bring a nurse to stay when I was too sick to get up. Told me it was Bureau work, but of course she was busy running her business. As I know now. The morning she left I went into the kitchen. She'd laid out some breakfast and the newspaper, and the newspaper was the *New York Times* from a week or two earlier, and it was folded open to your marriage announcement. Informed me the happy couple was leaving immediately for an extended wedding trip in Europe."

"Lord have mercy."

"Yes. But I figured I deserved it, too. It was all my doing." He pauses. "I don't think I slept more than a couple hours over the next two days. I kept imagining the two of you together. When I slept at all, I dreamt about it. Then she returned. Full of sympathy."

"I'll bet."

"After supper, she followed me into my room. She had this bottle of French brandy she'd brought back with her. We drank a couple of glasses together. Then she asked if she could comfort me. Unbuttoned my trousers. I didn't even try to stop her, Gin. Didn't even *try*."

"No, I guess not. No reason you should, so betrayed as that."

"She went on her knees and had me off. I might have lasted a minute, I think less. Afterward we got in bed and we did it together. Had intercourse, I mean. Then I slept until noon." He knocks ash from the cigarette. "When I woke we did it again. Over the next few days, until the hour you arrived, we did it five—no, six more times."

"You kept count?"

"Not for the reason you think. Not because it gave me any joy."

"What, then?"

With his thumb he brushes the yellowed remains of his black eye. "Because I knew it was wrong. In my heart I knew it was adultery. I was counting my *sins*, you see? But the more we did it, the worse I burned. I took obscene pleasure in my own degradation. I think I wanted it to kill me."

"My goodness, no wonder you was skin and bones. I only had Bronstein but twice, the night before we married." I take the cigarette from his fingers and smoke it once before I hand it back. "Also, since we're confessing to each other, I brought off Standish on the seat of his flivver, to get that information from him."

Anson turns up his face to the sky and makes a noise like his last breath.

"I'm sorry. I don't mean to hurt you. I didn't much care about it at the time. I didn't much care about anything, once Willebrandt told me you was frozen dead at the bottom of that lake."

A gull swoops right before us to snatch one of them tiny crabs from the tide wash. Carries it off, calling in triumph. Anson sucks the last of his cigarette and blows out the smoke. Dissolves into the good clean breeze.

In that cold voice of his, he says, "If I could travel back to that day in October and shoot myself through the heart, before I could do what I did, I would. With pleasure I would shoot myself through the heart. But I can't do that. Can't bring my mother back or take back what I did with the woman who murdered her. All I can do is bring that woman to justice, as swift as possible."

"Then do it, with my blessing. Do whatever you need for your own peace."

He drops the spent cigarette in the sand and checks his wristwatch.

"I should be off. Have to be in Boston by evening. Thank you for allowing me to see our son. I—well, it meant more than I can say, just to hold him a little. I hope—maybe you won't mind if I stop off here this summer, whenever I can manage it? Spend some time with him?"

"*Mind?*"

"And, well, I know I don't have the right to ask, but—Patsy—I don't want her to think . . ."

"They Lord, Anson. What kind of woman do you think I am?"

He stuffs his hands back in his pockets and stares at his toes, curled in the sand.

"I think Bronstein was dead right," he says quietly. "God gave me His finest pearl, and I tossed her away."

"Tossed me *away*? Do I *look* tossed away to you? Look at me."

Anson turns his face reluctant in my direction. Bleak hollowed-out unshaven head, hair whipsawed by the salt breeze. Empty gaze, a thousand times worse than anguish.

"I am mad as *hell* at you, Oliver Marshall. I am so mad for all this I could spit. I could about kill you when I think of you in bed with that woman, no matter how bad your heart was broke. But I also know what it's like to have you dead and gone from me altogether, and I know which one I choose. I would a million times ruther you be alive and drenched in sin like the rest of us than to carry on without you virtuous as a saint, that's what. And if it takes ten years to forgive you, why, so be it. We're young yet."

From the house comes the noise of children caterwauling. Both of us turn together. Small golden-haired girl child comes pelting down the sand screaming *Anson! Anson! Anson!*

"Go to her," I tell him.

He turns and hurries up the beach to meet her. Goes down on his knees and takes the full weight of her hurling body against his poor frail chest. Near enough knocks him over, my wee round sweet apple. Stronger than she looks.

3

COMES THE summer and the summer people. My dear beach be crowded with them, swimming and searching for shells and what have you, while the sun blazes hotter each day and Johnnie grows big as a dolphin. June melts into July. Out in some federal courthouse in Boston, Luella Bronstein's arraigned on several counts of murder in the first degree and conspiracy and fraud and violations of the Volstead Act, among other crimes too tiresome to list. Anson works there as he has worked most of the time, week after week after hot, lugubrious week, from a desk in the Prohibition bureau field office and an even stuffier room—so he claims—in a Back Bay boardinghouse. I do swan, I read more about that husband of mine in the newspaper than I see of him. Trial of the Century, they're calling it, even though I can personally recollect at least three such-named trials myself only this decade.

Now it's the sixteenth of August, and last night Anson came home for a flying visit. Just the night, which he spent on the parlor sofa, for while this cottage be reasonable spacious—at least compared to the hovel I was bred up in—there are only so many bedrooms, and my daddy's visiting, too, even brung along my kid brother Charlie. All summer long Schuyler has sailed back and forth betwixt his two families, Cape Cod and East Hampton, while his wife pretends he's on business somewhere. His comings are always joyous. Brings a few bottles of champagne from the Schuyler cellars, which they stacked tight full of liquor in that hour before the Volstead Act became law, in order to keep the family in sauce until kingdom come. For this particular visit, he selects a prize vintage, for it happens we're gathering for what you might call a celebration.

Forty-three years ago this morning my mama came squalling into this world, and it seems only right we should honor her in joy instead of sorrow.

4

NOW I won't bore you with all the details. Frankly we never did celebrate my mama's birthday when I was growing up. I never so much as knew what day was the anniversary of her birth. Never occurred to me to ask, me being a child and all.

But Schuyler knows. Schuyler insisted. Having celebrated his beloved's birthday like a tragic drunk most years, he was going to make up for every one of those lost celebrations this time around. Secured Anson's faithful promise that no matter what developments in the Bronstein trial preparations, my husband would contrive for to join us on the big day. And lo and behold, Anson drove up late last night, carrying a bouquet of handsome pink roses for me, color of Johnnie's fat cheeks. Patsy ran shouting downstairs in her nightgown and you can imagine the uproar. Baby woke and everything. Took an hour or two to pack everyone back to his individual bed—me upstairs with Johnnie, Anson on the parlor sofa, as is our habit on the rare occasions my husband spends the night at all.

Rises early, too. Why, right this second Anson swims strenuous out on that Atlantic sea, as he likes to do the moment dawn fingers the horizon. Dives into the ocean water and swims a mile or two, builds back his strength and all. I stare at him through my bedroom window as he climbs back on the sand, dripping seawater from his pale skin. He has gained back some weight and color, at least. Compared to that bundle of empty nerves that drove here at the end of April, he's about bursting with health. Stopped with the cigarettes some weeks ago. Not a drop of liquor touches his lips. But he's not what he was. Some hollow space inside him that just won't fill. Some great weight that holds his spirit fast.

Johnnie has just about done with his milk. I bring up his air and carry him down the empty sand to his daddy. You should see Johnnie grin and stretch out his arms at the sight of that great dripping brute. Squeals with delight as Anson lifts him up in the air and blows raspberries into his belly.

"You're going to bring up all his milk," I tell him.

Anson lowers Johnnie to his ribs and apologizes. Kisses me on the cheek and smiles.

5

ACCORDING TO plan, Patsy and Anson are going to make the birthday dinner. Ruth Mary's taken aback, but I assure her they make a fine team together in the kitchen. Besides, you can't tear Patsy from Anson with a crowbar these days. Like a burr on a donkey's backside, she be.

You see, back at the end of May, when he was back from Boston for a couple of days, Anson sat Patsy down on the parlor sofa and asked if she would mind becoming his actual daughter, and Patsy just threw her arms around his neck and burst into tears. Then she asked if that meant he would stay with her always, and he said yes it would, he wasn't going anywhere, wanted to be her father more than anything, same as Johnnie, and she could call him Papa if she wanted or just Anson if she didn't. Then she looked guilty at me, who sat on her other side, and asked if it was all right if Anson was her own true daddy. I said Anson had my blessing, that way she could be his wee round sweet apple as well as mine. So he took out papers that very next day. Process does require some time, not least because first we had to reestablish Anson himself as an actual living person still married to yours truly, which is not the easiest administrative feat in the world, it turns out. Luckily the Department of Justice itself handled the case and the expense, on account of needing him to be legally alive in order to give testimony at the Bronstein trial.

Anyhow, by October my Patsy should become Miss Patricia Ruth Marshall if all goes well, sister and step-daughter all at once, and I guess we will hold an even bigger party for that memorable occasion. In the meantime, she clings to him ferocious whenever he arrives from Boston. Pure terrified he will not come back next time, no matter how many times he assures her otherwise. This latest three-week absence was specially hard to bear. Why, soon as Anson's come in from his swim, washed and dressed, she scoops him up and tugs him to the kitchen, getting the bread baked and the cake assembled. They've spent a fortune in telegrams arranging it all. Each time the Western Union boy cycled up she ran down to open her telegram, to MISS P KELLY CHATHAM MASS from MR O A MARSHALL BOSTON MASS. She won't let me see them, either. Keeps them stacked in a drawer in her bureau.

6

ONCE JOHNNIE'S settled down for his nap, I put on my bathing suit and join my father on the beach, where he reads a book under a striped umbrella as he likes to do. Charlie frolics with Ruth Mary's brood in the water before us. Schuyler looks at me over the top of his reading glasses and puts his book away. Folds the specs up careful and sets them on top of the book. "What's on your mind, sweetheart?" he asks.

"Can't you guess?"

Now, Schuyler don't know the vile circumstances of Anson's winter absence. Certain details you can't reveal to your own father, after all, no matter how worldly a fellow he be. But I reckon he divines more than he lets on, and naturally the man can read a newspaper, all right. Can add a few sums together. And the state of formal affection betwixt me and Anson speaks for itself, don't it? The parlor sofa and all. Especially now that Johnnie be nearly four months old and his mama back to her old self, more or less, except for a pair of leaky teats.

"Hmm," he says, a noise that seems to encompass the entire affair and all its dependent clauses. "So bad as that, is it?"

"No worse than I feared, to say the truth. But seems I can't just bear it like I thought I could. Can't bear to have so little of each other, when we used to have everything."

"Let me ask you this. Have you forgiven each other?"

I look in my lap. "I don't know that it's a question of forgiving. We can't do without each other, that's all. But we can't seem to find our way back, either. Not to where we were."

"My darling, I imagine you never will. Once you cross the Rubicon, you can't return. You can't forget what's happened. You'll have to find some new territory to build your lives on, that's all. If that's what you want, to remain together."

"But that's the trouble. Can't see my life without him. Yet I can't close my eyes without seeing her and him together. *Her*, of all people. I can forgive him, all right. I can feel all the pity in the world for him. I can feel his broken heart like it was my own, because it was. And I have lain with other men besides him, which I know must torture him, though he never said a word to me. Why, I once used to took his own brother to bed. And I had Bronstein, too. I can *forgive* him for lying with her, sure. But I can't *forget*, and neither can he."

"Do you have to forget? Isn't forgiveness enough?"

I toe some sand. "You see, I think it scared him almost to death, what he did with her. That he could go to bed with another woman besides me—woman he didn't even love—and do things—seems to me he did things with her that shocked him afterward—and until then he thought himself a man of virtue. He was proud of that, I believe. Never imagined he should commit some intentional sin to be forgiven for."

My father nods. "Sometimes it's easier to forgive others than to submit ourselves to be forgiven."

"I don't know that I forgive *myself* for what I've done. I only learn to live with it. To *accept* what's done. But he don't. Every day he wakes up and carries the knowledge of her on his skin. He can't bury the memory of what he did with her. Nor can I, to say the truth. I dreamt about it, before I even found them. Dreamt the two of them together, vivid and real like I was right there watching, and then it turned out to be true. You can't forget a thing like that. And I don't want to know everything they got up to, don't want to think about it, but it's there, all right, right there at the edge of my imagination, biting my skin like a fly, and I can't quite—I don't know whether it disgusts me or—or . . ."

"Or what?"

"Or the opposite." So soft as almost to say it to myself. Not even certain he hears me, for we sit there silent for a moment or two, side by side, sharing our miseries.

At last my father speaks, in his nice quiet voice. "Darling, what exactly do you want from me?"

"I don't know. A man's perspective, maybe. Can he ever again look at *me* without disgust?"

"Disgust? You think he looks on you with disgust?"

"Of course he does. He won't touch me. Won't hardly look at me. Like maybe he still imagines me with Bronstein, the same as I imagine him with her."

"Maybe he does, but I assure you he doesn't love you any less."

"How the devil do *you* know? Has he talked to you?"

"He doesn't have to. Let me tell you something. When your attention is elsewhere—on the children or some other task—that man looks at you as if the sun rises each morning from the crown of your head. He would sell his soul for you."

"Then why don't he touch me?"

"Because he feels *guilty*, for God's sake. Unclean. Unworthy of your attention."

"You're saying it's up to me to touch him first?"

Schuyler stares out to sea. "I'm saying when a man loves a woman as much as that, it's always up to her. Even when he knows better."

7

DINNER'S A smashing success, a fine beef Wellington with Madeira sauce brought off so perfect, even that experienced gourmand Schuyler pronounces it sublime. I don't wish to see the state of the kitchen, however. Then Patsy comes out bearing a chocolate cake stuck with candles, which she and I blow out together, in place of our mama. Schuyler looks on with a ghost of a smile. My kid brother Charlie snaps a photo with the Brownie he got for Christmas. Cute kid, that Charlie. Hair like our father. Bright blue eyes. Smattering of freckles across his nose and kind of a smart aleck, like your average filthy rich twelve-year-old boy, but I think he's got a soft heart inside. Anyhow, we contrive to make the occasion a happy one, as Mama would have wanted. Even Anson grins like his old self from time to time. Catch him once looking at me in such a way that isn't quite so respectful. He turns away quick, but I caught it.

Then the telephone rings. Everybody stops talking and looks at Anson. He wipes his mouth with his napkin and rises. "Excuse me," he says.

We pretend to make small talk. Patsy and Laura Ann spent yesterday constructing all these silly hats out of colored paper, which we trade around and that kind of thing. Mary Rose drops some chocolate frosting on her pink dress and cries. After some time, Anson slips back into the room and resumes his chair. Face pale, lips set. He takes a sip of water from his glass. When I catch his eye at last, brows raised to ask what's the matter, he makes the smallest possible shake of his head and turns his attention to Patsy, who puts a green paper hat on his head and claps her hands.

For some reason, the remaining cake turns to sawdust in my

mouth. We rise and clear the table. Ruth Mary shoves me out of the kitchen and says I'm not allowed to help with the washing up this evening. Anson rolls up the sleeves of his shirt and dries the plates while I put some music on the gramophone for the children. My father waltzes me around the parlor, eyes misty. When we have finished the whole side of the record, I notice Anson standing by the door, wearing his jacket, valise by his side. I steal out of the parlor to the dark entryway.

"Headed back already?"

"Something's come up. I'm sorry."

He leans forward to kiss my forehead. I think of what my father said to me on the beach. Boldly I put my arms around his waist and draw him close. He don't resist. Still his bone and muscle stands rigid as steel against mine. I lay my cheek on his shoulder and listen to the thud of his heart.

"I can't get it out of my head." His voice is so desperate quiet, I must strain to hear him. "What happened up there. Whenever I close my eyes, she's right before me. What we did. I want to bleach it from my memory, score it, burn it. But just when I think it's gone, she lurches back. Worse than before. Won't let me go."

"It's got to stop somehow, though. Can't go on like this always."

"I'm sorry. I'm sorry, Gin."

"Sorry for what? It's done now. It's past. She's got no hold on you anymore."

He shakes his head above mine. I pull back to squint at his face.

"Is it something to do with that phone call? Something happen?"

"Nothing you need to worry about. I'll handle it, all right? I'll find a way to make things right, I swear it."

Last final kiss upon my temple, and he's gone.

8

ON THE first of September, Ruth Mary takes her children back into New York to ready up the house for our return. Schuyler embraces me for the last time, ruffles my red hair, and sails off back to Long Island, with promises of cozy metropolitan evenings together over the autumn and winter. So we remain just the three of us, me and Patsy and Johnnie, for the end stretch of summer. Anson's still busy up in Boston. Trial's set for the fourteenth of September, as Mabel Willebrandt commanded. He comes home occasional to visit with the children and with me, though mostly with the children. I can tell things aren't going so well. How grave he is, how silent. I don't want to ask. When I do, his answers are mostly the same, anyhow. I am not to worry. Some trouble with witnesses, that's all, on account of certain interests not wishing to have their names dragged out in a public trial. He'll make sure that me and Mrs. Marshall have our justice, never fear.

Four days to go. Patsy's heart is broke. Wants to know can we come back to this house next summer, and I tell her I don't know why not. I've begun to pack up a few things, so as not to require us rushing frantic at the end. Anson's promised to drive down from Boston tomorrow and spend the last golden hours on the beach with us, then help us load the car and drive to Manhattan and settle back into the house on Christopher Street. After that, I expect he'll need to be on hand for the trial in Boston. Deliver his testimony and that kind of thing. That's all right. Trial can't last forever, can it? Then surely Luella Bronstein will be found guilty and sentenced to prison, and this weight will lift from his shoulders, this chapter will close.

We will be free, me and Anson.

Now I sit with the children under the umbrella on a cheerful striped blanket, enjoying the last of our holiday. Johnnie suckles at my breast, Patsy builds her sandcastle just outside the flattened ellipse of shade. They do say September's the best time of year out here, and I have to agree. Sun's not so blazing hot but the water might be a salt bath, if you close your eyes. People have mostly packed up and gone home to their everyday lives, Boston and New York and points between. The solitude is like heaven. A woman can nurse her sweet baby right out here under the beach umbrella, nobody to shock.

Yet by and by I come to feel someone is watching us. Patsy looks up sudden from decorating a turret with seashells. Squeals. Scrambles toward the house, where a man stands at the edge of the sand in his shirtsleeves, jacket over his arm. He goes down on one knee just in time for Patsy to tackle him to the ground.

"You're a day early," I tell him, when he walks up to join us, Patsy dangling from one hand. My nerves jangle and thrill. I expect my eyes are shining.

He squints briefly at the sun. Leans down under the umbrella to kiss the soft, round cheek of his son at my breast, then my own shocked lips. Expression on his face be too peculiar to make sense of. Wild or something. I would almost say he looks like a man released from prison.

"I just figured it was time to come home, that's all," he says.

9

THAT EVENING, after I have put Johnnie to bed in his cradle and returned downstairs, I discover Patsy and Anson conspiring in the parlor. Patsy's already taken her bath. She stands at the gramophone in her white nightgown, putting a record on. Looks up at me and delivers Anson a smart push to the small of his back. Anson holds out his hand. We dance to a couple of cornball Kalmar and Ruby tunes, cheek to cheek.

Telephone rings.

I pull back. "You want to get that?"

Anson looks down at me a moment. Right peculiar he has acted all day, crackling with some kind of unnatural energy, queer bright light burning in his eyeballs. Any other man you would think he was drunk, yet he don't touch a drop, speaks and moves as precise as you please, plays with the kids and makes dinner and washes up, won't suffer me to lift a finger to work. Now he walks right out into the hall and the telephone bell shuts off. He returns directly and finishes the dance. Then Anson turns to Patsy and asks for the honor. They waltz for a bit while I finish tidying the kitchen. I hear them clatter upstairs for bedtime and slip outside to the beach, where Anson finds me a quarter hour later. He takes my hand.

"I ask a boon," he says.

"Happens I am disposed to grant one."

"It's about Marie."

"What about her? Billy the Kid getting sick of parenthood already?"

"Something like that. She's kind of headstrong."

"Like her mother was, you mean? I noticed. She and Patsy do get along well, though. Thick as thieves, as I recollect."

He exhales softly. Lifts our linked hands and brushes my knuckles with his lips. "You really don't mind?"

"They Lord, house is crawling with ankle biters anyway. What's another mouth to feed? Anyhow I'm beginning to consider whether I actually do enjoy the chaos, for some reason."

"You were born to take in strays. Me, most of all."

I turn to face him. Spread my two palms over his chest. "This giant heart of yours. Thumping away tragic up there in that poor frozen house, with nobody left to love. She knew just how to get to you, didn't she?"

"I don't want you to forgive me. I don't deserve to be forgiven."

"Don't require me to quote the Bible at you, Oliver Marshall. Makes me sound like a preacher woman, when I am anything but. Anyhow I guess we both need forgiving, don't we? Neither of us clean from sin."

Sometimes Anson takes a while to answer me back. I used to think it was because he was choosing his words careful, words being important things and not to be undertaken lightly. But now I know him better—now I begun to take note of when he answers quick and when he takes his time—I think it's because he feels so much. Has to sort through it all. Bring it under some kind of firm regulation.

"Sometimes I can't breathe," he says at last, "watching you with Johnnie."

"Maybe if you hung around more, you might get used to it some."

Again he takes his time. Stares down inscrutable at my face. That peculiar fire has dimmed behind his eyes, like a man sobered up by the harsh noon light. In a warm, gravelly baritone, he says, "It's haunted me, what he said. Bronstein."

"What did he say?"

"How a man who doesn't put his wife and children first doesn't have a right to them in the first place. And he meant it. He would have died to protect you. He nearly did."

"God bless him, wherever he be."

"It should have been me."

"I'm glad it wasn't."

"What I want you to know," he says, "is that I would do anything for you. Whatever is necessary to protect you."

"I know you would."

"No, you don't. You see, I didn't understand what that meant, before. What was required of me, to put you and the children before everything else. Now I do." He puts his hands over my hands, against his chest. His face wears a queer beatific expression, like nothing I have seen on him yet. "Now I do."

"That's so?"

"That's so."

I rise on my toes and kiss his mouth. "Come upstairs."

10

J OHNNIE'S SOUND asleep in the dressing room where I moved the cradle last month. I check to make sure he's breathing. Anson stands at my shoulder.

"How is he?" he asks.

"Near enough perfect." I turn to face the man responsible. He stands right behind me in his shirtsleeves and checked vest and trousers and his necktie knotted neat, looking past my head at his sleeping son. I take his chin and point him back to me. "Lucky for us there's more where that came from, once he weans and all."

Anson gazes down at my face in such a way that my bones might melt altogether. I turn my back for him to unbutton my dress. He hesitates a second. Then his hands find the buttons and unfasten them nimble, so the dress drops to my feet, followed by my satin slip, and Anson's poor starved eyes are treated to the sight of my famous headlamps overspilling a fine lace brassiere.

For an instant, his hands hover near my shoulders. Then he stumbles back to sit on the edge of the bed. Braces his hands on either side of him and stares at the hollow of my throat, face all heavy with guilt. He speaks hoarse and whispery, like he's got a cold coming on. "I don't know how to do this anymore. I don't know how to touch you."

"Same as you used to, I guess. Same hands, same skin."

He shuts his eyes and slams his fists into the mattress, either side of his thick legs. Makes for to stand and head for the door, probably. I step forward just in time to cradle his head between my hands and hold him at my breast.

"Why, Anson. Don't you recollect how they rejoiced in heaven and on earth when the wicked son dragged himself home at last from his debauchery? Now behold your fatted calf, prodigal husband. Guess you might as well feast on me, since there's nobody else to do it."

He makes some noise in his throat. I pull my fingers from his rumpled hair and remove my brassiere. Shimmy my drawers to the floor and kick them away, so I stand naked before him, breasts full to bursting, belly yet soft, arms and legs smooth as cream. Anson lifts his hands to the buttons of his vest. Unfastens them one by one and shrugs the vest down his arms to the floor. Unwinds his necktie and collar, draws down his suspenders. Rises to his feet to remove his trousers and shirt and drawers, shoes and stockings, so he stands naked before me.

I put my arms around his neck.

"Never was sin between me and you, Anson. This is sacrament, that's all."

Finally we kiss. The old taste, the flavor. We kiss forever and ever, until Anson's knees buckle and we tumble onto the clean white bed. Naked as babes we lie together, skin against skin. Seems to me he is not the same as the man I took to my bed all the length and breadth of last summer—oh, my fine muscular animal of a bridegroom, rippled with sinew. Nothing to him now but bones and sorrow, lean and hollow, yet still my blood rises at the sight and feel and beloved scent of him. With his mouth and his hands he worships me. Salt breeze stirs us both. Moon grows ancient overhead. Finally we move into place, belly to belly. Anson joins us together, slow and heavy, kissing as he goes. How patient his rhythm. How soft his lips. I have *never*. Rapture steals up sudden. Like I am lifted up through the window to dangle in the moonlight. Then his shout of joy rings past my ears; my cup runneth over.

11

FOR SOME time afterward he rests heavy upon me, I don't know how long. Minutes, centuries. Tremor shakes him, every so often. Skin and bones nestle into mine. Warm sacred air holds us snug. Hearts beat against each other according to some eternal rhythm. Incoming tide washes the beach outside. Civilizations come and go, riverbeds turn to canyons before the wind returns them to dust. At last my beloved lifts his head; I kiss away the tears from his salt cheeks.

"Amen," I whisper.

He don't speak. Maybe he can't. Turns his lips to my kisses. My goodness, how the man makes up for lost kissing. Up on his elbows he rises again. How he finds the strength I can't possibly figure, though he always was a dirty carnal beast. Makes a question with his hips; I answer him with mine. Not a word passes between us. What we have to say to each other can't be expressed in vulgar prose, I guess. Still I understand him. What blessed sweet relief, what *liberty*, to know and be known so thoroughly well! Our mutual lust slips its traces and gallops amoral free until nothing's left of us, sapped out, wrung dry, drained limp, fallen to sleep in a heap like a pair of newborn puppies.

Though I do wake sometime later when Johnnie makes to cry. Soft little sobs turn determined. I poke Anson's ribs where he sprawls asleep on his stomach. He lifts his head groggy. "What? What is it?"

"Baby's crying."

Stumbles out of bed and shambles to the dressing room. Returns with Johnnie and hands him into my arms for nursing. Collapses back on his stomach and falls right to sleep.

Now surely I dwell in the house of the Lord.

12

WELL. NOW that's all settled at last, I guess the time's come to confess there is a particular reason I asked Schuyler to find us a cottage on Cape Cod of all places, which has nothing to do with the ocean beach and the pleasant weather and the various qualities of light and air and clambakes. It's weighed on my conscience for some time, and now that only a few more days of this seclusion remain to us, I must face the music before we pack up our things and return to New York.

I carry down Johnnie to the beach, where Anson and Patsy be making picnic of their breakfast, joined by a pair of dolls and Patsy's stuffed lamb, who still survives thanks to Ruth Mary's skill with needle and thread. Anson looks up to watch us approach, small wise smile at the corner of his mouth that makes me think of what we got up to in the night. I bend down and hand him the baby. "All full and clean," I tell him.

"Won't you join us, ma'am? Plenty of toast and jam around here."

"I'll join you later. Just going to cycle into town and pick up some groceries first."

"Don't trouble yourself. I'll do it."

"No, you stay here and play with the children. Make up for lost time. Too fine a morning to come in, anyhow."

"Guess I can't argue with that." He stands up to kiss me on my way. "Don't be long."

As I walk back up the sand to take my bicycle from the porch, I reflect how last night has done him a world of good. Eyes gleaming, skin pink, each hair bristling with new energy. I do believe there's nothing so soul-healthy as a husband tucked inside his lawful married bed. Certainly *this* husband, anyway. When he opened his eyes this morning, the old life was back inside them. Reached his hands for my hips and his mouth for my lips and joined with me again. Then he popped out of bed, fetched me the baby, pulled on trousers and shirt, and made everybody breakfast, whistling all the while.

Why, he even smiled just now for no good reason, as you saw.

I sling my business over my shoulder and climb on my bicycle. The sooner I finish this, the better. Return home to my dear strays gathered together, my own true family.

13

TOOK ME surprising effort to discover the exact location of the Hardcastle summer residence on Cape Cod, Massachusetts. You won't find them in the public telephone registry, and my own discreet inquiries produced nothing much, other than somebody thought it was near Chatham, wasn't it? Or Hyannis, maybe. Finally I broke down and asked my father about it. You can imagine he knows me well enough by now to suspect my motives. Raised an eyebrow or two and asked what for I wanted this particular information. And I said I couldn't tell him, but I meant no harm. Just some unfinished business, slung now over my shoulder in a messenger bag like them Western Union boys use for deliveries.

The day's fine, and the distance not far. Couple of miles on the other side of Chatham town, where I will stop for groceries on the way back. No entrance gate, just an opening in some high hedges, so narrow and inconspicuous you might miss it if you weren't looking, or the night was dark. Long gravel drive, neatly raked. Big white clapboard house at the end, near the beach. I lean my bicycle against a stone lion reclined watchful on a stone plinth. Straighten my hat and walk up the path to the front door. Let fall the brass knocker. Door's opened by a handsome tall young man about seventeen, looking like he was just off to slay dragons or something.

"Can I help you?" he asks. Seems to me his blue eyes are remarkable cold.

"Is Mrs. Hardcastle available?"

He looks me down and he looks me up, lusty young male eyes lingering just an instant on my overgrown bosom. Let me assure you I am dressed respectable, for all my hair might set the curtains on fire. Why, I even wore that pearl necklace my daddy gave me, said it was long overdue. So I look the part, I guess, because the young man steps back to let me through and asks whom shall he say is calling.

"Mrs. Oliver Marshall," I tell him.

His eyes flicker. He motions a hand in the direction of a small, bright room off the entrance hall. "Have a seat."

She arrives a few minutes later, once I've had time to observe the portrait of the thoroughly respectable man in the dark conservative suit that takes up much of the short wall facing the entrance hall. He looks much like the young man who showed me in, except older and more concerned with matters of state. Why, you would never believe this venerable figure ran the largest bootlegging racket on the Eastern Seaboard and died with his mistress's dagger through his stone heart.

"My late husband," the woman says, hint of lockjaw, touching my hand briefly with her fingertips. She's dressed for tennis, looks sporty for a mother of eight children, let alone a widowed one. Tall and blond, though darker than Luella, so I guess Hardcastle had a type, didn't he?

"I've heard so much about him," I reply.

"Yes." She flicks a glance to her wristwatch. "You'll forgive me, but I have a match in ten minutes. Is there something I can do for you, Mrs. Marshall?"

I've left the messenger bag on the wicker chair next to me. I bend over it now and unfasten the buckles. Lift out a leather portfolio. "I believe this belongs to you."

She raises both eyebrows, thin high golden ones. Without a word she takes the portfolio and opens it up. Riffles through the contents. Keeps her composure, though her blue eyes can't help but glint with greed. "Are these genuine?"

"So far as I know. They were given to me by a man named Bronstein. I understand they belonged to your late husband. They would have gone missing around the time of his death. I'm awfully sorry not to have returned them to the family earlier, but you understand a package like this has to be delivered personally, and I had a baby son last April. Kept me busy, as I'm sure you understand."

She closes the portfolio again and tucks it under her arm. "I appreciate your trouble, Mrs. Marshall. Indeed, I'm very grateful. The loss of these certificates has caused me no small consternation, as you must have imagined."

"It has weighed on my conscience daily, I assure you."

Her blue eyes appraise me with care. I turn to buckle up the empty messenger bag and tell her I won't detain her any longer. Must return to my family before I'm missed.

Mrs. Hardcastle clears her throat delicate. "Would I insult you if I ask whether you will take some mark of my gratitude?"

"No insult taken, and no mark necessary. Grateful to have them off my hands, to be honest."

She holds out her hand. "Then consider you have a favor owed you, whenever you choose to ask for it. This family always pays its debts."

I shake her hand and thank her for her civility. Wish her and her family the best. Then I turn and walk out of the house, take my bicycle and ride back up the long driveway, certain I am being watched from some window until I disappear behind those tall hedges.

14

WHAT A relief. Realize my hands do shake some, as I steer the bicycle down the lane toward town. Wasn't quite certain how that transaction might go, what kind of woman she be. I guess any woman married to Louis Hardcastle all those years, bearing him eight children at the same time as he kept a mistress such as Luella Bronstein and ran a business so extensive and illegitimate as a boot-legging racket, must naturally have the patience of Job and the sang-froid of a queen. No doubt she'll invest the dough wisely.

Yet my heart is as light as air. My God, what a millstone it was, that dough! Why does anybody covet treasure, is beyond my guess. Enough to get by, that's all I want. I pedal so happily into Chatham, sun baking the straw of my hat, I near forget to stop for groceries after all. Lucky I pass the store on my way. Stop the bicycle, pick out some nice fresh peaches, some green beans, eggs and bread and more coffee. That kind of thing. Put them all in the bicycle basket and stop off at the butcher for a chicken to roast for dinner, then the newsstand for today's *Boston Globe,* which Anson usually picks up. Be wondering where I am by now. Have to make up some little excuse that isn't quite a lie. Never could lie to Anson, and he knows it.

Another twenty minutes of pedaling and I turn off on the familiar drive to our sweet rented cottage. Patsy was right, we must certainly return to it next year. Fill the place to bursting and laugh all day and night. As I bring my cycle to a halt, the Western Union boy cruises into view. I wait for him to draw close, holding up the bicycle with my two hands. "Why, hello, Sam," I say. "What have you got for us today?"

"Good morning, Mrs. Marshall. Telegram from Boston, the usual."

He hands me the yellow envelope, I toss him a nickel. They do send Anson telegrams regular, those officers and agents in Boston. He likes to be kept up to date on all the little developments. I prop the bicycle back against the porch and wave the bright telegram to Anson and the children, still on the sand. Anson's put up the umbrella and set Johnnie on his stomach on a beach blanket. Patsy builds a castle. He sticks up his thumb to say he'll be inside in a bit, soon as this castle is properly finished. I take the basket into the kitchen, where it seems my husband has started fresh coffee in the percolator, just to demonstrate his renewed devotion.

Outside I hear some delighted squeal from Patsy, some rumble of actual laughter from Anson. Laughter, I tell you! Kitchen smells of coffee and ocean. Three more days until we head back to Christopher Street. Had a letter from Ruth Mary just yesterday. Assured us the house is all freshened and ready. Mentioned Bruno has turned the joint next door into a private club, paid members only, not so rambunctious, so as not to corrupt the children's morals or embarrass Anson's standing at the Bureau. Three more halcyon days on the shore, and tonight I shall welcome my husband into bed again, and our bliss will have no end.

Groceries all put away. Pour myself a cup of coffee and unfold the newspaper, and that's when I come across the headline that's been screaming at me all this time, if I wasn't so distracted by my present hard-won contentment to notice it.

BRONSTEIN DEAD

Accused Murderess and Bootlegger Found Lifeless in Prison Cell Yesterday Afternoon; Cause of Death Not Yet Determined

Trial of the Century Takes Explosive New Turn

Recent Examination Revealed Bronstein Was with Child, Sources Say; Full Investigation Pending, Says Willebrandt

ELLA

East Hampton, New York, 1998

EVENTUALLY THE ushers had to stop seating people according to bride or groom affiliation, because they ran out of room on the bride's side. Schuylers and Salisburys had turned up in force, Aunt Viv and Uncle Paul and the older kids and their spouses, plus the two toddler grandchildren. Aunt Tiny and Uncle Caspian had flown in from California with all their kids. Even Granny Annabelle and Grandpa Stefan had arrived from their idyllic home on Cumberland Island, off the coast of Georgia. Mumma and Dad, of course. Ella's brother, Charlie, had driven in late the night before after taking the last ferry from Martha's Vineyard, where he owned a bar. Then there were all the assorted cousins, Uncle Paul's colleagues at the hospital, Aunt Viv's colleagues from *Metropolitan* magazine. That half of the club on speaking terms with the Schuylers. Lizzie's Nightingale-Bamford friends, like a flight of sparrows in perfect synchronization. Aunt Julie stalked in on Uncle Paul's arm and collared Ella.

"Why the devil haven't you come back to help me? It's been *weeks*!"

Ella spoke in an undertone. "Because my husband's in the hospital?"

"*Husband?* Ha. So *that's* all a fellow has to do to get his wife to forgive his affairs."

"I haven't—oh, for God's sake. Never mind."

Uncle Paul was dragging her to her seat. "We'll speak later!" she called over his shoulder. "At the party!"

Ella remained outside the door. She was waiting for Joanie, who still hadn't arrived. Last-minute delay—she'd had to change flights—something came up, the usual. She'd been due to land at JFK midmorning, and was probably now racing down the Long Island Expressway at her usual breakneck speed. Mumma was saving seats for them both. Ella checked her watch—five minutes to one, when the service was supposed to start. Latecomers still straggling in. And here she stood in her cheerful berry-pink empire sheath, nascent bump clearly outlined on her somewhat emaciated frame, having to face everybody, all the questions—*How's Patrick? When are you due? So where's this Hector fellow?*—that made it clear the family gossip engine was running full steam.

Possibly Ella was going to kill Joanie, if her kid sister hadn't already killed herself going a hundred on the LIE.

"Ellsie!"

A pair of arms caught her from behind and spun her around into a tigerish embrace.

"Joanie!" she gasped. "I can't breathe!"

"Oh. My. God. Look at you. Holy *fuck*. That's a *baby*."

"I told you."

"*You* didn't tell me. Mumma told me. I thought she was kidding. I'm going to be a fucking *aunt*!"

"Would you *stop*? We're in *church*."

"Oops. Sorry, Lord!" Joanie crossed herself with her left hand and looked at the blue sky. The right arm was in a sling.

"What happened to your arm?"

Joanie took her by the elbow. "Oh, nothing. Come on. Mumma saved us seats, didn't she?"

It seemed to Ella that the entire congregation turned to look when she entered with Joanie, arms linked in sisterhood. Joanie had their mother's catlike eyes and broad, deep cheekbones, those dramatic eyebrows and the lush blond hair, to say nothing of her tall figure spilling out of an un-Schuylerlike dress of snug, short vinyl the exact yellow shade of a traffic sign. If you didn't know her any better, you would think she was trying to upstage the bride. If you did know better, you understood she was just Joanie.

Also, you knew that any man who figured he might cop a feel of that copious exposed skin stood a decent chance of requiring an MRI before they allowed him out of the hospital.

All the way up in the second pew, Mumma's arm shot up and waved frantically. Dad turned around and stood, beaming, to let them in. Joanie let go of Ella and bounded up to their father. *Daddy!* she screeched, throwing her good arm around him.

He laughed and asked her about the sling—*Oh, nothing!*—and hurried them into the pew, in between him and Mumma. Charlie leaned in from Mumma's other side and kissed Joanie's cheek. "What the hell, Dommerich? Even *I* made it on time."

"Asshole. I *am* on time. As long as the bride's not walking down the aisle already."

When she sat, Joanie's dress came all the way up her thigh, displaying the edge of a fresh purple bruise. Joanie caught Ella's stare and shrugged, grinning.

"So where's Hector?" she whispered in Ella's ear. "I'm dying to meet this guy."

"He's in L.A., finishing the movie."

"With Louisiana Goring, right?"

"How did you know that?"

"I know stuff. I thought he was supposed to be here today."

"We decided the time wasn't right for his big debut. With Patrick and everything."

"I'm so sorry about that. I mean, he's a dick and all, but losing a leg is not justice. His *balls,* on the other hand—"

"Joanie, we're in *church.*"

"Well, I'm sorry. When your future brother-in-law tries to slip you one at the engagement party—"

"*What?*"

"Oh yes."

"Nobody *told* me. Why didn't anyone *tell* me?"

"Honey, if you can't figure that shit out for yourself, no one can help you." Joanie clapped a hand over her mouth. "Sorry."

Charlie leaned over. "Would you two give it a rest? Everyone can hear you."

"Oh, please. The rank and file need a little entertainment. Anyway, it's only what everybody's thinking."

"If only they would start already," Ella moaned.

Dad checked his watch. "Five minutes late."

"Weddings always start late," said Mumma. "Well, except that one at the Naval Academy. We waltzed in at three minutes past and the bride was already halfway down the aisle. That's the military for you. Say, there's an idea."

"What's an idea?" Joanie asked.

"If anyone here was in the military. I bet they'd know how to open Aunt Julie's safe."

"What safe?" asked Ella.

"Oh, you know how she's been turning the house upside down,

looking for some of Grandfather's old papers. She finally found a safe behind some shelf in the library and she's sure that whatever she's looking for is inside. *Except* she doesn't know the combination."

"Oh God. This is such an Aunt Julie dilemma."

"I'll bet Joanie could crack it for her," said Charlie, poker-faced.

"*What? Joanie?* You know how to crack safes?"

"Maybe."

"Well, if you can crack this one, I'll give you a bottle of champagne," said Mumma. "Good Lord, is that Harry Macallister?"

"Looks like it," said Dad.

"*And* that *paramour* of his."

"She's not a *paramour*, Mumma," said Ella. "Jeez, what is this, 1950?"

"I don't understand why he doesn't marry her. It's been ages now."

"Maybe they just like things the way they are," said Charlie.

"Anyway, *you* should talk, Mumma," said Joanie.

"*Me?*"

"Oh, I've heard *stories*. Before you met Dad."

"*Now look here*," Dad said, thunderous.

"You don't need to defend my honor, darling. I was a little tramp, I admit it, but—"

"Would everyone in this family just *please shut up*," Ella whispered, teeth clenched.

"—you have to admit Cousin Harry has the most *interesting* taste in women—"

"Ella?"

Ella looked up. Uncle Paul stood at the end of the pew, staring at her. He had a peculiar expression on his face, the kind of expression she imagined he wore before a high-stakes surgery.

"Can I borrow you for a minute?" he said.

Ella rose in relief. "With pleasure," she told him.

LIZZIE SAT IN THE small, circular room that served as the bride's antechamber, at the center of a cloud of white tulle on the ancient settee. Her face was pale, her eyes were red. The room smelled of panic and Chanel No. 5. Aunt Viv sat next to her youngest daughter and patted her hand helplessly. She looked up at Ella's arrival. "Thank God. Maybe you can talk some sense into her."

"What's wrong?"

"She won't tell me." Aunt Viv rose. "I'll leave you two alone. Five minutes, all right? Or else we're going to have to start serving refreshments."

She and Uncle Paul exchanged a glance. He ushered her out of the room to the vestibule, where the bridesmaids milled uncertainly like horses waiting to fill a starting gate. Ella sat down next to her cousin, carefully avoiding the gigantic tulle cumulonimbus. She pulled an emergency Kleenex out of her pocketbook and handed it to Lizzie.

"What's wrong, honey?" she asked.

Lizzie dabbed at the corners of her eyes. "It's my fault," she said.

"What's your fault?"

"Patrick."

Ella took her hand. "Lizzie, we already talked about this. What happened to Patrick was a random accident. It could have happened to anybody. He was just in the wrong place at the wrong time."

"Because of *me*!"

"Not because of you. Because of me, if anybody. I'd asked him to run an errand for me at the DA's office—"

"That was *after*." Lizzie turned to Ella. The tears bubbled up at the corners of her eyes.

"After what?" Ella whispered.

"He came to the city that day to see *me*. I'm so sorry, Ella. I met him in his apartment that morning and we had sex." Lizzie burst into tears. "*Twice!*"

IT FELL TO UNCLE Paul to stand in front of the entire congregation and explain that the wedding had been—er, postponed. He was very sorry for the trouble and of course everyone was welcome to come back to The Dunes and eat up all the canapes and drink all the booze. Also, the band was booked until midnight.

"What the *hell*," Joanie whispered to Ella.

"Can I borrow your car to drive back to the city?"

"Sure, if you give me the shit on this."

One thing about Joanie, she could keep a secret if you told her it was a secret. She had a strict code of honor. So as they drove Joanie back to The Dunes, Ella explained what Lizzie had confessed to her in the anteroom: that Lizzie and Patrick had been enjoying an on-again, off-again affair since they first met at Ella and Patrick's own wedding, which had been off again since Ella and Patrick separated—Patrick trying to master his demons and all—but had picked up again the night after Ella left for Los Angeles, during a spontaneous after-dinner copulation in the broom closet of the club.

"That's so Patrick," Joanie said. "I'll bet he's been using that broom closet like a cheap hotel room."

Ella was driving Joanie's convertible, because of the sling. The car had a stick shift and Ella didn't even *want* to know how Joanie had driven it all the way from some friend's garage in Queens after a nine-hour plane ride. She turned down the long gravel drive toward the sea. "So they made this arrangement to meet at his apartment in the city Tuesday morning, which they did, and he figured he would walk downtown afterward because the weather was so nice."

"Ah, the fatal error."

"Not *fatal,* thank God."

The sun glimmered high and hazy overhead. The thick hot air rushed over the windshield and destroyed Ella's hair. Every summer day she'd ever experienced here at The Dunes seemed to live in her head right now, each one separate all at once, infinite and intimate. She wanted Hector so much her chest hurt. But he was on the other coast. On the edge of another ocean.

"She says she's in love with him," Ella said. "Can you believe? All these years she's been fighting her mad, tragic love for Patrick. She said she only started dating Owen because he was Patrick's friend. She got engaged to Owen literally out of despair because she realized Patrick wasn't going to leave me. The whole time feeling terrible because we're cousins. And then I left Patrick, and she was stuck marrying a man she didn't love."

"Are you actually feeling *sorry* for her?"

"She's just a kid, Joanie. She thinks he's the love of her life."

"And he *let* her think so, the prick."

"Look, I was stupid enough to think the same thing, once. We're all stupid until we know better."

"Sure we are. But we don't go around sleeping with our cousins' husbands, do we? I mean, aren't you pissed as *hell?* You should be pissed as *hell.*"

Ella flipped up the sunshade. The edge of the tent stuck out from behind the corner of the house, sharp and clean against the ocean.

The water was calm today, like a millpond. A few gossiping voices drifted from the lawn. She thought about her cousin Lizzie having guilty, desperate sex with Patrick—with Ella's *husband*!—probably under this very roof in front of her now, some dark corner or attic bedroom, and all she felt was sadness.

"It's a shame you're missing all the food," said Joanie.

"I just couldn't face everybody asking me what happened. *Plus* Aunt Julie. Were you kidding back there? Can you really open a safe?"

"Maybe."

"Well, don't do it. Please. She needs to stop. You need to tell her to stop. I mean it."

"Stop what?"

"She's trying to take down the Hardcastle family."

"The *Frank* Hardcastle family? Why the hell?"

"Long story. She's had me investigating all this financial malfeasance. Apparently it goes all the way back to some bootlegging stuff in the 1920s."

"Well, yeah. Everybody knows the Hardcastles have some serious shit in their closets. But what's it to Aunt Julie?"

"You know her. She knew them all back in the day, she's got some old bone to pick. I don't even care anymore, I'm sick of it. You know Patrick was doing some digging for me when he got hit by that car?"

"Seriously?" Joanie whistled. "Sounds like somebody's not messing around."

"Exactly. Which is why Aunt Julie needs to let it go with all the vengeance crap." Ella parked the car outside the house and waved away the valet. Joanie reached in back with her good arm and pulled a duffel bag from the tiny bench seat. She opened the door and got out just as Dad came out the front door with Nellie on her leash.

"*Doggie!*" Joanie squealed. She dropped her duffel bag and squatted on the gravel to take a full barrage of King Charles tongue. "You got a *dog*, Daddy? Why didn't you *say* anything? Who is this *sweet puppy*?"

"Not our dog, I'm sorry to say. It's Ella's dog."

"Hector's dog, to be fair." Ella took the leash. "This is Nellie and I think she's going to be extremely disappointed to have her beach vacation cut short. Um, Joanie?"

Joanie looked up from the silky fur at Nellie's neck. "Can I have her?"

"No, but you can see her again if you visit us. Christopher Street. Number 11, top floor. *Mi casa es su casa.*"

Daddy held out his arms and kissed her cheek. "We have to talk, sweetheart," he said in her ear.

"I know. When things have settled down, okay? It's all right. Love you."

Ella carried Nellie to the car and settled her in the back seat. The dog whined and looked at Ella anxiously. She stroked the soft, curving head and gossamer ears. "You'll be okay. We'll be okay. He'll be home soon, right? All together again. Snuggled up in bed on Sunday mornings like old times."

Nellie laid her head on her paws. Ella started the engine. Joanie came around to the driver's window and leaned her elbows on the door.

"Are you going to be okay? You look wrecked."

"I *am* wrecked. But I'll be okay. Always am."

Joanie squinted to the side for a second or two, pondering something. She turned back to Ella. "This Hardcastle thing. I might be able to help you."

"I don't want help. I'm out. Done. It's not worth people dying."

"But what if it is?"

Ella stared at her sister. People always expected her eyes to be blue, but in fact they were brown, tending toward hazel, inherited from Dad. They stared back at her now, dead serious. Not even kidding.

"I don't want people dead, that's all," Ella said. "End of story."

Joanie straightened. "Okeydokey. Call me when you get in, okay? I mean, just so I know my car is all right."

"Right-ho."

"And Ella?"

"Joanie?"

"Stop blaming yourself for the shit other people do, okay? It's a waste of time."

BY THE TIME ELLA parked Joanie's car in the nearest overnight garage and walked Nellie back to Christopher Street—Mrs. Gilbert could frankly think whatever the hell she wanted at this point—it was nearly dinnertime, but Ella wasn't hungry. Her insides were too jammed with thoughts and emotions and nerves. Most of all she wanted Hector. She hated standing here in the middle of the apartment, surrounded by all the furniture and cabinetry he had made with his own hands, his piano, his music, his dog, the sound of his voice floating in the air—everything but him. Missing.

Hector had returned to California after Patrick woke up. They'd agreed it was best—he had to wrap up all the sound editing, which was painstaking, and Ella had to concentrate on Patrick. Ella had spent every day at the hospital, keeping Patrick company as he came out of the medication, as he dealt with an infection that mercifully cleared within days, thanks to some powerful antibiotics; as he dealt with the life-changing news that didn't seem to fully dawn on him yet, like he figured this was all part of some weird dream he was having and he should stick it out until he woke up. She'd spent every dutiful night at Patrick's apartment. She had set aside every thought of Hector, every possibility of Hector.

Now her discipline broke. She wanted Hector so much she couldn't breathe. She wanted to tell him everything that had happened. She wanted to hear what he would say about it—about Patrick and Lizzie and Joanie in her traffic-yellow vinyl dress, his humor and perspective and understanding. She wanted to lie against his shoulder. She wanted his hands on her skin, she wanted him to make love to her, which they hadn't done since Los Angeles. Hell, she would settle for the sound of his voice. Just his voice! She would do anything to hear him say her name, that was all.

She tried calling Hector's cell phone, but it went straight to voice mail. She fed Nellie and cuddled her until the dog fell asleep on the sofa, nose buried drunkenly in Hector's favorite cushion. She showered and changed into pajamas. *You have to eat,* she told herself, so she ate an overripe banana and drank a glass of orange juice. Put some bread in the toaster.

Her cell phone rang.

"*Hector.* You have no idea."

"Guess where I am."

"Not Los Angeles?"

"In a car on the LIE. I figure no one will notice if I sneak in after dinner, right? Dance on the beach with my girl, under the stars? I just miss you too much. Couldn't stay away any longer. I'm sorry." He paused. "What's wrong? Did I mess up?"

Ella swallowed the banana and shoved away the tears with her sleeve.

"You did not mess up. But you're going to have to turn the car around."

THERE WAS NO MARATHON. No quickie, either. Just tender, un-hurried sex in a bed, face-to-face, sublime in its normalcy. At the end, Ella nearly laughed with relief. Her chest quivered and she flung her arms around Hector's neck to hide it.

"What was that about?" Hector wanted to know when he rolled away a moment later.

"What was what about?"

"That insane giggling during a very tender moment for me."

"I'm glad you're here, that's all. Just grateful to have you back."

Hector gathered her up in the nook of his shoulder. "Come here, you crazy kid. Giggle all you want, I don't care. Just don't get up and go anywhere."

"Me? You're the one who keeps flying off to the other side of the country."

"How else am I supposed to make you realize how much you miss me?"

"I miss you when you're in the other *room*, Hector."

"Well, I miss you when you're on the other side of the *sofa*."

Ella lay there listening to his heartbeat. Then her chest quivered again. "I'm sorry," she choked. "Her face, that's all. Poor Aunt Viv. Her *face* when I told her. It's a good thing Patrick was safe in the hos-pital in Manhattan. Oh my God, the *broom closet*. Poor *Owen*! Why am I *laughing*? I must be sick. It's terrible. It's the most horrible—horrible thing. I'm a terrible—I'm a terrible person—"

"If you ask me, they amputated the wrong limb."

"Stop!"

"Someone had to say it."

"Oh God. If I didn't laugh, I'd cry. I *was* crying. I've been crying and crying. Oh God. It's so terrible. Poor Patrick. The next few months are going to be awful. It's going to be a nightmare. I'm so sorry."

"Sorry for what?"

"Sorry to put you through them."

"Look, let's be honest. The *last* few months weren't exactly a picnic. It's just the kind of drama-packed, soap opera life I've come to expect from you, Dommerich. One damn thing after another. When's the honeymoon, that's what I want to know."

She found his hand and wound her fingers through it. "Second thoughts?"

"Not a chance."

"I'm going to have to go out every day and be strong for everyone and come home and fall apart. Could be messy."

"I'll put you together again. Nothing a few screws and some solid nailing can't fix."

"Was that a double entendre?"

"Me? Hell no. Just that dirty mind of yours."

"This." She snuggled herself into a comfortable position and closed her eyes. "*This* is what fixes me. Skin on skin."

"Nothing in the whole damn world feels as good as being naked with you."

"Just to be under the same roof again. Same bed. Same blanket."

"You and me. Little wee baby you're growing for us."

"Nellie. Don't forget Nellie."

"The Murrays of Christopher Street."

Ella looked up.

"Or the Dommerichs," he said. "I could get so much more respect as a German composer."

Ella turned on her side to face him. His warm, steady expression made her think of a fire simmering in a hearth. He drew her hand to his lips and kissed the fingers, one by one, until he came to her empty fourth finger and stopped. Rubbed the joint with his thumb. Kissed the skin above her knuckle.

"Murray's easier to pronounce, though," she said.

"So we'll flip a coin."

"Hector?"

"Yes, my goddess?"

"Do you know what I love most about you?"

"Well, heck. Where do we start? My carpentry skills?"

She shook her head.

"My sophisticated sense of humor? Genius way I load the dish-washer? Divine smell of my shaving cream?"

Ella brushed her thumbs along his eyebrows. Like a bird she kissed his lips. "Literally every single thing," she whispered.

The faint notes of Ella's cell phone drifted in from the living room.

"Don't you *dare* get that," Hector said. "I swear I'll divorce you."

"Not going anywhere, trust me."

On and on. Then it stopped. Then it started again.

"Don't give in, Dommerich. It's just more crazy melodrama from your crazy family. It can wait until morning."

"What if it's Patrick?"

"Patrick's mommy can take care of Patrick."

Ella closed her eyes. The phone rang again.

"Shit," she said.

IT WAS AUNT JULIE.

"I found it!" she announced, triumphant.

"Found what?"

"It's all here! It was all in the safe, just like I thought! Joanie opened it for me."

"That bitch." Ella looked at Hector, propped up on his elbow in the bed, adorably naked. "So what was it?"

"The Bronstein files, of course! Didn't I tell you?"

"The *Bronstein* files? But those were stolen! Patrick said—"

"Of *course* they were stolen!" Aunt Julie cackled with joy. "My brother lifted them himself from the FBI building in Washington back in 1928. And I'll tell you what, honey. Those Hardcastles aren't going to know what hit them."

ACKNOWLEDGMENTS

When I started researching the book that became *The Wicked City*, I quickly realized that no single novel could do justice to the sprawling, complicated history of Prohibition and a legacy that still reaches us across the decades since its repeal in 1933. Moreover, in Geneva Kelly, I discovered a voice and a character that both challenged me and gave me huge joy to create—how could I leave her after only one novel? Instead, I masterminded a crafty plan. I ended *The Wicked City* with a few dangling plotlines that tantalized (some might say irritated) readers and required me to write a sequel, *The Wicked Redhead* . . . which didn't quite resolve the story, either. Whether my long-suffering editor, Rachel Kahan, realizes exactly what I've been up to remains to be seen, but I couldn't have continued to write this series in between my other books without her unwavering support. Gin Kelly continues to be my favorite character among all the many I've created. Every time I return to her, she gives me more, and—sorry, Rachel!—as you may have noticed, her trials aren't over yet.

My research stack for this series has reached Himalayan scale at this point, but I do want to single out one particular book that inspired my interest in Mabel Walker Willebrandt and her extraordinary role in the story of Prohibition. Karen Abbott's *The Ghosts of Eden Park* brilliantly captures Willebrandt, the investigation and trial of George Remus, the so-called King of Bootleggers, and the complicated problem of Prohibition enforcement. If you're eager to learn more about the world depicted in *The Wicked Widow*—or just skeptical that I maybe overdid things—Abbott's book makes for eye-opening reading.

Confession time. I wrote this book in the late summer and early autumn of 2020 as a kind of therapeutic catharsis following the upheavals of the previous months, and the escape into Gin's voice and world hauled me back from the brink. So I'm extra grateful to everyone who had a hand in its creation, from the wonderful folks at HarperCollins (who, by the way, have carried on like heroes while the publishing industry scrambled to find ways to get books printed and delivered into the hands of readers in as much need of escape as I was) to my equally heroic literary agent, Alexandra Machinist at ICM, to my dear friends Karen White and Lauren Willig, who were in on the secret from the beginning and kept me going through endless motivational text chats.

Most of all, thank you to my band of loyal readers, whose love for the Redhead inspires me to keep writing her story. This book is for you.

ABOUT THE AUTHOR

BEATRIZ WILLIAMS is the bestselling author of fourteen novels, including *Our Woman in Moscow, The Summer Wives,* and *Her Last Flight,* as well as *All the Ways We Said Goodbye,* cowritten with Lauren Willig and Karen White. A native of Seattle, Beatriz graduated from Stanford University and earned an MBA in finance from Columbia University. She lives with her husband and four children near the Connecticut shore, where she divides her time between writing and laundry.